REBIRTH BOOK ONE

# THE GOD QUEEN

## M. L. TISHNER

M. L. Tishner
c/o AutorenServices.de
Birkenallee 24
36037 Fulda

ISBN (eBook): 978-3-9821129-0-9
ISBN (Paperback): 978-3-9821129-1-6
ISBN (Hardback): 978-3-9821129-4-7

Edited by Tiffany White at Writers Untapped

*For my husband,*
*For my parents,*
*For Abner*

PART ONE
THE WOMAN

# CHAPTER 1

THE SCREAMS DREW REI'S ATTENTION. SHE STOOD AT the steps of the boarded-up temple when the first one pierced the quiet of their small town. It came from the restaurant on the other side of the square.

She dashed down the stairs and onto the street, jumping inadvertently in front of a hover car whose driver honked and yelled. She didn't listen as she rushed past the long-dead fountain, now filled with sand and earth. Gravel crunched beneath her feet as she approached the ever-growing crowd. Not a cloud dotted the clear blue sky, the sun beat down on them mercilessly, and the smell of sweat and dirt filled Rei's nose. She pushed her small frame to the front to get a clear view, heart hammering in her chest. He had been threatening this for months, yet Rei prayed he wouldn't actually go through with it, but disappointment pooled in her belly as her fear was confirmed.

"Drops of Jupiter," someone muttered. "Why couldn't the cleric give him a quick death? That poison takes too long."

The boy lay writhing on the ground, blood running from his nose and ears, sand caking his dark hair. Rei turned to leave, blood pounding in her ears, but the crowd was now too thick around her and she couldn't move.

"He prayed to false gods," her neighbor, an elderly woman, said under her breath. "The cleric said this would be the fate of those who won't worship the One True God."

Ever since Earth voted to remain a part of the Domin-ion, the other gods were outlawed, despite the fact the holy city lay only a few hundred kilometers away from where Rei stood.

She fought to breathe as her heart raced. She never intended to convert, and the threat of not doing so had become too real.

The victim's scream brought Rei's eyes back to him. Folks said the poison fried the nerves, giving the victim the sensation of being electrocuted as the poison opened all the blood vessels in the head and caused blood to leak out of the nose and ears.

The cleric overseeing the execution sat in one of the outdoor tables of the restaurant, his dark eyes hard. His full lips turned down in a sneer at the poor soul in agony before him. It was a contrast to the cheerful, blue- and white-checkered umbrellas and table covers.

Rei's stomach turned in knots. "Drops of Jupiter is a horrible way to die," she whispered.

Eventually his writhing stopped, and the boy's eyes stared at the heavens while his mouth opened in a silent scream.

"Let this be a lesson for those who still follow that blasphemous religion," the cleric said. "The rest of you have until the end of the week to join the correct religion, or else." He combed his fingers through sleek blonde hair before leaving. The crowd parted as he walked past, until he caught Rei watching him. She averted her gaze, kicking herself for attracting his attention.

She peered at her watch, trying to appear bored as the cleric approached her. The holographic hands reminded her she was running late, but she never ran from a fight. She pulled her dark hair up in a knot as she began to perspire. Her lips pressed together until there was nothing more than a line after the crowd dispersed and left the boy's body on the ground.

"I hope you're satisfied," the cleric said. "His death is on your hands."

Rei's nails bit into her palm at the accusation. She wasn't the one who decided which religion was the correct one and who should die for it. "Mine?" she growled.

"Yes, you and the others who so heinously turn your backs on the One True God."

"Why are you so threatened by a boy who believes in many gods instead of one?" she asked, finally meeting his gaze.

"I am not threatened. The One True God wills it. The Dominion wills it."

Rei's legs grew weak, but she refused to back down as they locked eyes.

"And what of the will of the god queen?" she asked, standing a little straighter.

The cleric cackled. "She doesn't exist and neither do those other false idols."

"I believe she does."

"You believe wrong."

She rolled her eyes. They had been going back and forth like this for months. At first, Rei wanted to leave him be. She may not have agreed with his religion, but she respected his right to worship as he saw fit. But once he started trying to force his religion by boarding up the temple, bringing in Dominion soldiers to rough up locals who were caught worshiping during holy days, smashing the ceramic statues of the gods around town—including the one her brother bought for her—it became personal.

"I know you're one of the reasons why many won't follow the One True God." His voice was dangerously low.

"The people see you not converting, and they think they don't have to either."

"They shouldn't have to."

He crept closer to her, the smell of his cologne choking Rei. "You will convert. Even if I have to tie you down and perform the rite myself."

Rei chuckled. "Tie me down? Kinky. Your threats don't scare me. Try harder." She spun on her heels and walked away, gritting her teeth. It took all of her willpower to not punch him in the throat.

"Remember you have a week," he called. "A week until I make you the next example."

She continued through the alley that opened to the two main roads intersecting at the center of town. She walked along the wall of the basilica of the One True God, where someone had decorated the outside with graffiti. The bright greens and blues contrasted against the pale earth-colored bricks.

Once she was sure the cleric hadn't followed her, the adrenaline rushed from her legs and she leaned against the wall for support. Her heart pounded in her chest. She shouldn't have allowed him to get so close.

"I wish someone would tie him down," she muttered as she cut across the intersection, and one of the hover cars honked as she passed. She needed to get to the bar. It didn't matter what the cleric threatened; he would never set foot in her place of business. She was safe there.

The cleric came into town shortly after the most recent elections and constantly flexed his powers, knowing he had the full weight of Dominion support behind him. She never bothered learning his name—that would have required humanizing him, and she wanted to do no such thing. Both religions had lived peacefully in the town of Ballarat for years. Rei didn't understand why that had to change now. That wasn't true. She knew it was a question of control. It was what the Dominion did best.

Rei wondered if she should go ahead and convert. The action would be hollow since she knew the gods existed. She knew they would return to save the star cluster—one had already been reborn.

She shook her head. If she gave into that monster's demands, her influence would turn away more people from the gods. The idea fueled her anger and drove her to want to take action. No one should choose a religion based on what she did, anyway. People should believe what they wished.

# CHAPTER 2

Rei meandered down the sidewalk, passing between the parked cars along the sidewalk and the low adobe buildings with curved aluminum roofs until she arrived at the business she owned with her mother, Coronta Bar, with its flickering neon sign of a blooming flower. They couldn't afford a holographic sign, but Rei liked the way the flower shone at night. She pulled aside the deep green cloth that served as the door, feeling its rough texture in her hand, and entered.

Rei took a moment to let the events of the last few minutes settle around her. She didn't hate living in Ballarat, right at the edge of the Great Basin—the one on Earth, not the famous one on Proxima Centauri II. Yet ever since the last election, Rei grew more and more anxious to leave. She didn't mind living on a Dominion planet before, but her religious freedom wasn't impeded on before either. Unfortunately, she didn't know where she could go.

She pushed down those feelings and continued down the steps into the bar. The main body dove deep underground where it was naturally cooler.

It was a slow day, but there was plenty of laughter and talk that echoed off the walls and rang in her ears. It was a welcoming sound. The place boasted enough chairs and tables to fit most of the village, and to her left was the bar, a curved structure already filled with a few customers on stools. Her mother, Hotara, stood on the other side, filling orders with a speed and skill that bordered on magic while laughing at some joke.

Eyes shifted to Rei as she entered. Not all of them, but some. She was used to it. Most of the town inhabitants were capable of tracing their family lineage back several generations. With a population of no more than five hundred, their gene pool wasn't large or varied. Almost everyone shared the same Ballaratan dark eyes and black hair, making Rei's pale green eyes and brown hair an oddity. Of course, that wasn't the only thing that drew stares, judging from the way their gazes looked her up and down, lingering a little longer than they needed, but it was one of them. It made her "exotic," or at least that's the way she put it.

Hotara, on the other hand, was considered more alluring with her porcelain skin, despite years under the harsh sun, and raven hair, which she always kept in a practical braid. Rei could count on one hand the number of times she had seen her mother's hair loose. It cascaded like the shiny silks Rei saw in the market. Her mother's face also had an ageless quality that made patrons always try to guess how old she was. At first glance, Rei and Hotara appeared to be the same age, but it was Hotara's eyes that gave away her years. Rei couldn't help but be jealous, especially of her mother's lilac irises—an even rarer attribute to all the known planets of the star cluster.

Rei approached the bar where her mother poured several shots of Coronta—a deep violet liqueur Hotara personally distilled—on a tray sticky with the remnants of other drinks. Rei snatched two of the shots, quickly tossed back the first one, and gasped. The temporary burning gave way to warmth that started in her belly and flowed through the rest of her body. She sipped the second one slowly. All the while, her mother didn't comment, simply pouring two more shots. She picked up the tray and handed it to Rei. "Table four, and I am taking those shots out of your pay."

Rei took another sip. "You don't even pay me."

Her mother gave Rei an impish grin. "Oh damn, you're right. Just take that tray, and there will be another one waiting for you when you get back to me."

She did as she was told and returned to find Hotara holding another shot. Rei took it gratefully.

"Do you want to talk about it?"

Rei let the burning liqueur warm her tongue before she swallowed and spoke. "There was an execution. The baker's son who refused to convert."

Hotara was silent for several seconds, staring at the far back wall. "Gods. What is happening to this town?"

"Apparently, I am to blame since I won't fall in line. If I don't convert and convince the others to do so, I will be the next sacrifice." Rei leaned in closer to her mother. "It's not safe for us to stay here anymore. We should leave, but I don't want to leave Ballarat at the mercy of that asshole."

"We're not leaving." Hotara took the used glasses and ran them through the motorized brush, the soapy suds covered her hand. "It's safer for you here. We can deal with the cleric together."

Rei's face fell. "Safer? Are you serious? He singled me out."

"There are more dangerous monsters out in the star cluster than a cleric who has to pick on small women to feel strong."

Rei leaned against the bar and crossed her arms. Her mother was referring to the stranger who'd been hunting Rei her entire life, who killed her parents.

Rei set down her unfinished shot and took the cleaned glasses from her foster mother to dry them before putting them back on the shelf. "You have yet to tell me who this monster is. An invisible threat was scary when I was a child, but I'm twenty-two."

"I never told you who it was because I wanted you to have a normal childhood. I didn't want you consumed by pursuing someone who will never find you here." Hotara jammed a glass vigorously onto the brush.

"You told my brother."

Hotara stopped and let out a loud breath. "And look where that got Niklaryn. He was so consumed with revenge that it killed him."

The hair on the back of Rei's neck prickled. "Technically he was murdered by his best friend—"

"Don't get smart with me; you know what I mean. You are safer here. End of discussion."

Rei sighed, reached for her unfinished shot, and kicked back the rest of it. There were few things that scared her mother and whoever hunted Rei did. That alone gave Rei pause. Without this unknown threat hanging above her head, she would have left to avenge Niklaryn years ago. Instead, she had to stay because her brother died to keep her safe. Perhaps Hotara was right, there was no need to run. They would handle the cleric—he was just one man. She continued drying the rest of the glasses while Hotara drifted between tables for more orders.

Rei's gaze wandered around their little bar. Since the main room sat so low underground, the only lights came from old lamps stained from years of patrons smoking. The walls boasted a few old posters of bands who used to perform as they passed through. Other posters displayed advertisements, including one for the Ettowa Star Line—her family's most well-known business endeavor: luxury starships. But they were relatives she'd never met. No one in her family was aware she hid out here. She didn't dare even speak the name *Ettowa* out loud without Hotara worrying whose attention they would attract.

Rei used to daydream one of her relatives would find her and bring her back into the family, but the likelihood grew slimmer as she grew older. If an Ettowa were ever to come to Ballarat, now would be the best time. With their money and connections, Rei would use them to avenge her brother, or at least get away from the cleric. Yet, she knew she would never leave Hotara behind, and the stubborn woman refused to leave.

Across the bar sat one of their regulars, Sagitan Bronto, a retired Daer Knight, who wore his white hair short, which contrasted against his dark brown skin. His clothes fit his body well, accentuating that he was still in shape despite his age. For someone who spent a good part of the day at Coronta Bar, he rarely drank. He claimed he "simply enjoyed the company."

He watched one of the popular video logs on his touch screen, his back was to her so she had the perfect view.

Even though Rei didn't hear what the reporter said, the flash of bombs in another nameless city gave her a hint of what Sagitan was watching.

"More news on the civil war?" she asked.

Sagitan turned and put the screen down on the bar. "Yes. Trappist V wants to become Federation, but there is a strong Dominion base. They have elections coming up, but the violent ones can't wait. I'm interested in seeing how that plays out."

Another image of dark figures in red robes appeared on the screen, along with the byline about Infiernen Jessar and his Infinity Dogs almost making an appearance on Trappist V.

"Hasn't that man done enough damage? People should vote as they want, not because of fear," muttered Sagitan.

Rei's hatred for Infiernen ran deeper than his love of violence, and watching him use the same fear tactics as the cleric set her teeth on edge.

"Apparently not," she muttered. Her hand reached for the ring she wore on a cord around her neck. It belonged to her brother and was all that was left of him. "I wish the god queen would hurry up and return. She could rid us of the Dominion, and we can get some peace and quiet. He can die first." She pointed to the image of Infiernen on the screen.

"Who says it has to be the god queen?" asked Sagitan. "Or any of the gods? People can also move mountains, even if it is one stone at a time. You simply need to put yourself into a position where you can govern the change you want to see."

"Me? I am pretty sure you heard Hotara. Putting myself in such a position would require I leave Ballarat, and I am not going anywhere."

"Like I said, dear, one stone at a time. There's good you can do here and still defy the Dominion."

He was right. She hated the Dominion's current war on religion, among other things, and they needed someone to teach them a lesson. She may not reach the likes of Infiernen, but the cleric was close enough. An idea formed her in mind. It was simple, but it would be a start.

"Hotara," Rei called across the room. Her mother had been chatting with customers and her head jerked up at the mention of her name. "I hope you don't mind getting less sleep tonight. I have a stone I want to move."

# CHAPTER 3

REI YAWNED AS SHE SURVEYED HER HANDY WORK. SHE, Hotara, and Sagitan stayed up most of the night ripping up boards from around the temple windows and doors before piling them in front of the basilica of the One True God on the other side of the square. Rei continued on her own later, sweeping the temple, lighting the incense, and laying flowers at each of the twelve statues inside.

The temple matched the buildings around it with its low walls and aluminum roof, but the stained-glass windows made it unique. Its large weathered wooden doors were open. One image portrayed the God King Manden with a war hammer held high, while the other portrayed the God Queen Mica with her bladed staff. The soft smoke of incense spilled out down the steps and around several locals already gathered around the entrance. Most of them fervently wiped their faces of the dirt that permeated every inch of the town before entering. It didn't help.

Ballarat was cradled at the base of the Panamint Mountains, just at the outskirts of Death Valley. There were a few plants that managed to thrive in the heat, but they all had a perpetual layer of dust that allowed the vegetation to blend in with the dry earth around it—just like Ballarat's residents.

Rei picked the petals off a Golden Evening Primrose from her perch at the dead fountain as she continued to observe. The crowd had grown steadily since she arrived after breakfast. A few were even the recent "converts" to the

One True God. She smiled. One stone at a time. Niklaryn would have been proud. Even from this distance, the smell of Princesplums and incense from the temple tickled her nose.

"Rei, darling." Virga, Sagitan's wife, appeared at her side. She planted a soft kiss on Rei's cheek. She wore a bright scarf with pink and purple flowers, and her light blue eyes twinkled when she smiled. She had a round face made more prominent by the scarf. "How are you?"

Rei stifled another yawn. "Tired from doing the gods' work, but good. Yourself?"

"I'm well, thank you." Virga gave her a knowing smile.

Rei glimpsed another familiar face towering over the older woman. His attention fixated on the touch screen in his hands.

"Hello, Arram."

Virga's grandson was a head taller than she was, yet a few years younger. He slouched as though he didn't want to draw attention to himself. Like a shadow, he always kept to his grandmother's side. He met Rei's gaze and blinked at her with violet eyes. However, he didn't respond.

"Arram," Virga muttered.

"Hi," he said, although it sounded more like a grunt.

"I don't know what to do with this boy." Virga linked arms with the younger woman, pulling her off the fountain. "Shall we?"

Rei hesitated. She knew she probably shouldn't linger at the scene of the crime, so to speak. It was enough to reopen the temple for Ballarat, but she wasn't sure how much she should push her luck. The cleric didn't look pleased when he found the pile of wood at his doorstep this morning. It would only be a matter of time before he retaliated, and she would have to watch her drinks for poison from now on. For now, she would rather remind him these people belonged to her gods, not his.

"It's not a good idea. I'm supposed to be converting."

Virga laughed and released Rei's arm. "Sagitan told me. Next time you plan a stunt like that again, let me know. I love to rebel."

Rei covered her mouth in an attempt at feigned shock. "Stunt? Virga, I don't know what you're talking about. The temple was open when I arrived here this morning. Maybe our darling cleric finally realized we can all live in harmony?"

Both women glanced at the cleric, who scowled from his post at the entrance to the basilica, its hideous structure towering high above the buildings around it. Its golden roof reflected a sun beam into Rei's face.

Virga chuckled softly. "Of course. You are a model citizen and incapable of doing anything illegal." She cupped Rei's cheek. "Then run along before the cleric decides he wants a word with you. Your mother invited us over for dinner tonight, so we'll see you later. All right?"

Rei nodded and Virga turned to leave. "Come along, Arram," she called to her grandson.

"I'll be right there." His head tilted to the side as he edged closer to Rei.

She never liked the way he studied at her, the same way the cleric would look at a bug before squashing it under his shoe. She didn't know where Arram and his grandparents lived before they came to Ballarat, but she smelled privilege and it reeked.

"Why does it matter who worships many gods or one god?" he asked.

Rei blinked. "That's a question for the cleric. He's the one who believes we should choose one over the other. I don't care who people worship."

"You do, you little hypocrite. The two of you have been butting heads since before my grandparents and I arrived in this one-horse town. Why does it matter to you that people worship many gods?"

"Because they're real, Arram!" she growled, her face growing hot. "The Volocio are real. One of them has already been reincarnated, and it's only a matter of time before the god queen returns."

Arram raised an eyebrow. "You mean Kazimir Ettowa, claiming to be the god of illusion?" He snorted. "If that Ettowa is the real thing, I'm the son of the death god."

Rei's heart stopped at the mention of the name. Her name. "What does being an Ettowa have to do with it?"

He leaned against the side of the fountain and ran a hand through his hair, the same shade of brown as hers. "That family is rich, disgustingly rich, and I wouldn't be surprised if they paid the holy father to give him the title."

Rei pursed her lips. She knew the brotherhood who raised Kazimir was humble and lived a life with little to no earthly possessions. She didn't think these monks were so easily bought by her family's money. She liked to think they were men who took the religion seriously, unlike other monasteries with their jewel-encrusted walls who used their religion solely to make a profit. She never told anyone her relation to Kazimir.

"Well, my brother saw Kazimir's powers work," she said. "I believe him."

He chuckled. "Of course, the brother you bring up all the time and yet I've never met. He's probably some other illiterate yokel from this backwoods town," he sneered and barked a laugh. "You've convinced me, Rei. But please, satiate my curiosity: what's your brother's name?"

Rei felt the name Niklaryn Ettowa on the tip of her tongue. She wanted so much to say it, to boast about it. He was legendary; he was the best of the Daer Knights. She was so proud to be his sister. But unfortunately, everyone knew who he was, and revealing her relation to him would also reveal who she really was.

He smiled. "That's right. You never say. Makes me wonder if he exists, or he's some lie you use when you know you're losing an argument."

Rei shook and her muscles quivered. Her hand itched to slap his face, but she knew she had to take the higher ground. It's what her brother would have wanted. She breathed in loudly through her nose, trying to compose herself.

"This conversation is over." She pointed toward the temple, where Virga had long disappeared. "You should catch up to your grandmother. She appears to be missing her shadow." Now it was her turn to flash her teeth at Arram. "Now fuck off."

"Duly noted." He pulled away from the fountain and sauntered over to the temple. "See you at dinner later."

Rei rubbed her face and held back a yell. Any euphoria she had left was gone. She hated how much he got under her skin.

She crossed the square with the intent of heading back to the bar, replaying their conversation over and over in her head. She didn't stop until she reached the other side of the square, next to the pantheon of the One True God. Its hideous gold-painted roof left her angrier. It only reminded her how much this religion and Arram were monumental thorns in her side, and she was not looking forward to dealing with more of the young man's colorful remarks over dinner. The day had started out so well.

Rei turned the corner and collided with a figure.

"Ope, careful, little lady," said a light accented voice.

"Sorry." She stared at the stranger, her jaw dropping. His hood had fallen off, revealing a head of deep-red hair. He was older than she was; there were lines around his bright green eyes that smiled as he met her gaze. But the feature that drew her attention most was that every inch of visible skin was covered in freckles.

She had experienced this before. Her eyes relaxed as her vision multiplied, as though she were in two places at once. Swords clanged in the distance, crashing together, and her nose filled with the metallic scent of blood. The man stood in full battle gear, covered in blood that was not his; some had even splattered onto his face. He raised his war hammer, Nature's Wrath, as he yelled. His green eyes locked with Rei's as she held her own bladed staff high in the sky and she screamed in response. Lightning flashed above her, dancing across the clouds while the thunder clapped. Around her periphery, she could see long vines writhe and thrash.

She knew him. The gods had sent her this vision. They used to send more when she was a child, but their silence the last few years had caused her to doubt their faith in her. They wanted her to meet this man and her heart raced at the thought of it. She shook her head, the vision disappearing. She gave the stranger a shaky grin.

"I'm sorry." Her voice cracked. "This may sound odd, but I feel like I've met you before."

He let out a huge breath and a slow smile crept across his lips.

"I have the same feeling too," he said.

A lightness bloomed in her chest like she waited years for this moment. She was unaware of what the moment was, but she knew she had to trust the gods. She extended a trembling hand.

"I'm Rei."

# CHAPTER 4

The redhead took Rei's hand, and his calloused fingers gave hers a gentle squeeze. "I'm Manden."

"Manden? Like the god king?"

He shrugged. "My parents had an odd sense of humor."

Rei beamed. "Apparently."

His grin remained and his eyes roved all over her face as though trying to remember every detail. Eventually his gaze drifted to something behind her and his face fell. "Is he giving you trouble?"

Rei turned to see whom he referred to. The cleric stood in the shadow of the pantheon. His gaze never wavered from her face, and his mouth turned to a sneer.

"Nothing I can't handle." She turned back to Manden. "Then again, I do have the god king by my side."

"Good one," he said with a snort, running a hand through his hair, leaving it mildly disheveled. "Do you want to get out of here?"

"Here?" she squeaked.

"The square. I'm meeting up with a friend at a local bar. Would you like to join us?"

She still couldn't place where she had met him before. "Sure. I know the best bar in town."

"Coronta Bar, right?"

"Ah, so you know it."

"I have history with Hotara." He winked.

Rei grew cold. She had never seen Hotara with a man her entire life and puzzled over what made him different. If he was so important, Hotara would have mentioned him. "Uh, well . . . okay."

"Shall we?" He took one of the less-crowded side streets that opened to the big intersection and Rei followed. His companion waited close by. Her wild golden hair moved in the breeze as she leaned against the wall of a kiosk. With her back turned, she didn't see them as they approached.

"Hey!" Manden yelled as he stood just behind her.

"Shit the bed!" she exclaimed, spinning around. Her hazel eyes sparkled as she playfully punched Manden in the arm. "You scared me."

"You should pay more attention."

"Oh trust me, I was." She turned back and gestured to something across the street.

Rei followed their gazes. There was nothing except a couple of women standing near the open doorway of the local brothel with holographic butterflies hovering delicately around the entrance. The women had the typical dark features of the locals of the town. Their amber skin was visible as their long robes opened to reveal the curves of their breasts.

"Well, I see your tastes have improved, Bernie," Manden said.

"I have always appreciated beauty. It's not my fault you can't see it." Bernie giggled. "Do we have time to say hi? All work and no play makes me a dull girl."

"I would really like to get to the bar sometime this year," Manden said, wrapping an arm around the woman's shoulders and pulling her away.

"Killjoy." She blew a kiss at the women and finally faced Rei. The blonde raised an eyebrow. "Well, hello, beautiful."

"Hey, now," jumped in Manden. "This one you can't flirt with."

"Must you block me at every turn?" Bernie pouted. "What's your name, beautiful?"

"It's Rei."

"Hello, Rei. Bernie." She pointed to herself before extending a hand. "Well, introductions have been made, so let's go to this bar you wouldn't stop talking about." Bernie grabbed Manden by the arm and pulled him between her and Rei.

They passed the basilica and the cleric who had yet to leave his post. "You should smile more," Bernie said to him. "I'm sure you look prettier when you do." The cleric's scowl only deepened as his face turned a dark shade of red.

Rei held back a laugh. She stared in awe of this woman.

They walked along the main street in the shade of the colored tarp that protected them from the noonday sun. They passed a small stand with fabric hanging on a line.

Once they reached the intersection, Manden led the way with a confidence that boasted he had been here before. Perhaps he didn't lie about his history with Hotara, yet Rei worried about why her mother never mentioned a redhead. She wondered what sort of history they shared and prayed it wasn't grim. She dismissed the concern. Her instincts told her Manden wouldn't harm her mother.

Rei caught him watching at her. "You okay?" he asked.

She nodded. "I'm just surprised at how well you know your way to the bar."

"I've been here before."

They arrived at Coronta Bar within minutes. Rei followed Bernie, though when she was halfway down the steps, she realized Manden remained outside. She returned to the entrance to find him staring at the cloth door that hung limply in the ever-brightening sun.

"I guess it's my turn to ask if you're okay?" she asked.

Manden blinked. "Sorry. It has been a long time since I've seen her, and I'm nervous."

"Who is Hotara to you?"

His face fell. "Did she not tell you about me?"

Rei shook her head.

He pressed his lips together until all that remained was a line. Then he shrugged and patted Rei on the shoulder. "Well, then you're in for a surprise." He disappeared behind the curtain.

Rei furrowed her eyebrows. "Weirdo."

She pulled back the curtain, sweat and alcohol filling her nostrils. It was never the loveliest of odors, but it was familiar and it was home.

Several unfamiliar faces filled the bar. They stood out in their clean desert garb. Rei assumed they were passing through, but she'd never seen so many at one time.

She took note that many of them watched Manden tromp down the stairs. A hush calm came over the clientele —a redhead was a rarity.

Hotara's hair was in its usual braid, but a strand had come loose and hung in front of her face. She concentrated on mixing a drink, not noticing the most recent visitors right away. Bernie was the first to reach the bar and drew Hotara's attention. She looked up to take Bernie's order and saw Manden approaching. Hotara's eyes widened and her mouth hung open. The drink fell from her hands, and the clink of glassware hit the ground.

The palpable tension radiating between the two stopped Rei in her tracks. Hotara's cheeks grew red as she fidgeted with her braid over her shoulder. Her orchid eyes shone as they beheld Manden. Whatever they were to each other, the bond was strong.

Hotara turned around and pulled back the curtain to an entryway that connected their home to the bar, disappearing behind it. To Rei's surprise, it didn't take long for Manden to follow her.

Rei bound down the steps two at a time and passed through the curtain, but stopped. At the end of the hall, the couple embraced, murmuring in each other's ears. They pulled away and Manden ran a hand over Hotara's hair, then wiped away a tear that rolled down her cheek. Rei's mother pressed her lips against Manden's and pulled him close like he was her lifeline. They fit together like they were one being, and Rei felt she intruded on a moment she shouldn't, but her curiosity quelled any awkwardness.

"I missed you, Tara," Manden whispered.

The feeling of déjà vu returned. Rei never expected to see her mother so intimate, and yet everything about the scene unfolding in front of her felt right. She had seen this all before.

As Hotara and Manden broke the kiss, he held her hands in his. They both noticed Rei standing at the opposite end of the hallway. The rose color returned to Hotara's cheeks when she refused meet her daughter's eyes.

"I'm sorry, I didn't know what I was expecting," Rei said. "I am just very confused what this"—she gestured to the couple—"is. What is happening?"

"Rei," began Hotara but faltered.

"Who is he?" Rei's heart beat unnaturally fast.

"You never told her about me—" Manden began.

"You!" Rei cut him off. "You don't talk. I am asking Hotara because I don't understand what is happening." She looked at her mother, who still appeared unable to respond.

"Mom?" Rei hadn't called Hotara by that name since she was a small child.

Hotara glanced at Manden, who stared at Rei as if not sure what to do with her. "Manden, can you take care of the bar? Rei and I need a minute"

Manden nodded, shuffling sideways as he walked past Rei. He gave her one last look and a smile as he lifted the curtain and left.

The curtain didn't completely block out the noise of the rowdy patrons on the other side, but it muffled the sound. Rei and Hotara peered at each other for several minutes while she waited for her mother to give a response.

"Manden is my husband," Hotara finally confessed.

The earth shifted beneath Rei's feet. She rubbed her temples, a habit at times she felt overwhelmed.

"Why didn't you tell me you were married?"

Hotara didn't respond at first. That's what hurt. Rei didn't have many friends, and she expected more from Hotara. Her mother was her best friend, and yet she had kept such a vital piece of personal information from Rei.

"It was hard," Hotara whispered.

"What was?"

"Being far from him for years."

Rei bit her lip and frowned. "But you could have contacted him, right?"

Hotara shook her head. "Manden has a high rank within the Federation, and he didn't want them to know his background. He's been playing the bachelor all these years because if we messaged, anyone in the Dominion or the Federation might come sniffing around to find out who I am. And if they found me . . ."

Rei took a shaky breath. "They would find me."

"Exactly."

The truth weighed heavily on Rei's chest. Hotara's hands returned to her braid and fidgeted with the end. Her mother was taller than Rei, and yet in this moment, she looked so small, so vulnerable. Her eyes didn't have the same fiery glow, and her lips trembled as she held back tears, making Rei regret being so harsh. "But that doesn't explain why you couldn't tell me."

"Because if I even mentioned him, then I would think about him." Hotara's voice shook. "I missed him. It was easier just to focus on you and our life here. I needed to not speak of him to help ease the pain."

Rei couldn't imagine loving someone so deeply that being away from him hurt that profoundly. The only time she felt anything close to that kind of loss was when her brother had died, but that was different. He was all she had as blood family.

Rei leaned against the wall and stared at the curtain, open just enough to reveal Manden on the other side. He chatted with Bernie, who stood near the large music player. The green light reflected off her face as she pushed a few buttons, and the twang of a guitar erupted from the speakers. The blonde must've said something funny because he threw his head back and laughed.

When Rei glanced back at Hotara, tears filled her mother's eyes.

"I am sorry I didn't tell you before. I know there are a lot of things I haven't told you concerning my past, but there will be a time when everything will be made clear to you. Manden's coming here is the beginning of that."

The feeling of betrayal reduced to a dull pain in her chest. Rei kept her mouth shut, knowing that if she spoke, she would say something hurtful. She loved her mother so much. This woman who let her husband leave to "play his part" so she could live on the edge of the star cluster to raise a child who was not her own. Rei knew not talking about Niklaryn helped her deal with the pain at times. She understood Hotara's motives.

"How long will he be here?" Rei asked, never taking her eyes off him.

"He's passing through to do some recruiting. They leave tomorrow night."

Rei nodded. "Well, that doesn't leave you much time." She pulled the curtain aside and entered the bar.

"Wait, Rei." But she didn't stop to listen. She approached Manden, who leaned against the other side of the bar. His back was to her, and it was Bernie who pointed her out from where she stood near the music player, eyeing the Ettowa Starline advertisement.

"Yes, little lady?" Manden asked, turning to face her.

"You should go to her." She looked him in the eyes. "She needs to be with you."

Manden didn't hesitate. He dashed through the curtain, gone in moments. Rei closed her eyes and let everything wash over her, the sound of the crowd, the clink of glass as guests cheered, patrons arguing—but not loudly enough to discern over what—and the smell of beer, salt, and citrus.

"A little overeager, no?" asked Bernie, taking a swig of a Coronta Sour from a dainty blue glass. She approached the bar and swung a leg over an empty stool.

Rei looked for her tray to start filling orders when she noticed Sagitan had already taken over helping serve their patrons for the night. This was not the first time he had done this, but tonight she couldn't be more grateful.

Rei took a glass and poured some Coronta. She added a splash of water before taking a sip. "Apparently, they haven't seen each other for years."

"I know. Manden wouldn't shut up about her the whole flight here." Bernie stared at her glass. "I mean, I'm glad that he is reunited with his lady love, but I wish he would have talked someone else's ear off."

Rei grinned. She felt seconds away from being overwhelmed, but years of working at a bar taught her to keep her personal problems hidden from the customers. She pushed down the feeling.

"So what kind of a name is Bernie?" Rei took another sip, the burn from the drink filled her tongue, making her gasp.

"What kind of name is Rei?"

"It's short for Reina."

"Pretty." She pointed to herself. "Bernadette."

"Got a last name, Bernadette?" Rei took another sip.

"Boyard."

It turned out that the day was not finished in serving Rei surprises. Rei almost choked on her drink. That was not a name she expected out here in the backwaters of the star cluster. Boyard was practically royalty among the Federation, considering their patriarch. "Are you related to Urius Boyard?"

"He's my uncle."

Rei's eyes grew wide as she took in a new appreciation of the blonde in front of her. No wonder she wasn't afraid of the cleric. He knew who she was and what it would mean for him to harm Federation military royalty.

She looked back at the curtain where Manden had disappeared moments before. "Manden must be very important to the Federation if he is working with a close relative to Urius Boyard."

Bernie finished the rest of her drink. She reached over

the bar to take the bottle of Coronta and poured herself some more. "I wouldn't know. We only just met."

Rei smelled the lie. The two appeared too at ease with each other to be casual acquaintances. Hotara had just told her Manden lived publicly as a bachelor so he had to trust Bernie enough to bring her out here. They were planning something, two high ranking officers wouldn't come to the backwaters of the star cluster for mere recruiting, but their timing couldn't be more perfect. Perhaps they could help her with the cleric or at least keep her out of harm's way in case the cleric decided she needed a dose of Drops of Jupiter. Then the realization dawned on her: maybe she could help the Federation track down Niklaryn's killer. Her brother was their shining star, after all.

Rei took another sip of her drink. "I hear you're recruiting."

"We are. Do you recommend someone?"

Rei leaned in with both hands on the bar. "Yeah. Me."

Bernie raised her eyebrows and leaned back, crossing her arms. "Did not expect that. I like your moxie."

Rei smirked. Bernie was easy enough and Hotara was going to hate this idea. Manden was the wild card. She needed him on her side to convince her mother. Her little war with the cleric was nothing compared to what she really wanted: Infiernen's head on a plate. It was safe to assume Bernie and Manden would also be joining them for dinner, and she could work on them then. She raised her glass. "To the Federation?"

The officer raised hers. "To the Federation."

# CHAPTER 5

"WHAT IS WRONG WITH YOU?" ASKED HOTARA AS SHE and Rei pushed together tables in the bar, enough to fit their guests. "Weren't you listening when I told you that it's safer here in Ballarat?"

Rei lugged a pile of plates from behind the bar. "Yes, but that was before I discovered you have a husband who's a high-ranking officer working alongside Urius Boyard. I mean, it's the Federation! Whoever killed my parents is in the Dominion because Niko fought alongside the likes of Bernie against whoever they are. I am sure Manden can keep me safe."

"Yes, but then this person will know where you are." Hotara aggressively folded a napkin before handing it to Rei to place. "At the moment, he thinks you are simply hidden somewhere in the Tyre Star Cluster. That's anywhere on fourteen planets. The minute you align yourself with the Federation, he'll know you're with them. Only three planets have voted for the Federation in the last decade, Rei. Three!"

Rei's skin tingled. This was the most they had talked about her parents' killer, and the threat felt like more than a dark shadow hanging over her head. "So my hunter is a man?"

Hotara's face grew red. She flopped down into the nearest chair and put her head in her hands. "I swear, you're not listening to what I'm saying."

"I am." Rei sat down next to Hotara and pulled the

woman's hands from her face. "I am. Look, you don't have to tell me who it is. I have no intention of going after him."

"But you have every intention of going after Infiernen, right? You always lose your head where your brother is concerned. Killing him is not going to bring Niko back."

Rei sighed and picked at folded napkin in front of her. "Nothing will bring him back. I just feel useless out here."

Hotara cupped Rei's cheek. "You are destined for great things, darling. But the timing isn't right. Until then, I want —no, I need you safe."

Rei pulled away. "Timing?"

"You're not ready yet."

"How am I not ready? You've made sure I know how to handle a bladed staff. Niklaryn drilled me on whatever knowledge of guns and weapons he learned from his years at the Daer Academy. You both wanted me to know how to defend myself and I can. What more do I need?"

They were interrupted by someone clearing their throat. "Bad time?" asked Manden from the top of the stairs. Bernie stood next to him, a bottle of wine in hand.

"No," Rei said, leaving her chair to continue setting the table.

"Tara, can I speak with you a moment?" he asked, gesturing to the back of the bar.

Hotara nodded and followed. The two disappeared behind the curtain

Bernie placed the bottle at the center of the table. "Do you need help?"

"Sure," Rei replied. "Just fold some napkins and I'll grab some silverware." They were conveniently behind the bar, not too far from where Hotara and her husband were likely arguing about Rei's future. She hovered close to the curtain.

"She's still vulnerable, Manden," Hotara snapped. "The time isn't right."

"I know. But Urius is adamant about having her join. I was already sent to pick up Arram and his grandparents. He sent Bernie along with me to make sure I picked her up as well."

"*Aun no he semanifestao.*"

Rei gasped at the last sentence. When she was a child, Hotara taught her a secret language. It was their code. Rei thought it was all made up but now wondered if Manden knew as well. *They haven't manifested yet,* her mother said. She never realized something was supposed to manifest. She rubbed her temples as a headache pierced the area between her eyes.

"We can keep her safe until then," Manden answered in the same language.

"Like you kept Niklaryn safe?"

Rei inched closer to the gap between the curtain to better see. Manden leaned against the wall. "There was nothing to be done for Niklaryn. Can—can we just get through dinner? It's our last night together, and I don't want to waste it on anger."

Hotara sighed. "I know. I think she needs more time. I don't want to send her out until she's ready."

He tucked a strand of her hair behind her ear. "Like I said, Urius is adamant. Unless you want to fight him for her."

She laughed. "That wouldn't be fair to him. You know I'd win."

Manden chuckled. "I know, love."

Rei hurried to the bar to grab the silverware and scurried back to the table before the couple returned.

"Hear anything interesting?" Bernie raised an eyebrow.

"Perhaps a little too interesting."

Hotara and Manden returned to the bar and the four continued setting the table. Rei's thoughts wandered back to the secret conversation. She didn't understand why Urius wanted her to join the Federation. It was likely because she was Niklaryn's sister and a guaranteed ally. They only had three planets in the star cluster and needed as many people on their side as possible.

Her thoughts returned to the talk of something manifesting. Rei's heart pounded as she considered what was supposed to appear. Nothing she came up with would signify her being "ready" to join the Federation. The headache remained, like a pick shooting between her eyes. This was all too much. She just wanted to get off the planet. It shouldn't be complicated.

"We hope we're not too late." Virga's voice popped into Rei's head. She and Sagitan descended from the entrance above, their grandson not far behind and toting a large bowl of cream. Though Rei knew Virga's famed dessert had layers of fruit swimming underneath.

"Not at all." Hotara took the bowl from Arram. "You're just in time."

Everyone helped to place the food on the table, and Rei settled between Bernie and Virga while Arram sat across from her. The young man reached out to grab a rosemary chicken leg, but Virga lightly slapped his hand away. "We need to pray, dear," she said. "Rei, child, would you do us the honor of saying grace?"

They bowed their heads in prayer and she said a short one. Afterward, Virga began to pile Rei's plate for her, spoonfuls of rice, covered in sauces and herbs.

Rei raised a hand. "Ma'am, you don't need to make my plate."

"Don't bother trying to stop her," Sagitan said with a wink. "Virga will do as she pleases."

"That's right," Virga said. "I enjoy doing it, and besides, Rei, you're so skinny and could use some more food. I worry that if I don't feed you, you won't put enough on your plate." She piled on more rice and sauce before proceeding to Sagitan's plate. As she did, she leaned in and gave her husband a soft peck on the lips.

"Thank you, my dear," he said with a grin.

The meal was marvelous, but Rei found the company better. Virga was so vivacious with an infectious laugh. After dinner, Sagitan and Virga argued over how they met, each of them butting in to tell the entertaining story. Manden and Bernie frequently refilled glasses with wine until Hotara had to run to the bar for more. Rei's cheeks grew warm with each sip.

Rei raised an eyebrow as she looked over at Arram, who leaned back in his chair and took a long swig of his wine.

"Are they always like this?" She gestured to his grandparents.

He nodded. "Yup. They are really that sweet. I never get tired of it, though."

Rei gave him an incredulous stare. "And here I thought you didn't have a heart."

"Don't tell anyone." He gave her just a hint of a smile. His eyes shone from the light above the dining table and, from a certain angle, he reminded her of Niklaryn. He had the same eye shape and nose. Or maybe it was her own mind playing tricks on her. The moment was gone when his scowl returned. She recalled Manden saying he was there to pick up Arram and his grandparents and wondered why Urius wanted someone like him. She gritted her teeth at the unfairness of it all.

"Why do you get to join the Federation?" she asked and the table grew quiet.

Arram's eyes widened when he realized the question was directed at him, but it was Bernie who responded. "Um . . . why do you think Arram is joining the Federation?"

Rei threw her fork on her plate with a loud clatter and turned to Hotara and Manden. "I heard them arguing about it."

No one spoke, but a few shifted in their seats. Arram ran his hand through his hair until it was a disheveled mess. His eyes darted to his grandparents as though they held the answers, yet Rei's gaze never left his face, waiting for him to respond.

"Why—why not?" he stuttered. "Anyone can join the Federation."

"Not everyone gets a personal escort from Urius Boyard's own niece. What makes you so special?" Rei rubbed her temples again as the pain in her head grew more intense.

"I'm not special."

"I know you're not," she growled. "So why?"

Virga put her hand on Rei's shoulder. "Rei, sweetheart, are you all right?"

"No. I want someone to answer me!" she cried. "Why is it important that he goes, and I have to wait until it's the 'right time'?" She breathed hard.

"Infiernen's hunting me!" answered Arram with a tremble in his voice.

The air rushed from Rei's lungs at the mention of her brother's murderer. "What?" she whispered.

Arram pulled back the collar of his shirt with a shaking hand, revealing a puckered scar—he was branded with an infinity mark. It was the symbol of Infiernen and his Infinity Dogs.

"I thought the brands were just a rumor," Rei said.

"Wrong place at the wrong time." Arram straightened his collar.

"Don't they do that to mark homosexuals?" Those who didn't follow the Dominion's preferred religion weren't the only ones suffering persecution.

"They do."

Rei stared at Arram, his violet eyes dimmed as he stared at his hands. What kind of monsters would mark someone like him?"

"It's how a lot of dictators manage to get their foothold when they want power," Sagitan said. "They create an enemy for the people to rally behind. In this case, Sovereign Praymer chose a minority of successful people who already had a long history of persecution and literally gave the people permission to treat them like second-class citizens." He sighed and took a sip of wine. "Desperate people believe the lie because they want it to be true, and it distracts them from their own problems."

"I was outed by a concerned neighbor." Arram spat the last word. "It was Infiernen who did the deed. We managed to escape, and since then we have been on the run."

She didn't know if she should pity Arram or remain jealous that he was able to leave. Perhaps both. Rei wrung her hands as she stood, adrenaline pumping through her legs. The ground lurched beneath her feet and colors formed along the edge of her vision. The pain in her head spiked.

"Rei, are you all right?" asked Hotara.

"I have this horrendous pain." A pressure formed behind her eyes. She must've had too much to drink.

Perhaps she should rest. Her eyes fluttered closed and the rush of adrenaline fled from her body; she felt like she was in a free fall. Someone distantly called her name.

Her eyes snapped open, and she no longer sat in the bar.

She stood on a balcony overlooking a brightly lit city sitting on the edge of a vast lake. Two moons hung like lanterns in the sky. The bigger one was silver, and its light revealed a land of rolling hills and forests beyond the city walls. The smaller one had a violet hue that reminded Rei of her mother's eyes.

What a strange dream.

The sharp stroke of a fiddle and the raucous laughter of people cut through the silent night as Rei saw people dancing and drinking below, but it felt far away. She was too focused on the fact that she wasn't alone. A lock of his dark hair fell into his darker eyes. He brushed the strand away. The sword peeking out from the strap on his back and the pistol resting on his hip outed him a Daer Knight. The simple sight of him was enough to make her pulse race, and her heart almost broke with every moment he wasn't hers.

Somehow, Rei knew this secret meeting of theirs was forbidden.

She didn't care.

All that mattered was the stranger with the deep, dark eyes. Her hands moved of their own accord to remove a satin glove that ran up to her elbow. The fabric felt expensive, but her interest in the man washed away any desire to inspect them. The simple act of taking off these garments felt taboo; the gloves marked her as another's, but she was no one's property.

"Micaela," he breathed.

A vague memory played in the back of her mind. Her parents would also call her Micaela. But it was always when they were alone at home and in hushed tones—almost as if it were a secret, very much like this meeting.

"Shh," she whispered, placing a naked hand over his lips. *By the gods, they are soft.* Her hand moved to his chest, feeling his heartbeat steadily under her touch.

"What about…" he began.

"It doesn't matter," she whispered. She moved closer to him until they were only inches apart. His mouth parted only slightly, and he breathed hard from the hunger she saw in his eyes.

"It does," the handsome man said. "If your husband finds out."

"He won't find out, and frankly I don't care if he does. I love you, Atrius."

Rei didn't know who this husband was, but he might as well not exist. She wanted to see where this fantasy would lead. The way this Atrius looked at her made wave after wave of emotion crash against the shore of her mind, each one more devastating than the next. The fire in his eyes threatened to consume her and she welcomed it.

He leaned in and softly pressed his lips against hers. Her pulse raced as she took her ungloved hand and placed it behind his neck, grasping his soft hair. He wrapped an arm around her waist, pulling her closer. Passion coursed like a boiling river through her veins as he pulled her other glove off.

Atrius's protests had been a gauzy veil of propriety, and the heat of his need for her burned it all away.

His kiss grew deeper, leaving her wanting more. She arched against him, pressing against his strong body as his hands ran down her back, tugging at the thin fabric separating his fingers from her skin.

Rain splattered on her skin, falling hard enough to

plaster her curled hair to her head. Rei no longer felt Atrius's arms. Angry, plump clouds crowded the sky above. She stood in a courtyard as it showered around her.

Atrius lay in her arms, wincing as each drop fell on his face. Blood ran from his nose and ears, and he shuddered. Poison. Drops of Jupiter. It was a horrible way to die.

"I'm sorry. I tried to kill him," Atrius said between labored breaths. He clenched his teeth as the poison slowly destroyed his nerves.

Rei said nothing. Her vision blurred as tears filled her eyes. Anguish ripped through her as she watched her love's life fade before her. She held him tighter, wishing to take his pain for her own.

"You will get through this," she whispered. "There has to be an antidote. I already lost Max and the others. I can't lose you too."

His eyes filled with words unspoken, and his pain tore Rei's heart anew.

The light faded in Atrius's eyes, and his body relaxed in her arms.

"Atrius?" she asked. "Atrius!" This time she yelled louder.

Rei's eyes snapped open from where she lay on the sticky wet floor. Atrius's name was still on her lips as she brought a hand to her face, wet with tears. Her heart ached at the memory of him. Her vision grew more focused and six pairs of eyes stared down at her.

"Atrius?" asked Manden.

Rei's face burned at the memory. He and Sagitan helped her to stand and Virga handed her a damp napkin to wipe her face. She briefly locked eyes with Arram, and he gave her sad smile. The headache had evaporated, but an ache in her chest took its place.

"Did you hear what she said?" Manden whispered to Hotara. "I think it's time."

Bernie put a finger to her lips. "And the timing is bad." No one moved as they listened. A deep roar dotted with a piercing scream and the pop of gunshots rattled Rei to her core.

She scrambled up the steps to the entrance above, and the screams grew louder as she drew nearer to the curtain, the noise outside competing with the thunderous beat of her heart in her ears. She drew back the cloth and discovered a large hooded figure with a sword raised high racing toward her.

# CHAPTER 6

Rei screamed and backed away from the curtain. An explosion rocked the earth, and Rei lost her footing and tumbled down the stairs. Arram rushed to her side, helping her stand and drawing her back as dark figures entered the bar. Only Negander dressed in that shade of blood red. Sagitan approached the fighters, a pistol and gladius having magically materialized in his hands.

"That's him!" One pointed at Arram. "Infiernen wants him."

One of the newcomers aimed his gun at Sagitan. A shower of bullets rained on the master, but he twirled the blade in front of him, and the shots bounced off with little spectacular sparks. Sagitan's movements were a blur, like he merely swatted away flies. Niklaryn used to tell her that Daer could deflect bullets, but she always assumed he lied.

"Run!" yelled Bernie, coming to their side, a large rifle in hand. "We'll hold them off! Sagitan and Virga will get you out." Rei almost ran but saw Arram hesitate out of the corner of her eye.

"Arram, come!" bellowed Virga, pulling him toward Rei.

Manden, Hotara, and Bernie approached the Negander as Rei, Arram, Sagitan, and Virga bolted for the hall behind the bar.

They raced through the kitchen. The bullets Sagitan's blade didn't deflect whistled by them, chips of plaster flying from the wall next to them. The room filled with dust from the broken bits of clay, and the smell of gunpowder filled

Rei's nose. Bile rose in her throat, but she pushed it down. She kept her arms on Arram's shoulder, pushing him forward as they fled out the back door.

Outside was no safer. People screamed and ran, followed by more figures in red cloaks who cut down any local they caught. A huge explosion rocked the ground beneath them, and the whole town erupted in pandemonium: buildings caught on fire, cries echoed, and the smell of smoke hung in the air. Rei stood in shock as she watched the flames devour her town.

Sunrise wouldn't arrive for hours, the only light dancing from the flames of nearby buildings. Rei took Arram's hand and pulled him away from the house and down the street.

"Keep going!" yelled Sagitan as more bullets sparked off his blade. Virga remained at his side, his pistol in her hand as she picked off some of the soldiers as they approached.

Rei pulled Arram and they dove between two buildings. The other side revealed a blazing intersection, the fire scorched Rei's cheeks as the smell of flesh reached her nose. Her heart reached her throat at the thought of her neighbors trapped in this inferno.

"There they are!" Another figure in red pointed at them.

Arram yanked Rei back to where they came, only to discover it engulfed in flames. The Negander had cut off another means of escape. They had no choice but to dash down the intersection toward the large basilica that remained untouched by the fire. Rei took Arram's hand and rushed toward the square. People were lined up and gunned down by more figures in red. The rage of unsatisfied revenge boiled her blood. Her stomach turned over and her eyes stung from unshed tears.

"Out of my way!" bellowed a man, shoving Rei against

the wall as he passed them escaping the carnage at the square. His head exploded in a burst of red. Bits of his brain landed on Rei and she screamed. The man's headless body crumpled in a heap at Arram's feet, and ahead of them a Negander pointed a platinum pistol in their direction. The light of the fire behind Rei and Arram illuminated the knight's face. Her cloak fell back to reveal a heavy square jaw and a milky-white scar that ran from her right ear across her nose to her left eye.

The Negander turned to someone out of view. "I found them!" The woman then cocked her head to the side. "Who are you?"

A gun cracked. The Negander spun her sword and the bullet met her blade with a flash.

Rei watched in horror as vines grew around the woman's legs, and she was suddenly yanked out of sight with a scream. Rei turned to Arram, his cheek red from the blaze behind them. They readied their guns and inched toward the end of the alley.

"Rei?" It was Bernie.

They turned the corner to find Bernie, Hotara, and Manden with the unconscious Negander lying between them, wrapped in the mysterious vines.

"Thank the gods you are alive." Rei threw her arms around Hotara's neck.

"I wish we had more time," her mother whispered.

"It doesn't matter." She pulled back and met Hotara's gaze.

"Finish this later. We gotta go," Manden said, hand outstretched toward the unconscious Negander while holding a beautiful long staff with swirls carved into its body and a half-foot long blade on one end. "This is for you," he said handing it to her. "You'll need this."

Rei grabbed the staff, and her eyes shifted between it and the gun. While she knew her way around a staff, she didn't understand what Manden expected as gunfire popped around them. "Really?" she asked.

"Trust me," the redhead said with a smirk. Rei slung the staff over her shoulder.

"Did you see my grandparents?" breathed Arram.

"What?"

"At the bar, did you see my grandparents?"

"The bar is gone," Bernie said. "The Negander burned it."

Arram turned to Rei. "We have to go back. I think something happened."

Rei watched the world burn around them. Despite their feelings for each other, she and Arram were on the same side, and they had to stick together. She knew the distant look in his eyes. It wouldn't be long until Arram would try to return for his grandparents. Arram nodded as though reading her thoughts and the two bolted down the street to return to where they last saw Sagitan and Virga.

"Goddamnit!" Manden yelled. "Wait!"

"There they are!" a Negander cried, running alongside them. One ran next to Arram—too close for Rei. She fired her gun at the figure, but the bullet ricocheted off the blade. Rei yelled as the bullet grazed her arm, knocking her to the ground. She scrambled to find the gun but lost it in the kicked-up dirt. With no choice, she grabbed her staff and kept running. Arram was already far ahead of her.

"Careful!" cried one of the figures. "She's not to be harmed!"

"Faster!" Rei cried. "They're going to cut us off!" The burning inside her roared. She wanted to kill them. She wanted to throw everything she had at them.

"Rei! Arram!" Hotara cried. Bernie and Manden weren't too far behind. The ground shuddered beneath them from another explosion, and it threw Arram and Rei to the ground.

"Grab them!" someone yelled.

The Negander circled them like hawks, cutting off another direction to escape. Soon there would be nowhere to go.

"Bernie, be careful!" Manden yelled.

"Manden!" cried Hotara, swinging her staff toward the enemy, warning them to stay back.

The world slowed down, and everything crystallized in horrific detail. The smell of burned flesh filled her nostrils, and bodies lay strewn across the streets. Some were Negander, but most were people she had known since her childhood.

Spots littered Rei's vision as she ran, but they didn't shield her from the constant onslaught of images of the destruction of her home. Some of the Ballaratans helped Bernie and Manden fight the Negander, but the locals were getting in the way.

One Negander swung for Rei's head with the hilt of his gladius. Rei ducked and thrusted the staff blade into the man's back.

"Manden, Hotara, I need help," Bernie yelled as she took a shot.

Another Negander approached Bernie from behind. Rei ripped the blade from the dead man, changed her grip on her staff, and launched it. Her weapon landed with a loud thud against the man's chest, pinning him to the ground.

Hotara threw her hands toward the blonde, and the ground rumbled beneath them, opening and swallowing the

Negander whole. Rei's head grew faint; her eyes were playing tricks on her or the smoke had grown too thick.

She lost track of Arram, only to find him turning the corner toward her house. She followed and found him standing over Virga and Sagitan. The older woman lay in a heap, the blood on the floor encircling her head like a halo, while Sagitan's eyes were closed, and his hand wound tightly around hers; a large hole in his stomach leaked vital fluid into the crimson pool of blood surrounding them.

Something inside her burned and she shook. Why did the Negander do this? Virga and Sagitan had done nothing. They were innocent. They didn't deserve it. No one deserved to die like this.

Her thoughts went to the Ballaratans, to the man whose blood stained her shirt, to those who burned in the fire. Anger from her brother's death resurfaced. These same monsters who took Niklaryn were not satisfied. Now they came for Arram's grandparents, and only the gods knew what they wanted with her and Arram.

The air filled with ash that fell like rain around her. Only Manden, Hotara, and Bernie stood between her and their captors. The redhead's eyes were vacant, and Bernie's shoulders hunched. Hotara's black hair whipped around her, sticking to her face, now wet with tears. They had failed. Everything Hotara did to protect Rei was all for nothing. And now they'd have Arram too. Her heart pounded in her chest, threatening to burst.

"I have him!" cried the cleric, grasping a fistful of Arram's hair. He held a large bloodied knife at the young man's throat, a thin line of red dripping down. "Infiernen told me he wanted the boy dead."

Something snapped inside Rei. Color filled her vision until all she saw was white light. White cleansing light. She clenched her fists, turned her head up to the heavens and yelled, letting loose all of her sadness, anger, and frustration.

She screamed and screamed, her voice becoming unearthly and powerful, taking on a strange tone. The sound echoed from some unknown place, then multiplied, taking on the form of all the victims who had lost someone they loved to violence. She cried harder and harder, straining her lungs. She raised her staff in the air, calling on the heavens to aid her. She was their champion.

As she felt the end of her breath, she threw her hand up and shoved it through the air. In response, the air crackled as she surrounded herself in the white light. She wanted to cleanse the world in fire.

Then lightning struck her staff, filling her with power. She threw her hands forward. Lightning came, flying toward the cleric, throwing him away from Arram. His body blackened until all that remained were ashes that scattered into the air. She swept her hand over the closed ranks of Negander savages. Their screams filled the air while their bodies slowly blackened to charred husks. She took a step forward—or tried to. Instead, her eyes rolled back in her head and she fainted.

# CHAPTER 7

Bronx stood in a golden forest. Shimmering leaves that reflected the sunlight covered the ground around him, yet he saw no sun. Black tree trunks reached the height of at least three men before the first golden branch appeared. A gentle breeze moved through the woodland, carrying with it the soft scent of lavender. He took a few steps forward, daring to venture in further. The soft ground absorbed the sound of his footsteps. He didn't see a single living thing around him, and the silence wrapped him like a cocoon.

The crack of a branch echoed in the distance, and Bronx whipped around but saw nothing. He wasn't alone.

"Bronx?"

He snapped awake. Crona peered down at him. He must've dozed off. Documentation was the most boring part of being a combat medic for the Federation, but Bronx preferred the monotony over returning to the battlefield. He wasn't ready for that yet.

"Interesting read?" she asked, gesturing to the mountain of paperwork.

"Riveting."

"Yeah, the snoring was a good indication." She pulled out the chair opposite him and sat down.

He chuckled. "It's the only way to let people know. In case they're curious about what I'm reading."

"I'm well aware of the practice. I believe I have done my fair share of snoring after reading some captivating reports on supply chains." She snorted, taking a handful of papers and placing them in a folder.

"Must run in the family, then."

"At least on Mom's side. From what I knew of your dad, he would have actually stayed awake for this sort of thing." She cocked her head to the side. "Professor of Anthropology, right?"

Bronx nodded but bit his tongue. Crona never met his father, but he knew hers. He never got along with his half-sister's father and was quite certain that anything he said in her presence would come off as an insult.

He returned to his paperwork.

From where they were stationed on the planet Gliese VI, they saw little action in the current civil war with the Dominion. However, they were close enough to get the wounded from nearby planets, the ones still fighting to be free of the hold of their leader, Sovereign Anekris Praymer. Bronx currently filled out a form in the medical wing for a soldier who was flown in the day before. First Petty Officer . . . something Prue; he couldn't recall the soldier's first name now. He'd been brought to Gliese VI because it was the closest facility and currently lay in a bed, the steady beep of his heart monitor the only sound that echoed in the medical wing.

It wasn't a very large facility with its six beds and various monitors and machines, with desks for the medics on the far end. Despite being underground, the shiny metal plating surrounding them made it easy to keep clean and avoid infection.

"Manca! Sandern! I was just looking for you two. I have news!" Kazimir Ettowa entered the medical wing with a large piece of paper. He ran a free hand through his unruly black hair, his blue eyes bright.

"Your family, Kaz?" asked Crona.

Kaz nodded and handed the message to Bronx.

*Found them. Had a little run-in with Negander while on Earth. Will be arriving on Gliese VI within the hour. Have Bronx bring a stretcher.*

*—M*

"What does it mean?" asked Crona, who read it over Bronx's shoulder.

"Obviously, someone's hurt," Kaz said.

"Or worse," said Bronx quietly.

"No need to be negative just yet." Crona pointed at the time stamp on the message. "Let's go. They'll be here soon-ish, and I want to welcome our new friends to the party."

"I'll help with the stretcher," Kaz offered.

Bronx threw other necessary supplies—a pulse scanner, gauze, and tools for stitches—into a bag and slung it over his shoulder. He joined Kaz in helping with the stretcher

The beeping from Prue's heart monitor grew erratic, and the petty officer breathed irregularly with labored and painful sounds that stopped as quickly as they began.

Bronx dropped his bag, sat down at the edge of Prue's bed, and took off his gloves, unsure why he did it, as if his actions were not his own. His heart hammered in his chest, knowing what was about to happen, and yet he didn't fight it; some part of him knew this was the right thing to do.

"Uh . . . Bronx—" began Crona as she approached him, but it was too late.

Bronx reached out and took the man's hand. Some force pulled on what felt like a string. Teasing him, taunting him. He tugged on it hard and everything unraveled. Dread pooled in his core. He knew what he'd freed—a soul. A plume of black smoke appeared above Prue's body, curling upwards before it dissipated in the air. Prue took one last deep breath and with a heavy sigh, he died.

"Shit," muttered Bronx as he regained control of his body, releasing Prue's hand like it burned him. He leaped from his seat and backed away, knocking over a tray of scalpels and tongs. The metal clanged as each of the pieces hit the ground. This was not the first time, but he always prayed it would be the last. He looked over at his sister; Crona said nothing as she put a hand to her mouth, stunned.

Bronx felt his sister approach. "Are you alright?" she asked.

Bronx's eyes darted in her direction. His face lost all feeling, his legs weak. He'd done it again, and this time, there'd been witnesses. Shit.

Bronx rubbed his face. "I—I don't know what happened. I don't know what I was thinking."

"I'm sure you had a good reason," Kaz said.

"That's the thing." Bronx paced, adrenaline rushing through his legs. "I didn't have a good reason. I just felt compelled. Like I could ease his suffering if I did something." He rubbed his face again.

"Well, you certainly eased his suffering. As well as any other ailment he would feel in the future," mumbled Crona, leaning on the bed next to Prue's.

Bronx glanced back at his sister. "You're not funny."

"I'm not trying to be. This is serious."

"Of course this is serious. A man just died." Bronx's voice shook. He took a deep breath. "Sometimes I wonder what I'm doing here. Everything I touch dies." He sat down in a chair next to Prue's bed and put his head in his hands.

"That's not true!" Kaz said.

Crona approached him, getting as close as she dared.

She reached out to him, but he pulled back. "Bronx, I've managed to hug you loads of times before, and you haven't killed me yet." She pointed to her eyes. "I can see the future, remember?" She reached out quickly and pinched his cheek. "See? Haven't killed me yet."

Bronx pulled back and swatted her hand away. "Stop it."

"No, you stop it." She tried to lock eyes with him, but he refused to meet her gaze. "I'm sorry Prue died. I know you didn't do it on purpose, but face the facts. Look at the bigger picture. You kill people with a touch—that's your gift. I know you have no idea what you're doing, but we will get through this, and you will learn how to control it."

"Your sister's right, Bronx." Kaz hadn't moved from his position at the foot of Prue's bed. "We're all still figuring things out. I know we sound like we don't understand since our powers aren't as deadly, but we are on your side."

Bronx stared at his sister, his pulse rising. He knew she was right, and he hated it. It frustrated him. He wished she would just leave him alone on the subject. He may no longer wear the uniform, but his own Daer instincts still kicked in.

He took a moment to take several calming breaths before responding. "You're both insufferable."

Crona shrugged. "And you're acting like a little shit. What do you want me to do? Agree with you? Oh, woe is you, Bronx! Yes, everything you touch dies. Maybe you are a freak."

"That's a bit much, Crona," muttered Kaz.

"Stop it!" Bronx snarled.

"No," she said flatly. "Because it's not true. You are not a freak; you are doing so many good things here. Not everything you touch dies. You're the one with the magic touch.

You have a higher success rate of saving people than any other corpsmen. I know, I've seen the stats."

He refused to meet her gaze. He knew he was being stubborn, but he didn't want to listen to her.

Crona rolled her eyes, then turned to Kaz. "Come on. He stops being fun when he's like this." She walked to the stretcher. "I'm sure Manden and the others will be here soon."

Bronx removed his other glove and threw both away in the trash with enough force to tip it over. "I'm coming." He grabbed a second clean pair, put them on, and stood to help Kazimir once more with the stretcher.

"But first, can you help me put him into cold storage?" He gestured to Prue. "I'll worry about the paperwork when we get back."

# CHAPTER 8

The medical wing sat at the end of a long and shiny metal-plated hallway where the Federation soldiers slept. This floor was only for women, while the men stayed below.

Bronx and Kaz carried the stretcher down the hall as Crona ran ahead to a different tunnel to grab the keys to their vehicle for the long drive to the hangar. The tunnel to the hangar was still underground, but without the metal plating. Its long row of UV lights along the low ceiling was the only hint of technology present, aside from the few cars parked at the entrance. The musty smell of fresh earth and car exhaust was more pungent here, but the stench lessened once they started driving.

As Crona drove, Bronx decided to push his current problem out of his mind and tried to think about what awaited him at the other end of the tunnel: Rei Ettowa.

When he had apprenticed with Niklaryn all those years ago, he frequently saw his mentor sneaking glances at a picture of his little sister. Niklaryn never told a soul about her, but he trusted Bronx. Bronx had heard so much about her that he felt he already knew her, yet he never thought that he would meet Rei after what happened.

Part of him expected to see the same young girl from the photo—with pigtails and missing front teeth—but he knew she was only a few years younger than him and was prepared to meet a young woman. What he hadn't prepared for were the questions she was bound to ask about the day her brother died.

"Bronx?" Crona's voice rang through his head like a bell. "Oy! Wake up!"

Bronx snapped out of his reverie to find that they had already arrived at the hangar. It was hidden deep within Mount Environ, several kilometers away from their base. The underground tunnel they had just traveled through allowed a veil of secrecy for the comings and goings of their soldiers. Bronx jumped out of the bed of the vehicle and approached Manden's ship.

According to their friend, the *Luciernaga* was several thousand years old and resembled a hodgepodge of scrapped ships, metal pieces—some of them gold—and a few ion cannon stations that appeared to have been placed randomly, yet had been essential. Bronx swore the end result made *Luciernaga* look like a face with the cockpit as the eyes and the front hatch as its mouth.

The hatch opened like a long tongue, and their redheaded friend strode out to greet them. Crona ran to Manden and almost knocked him down with a big hug. Kaz followed with a hand extended.

"Are you kidding?" Manden pulled Kaz in for an embrace. "Come here, you."

Bronx stayed behind as usual.

"Bronx," Manden said, giving the medic a nod.

"You look familiar," said a young man who came into view from the hatch. He was as tall as Bronx with brown hair and light eyes. For a moment, the medic thought a ghost had come back to haunt him. *Niklaryn?* he wanted to ask. The newcomer's violet eyes flashed. He was someone different, and yet it still took several moments for Bronx's heart rate to return to normal.

"Do I?" asked Bronx. "I'm sorry, I don't know your name."

"Arram Bronto." The young man extended a hand to Bronx, who only stared at it.

"Bronx, doesn't do hand shaking," muttered Manden.

Arram pulled his hand back. "Sorry."

Bronx shook his head. "I'll explain later."

"Okay." Arram stepped out of the way, clearing the path for Kaz and Bronx to enter the ship. "You're a Daer Knight, right?" he continued.

"I was once." Bronx readjusted his grip on the stretcher, his heart pounding in his chest. This was the moment; he was going to meet her. The stretcher must be for either Bernie or Rei.

"He still is a Daer," added Crona.

"Well, I-I'm sure Rei will be excited to meet you," was all Arram said as his eyes stared at the floor, the muscles in his jaw flexing.

"Where is she, by the way?" interjected Crona.

"She's probably with Bernie," Manden said, walking toward his ship.

Bronx, with Kaz helping on the other end, continued hauling the stretcher up the ramp into the first room of the ship—the cargo hold.

"We're in the infirmary." Manden's voice echoed from the belly of the ship. The infirmary sat behind the cargo hold, currently filled with plants from every corner of the star cluster. A mix of lilac and magnolia filled Bronx's nose.

The men maneuvered the stretcher around the mesh metal staircase that led up to the rooms, kitchen, and cockpit.

Bronx sneezed as they ventured through what appeared to be a small forest, lightly brushing against several pots of vines overflowing onto the floor. He continued to the infirmary where Manden and Bernie stood on either side of a bed.

"I didn't want to leave her alone in case she suddenly woke up. That's why I didn't come out earlier," Bernie said quietly. She turned and saw that the combat medic had entered. "Hey, Bronx, Kaz."

Bronx didn't answer. All his thoughts focused on the unconscious woman lying before him in blood-splattered clothes. Rei Ettowa appeared to be asleep, her dark hair framing her face. His pulse raced.

Not long after Niklaryn was gone, he dreamed about a beautiful woman who made his heart stop with a smile. Time had since obscured many of the details, but he clearly remembered Rei's face.

He never told anyone about it, thinking that she was some subconscious fantasy. But somehow his brain must have created the woman of his dreams from memories of Rei. Thank the gods Nik wasn't here. He knew he shouldn't have impure thoughts about his mentor's kid sister—no matter how attractive she may be.

He pulled the pulse scanner out of his bag, placed it on her neck, and read the little screen. The lines blipped, showing a strong and steady heartbeat.

He lowered his face toward hers to better hear her breathing—slow and steady. He pulled away, using all his willpower to not lean in closer. His eyes glanced over the rest of her body, trying to the find the source of the blood on her clothes.

"I don't see a wound," he said.

"Just a graze from a bullet. I already patched her up." Manden pointed to Rei's other side.

"Very nice." He admired the tiny stitches. It was no

surprise knowing Manden's history on the battlefield. "And the rest of the blood?"

"Unlucky victim," Bernie said.

Bronx helped Manden move her to the stretcher; he double-checked that the gloves reached his sleeves so that not an inch of skin was exposed. One could never be too careful.

"What happened?" Bronx took one end of the stretcher while Manden held the other, leading it out of the infirmary and through the cargo hold.

"As I said in my message," Manden said, "we had a run in with the Negander. They attacked the town, trying to get to Rei and Arram. Bernie, Hotara, and I managed to save them in time; however, the Negander had already killed Sagitan and his wife." He gazed down at their unconscious newcomer. "This little lady was angry. Her powers came out for the first time and fried them."

"It was quite a sight," Bernie said.

"She used too much energy and passed out," Manden said. "It happens to people like her at some point in their lives."

"Where is Hotara?" Kaz asked.

"I sent her to Tas'und'eash. With any luck, she can rally the rest of the Volocio to help with our cause."

The group continued out of the ship and back toward the vehicle. Arram took Rei from Bronx and helped Manden carry the stretcher.

They brought Rei to the medical bay and laid her down on an empty bed. Bronx made sure it was far away from where Prue had passed earlier.

He placed a heart monitor on her finger and waited for the steady beep to fill the silence in the room. Arram stood nearby, his eyes never leaving Rei's face. Bronx imagined how concerned he must have been.

"Come, Arram." Crona linked arms with him. "They're still serving dinner in the mess hall. You look like you could use some food."

"I feel uncomfortable leaving her here," he said quietly.

"I'll stay," offered Bronx. "I'm still on duty here."

Arram nodded and allowed Crona to lead him out the room with Kaz following.

Crona stopped at the door and quickly glanced in Bronx's direction. "Should I bring you something, too, Brother?"

Bronx shook his head. "I know where Ayres hides his snacks. I'll be fine."

Manden stayed behind, watching Bronx thoughtfully. The redhead always did that when he studied one of them —as though he were trying to see more of Bronx than what was there.

"Yes, Manden?"

He cocked his head to the side. "I'm desperate to know what you're thinking."

"Thinking?"

"About her." Manden gestured to Rei lying between them.

Bronx couldn't shake the feeling of having met her before, but that was impossible. "Well," he finally answered, "she's a great conversationalist."

Manden chuckled. "Jokes aside, smart ass. I really want to know. I've been looking forward to the two of you meeting for a long time."

The medic shrugged. "Kind of hard to have a meeting when one's unconscious."

Manden waved his hand dismissively in Bronx's direction "Bah. Details."

"Does this have to do with *him*?"

"Yes."

Of course it did. Everything in Bronx's life the last few years always came back to that man, and a part of him resented it.

"I'm sure you've felt some of his memories. As dreams, perhaps?"

Bronx clenched his sweaty palms, which stuck to his gloves. "Dreams?"

"Your sister once told me about dreams she had before her powers manifested. Kaz, too. That's what they are. Memories. I watched Rei go through hers, so I'm just taking a leap here."

It was bad enough Bronx shared the same gift and the same face as the man in question. But Manden suggested they had the same taste in women. The idea didn't sit well with him, but his body already betrayed him whenever he looked in her direction. His pulse elevated and his mouth had gone dry.

Manden still watched him, waiting for a response. But Bronx didn't want to talk about that, so he stuck with a truth he was comfortable with.

"I'm relieved she's here and she's safe."

"Oh?"

"You remember me telling you how I knew Niklaryn? We were close friends. Close enough that I was the only person he told about her. Not everything—only that she needed to be protected. He made me vow to protect her if something happened to him."

"You've done a great job doing that all these years," Manden said dryly.

"Niklaryn forgot to give me the minor yet crucial detail of where she was hidden. I knew Earth, but that was it. Then there was the problem that no one else knew about her, so who could I ask? It turned out your wife hid her all along." Bronx laughed. The universe really wanted them to meet. He believed it was some cruel joke.

"You'll have a chance to uphold that vow now, Bronx. I don't know how she's going to react when she wakes up. The last few days have been overwhelming for her. You saw how Arram is handling things and he just lost his grandparents. Rei lost everyone she knew and grew up with. Infiernen and his Negander destroyed her entire town. Her powers manifested out of pure rage. She brought down countless Negander and turned them into charred husks."

Bronx's eyes widened, and his heart stopped at the mention of Infiernen. He hunted her, too? It made sense. The Negander had been hunting Bronx and the others for years now.

He studied Rei. He didn't think she would be so dangerous—almost as dangerous as he was. The idea of no longer being the only one with lethal gifts gave him a little comfort, especially if it meant protecting the others against the Negander.

"You and I are the ones with the most battle experience," continued Manden. "We've seen the most. We also know what happens to those who experience trauma and have no support group to help them through it. These two are the only survivors of that massacre. Just be prepared."

"Of course." Trauma was something Bronx knew plenty about.

# CHAPTER 9

Rei's eyes refused to open. The light shined on her, too bright. She tried to lift her hand to cover her face, but it was heavy. Eventually, her body surrendered to her will, and her eyelids opened slowly, revealing a room filled with a fluorescent glow. She moved and heard the rustle of cotton sheets. The smell of astringent cleaning supplies and latex filled her nose. When her eyes came into focus, she saw a box of gloves on a table, and next to it a steel stand with a bag of fluid hanging down. The steady beep of a heart rate monitor interrupted the silence.

Panic surged through her. She was in a hospital bed, but she didn't know where. Perhaps she had been captured by the Dominion; the thought made her pulse spike. She sluggishly turned and found a figure walking toward her.

"So you're finally awake," he said. She stared up into the eyes of this stranger. She had never seen eyes so dark. He had strong features, ivory skin with a bit of stubble on his chin. He brushed a lock of brown hair from his eyes, and Rei saw a hint of a smile when their eyes met. Something about the gesture felt familiar.

"Where am I?" she croaked.

The young man fetched her some water from a nearby desk. A large vase with yellow flowers sat next to the pitcher.

"You're on Gliese VI," he responded.

She watched, enjoying the way his body moved under his tightly fitted uniform. He returned with a glass and placed it on the table next to Rei.

"Is this a Federation planet?" Her voice was a little stronger.

"Yes."

She noticed the silver twelve-pointed star and a red cross over his heart—he was a medic. She tried to sit up, the action requiring a lot more effort than she thought.

The stranger jumped to her side with pillows from a nearby bed and placed them under her back. She sank into them with a sigh of relief, reached for the glass of water, and drank, keeping her eyes down, fighting the urge to stare at him again.

"How long was I unconscious?" she asked.

"Just over a day," Manden said from the doorway that hissed closed behind him. Rei's throat tightened as he approached her bed. He threw his arms around her and squeezed. All the tension in her shoulders released, and she hugged him back.

"Where's Mom?"

"I had to send her away," he whispered in her ear. "But she's safe."

Rei's eyes burned from unshed tears. She needed Hotara.

Manden squeezed her tighter, as though sensing her distress. "You can do this. I'm here for you."

She closed her eyes and pulled away, quickly wiping the tears from her face.

"You okay?" he whispered.

She would have to be, but the words refused to escape her lips. Rei only nodded. She dared a peek over at the medic, who picked some unseen lint from his uniform.

"That's Bronx." Manden's voice cut through her thoughts.

The doctor looked up upon hearing his name and locked eyes with Rei. He gave her a small wave. "Hi."

"Hi," breathed Rei.

She turned back to find the redhead also watching her. A broad smile spread across his lips as though he pieced together the final piece of a puzzle, though Rei didn't know what.

He clapped his hands. "Now that she's awake, I think we should get this meeting started, eh?"

"Perhaps." Bronx turned to Rei. "If you're up for it."

"What meeting?" asked Rei, wiping her eyes.

"There are things you need to know. But I wanted to wait until you were awake," Manden said. "I think everyone is still in the lounge. Should I tell them to come here?"

"It would be best if she doesn't move too much right now," Bronx said.

Manden nodded, then sprung from the bed and left.

"Maybe grab some food for her. She needs time to adjust," Bronx called. The medic glanced at Rei with a raised eyebrow. "I don't think he heard me."

Rei's eyes never left the door. "What was that about?"

He chuckled. "You don't wanna know."

She liked the sound of his laugh.

Her eyes followed him as he returned to his desk and his smile disappeared, his lips pressing together into a line. A little voice whispered in the back of her mind, urging her to discover what about him felt so familiar. She would have attempted small talk, but her voice failed her. Her thoughts were trying to piece together the events of the last twenty-four hours.

She fidgeted with her sleeve and realized she still wore her old clothes. The collar of her shirt itched. The blood on the cloth darkened to a brown and crusted; the stain would never come out. The image of the man's head bursting was forever in her mind's eye. Her vision filled with red as she pulled at the collar, suddenly feeling unable to breathe.

"I have to take this off," she gasped. "I have to take this off." The image continued replaying in her mind. She tried to pull the cloth away from her skin, but it felt so tight.

"Hey." Bronx approached her and reached for her hands, pulling them away from her collar. "It's okay. Deep breath."

She listened. He breathed with her—in through the nose and out through the mouth.

"Again." His dark eyes never left hers.

"One more time in." He continued in rhythm with her. His gloved hands gently squeezed hers, and his thumb ran over her knuckles. "And out." His voice was soft.

Her heart pounded, but she wasn't sure if it was due to panic. Her breathing slowed and the anxiety faded away. His gaze shifted from her face to their adjoining hands and he let go. Her fingers grew cold where he had touched her, his warmth quickly disappearing.

"There's a shower in the back and a change of clothes," he said.

Rei nodded, feeling a little more herself, but the blood on her shirt felt heavy.

"Full disclosure: I only have scrubs for you. But at least they're clean." He smiled and she found herself smiling back. "Can you stand?" he asked, pulling away to give her space.

Rei slowly rose from the bed, but dizziness overcame her. He reached for her again, and she waved him away.

Her muscles screamed as she hobbled close behind the medic. Bronx passed a large wooden desk covered in stacks of papers. He showed her to a back room with smooth metal walls and a shower with an opaque glass partition and a shelf full of scrubs, all a comforting shade of blue.

"If you want, I'm sure we can clean the blood out." He pointed to her clothes.

She shook her head. "I'd rather they were burned." She felt his eyes on her while she searched through the scrubs for a pair in her size. The fabric was thin, but at least it was soft. They didn't smell like anything, but it was better than the hint of smoke still in her nose.

"I'll take care of it. Just leave them on the chair." He left, closing the door behind him.

The warmth from the shower reached into her soul. Her wounded arm ached, reminding her of the bullet and how the Negander evaded it so easily. At least it no longer bled.

She scrubbed herself raw with the fresh bar of soap, but for a long time she swore the water continued to run red. She wasn't sure if her eyes played tricks on her or if there was really that much blood to wash off. In the end, she stood under the cascade, not thinking about whether she wasted water, instead praying that it would cleanse the images away. It didn't.

Her clothes were gone, replaced with a threadbare towel, scrubs, and a pair of slippers. The scrubs were thinner than she originally thought. She rubbed her arms to maintain the warmth from the shower.

Once dried and dressed, she returned to the main room. Arram and Manden had arrived, standing between the rows of empty beds. The room wasn't very large. She counted only six beds, a few monitors, and a few well-worn chairs between them.

Bronx stood next to her, pouring more water into her glass before returning it to the bedside table. Manden held a small plate of steamed potatoes and minced meat. The herbs made her mouth water, and she wondered how many hours it had been since she last ate. She squeezed her eyes shut. Dinner with her mother, Sagitan, and Virga. Manden placed the plate next to her glass.

Rei observed Arram from his post between the beds. They had been through too much together, yet she couldn't find the strength to approach him and embrace him. His familiar scowl returned to his features, warning any who dared come near. Rei understood and kept her distance, giving him the space he needed.

He reached out to her, and she almost did a double take. Perhaps she was wrong about him. She took his hand and gave it a gentle squeeze. They were soft, a scholar's hands. She pulled away and neared the bed where the smell of the food left her salivating. Within moments, she had shoveled most of it into her mouth.

While she finished, she watched as other people entered. Bronx leaned against a desk next to a fidgety younger woman with dirty blonde hair who sat on the wooden chair next to him.

Rei's attention snapped to a regal, blue-eyed young man. She recognized the commanding profile of Kazimir from news articles on the Nexus. With ease and confidence, he approached her bedside.

"Hello, Cousin." He extended a hand to her. "I'm Kaz."

"As in Kazimir? *The* Kazimir Ettowa?"

He pulled up a chair next to her bed. "The one and only."

"And you know who I am? Did Niklaryn tell you? He told me he met you once."

He shook his head. "No, he never said anything. It was Manden."

"Oh." She turned to the redhead with a flash of annoyance. "You seem to tell a lot of people about who I am. Did Hotara know about this?"

"I only told the people I trusted with your safety. Sagitan, Virga, and these fine people."

Rei scanned the other witnesses in the room: Kaz, Bronx, the mystery blonde. "So they're all expected to protect Arram and me? Or what?"

"We're all in the same boat, actually," the woman said. Then she pointed to herself. "I'm Crona, by the way."

"What exactly is this 'meeting' about?" Rei asked, ignoring the greeting. The rest of them looked at each other, as if wondering who should start. Dread pooled in her stomach at the thought of another surprise.

"It's probably best to start at the beginning," Crona said. "Volocio. What do you *think* you know about them and the Second Coming?"

"They're the gods." Rei glanced at Arram. "It is said that those who were killed by the ancestor of the Dominon Sovereign would return to finish what they started."

"They're real," Crona said. "In reality they are a race of beings from a planet far away from our star cluster; it's called Tas'und'eash."

Rei's skin tingled. She half expected Manden to tell her it was a joke, but his face remained neutral.

"So it's all true?" she asked.

Crona nodded. "All of it."

Rei turned to her cousin. "Are you really the god of illusion?"

Kaz made a face. "Yes and no."

"What do you mean?"

"There's more." Kaz walked to the desk next to Bronx to pour himself a glass of water.

"About two thousand years ago," began the medic, "a

group Volocio traveled here to the Tyre Star Cluster, to Earth, and fought in what we know as the Battle of the Badlands. I believe it was near your village. Anyway, the humans here saw them and began to worship the Volocio because of their gifts. That was the birth of Tyre's religion."

The room grew warm around Rei and she frowned. She didn't like what the medic was insinuating. "You make it sound like they're just people."

"But they are."

Rei's mouth went dry. That didn't sound right. "So they're not gods?"

"No," Manden said. Rei's eyes darted to him, still waiting for him to crack a smile. There was none.

"So you mean that the gods are really . . . what? Aliens from another planet?"

"No. Volocio are still human." Manden chuckled. "Just evolved differently."

"Oh." Rei's stomach turned to ice. "So the religion is false?" she muttered to herself.

"Yes," Crona answered with a snort. "It's quite funny when you think about it."

Rei's found the whole situation anything but. The collar of her scrubs grew too tight and her breathing more strenuous.

Manden laid a hand on her arm. "Are you alright?"

"Honestly, no." She closed her eyes and tugged at her collar. Her gaze darted to Bronx. His dark eyes widened with concern, and she heard his voice whisper in her ear, reminding her to breath. She took several calming breaths before continuing. "But there's obviously more so . . . continue." She waved her hand dismissively.

"Well, this ancestor of the Dominion Sovereign hated

the god queen—or who we know as Micaela. In his attempt to be rid of her, he killed her and five other Volocio."

"At their funeral," began Manden, "an oracle made a prophecy that the six would return during another great war. They are to join the god king and finish what they started."

"The Sovereign, Anekris Praymer, knows that the prophecy is about him and the destruction of his line," Bronx said. "The Sovereign doesn't want people to know the whole truth. It's part of the reason why he dug up the old one-god religion."

"Then how do you know the truth about the prophecy?" Rei asked.

"I was there," Manden said.

Rei gasped and Arram almost fell off the bed, mouth falling open.

"You would have to be—" she began.

"Four thousand and forty-four years old." Manden gave them a large toothy grin.

"You were at the Battle of the Badlands?" Arram said.

"But that would make you . . ." Rei said.

Manden smirked. "Yes, my child. I am your god king."

# CHAPTER 10

Manden raised his arms out to the side with the palms facing up, mimicking a very common statue of the god king found all over Tyre.

Rei rolled her eyes. "Bullshit."

"It's true! I am the same Manden from the legends and myths. They named me god king because of the awesome power I wielded."

"By power, he means his weeds," muttered Crona from her chair next to Bronx.

Manden stuck his tongue out at Crona. "Mean."

"Prove it," Rei said.

Manden narrowed his eyes as he reached into his pocket. He opened his palm, revealing several seeds that he tossed to the ground between them. They clinked softly as they hit the floor. He pointed a hand to the yellow flowers sitting on the desk behind Bronx. The flowers began to brown and wilt, followed by a small pop. The seeds grew, blooming into vines that twisted and writhed like snakes on the floor.

Rei's heart leaped into her throat. "By the gods!" She backed away as far as the bed would allow, but it wasn't enough.

An unbidden memory surfaced from the attack in Ballarat. The Negander who found them was snapped away and found unconscious, wrapped in vines. Her heart thundered in her chest.

Arram's eyes widened; his mouth dropped open, but no sound came out.

"Do you need more proof?" asked Manden.

Rei shook her head. "I'm still not seeing the connection with us," she whispered. It was a lie.

"The rest of us are the Volocio from the prophecy," said Bronx gently.

"And so are you," Crona said.

Rei's eyes darted to Arram, whose face remained neutral. How could he possibly be calm? "Excuse me?"

"You are the reincarnation of Empress Micaela Roya," came Kaz's voice next to her. "Arram is her younger brother, Maximilian, though you were better known as God Queen Mica and her brother Max—both lightning Volocio. Those of us who knew the truth speculated your identities for years, but we weren't sure. When Manden saw you wielding lightning, we were certain."

Rei was not amused. "No." She put her hand to her mouth. "You expect me to believe that I am the god queen?"

"Yes," Manden said without hesitation.

Rei looked at the redhead. She wanted to refute it all.

"Remember when you fainted at the bar? You saw something, didn't you?" Manden's green eyes remained focused on Rei as she remembered. "Those were Mica's memories coming through."

"The Battle of the Badlands," she whispered. The memory of her facing him on the battlefield surrounded by vines and lightning was still fresh. Yet it all felt unreal.

"I told you, I was there. It was the day we met." Manden smiled. "You look just like her. I was so happy when I met you. I waited two thousand years for the chance to see her again."

Rei lost feeling in her face. No wonder he smiled the way he had when they ran into each other—with relief, like finally reaching home after wandering lost for so long. She remembered telling him that she had met him before and she had—as Micaela.

"Okay." Rei turned to Kaz. "So how did you know who I was?"

"Well, everyone knows who I am," her cousin said with a shrug. "When we were reincarnated, we Royas maintained the same familial relationships. We are still cousins, and Arram is your brother."

The air rushed from Rei's lungs. She must've misheard. Niklaryn never mentioned that they had another brother. Rei wrapped her arms around herself as she shook.

Arram fell hard on the bed behind him. "She's my what?" He stared at Rei as if seeing her for the first time. "This can't be happening," he whispered. His violet eyes were wild. "They lied to me."

"They never told you?" asked Manden, rubbing his chin.

Both Rei and Arram shook their heads.

Manden pinched the bridge of his nose with his thumb and forefinger. "God bless it. I told them to tell you the truth."

"Was that why they wanted us to meet?" asked Arram, his eyes filling with tears. "That was why it was so important to Grandmother that I try to be your friend." He stood. "And I couldn't even give her that." He stormed out of the room, the doors swishing shut behind him.

"Damnit, Virga," Manden whispered.

"Perhaps they thought they had time?" Rei's voice shook.

"But you didn't have time!" yelled Manden. He put a hand to his chest as his face fell. "I'm sorry. I didn't mean to yell. Infiernen has been chasing them for years. They never stayed in one place for more than a month, maybe a month and a half. They were in Ballarat for two. They took too long to gain your trust and bring you both into the Federation. I think they were worried Urius would pull you away from them once you joined, so they delayed things. That's why Bernie and I had to come—Urius grew impatient. We tried to buy you time and sent the Negander in the opposite direction, but somehow, they saw through it."

Rei's eyes filled with fresh tears as she thought back to those kind people. It was no wonder Sagitan always came by the bar, or why Virga fussed over spending time with Rei at temple—they wanted time with their granddaughter. Her heart ached for Arram, kept in the dark the whole time. He was her brother and all she had left now.

Rei's patience was depleted. There was too much information to digest at once. A few tears fell down her face, which she quickly wiped away.

"Thank you for telling us everything," she said to the group as she stood. "But I have to find Arram." She refused to meet anyone's eye as she left the medical wing.

Outside of the room she walked through a long hallway with sterile metal walls, brightly lit with little lamps along the way that disappeared as the corridor eventually curved to the left. She followed the path, letting her feet decide her destination. Her slippers whispered on the floor's smooth surface.

"Arram?" she called, her voice echoing down the hallway.

She continued until she found a crossroad, a hallway to her left, a sitting room to her right with a few people in Federation uniforms, and in the middle, stairs. Arram was hunched over at the bottom, his head in his hands.

She sat down a few steps above him and touched his shoulder. He flinched.

"Go away," he said through a sob.

"Arram," she said in the same calming voice Hotara used on her.

"I said go away!" He faced her, his red eyes making the violet of his irises more brilliant.

"No."

"Why?"

Rei furrowed her eyebrows. "We're family, obviously."

He scoffed, "You're a stranger," and turned away from her again.

Rei let the comment roll off of her and leaned against the railing. Her hand went to Niklaryn's ring around her neck, the only piece of home she owned. "You're trying to push me away. It all makes sense now. You moved around so much, you felt like you weren't in control of your life. Being an asshole worked twofold: you were in control of the situation and able to keep people at an arm's reach." She began to pick at her fingernails. "I was that way for a while when Niko died. I was so angry. But Hotara was relentless, and she stayed by my side while I worked through my pain. I'm going to do that for you."

"Because we're family?"

"Yes."

He stood and turned to face her. His eyes were still wet with tears, which he furiously wiped away. "Last time I checked, you didn't like me. And now because we share blood, I'm worthy of your pity?"

Rei winced. He was right in a way, but after the destruction of Ballarat, they were bound by more than blood. "I will admit, I'm still unsure how I feel about you." She stood with a groan over her stiff legs. "Since we've met, you've done nothing but antagonize me with your asinine comments and your superiority complex over me and the rest of Ballarat. If I don't like you, it's due to you trying so hard to be unlikeable. Well done. But we just went through a nightmare together, and you can't deny we are bound together now."

"Yours was the first hand available." His lips trembled. "I could have easily held hands with that handsome medic. He seemed sympathetic enough."

Rei rolled her eyes. "That is bullshit and you know it. I saw you with your . . . I mean, our grandparents. Family means a lot to you, and I know you think you lost it when they died. But you didn't—you have me. I'm not saying that I'm going to hold your hand through the whole thing and sing happy songs, but I'm here, even if you just need someone to listen. We should at least try—we owe our grandparents that."

He said nothing, but his eyes never left hers. They were blank as he placed his hands in his pockets. "I don't need you." His voice was flat. He turned and continued down the stairs, leaving Rei alone.

"But I need you," Rei said. She didn't think he heard, but he did and stopped at the bottom of the stairs. He didn't turn around. "It was so lonely in Ballarat after Niklaryn died. I always had Hotara, but it wasn't the same. I felt something was off, that I wasn't like the others. When we first met, I felt the same with you, but you never let me get close. I understand now. We are more than just siblings—we are these Volocio. We are different, but we aren't alone. I know this is a lot to take in, and you're probably over-whelmed. I know I am. But we don't have to go through this alone. We can't."

She waited for Arram to respond, but he didn't. He

continued down the stairs and disappeared. Rei stood on the stairs for several more minutes before wiping her face and climbing the steps.

Rei never felt more alone in her life.

# CHAPTER 11

REI'S ROOM BOASTED FEW ITEMS: A BED, A DESK, AND A lamp. There was also a shelf for books, but it was empty—precisely how she felt at that moment.

She knew she should try to sleep, but it eluded her. Too many thoughts swirled through her mind, and every time she closed her eyes, she saw fire and blood surrounding the bodies of her grandparents.

She walked out of her room to find the hallway lights dimmed, but a glow came from around the corner. Someone was probably in the medical wing. Rei wrapped her blanket around her shoulders and walked toward the light. The room was empty, but she heard the clatter of metal being thrown in a bin. Bronx entered the room from the back and stopped when he saw her in the doorway.

"Are you okay?" he asked.

She shook her head. "I couldn't sleep. A lot to think about."

"Shall I make you some tea?"

Rei nodded gratefully.

He gestured to a chair at the desk as he rummaged through the drawers. Rei sat down, and Bronx pulled out a small light-green box. He stared at it with furrowed eyebrows.

"It would appear I only have mint." He looked at Rei with a shrug.

"Mint's my favorite."

He smiled. "Great."

A smile crept across her lips as she watched him start the kettle.

"What about you?" she asked. "Shouldn't you also be sleeping?"

"My shift is over in about"—he leaned over the desk and peered at his tablet—"twenty minutes. I just have to wait for Ayres to relieve me."

"So you will get some sleep soon, then?" Disappointment pooled in her belly. If he left, she would be alone again.

He shook his head. "Today's been a big day for all of us. But I've always had trouble sleeping. I find it overrated, anyway," he said with a wink.

"Dreams?" she asked.

"Weird ones."

"Such as?"

The kettle beeped that it was ready. "On a good evening," he began as he poured, "I dream about a golden forest, a gate made of pearls, and figures with black and white robes. I always feel at peace there. But the memory doesn't feel as sharp when I'm awake, when I try to remember."

She was grateful that he talked. It was a welcome distraction. "And on bad evenings?"

Bronx took a deep breath. "Battles I wish to forget."

"Oh." Rei could only imagine what he'd seen.

He handed her a mug, this time with gloveless hands. He noticed it as well; after placing the mug on the table in front of her, he quickly put on a pair attached to his belt.

He grabbed his own mug and sat down on the chair on the other side of the desk. "So usually when I can't sleep, I annoy my sister."

"Sister?"

"Crona."

Rei narrowed her eyes. She didn't remember them looking alike. "Is she a night person?"

"No, and it pisses her off when I wake her up. But she forgives me every time because she loves me." He paused with a smirk, but then his dark eyes grew serious. "How are you feeling about today? About being Micaela?"

Rei pondered for a moment, trying to find a way to answer. She held the tea to her nose. The smell of mint reminded her of home, and she missed the comfort, but now the memory of home was tainted.

"Overwhelmed. I'm still trying to wrap my head around the fact that the Negander destroyed my town, killed my grandparents—except I didn't know they were my grandparents. Also, I can suddenly wield lightning because I am the god queen and Arram—who, by the way, is a huge asshole— is my brother. And to top it off, everyone knew about this except us." She stared at her mug as the leaves swirled lazily. The whole thing sounded ridiculous now that she said it out loud. She pulled her knees to her chest as the words ran over and over in her mind.

"So . . . a completely normal day for you?" he asked, interrupting her thoughts. She glanced up and found him raising an eyebrow.

Rei barked out a laugh. "Yeah, if you call a soap opera normal."

"You really didn't know any of this?"

Rei shook her head.

"I'm sorry you had to learn the truth like that. But we are all in this together. My sister, Kaz, and I are here if you or Arram need it."

Rei smiled as a small weight lifted off her chest. She didn't realize how much she needed to hear that.

He stared at the wall for a few moments. "I can't imagine what that's like, realizing every person put in your path was placed there to groom you for this life." He leaned back in his chair and propped his boots on the desk before taking a sip of his tea.

"No?" She recalled the hushed argument between Hotara and Manden. It was true her destiny always lay with the Federation.

He pointed to himself. "Born and raised an atheist. I thought the myths were just that, nothing more than stories to scare children into eating their vegetables. Then my powers manifested for the first time." He grimaced.

"What are your powers? If you don't mind my asking." Rei took a long drink of her tea. The heat warmed her belly. Her eyes never left his face.

He blinked. "That's a more serious conversation for a second date."

Rei's heart fluttered. "Oh, we're on a date now?"

"Well, we're having drinks, right?"

"Oh, you poor dear. If this is your idea of a date, you must not get out much." Rei laughed, feeling lighter for the first time in days.

"Why are you laughing? I was serious." He tried to narrow his eyes, but his face broke into a smile and he laughed with her.

"I needed that. Thanks," she said when the laughter quieted down.

He raised his mug. "Glad to be of service. After a day like today, you looked like you needed a good laugh."

"I did. But I can also use a good drink."

"You'll have to go to Yticol for that. It's the nearest village."

She suddenly felt bold with the handsome man in front of her. "Second date?"

His face fell. He locked eyes with her and bit his lip, then gave her a look that sent a shiver down her spine. "Second date," he purred.

Rei took the last swig of her tea, warmth filling her. She told herself it was from the tea. "So you won't tell me about your powers. What can you tell me about yourself? Or would you rather remain cloaked in mystery?"

"Cloaked in mystery. I like that."

They grew silent, but Rei's eyes never left his. She studied his face, still trying to pinpoint where she had seen him. The truth sat on the tip of her tongue. She knew that when she found out, she would feel silly that she hadn't thought of it before, but the onslaught of information over the last few days had simply left her frazzled.

"I was born on Wolf X," he said, his voice low. "I was sent to the Daer Academy when I was six, apprenticeship at sixteen, and knighthood at eighteen. The usual. I knew my destiny was to fight alongside the Federation—to fight tyranny, to fight for human rights. Then one day I met this redhead who told me that I was the reincarnation of a man named Atrius Duque. Since then, my life has been one big clusterfuck." He brushed a lock of his dark hair from his eyes with just the hint of smile.

That was it. How did she not notice before? Rei felt the hair at her nape rise, and her lips parted at the mention of his name. The memory of the kiss and his touch crashed into her mind, leaving room for little else. She brought a hand to her lips, to her face, and flushed. It was true, those dreams were true. She wanted to ask him about it but didn't know how to breach the subject.

"Is everything alright?" he asked.

"Yup," she lied, trying to force a smile.

"Oh, I didn't realize you had a guest," said a new voice behind Rei. She turned and saw a young man with dark skin and warm eyes in the doorway. "I can come back, if you need more time."

Rei had forgotten Bronx mentioned someone taking over his shift. She turned back to the medic, whose eyes were still on her. "Maybe it's time I try to get some sleep," she said, even though she guaranteed that wasn't going to happen tonight.

Bronx nodded and reached for her. "I'll take your mug."

She couldn't tell if he was disappointed or not; his face remained neutral. She handed over the mug, hoping to brush hands, but he still wore gloves. He hooked his finger around the handle and brought the mugs to a nearby sink.

"I'll walk you to your room," Bronx said when he returned. "Have a good shift, Ayres," he said to the young man as they passed.

"Yes, the graveyard shift, my favorite." The newcomer took a seat in Bronx's chair. "Get some sleep, friend."

They walked side by side, and Rei watched him out of the corner of her eye. She was glad for his offer to walk with her. She wasn't quite ready for their night to end, yet they reached her room all too quickly.

"You said you were knighted. Are you a Daer?" she asked, looking up at him.

He leaned against the wall next to her door. "Technically, but I don't wear the uniform anymore."

"Did you know my brother? Niklaryn?"

He sighed, eyes cast down at his gloves. "Yeah, for a time."

She reached for her door and turned back to Bronx. His

eyes softened when they met hers. A small smile formed on his beautiful lips. Her mind went blank as she stared.

"This was fun. We should do it again sometime."

She lost her voice for a moment, but then managed to answer. "What? The two-second conversation we just had?"

"Uh . . . yeah. Maybe next time we should extend it to six." He winked.

She grinned. "Oh, how adventurous."

They chuckled.

She entered her room and pressed her body against the closed door, hoping he did the same.

Rei sighed. "Gods, I'm such a smiling fool."

# CHAPTER 12

Rei opened her eyes and saw the staff leaning against the wall next to her bed. She rose and pulled it toward her, running her hands over the elegant carvings. She recognized the grain—sandalwood. Her brother had always worn the oil of this tree instead of cologne. She held the staff to her nose to find the creamy spicy scent brought back memories of her brother's hugs and the way he used to make her laugh. The tang of metal tickled her nose as well; the staff also felt heavier than the wood should have been. She remembered how lightning struck the staff, filling her with power, yet the wood showed no signs of damage. It was made for someone like her and the thought sent a shiver down her spine. It was made for the god queen.

Rei was torn. Suffice it say that this was home now, but she wasn't ready to settle in. Her feelings were still all over the place. The bloodstains on her staff reminded her that it was hard to wash the memories away, but also, that she couldn't go back to before.

A knock interrupted her thoughts. Rei opened the door to find the blonde from yesterday standing in the doorway, holding a bundle.

"Hiya!" she said, with a large toothy grin.

"Hi. It's Crona, right?" asked Rei.

She nodded vigorously. "Yup. Come on and get dressed. I'll take you to breakfast."

Rei looked down at her clothes. She still wore the scrubs and slippers. "Um . . ." she started, not sure what to do to "get dressed."

"Oh here." Crona handed Rei the bundle in her arms. "I got you a Federation uniform, but I had to guess your size. I think we might be about the same, except that you're a bit bigger around the chest than I am. Go ahead, I'll wait outside." Crona pulled the door closed.

Rei unfolded the bundle on her bed. It appeared to be the same type of uniform that Crona wore: dark-blue trousers and a long-sleeve shirt with a steel-gray jacket. She welcomed the heaviness of the fabric as she put the clothes on. She studied at the Federation symbol embroidered over her heart—a silver twelve-pointed star inside a blue hexagon. When she was dressed, she walked out of her room, and Crona nodded in approval.

It occurred to Rei that by putting on the uniform, she now committed to the cause. She wasn't sure what would be expected of her as a Volocio, but she was happy to join the cause that may finally help her get the revenge she so often dreamed about. Still, she expected her initiation to be a little more... grand?

"So, do I need to pledge an oath or something?" she asked, putting a hand over her heart.

Crona giggled. "No. Let's go. I'm starving."

Rei followed Crona down the corridor of the women's dormitory. The only sounds were their footfalls and the soft whir of a nearby fan circulating the air underground. The UV lights were brighter now. Rei assumed that was to let the dwellers know it was day.

They walked past the medical wing just as Kazimir and Arram climbed up the stairs to meet them. Arram also wore a Federation uniform, and the color made his eyes appear bluer. He gave her a small smile as he tugged at his collar. Arram was probably destined to join the Federation someday, but Rei wasn't sure if now was too soon. He looked too young in the uniform.

The four continued down several alcoves that strayed from the main path, all dotted with the same lamps and shiny walls. Everything looked the same to Rei, and she secretly prayed she would be able to find her way back. Kaz and Crona led the way while Arram walked at Rei's side.

She eyed her younger brother. "How are you feeling?"

His eyes remained forward. "Fine."

She furrowed her eyebrows. She had hoped some progress had been made between them after last night. But the way he set his jaw and pressed his lips together told Rei he was determined to remain as before.

Crona turned and walked backward, giving them a toothy grin. "Welcome to the Underground."

"Apparently," Arram said, "we're situated under a lake, so heat sensors won't find us."

"The Underground was built as the first fortress by the Federation when it was still an underground movement." Kaz paused. "Pun intended," he added.

As they continued down the hallway, Kaz pointed out other areas of interest until they arrived at a large meeting area with tables and chairs, most of which were empty. "And of course, we have Crona's favorite room: the Mess Hall."

She followed Crona, Kaz, and Arram to the line to get food. Arram took a tray and started piling eggs, toast, and a few links of sausage on his plate. Rei dumped on as much food as she dared, briefly wondering if she had taken too much. But when she looked at Crona's plate and found a mound of food larger than hers, she didn't feel as bad.

Manden already sat at a table in the back corner, his red hair a beacon in a sea of dark and light hair.

"Where's my brother?" Crona asked, placing her tray on the table.

"You just missed him. He wanted to head into Yticol to look for some book or something." Manden popped a piece of melon into his mouth. "I was only half paying attention to what he said."

Rei smiled upon hearing Bronx mentioned but immediately quelled it, hoping no one else noticed.

She sat between Arram and Crona as the blonde immediately began forking large quantities of bacon into her mouth until her cheeks puffed out like a squirrel, then she rocked side to side and hummed. Manden looked over at Crona and shook his head, a small smile on his face. Crona simply responded by giving him a big grin, cheeks still full. "Whatever, I'm still your favorite."

"Of course," Manden said. She took a big bite of bread. "My favorite marmot."

Kaz laughed, but Rei and Arram didn't. She had never heard of a marmot. Arram was probably just being Arram.

Crona narrowed her eyes. "I would make a damned adorable one." She pointed her forkful of potatoes at Manden. "And don't you forget it."

Manden snatched the fork and stuck it in his mouth. Crona squawked, causing the whole table to roar with laughter; this time even Arram cracked a smile.

"Can we also go into Yticol?" asked Rei once her plate was empty of a second helping. "I must admit, I would like to feel the sun on my face."

"Today's cloudy," Manden said. "Which would be a good day for you to get out. There is at least one Dominion satellite orbiting, so we make sure to not go out unless we know our movements can't be tracked." He gestured to Kaz and Crona. "Can either of you take Rei? I need to run some diagnostics on my ship."

"I would, but I have a video call with the council," Crona said.

"I can take her," Kaz said. "It'll be a great opportunity to get to know my cousin."

"Arram should come, too." Rei watched the look of realization hit her brother's face. "How about it?" Her gaze never wavered.

He threw his fork onto his tray. "Sure."

Kaz led the two out of the food court and toward the underground tunnel that led to the hangar. He explained more of the Underground's layout and connection to the hangar as they approached a staircase that led upwards. The steps were stone, mostly clean aside from the cobwebs in the corners. After several agonizing minutes of climbing, with Rei sweating and panting, they reached another door with a small scanner.

Kaz's thumb unlocked it, and the door clicked open softly. On the other side was a large library, the entrance situated in a small space between a wall and a bookshelf. A quick glance around the room revealed worn and old furniture, possessing a thin layer of dust, as did all the books.

"Where are we?" asked Rei.

"This is Urius's family estate. Back before the civil war started," said Kazimir, leading them out of the library.

"How many soldiers are in the Underground?" she asked.

"Maybe about fifty or so. Urius doesn't want to make our presence entirely known to the Federation yet, so we stay here. It's small and almost completely unknown aside from a few people. The less people know about us here, the better."

"Does Urius visit?" asked Arram.

"He does. Rarely. He claims not to for the Dominion's sake," Kaz said.

Their cousin led them through the house where Urius once lived. Just like the library, the rest of the house was in a state of disuse and in need of repair. Dust or cobwebs covered almost every inch, and the only sound they heard was the scurrying of little animals across the floorboards. Rei wanted to see more of the house, but Kaz kept moving ahead.

As they walked out of the building and onto the grounds, Rei gasped at the sight in front of her. She had never seen so many shades of greens and blues in her life. What once must have been a beautiful garden sat off to the right. Now weeds and wildflowers overtook it. Sunshine pierced through a small opening in the clouds and glanced off the dew-bright leaves, making the blue, yellow, and purple flowers pop as the light hit them. Rei wished she knew what the flowers were called but appreciated the beauty, nonetheless. Bees hummed and birds twittered somewhere in the trees above them. The sweet flower perfume overwhelmed Rei as she breathed deep.

"It's so beautiful," she whispered.

"Did you only know the badlands?" asked Arram, coming to her side. She nodded and he let out a whistle. "I was jealous of you, for being able to stay in one place for the entirety of your childhood. But I must admit, I got to see some beautiful places in the star cluster with my grandparents."

"Our grandparents."

"Hm," was his only response before he continued on.

Rei clenched her jaw. "They were my grandparents, too," she grumbled, but she didn't think Arram heard her.

The lake that ran over the Underground stretched out before them. The sun rose, its rays peeking through the clouds and reflecting like glass off the surface.

Kaz walked down the path and toward a dense forest. "Come on, you two."

Rei quickly caught up, her eyes glued to the sights around her.

Somewhere in the trees, an angry creature chattered, but Rei didn't recognize the animal. She whirled around to find a small brown critter with big eyes and long floppy ears. Yet all she saw was a towering creature with horns and pointed bloody teeth. It hopped in her direction and she screamed and ducked behind Arram.

"What is that?" asked Rei.

The creature grew louder behind Kaz. "Um, a rabbit."

Arram lifted an eyebrow. "You mean to tell me you're afraid of that little thing?" He wandered over and picked up the creature. It appeared docile in Arram's arms, but she knew that it was only to give its victims a false sense of security. Her cheeks burned from embarrassment that such a thought even crossed her mind. She couldn't bring herself to look at it. Snakes, scorpions, or desert raiders didn't bother her, yet this little thing turned her insides to ice.

She waited for Arram or Kaz to tease her, but they didn't.

"It's probably a memory from your previous life. I get them once in a while," Kaz said as he watched Arram stroke the creature behind its ears. "Manden used to tell me stories of battling these giant rabbit-like creatures from his home world. He told me he would get spooked by rabbits when he first came to Tyre because they reminded him of the baby version of the great harinchen on Tas'und'eash. Seeing a small one usually meant the larger parent wasn't far behind."

Rei's stomach dropped. *Those damned things are real?* She had to admit she felt less ridiculous about her reaction.

Arram placed the rabbit back on the ground, far from Rei, and they watched as it hopped away. He turned back to his sister and cousin, and his eyes narrowed as he briefly chewed on his lip.

"Have you ever been to Tas'und'eash?" he asked.

Kaz shook his head. "No, but I hope to see it someday."

"Me, too." His shoulders relaxed. "I used to get a lot more of these memories when I was younger. Before I knew who I was."

"When did you first find out?" Kaz gestured for the two to continue walking with him.

Arram picked up a delicate white puff that blew apart as the wind hit it. "When I was sixteen and had my first encounter with Infiernen. I had to fight my—our grandparents to tell me, I didn't understand why Infiernen wanted to hurt me."

Heat radiated through Rei's chest when he made the correction. He must've heard. Rei's eyes went to Arram's shoulder where the brand lay hidden under his uniform. Arram glanced in her direction as though he felt her staring.

"Your grandparents didn't want you to know?"

Arram shook his head.

"What about you, Rei?" Kaz continued. "Why do you think Hotara never told you?"

Rei's thoughts returned to fights she had with Hotara. Hotara's omission wasn't just protecting Rei from the truth about the man hunting her. "She said she wanted me to have a normal life. I guess she didn't want me to feel burdened with the truth."

"I know that feeling." Kaz tugged on the button of his uniform. "I found out my parents were monetizing on my celebrity. I guess I shouldn't have been surprised. We know how our family can be. They thought they were protecting me, but all it did was make me look the greater fool once the truth came out."

Arram stopped in his tracks. "I-I didn't know."

Their cousin grimaced. "I love our family dearly, but they have no qualms with dragging the rest of us down to their level. Growing up away from them was a good thing."

"You can love family, but you don't always have to like them," Arram said with a small smile and Kaz beamed back. Rei felt a lightness in her chest watching them bond.

Their cousin continued meandering down the path.

Once he was out of earshot, Arram's lips turned into a sneer. He glanced at Rei, face flushed and nostrils flared. "I know what you're trying to do, Rei. Stop it."

"Stop what?"

"You think because Kaz and I spend the morning together that we're automatically going to be best friends or something."

Rei pinched her lips together.

"Did I force you to talk to him? No. Would it kill you to get to know him before you pass judgment? So far I think he's nice."

"He's an Ettowa. They're only nice when they want something."

Rei let out an exasperated sigh and gestured between the three of them. "And yet we're all Ettowas."

Arram rolled his eyes. "Don't remind me." He spun on his heels and followed Kaz, who stopped once he realized that neither Rei nor Arram had followed. Her brother clenched his fists as he walked, his shoulders tense. He was trying to remain cold, but she already saw the crack in his armor. She knew her brother needed more time, but at least this nudge helped.

# CHAPTER 13

They continued in silence until eventually they came across the sound of people, the sound of civilization. As they rounded a bend, a village appeared before them with a number of vehicles parked outside.

"This is Yticol," Kaz said. "It's an old city, like the ones from Earth that predated the modern automobile. Its streets are so narrow that no one is allowed to drive."

The picturesque old city sat on a tiny island, touching the main land by a little thread of a bridge. Water wasn't the only thing to surround it; a great stone wall wrapped around the edge where small waves lapped against the facade. Scorch marks blackened the gray stones near the entrance.

"What happened there?" asked Rei.

"Infiernen and his Infinity Dogs attacked the city six months ago. No one was hurt, but I think he just wanted to remind the Federation what he's capable of."

And how untouchable he is, Rei thought to herself. The Negander always darted from place to place, and no one stopped him. No one had the firepower to do so, yet Rei did. She only needed to cross paths with him one time and she would destroy him. But she had no idea where to even start. She lived most of her life in the Dominion; she knew little of the other side.

Kaz led them through the cobblestone streets, each a different shade of gray, that carefully lay in angles that pointed Rei and her companions further down the narrow alleyways. The buildings were taller than those in Ballarat and appeared to almost touch each other at the top. A string of lights zigzagged between the off-white stucco walls that chipped and cracked from years of sun and rain.

They visited a couple of shops and wandered through the endless winding roads between the buildings. An older woman with laugh lines around her mouth and eyes stood behind the counter in a small store that was tucked in an alleyway. Odd knickknacks, scarves, hats, and little crystals that threw rainbows on the walls crowded the space.

Rei found a beautiful green scarf with little pink roses embroidered along the edges. Its shade of emerald had quickly become her favorite after this morning's walk. Unfortunately, she didn't have money.

Kaz pulled change from his pocket. "I'll get it for you."

Rei shook her head. "No. You don't need to do that."

Kaz pressed a few coins into her hand. "I insist! Think of it as a late birthday present." He wore a pained expression. "While you're here, you'll get a stipend as a member of the Federation. It won't be much, but it will allow you some luxuries from time to time. Until then, let me buy this for you."

Rei almost pressed that he shouldn't, but then she thought about his own upbringing. He, too, had spent most of his life away from family. He probably felt like he needed to make up for lost time. If she were in Kaz's position, she probably would have done the same thing.

The labyrinthine feel of the old city mirrored the Underground, and Rei hoped there was a pattern to this chaos.

The alley opened to a sunlit harbor—walled in, save for a small entrance guarded by a lighthouse and a statue of a lion. The lighthouse led the residents home, while the lion guarded the city from outsiders.

After living so long in the desert, this town felt alien. It served as a reminder of how sheltered her life had been thus far. Yet Arram, at her side, appeared unfazed by the beauty around him. It was likely the byproduct of traveling from planet to planet. They waited for Kaz to finish talking to an acquaintance they passed.

"Arram," Rei began, "did you live on any Federation planets when you were growing up?"

"Most of them were, why?"

Rei admired the view of mountains beyond the lake— the highest peak sat directly in her line of sight between the lion and the lighthouse.

"I'm going to need your help," she said. "The Dominion blocked out all Federation news feeds. You already have a good idea of who's who in our family, so I'm sure you are just as thorough with the Federation."

"You want to know everything." He scoffed. "Of course you want something from me. You're no different than the other Ettowas."

Rei sighed. "Needing your help is not the same as using you. We are on the same team, we have the same goal."

"Forget it. You can use the Nexus to find the information you need."

Kaz returned, his eyes darting between Rei and Arram. "Everything all right?"

Neither responded, but it was Rei who walked away first. She didn't understand why he couldn't see past his own prejudices.

A little cafe sat around the corner from the harbor. Rei saw him first, sitting at one of the tables, tablet in gloved hand. She watched Bronx as he used a naked hand to swipe, unaware that she was nearby. She saw his Daer ring on his finger. The memory of being in Atrius's arms clouded her thoughts, and she imagined what it would be like to feel his hands upon her.

"What brings you out here, Bronx?" asked Kaz, bringing Rei out of her head.

Bronx saw Rei first; his lips parted as their eyes met. He quickly stood and gestured for her to take his seat.

"I planned on going to the bookstore." Bronx pointed to the shop across the street before finding more chairs for himself, Kaz, and Arram. "I wanted to find a book on the medicinal properties of the Bryon species of fungus in the area. By the way, Kaz, Crona needs you back in the Underground."

"Religious dilemma?"

"Yup. With generals this time, too."

"Great." Kaz made a face.

"Why the fungus?" asked Arram.

"Potential antibiotic," said Bronx. "One of our last patients used up most of what we have. Connocillin is the standard, but it's harder and harder for us to obtain."

"Why? Where is it grown?"

"Connocillin is grown exclusively on the planet Trappist V. The people there lean Federation, but the planet is in the same star system as the Dominion capital, Ara'nden. It's a complicated situation." Bronx's gaze turned to Rei. His eyes left her breathless; they were so dark and framed by long lashes. When he blinked, their shadows fluttered on his smooth cheeks.

"I'll see you all back at the Underground," Kaz said, breaking the spell. "You're in good hands with Bronx." With a quick wave, their cousin disappeared into the crowd.

"I am truly having a hard time believing Kaz is that nice," Arram said once their cousin left and a server came with a carafe of water and three clean glasses.

"Oh, believe it," Bronx said. "Kaz is one of the nicest people you'll meet."

"Really?"

Bronx nodded. "He always tries to see the good in people. I think it's from his years in the monastery. The monks practiced love and peace. Although there are some people who don't deserve his kindness. His sister—Skylar—is a piece of work. She's an Ettowa and a Daer Knight, so there's ego and entitlement aplenty."

"Have you met other members of our family?" asked Rei. She hoped everyone wasn't so quick to judge an entire family based on the actions of a few. She really wanted Arram to trust her and see past her last name. "Are we all so terrible?"

"Yes," Arram said.

"No," countered Bronx. "Some of the business decisions made by Ettowa Star Line has affected certain neighborhoods on Wolf X and Proxima Centauri II with their fast expansion of launch ports and production facilities. As a result, they're not always popular. I've only met the ones who support the Federation. They've always been nice to me. From what I heard, the ones who support the Dominion are in deep—I mean, inner circle with the Sovereign."

"So why do you feel so much hatred toward the family?" She turned to her brother. "I understand dislike, but this? I don't understand the hostility."

Arram stared at his glass that he had yet to fill. "They're everywhere. They don't just have the Star Line, they are in politics, in fashion, in the judicial system, entertainment, you name it, there's an Ettowa succeeding in it. Nepotism at its finest. And somehow one of them turned out to be a reincarnated god... well, three of them, now. Kaz got to live openly with his identity with all its splendor and accolades." He filled the glass and quickly drained it. He met Rei's eyes. "I knew for years I was Max. I knew that was why Infiernen hunted me—why he branded me. My life was one of constant fear of being caught again, while Kaz got to have it easy—he didn't have to struggle, just like the rest of the Ettowas."

Rei crossed her arms as she bristled. "The rest, Arram?" She leaned in close to him. "Hotara and I struggled for years to keep our bar afloat. Where was my silver spoon when I had to clear vomit from patrons at the bar? Where was the privilege when the loneliness set in? I thought I was the last of our family after the death of our parents—our brother, Niklaryn." Her voice was dangerously low. "Do you know how grateful I am knowing I am not the last of our family? Even though you are a monumental pain in my ass. You aren't the only victim of Infiernen, Arram, but you and I are finally in a place where we can do something about him. So take care next time you make assumptions about someone simply for the misfortune of a last name you don't like."

Arram's cheeks grew red and he refused to meet Rei's gaze. Then he stood. "I need to walk. I'll just go on ahead to the bookstore. You can meet me there."

Rei slumped back into her chair. "I don't care what you do."

He winced and Rei almost felt guilty. Almost. He nodded and, with hunched shoulders, wandered over to the store across the street.

"He is certainly a bucket of sunshine," the medic muttered.

Rei nodded. "He's had to protect himself for so long. It's a hard habit to break."

She didn't blame Arram for his mistrust. Perhaps she was a little too harsh on him.

"From what Manden says, you didn't have it easy, either," Bronx said. "Don't try to force things. You both are on the same team. Your interests will cross soon enough."

"I know. He just brings out the worst in me. He has since the day we met."

"Just like an annoying little brother, right?" He raised an eyebrow.

She chuckled. "Exactly like an annoying little brother."

Bronx paid for his coffee, and the pair made their way to the bookstore. He broke away from her toward the medical section to find what he was looking for. She watched him walk away, noting the grace in his steps. Every step was precise and fluid, and she remembered that he was a warrior, too, like Atrius.

Rei walked between the shoulder-high aisles, touching a book here or taking one out to read the inside covers, feeling the soft leathery spine and the raised bumps of the book title. The place was quiet, save for the sound of people murmuring or the occasional crisp ruffle of pages being turned. The dry scent of paper and cardboard filled her nose as she wandered, searching for her brother.

She found Arram in a back corner, staring at a shiny golden book called *The Ettowa Families of the Tyre Star Cluster* by Felix Royalt.

"I didn't realize there was a whole book on us," Rei said.

"The author's good. I've read some of his other histories." Arram handed her the book. "I'm sorry I made those assumptions about you. Sometimes I don't think before I speak."

"Sometimes I don't either. Must run in the family," she said with a smirk.

Rei opened the book and ruffled through its pages until she found what she wanted: the family tree. Rei squinted her eyes until she saw the names of Niklaryn, Rei, and Arram in the far bottom corner. She ran her finger over Niko's name.

"You'll have to tell me about him sometime."

Rei smiled. "Gladly." She returned the book to the shelf. "I'm sorry that I tried to force a friendship with you."

He waved his hand dismissively. "We can still work together. You were right about Infiernen. He took so much from us and still wants more. He's killed our family and hunted both of us for years. It's time someone finally stopped him."

Rei pondered over Arram's comment. It made sense Infiernen would have been the one hunting her all these years. Yet she could not think of what that Negander hoped to gain by wiping out her family.

"That's why I wanted you to help me navigate the ins and outs of the Federation. As lightning Volocio, you and I can do some serious damage. I think we have the capacity to take down Infiernen ourselves. I want to have an idea before I try to organize a meeting with Urius. We'll need to get your powers to manifest as well, right?"

Arram's face fell. "They manifested once—when Infiernen attacked me. It's how I fought him off. But they haven't worked since."

"Okay. Then we'll add that to the list." She grinned.

As the sun made its way behind the mountains, they returned to the Underground. Bronx walked between Rei and Arram, but half a step behind them. He and Arram talked about the war, politics, science, things that Rei was not familiar with. She simply walked silently, envious of their conversation, wishing she knew enough to contribute, but enjoying hearing the two of them talk all the same.

As Bronx spoke, her eyes wandered over his gloved hands. She never once saw him take them off, and when he walked, he held his hands behind his back. Everything about his demeanor suggested a physical distance: the fact that he was still half a step behind them, his clothes, the gloves, the long sleeves, and the high-neck collar despite the warm summer air. Very little skin showed, and she wondered why but never asked. Perhaps it was just a personal preference.

When they finally reached the Underground, they found the other Volocio in the small lounge area, along with another familiar face.

"Hey!" said Bernie as they entered the common area. "The fun has arrived!" The officer approached Rei to give her a big hug. "You okay?"

Rei returned it but felt all eyes in the room on her. "I'm fine," she said too quickly. "Aside from the world of information dumped on me the last few days, I'll be fine. I have to be."

Bernie nodded, then studied both Rei and Arram. "I hope so. You're with the Federation now, so you have to be all right. We need you. Listen. I picked up my uncle on the way here. He wants to meet with you alone, Rei. He told me to tell you that he will be at the Rose House Inn in Yticol around noon tomorrow."

"He won't meet us here?" asked Arram

Bernie shook her head. "My uncle avoids coming here if he can. The Dominion doesn't know about this place, and they watch his moves via satellites quite regularly. But it's expected to be very cloudy above Yticol tomorrow, which should keep the satellite here from being able to see him. It's easier to brush off him visiting the town, but his homestead is supposedly abandoned, so he doesn't want to give a reason why it may not be. If you know what I mean?"

Rei bit her lip. She had a feeling that whatever reason Urius had for wanting to meet with her alone was not something she was going to like. "Of course. Can't wait to meet him." She gave her friend a half-hearted smile.

# CHAPTER 14

The Rose House sat in the plaza not too far from the harbor. It was an off-white building with red-rose bushes weaving through trellises along the outer walls.

"Best food in town," Kaz said when they arrived. "The owners are four sisters."

"This is *the* place to come for egg noodles and lentils, but be aware that they also serve a wise-ass comment as a side dish." Crona linked arms with Rei and pulled her through the door. A wall of sound hit them as they entered. "But don't worry. They treat all their customers like family."

Two women behind the bar spoke to an older gentleman seated on the opposite side, his face recognizable. Rei watched the Leader of the Federation with great interest. His muscular build was visible by the way his coat hung on his frame. He was tan with pale blonde hair, strong jaw, and light eyes—the same hazel as Bernie's. His eyebrows rose as he beheld Rei and the others standing in the doorway. She saw the familial resemblance between him and his niece.

The room was full to the brim and loud with the murmur of conversation, punctuated by the occasional laugh. A full restaurant didn't seem like the place for a clandestine meeting with a man who supposedly never visits this place.

"Why don't you two find a place to sit?" Kaz pointed to the man at the bar. "I need to ask Urius something first." He left Crona and Rei to navigate their way through the narrow spaces between the rows of mostly filled benches. Kaz took off his jacket and slung it over a nearby stool and chatted with the women and Urius.

While they waited, Rei watched the Federation leader out of the corner of her eye. She hoped that he would assign her somewhere where she could do some real damage.

A curvaceous woman with warm brown eyes came to them, pad in hand. "What would you girls like?" she asked.

"I would just like some tea, please," Rei said.

"You want a raspberry, mango, or lucuma tea?"

Rei raised an eyebrow; she had never considered fruit in her tea. She was accustomed to just mint. "Uh... raspberry?"

"And I'll have a big glass of orange juice, Kirsty." Crona made a big circle with her hands. "And I mean big, the biggest glass you can give me," she added. Kirsty wrote the orders down with a knowing smile, as if it was not the first time Crona had made such a request.

"Food?" asked Kirsty. Both ladies shook their heads.

As the woman walked away, Crona called, "You know what? Just give it to me in a maas!" Rei smirked at Crona, who drummed her fingers on the table. Crona responded with big innocent eyes. "I'm thirsty."

Rei chuckled, even though she had no idea what a maas was. She watched her companion as the blonde hummed. In daylight, Rei saw how she and Bronx shared similar features: long face, same nose, same eye shape—though hers were a glowing aquamarine to his inky black—even the same smile.

"Manden told us that you grew up in the desert," Crona said.

Rei nodded. "A little town called Ballarat."

"Do you miss it?"

Rei thought about it. She was so ready to leave when she lived there, but a part of her knew that even if she did, she could always come back. But it was gone now. "I miss what it represents."

"I hear you. To have that ignorance back, that innocence."

"Yeah." Rei thought about Hotara wanting her to have a normal life. Life was simpler when the idea of revenge was nothing more than a fantasy. But she was not going to let go of the possibility of avenging Niko.

"I miss my home sometimes," Crona continued. "I miss gardening with my mom, my fingers in the dirt. My mom and I were really close."

"Were?"

"Our relationship wasn't the same after Bronx's and my powers appeared." Her eyes grew distant as they stared at her empty hands.

Rei realized that she wasn't the only one to feel betrayed by a parent. The sting of Hotara lying about Manden and her grandparents still had a bite.

Rei had to admit that she was surprised, but grateful, by how open Crona was. She appreciated knowing someone else went through the same situation. She didn't realize how much she needed it.

Crona gave Rei a half-hearted smile. "If there is anything I have learned through my powers, it's that everything happens for a reason. I don't regret where my path has taken me, and I'm glad I'm not alone. Bronx is my best friend. Kaz and Manden make life interesting, and your brother seems nice, but honestly, I'm glad you're here. There are too many Volocio boys in our group. We need women."

Rei smirked. "So we can talk about boys and makeup?"

Crona wriggled her eyebrows. "To overthrow the patriarchy."

Rei laughed. Crona reminded her of Hotara, and the thought comforted her. She had a feeling the two women would get along just fine.

"I like you," Rei said and the women shared a smile. "Tell me more about yourself. You're the reincarnation of Alexia, right?" she asked, deciding to go ahead and get the question out of the way.

Crona made a face and still kept drumming. "Yup. Goddess of time. But what I really am is a seer."

"So you can see the future?"

Crona turned her head from side to side. "It's more like remembering."

"Remembering?"

"Yep. I still can't control it at will, and when it does come to me, it's like a memory. Sometimes, I have to listen for it, but I have to be in a calm state of mind." She stopped drumming and laced her fingers together. "Which, as you can see by my constant fidgeting, is hard. It also doesn't help that my talents are always requested in terms of tactics."

"So you're good?"

Crona shook her head. "Lucky. My powers are very temperamental. The visions come only when I'm calm, but the stress of not having my powers work or wondering if I interpret the visions wrong keeps my mind anything but serene. So I study what I can to make an informed decision when my powers fail."

"That sounds frustrating."

"Very."

"Is there a plan for Trappist V?" asked Rei. She and Arram had talked long through the night and she was now full to the brim with ideas. She had her sights set on this planet. She remembered Bronx's mention of their need for the antibiotic, and the fighting between the parties was a common sight on the Nexus. If she could cause enough of a stir there, perhaps it would tempt Infiernen to come to her.

"At the moment, no." Crona continued to tap her fingers on the table.

"But we need that planet."

"I know. No one has come up with a decent plan to sway the public to remain Federation without violence. Do you have a plan?"

Rei slumped. "It still requires violence. Infiernen's head on a platter."

Crona cocked her head to the side. "It would be effective if it could be done."

"You don't think I can do it?"

"I think Infiernen's too slippery. He has evaded our attempts more times than we'd like to admit."

Kirsty returned with drinks. Apparently, a maas was a gigantic ceramic glass that required two hands to lift.

"How much is in that?" Rei asked.

"A liter!" Crona took a long draw of her juice while Rei stared at her tea. She immediately regretted having ordered it as she watched the raspberries float lazily in the steaming liquid. Next time, she would stick to an herbal tea. She picked the fruit out and placed them on a nearby napkin. The water was still too hot, and it burned her fingers.

"So what you see, is it set in stone?" Rei stuck her fingers in her mouth, hoping it would dull the pain.

"The future, no. I mean, I can't control it, but I can influence it at times. Sometimes it's like I'm given options. Sometimes I'm given a direct course to get to the result, other times I have to guess. I see the future as a dear friend who likes to keep secrets. I am one of the few she trusts enough with some of them." Crona smiled, but it didn't reach her eyes.

Having finished his conversation with Kaz, Urius approached Rei and Crona.

"Be careful around Urius," Crona muttered before he arrived at their table.

Rei locked eyes with the blonde in surprise. What did she mean by that? But the Federation leader had already arrived.

"Hello, Rei. I'm Urius." He extended a hand.

Rei took it and shook it firmly. "I know who you are."

"I knew Niklaryn well. Your brother was good man," Urius said with conviction. He sat across from her, setting a glass of beer on the table. A ring of condensation already formed at the base.

"That he was."

"I'm going to join Kaz," Crona said quietly and left to sit at the bar, taking the maas with her.

"I must admit, I found it too coincidental that the sister of one our greatest Daer is also the god queen." Urius kept his voice low.

"Trust me, I was just as surprised to find out. Did Niko ever mention me?"

Urius shook his head. "No. Now that I know who you are, I don't blame him. That's why I want you safe in the Underground until we decide our next step. It was built for me by the goddess of the earth, Tara," said Urius, chest puffed.

"Tara?" So there was another Volocio here in Tyre.

Rei remembered Manden whispering the name "Tara" to her mother when they reunited. Hotara.

"Manden's wife." Urius took a large gulp from his beer.

Rei's heart sank. How much more did Hotara keep from her? She pushed the feeling down. She refused to dwell on it right now; she needed to focus on her goal. "I would like to discuss some ideas I have for my and Arram's roles in the Federation."

Urius cleared his throat and stared at his hands. "Ah, yes... well." He looked up at Rei. "I am sure you have fine ideas, but we already have made a decision of what to do with you."

"We?"

"The Council and myself."

Rei watched her tea before taking a sip. She had to be patient. She had faith in her ability to convince him of her and Arram's plan. She didn't think an ardent believer like Urius would ever deny his god queen.

"We'll need you to eventually be a figurehead for us. We need you to be the god queen."

Rei's rubbed her sticky palms together and furrowed her eyebrows. It wasn't exactly what she had in mind, but perhaps she could still use it to her advantage. "Figurehead? And what does that entail?"

"To be a person for the troops to rally behind. A lot of it will be show—you'll have to look the part. Costumes and such."

"Costumes? I assumed that I would be placed in the army somewhere. I can be useful with my powers."

He shook his head. "Between our Daer and soldiers, we have enough fighters. But you're different. You're more than just a grunt. Remember, the prophecy states that Mica will lead the armies, so obviously I'm putting two and two together here."

Rei's face went numb. "You expect me to lead?"

"Yes."

"Then I want to lead the Federation to Trappist V. I want Infiernen's head."

"No."

Pressure built in Rei's chest as the wind knocked out of her. "Pardon?"

"I said no. You will lead where I say you lead." Urius took another swig of his beer.

Rei lost feeling in her legs as the truth washed over her. "You deny the god queen? You won't even hear my plan."

"Because there is nothing to discuss, Ettowa. The decision was made long before you arrived." He jutted his chin. "And we both know you're not a real god."

Her blood boiled as control slipped through her fingers like water. So much of her life had already been decided before she was born, being in the Federation was no different than Ballarat. But she wasn't going to let that stop her. "You said this will happen eventually. Who decides when the time is right? You?"

"Yes. But if you must know, my timing is dependent on having all six reincarnated Volocio working with Manden. I only have five at my disposal."

The muscle in her cheek flexed. At his disposal. As though she was at anyone's beck and call. She flashed her teeth. "And if I refuse? I'm no general."

Urius gave her a knowing smile. "You're welcome to refuse. But I know you and your brother have spent most of your lives trying to avoid Infiernen's attention. Let's just say that doing this is the price for the Federation protecting you. You scratch my back, I scratch yours."

Rei's mouth fell open. She would have refused him right there, but he had the audacity to bring Arram into it. He knew it, too. She leaned back in her chair and stared at the leader. How dare he.

"Oh, don't balk." He rolled his eyes. "You and I have the same goal: disable Infiernen and dismantle Praymer's hold on his people. I know you have no military background, and you may be useful or useless in a fight. I don't know. I don't care. What I do care about is that your coming has been foretold, and I plan on using that. I use people's strength, and I know that'll be yours."

Rei said nothing. This was not what she had signed up for. "Oh yes, my face is a real strength," she muttered. "I don't agree with your plans for me. I am best suited for the battlefield. I destroyed a large group of Negander by myself. My job should be working on taking down Infiernen."

"That's noble of you to want to avenge Niklaryn. Bernadette told me what happened in Ballarat. And while that is impressive, you were also unconscious for over a day. You would be exposed and possibly captured. No. You must be protected. If it makes you more comfortable, I can assign someone directly. Bronx, perhaps?"

Rei furrowed her eyebrows, but her heart hammered in her chest at the mention of his name. "What? Why?"

"He was Niklaryn's apprentice. It would make the most sense. I'm sure he's told you."

Rei shook her head. "No," she said. Bronx had only said that he knew Niko "for a time."

The sound of shattering glass broke through Rei's thoughts. She spun to the bar where Crona and Kaz sat. The glass maas lay in several pieces on the floor. Crona's face was pale and glistening with sweat. Her light eyes glowed and her whole body trembled.

"Rei, behind you!" Crona cried.

# CHAPTER 15

Rei spun in her chair to find an empty bench behind her. Everyone in Rose House turned to stare at Crona. Kirsty rushed to her side, cleaning up the shards of the broken glass. Rei saw the worried looks in Urius's and Kaz's eyes. Crona didn't mean now. It must've been a vision.

"I'm fine," Crona said with a forced smile. "Carry on."

The blonde slid off her stool and quickly walked out the door. Rei, Kaz, and Urius immediately jumped from their seats and pursued her out of the inn, the bright sun stinging Rei's eyes. She covered them with her hand and kept walking, ignoring the grumbling of the patrons she passed.

"Why now?" Rei heard Crona asking herself. "Why not before? Fuck! FUCK!"

"Crona, what happened?" asked Urius, but she continued on. "Crona!"

She stopped and turned to face them, her eyes red with unshed tears.

"What happened?" asked Rei.

"I had a vision. A city—a plaza with a tall palace off in the distance and you were in the middle of a large crowd." She pointed at Rei. "You wore a white gown, and my brother stood on a stage in front of you in chains.

"Then I saw him. Infiernen appeared behind you with a triumphant smile on his stupid face. That bastard Negander raised his pistol high for everyone to see"—Crona put her hand in the air in the shape of a gun—"before pointing it at my brother's chest and pulling the trigger."

Crona breathed hard, and more tears fell down her face.

"I've been trying to see more of this vision," she whispered. "I can't. I have to know how to stop this from happening, but I can't see."

Crona rubbed her face, and an angry tear fell down her cheek.

Rei cast a glance in Kaz's direction. "This has happened before, right? A vision at an inopportune time?" she asked in a hushed voice.

Her cousin nodded. "It doesn't happen often, but she takes it hard every time."

"I have to get out of here, Urius," Crona said. "I need to go somewhere to think." She trudged away before the leader could answer. Rei followed her; perhaps they could work on this problem together—but she had no idea where to start.

"We're not finished, Ettowa!" called Urius.

She spun around and raised a finger to him. "According to you, I am just to wait here until you decide otherwise. I don't think there's more we need to discuss." She ran down the street to catch up to the seer.

"Crona, wait!" she called.

"Go back, Rei."

"This vision affects me, too. I want to help. I don't want anything to happen to Bronx either."

Crona slowed and held up both hands. "I don't know how you can help when I don't know what to do." She rubbed her face furiously. "I can't let anything happen to him. Infiernen has been after him for years, and we have always been careful. I can't bear the idea that something goes wrong, and we mess up."

Rei growled in frustration, louder than she intended, and some bystanders flinched and gave her a wide berth as they passed. "This is what I was trying to convince Urius of. We have to stop Infiernen before he can get to any of us."

"But he's always been so hard to find. How can we stop him?"

Rei ran a hand through her hair. "I had hoped to figure out a way to lure him to me." Her eyes remained on Crona's face as she contemplated. She pressed her lips together until all that remained was a line. "You said Infiernen appeared behind me in this crowd, so there is a moment in the future where our paths will cross."

"I think your paths will cross numerous times." Crona twisted her hands together as she bit her lip in concentration. "My visions are sometimes several points in the future jumbled together."

"Okay, so let's start at the beginning. I was in a crowd, tell me more about that."

Crona closed her eyes and breathed. "They worshiped you. But that's an obvious future, you're the god queen." She squeezed her eyes tighter, but then threw up her hands. "But I can't see past you in the white gown."

Rei raked her hand through her hair. "Okay. The gown is unnerving, but what can you see of Infiernen?"

"Nothing more than that stupid grin." The seer locked eyes with Rei. "I think I should talk to Manden. He may have a better idea how I can see more." She drew close, her aquamarine eyes glowed with determination. "If I figure out the way your paths cross, can you kill Infiernen?"

Rei narrowed her eyes and smiled. "Gladly."

Crona smirked. "Good." She sauntered away toward the bridge to leave the old town. "I'll get back to you. I look forward to seeing your work, God Queen."

# CHAPTER 16

BRONX DIDN'T HAVE TO LOOK UP FROM HIS BOOK TO know that Crona was nearby; his years of Daer training had taught him to always be aware of his surroundings. He was taking a break in the back room of the medical wing, reading the book he purchased the day before. Just as he feared, there was no fungal alternative to Connocillin on Gliese VI.

Even though he was deeply focused on the book, he sensed the energy that exuded from his younger sibling. Crona had made it a game to see if she could successfully sneak up on Bronx, but she had yet to be able to surprise him.

"Yes, Crona?"

"I need your help."

Bronx raised an eyebrow, his interest piqued. He turned to find her with a large bundle of blood-red flowers in her arms. "Did you pick every one of those flowers? I hope there's still some left."

Crona shook her head. "No. Manden made them for me. They are from Tas'und'eash, Stars of Saskia."

She sat in the chair next to his and placed the flowers on the table between them. Bronx took a flower and held it to his nose. It smelled like jasmine.

"Smells lovely."

"They are."

He tossed the bloom on the table with the others. "What do you need help with?"

Crona held up one of the blossoms. "Apparently,

Volocio like me use this flower to amplify their gifts and see more visions."

"What more do you need to see?"

Crona ignored his question and rearranged the flowers on the table until each were neatly spread out.

"Crona?"

"I saw Rei in a crowd as she watched Infiernen shoot you on a stage."

Bronx's legs grew weak. Given his history with Infiernen, the idea of meeting his end like that ripped through his core in a way he could never reveal to his sister. He wasn't sure what hurt more, Infiernen's bullet or the idea that Rei watched.

"You want to stop the vision from happening?" His voice cracked.

"Rei and I want to find a way to kill Infiernen first. Perhaps I can see a future where we have an opportunity to neutralize him."

His heart skipped a beat at the mention of her name. "Rei and you?"

"She wants to help. I know she has her reasons for wanting Infiernen dead, but she told me she didn't want anything to happen to you." Crona grinned. "I like her."

Bronx took another bud in his hand. "Is it dangerous?"

"Manden didn't mention that it was, but he did say the visions were intense."

Bronx narrowed his eyes. His sister was always a terrible liar. "You know I don't like you taking unnecessary risks. Especially for my sake."

"Saving your life is necessary, and you know I'm still going to do what I damn well please."

She was right. Crona was a spirited and independent woman, and he loved her for that. He respected her ability to make her own decisions about what she did with her body. The most he ever did was voice his worry.

"Well, at least you came to me. Perhaps I can be of some use in case something goes wrong."

"Exactly!" Crona dropped a notebook in his lap. "You can also be my secretary and write what I experience."

Bronx gingerly picked up the book. The cover had the profile of a woman with dark flowing hair surrounded by green, blue, and violet flowers. He knew that Crona had bought it simply because of the colors. His sister was always drawn to art of all forms, and the more striking the image, the better.

Of course, the young woman reminded him of Rei. He wondered what she was doing at that moment and almost asked Crona if she knew, but he didn't want to sound too eager.

"So what would be the lowest dosage? A flower? A petal?" Crona asked, more to herself than to her brother. She picked up a bud and studied it for a long time. "I guess we'll start with a flower."

The bloom was tiny, hardly bigger than his thumbnail. Bronx watched as his sister put the flower to her lips, took a deep breath, and put it in her mouth. She chewed the soft petals. "Mmmmm, sweet."

For the first several seconds nothing happened. Bronx's heart pounded as he waited for the visions to take hold. Crona's eyes met her brother's, her eyebrows furrowed.

"Hmm," she muttered. "Nothing's hap—" Her eyes rolled back, and she collapsed into the chair. Bronx rushed to her side before it tipped over.

"Shit," he muttered.

He opened her eyes, now full white. Her hands shook and eyelids fluttered. His hands trembled as he lifted her and brought her to the main room, laying her carefully onto a nearby bed. He fumbled with the heart monitor before placing it on her finger. The steady beat was a welcome sound but didn't slow down his own racing heart. He turned her onto her side and watched, helpless, as she convulsed. Hopefully these seizure-like spasms would be quick. He held her arms down with the adrenaline shooting through his own for several agonizing moments before Crona went slack. She took a deep breath, exhaled, and opened her eyes.

"Holy shit," she muttered. She rolled onto her back and looked at her brother, then to the heart monitor on her finger. "What happened?"

"What happened?" Bronx glared at her. "I'm calling bullshit. I'm quite sure Manden said this was dangerous, and you didn't want to tell me."

She rolled her eyes. "I'm fine."

"You had a seizure." He shined a light into her heavily dilated pupil. She swatted the light away, and he pressed his lips together. "I didn't like what I saw. What did Manden say about this flower, exactly?"

"He didn't say anything to me."

He hated how easily his sister lied. "I don't like this."

"But what a rush," she breathed. "Grab the notebook. Write this down."

Bronx grabbed the notebook from the backroom but hesitated before coming back. He really didn't want to watch his sister experiment further if this was a side effect. "One flower ingested. Epic visions!" she said when he returned.

"What does that mean?" he asked as he wrote.

"At first nothing happened, and then just as quickly, I was thrown back from this sudden onslaught of visions that reached into every corner of my consciousness. I couldn't focus on anything specific, but I saw everything. I saw Rei was hurt in the medical bay of the *Luciernaga*, but nothing serious. I saw an upcoming battle that we fight in. I saw Rei battle Infiernen, but I just have to figure out where. I saw people, so many people crying, dying, coming into the world, fighting, loving, and working. I felt like I saw into eternity."

She waited for Bronx to finish writing all she had just described before asking, "How long was I out?"

Bronx looked up from his notes. "Perhaps a minute, maybe two."

"So the effects fade rather quickly. I guess seeing the whole of eternity hardly lasts more than a few minutes."

"I really don't like this." Bronx's thoughts went to the flowers still in a pile in the backroom. "I don't think you should take a whole flower again."

"No joke," his sister replied. "This flower is powerful. There has to be another way to ingest this. I can see the appeal and, I think, a weaker-willed person would relish in seeing the future of everything."

Bronx raised an eyebrow. "But not you?"

Crona hobbled over to his desk where he kept a pitcher of water. She filled a glass and finished drinking it before she spoke. "No. It was too much. What would I do with information that went beyond my lifetime? A Volocio's lifetime? I don't need to see all of that. Only something I can work with. Something I can use to help people."

Bronx couldn't quell the voice in his head that told him if he had this power that he would use it to its full potential. At least with a gift like Crona's, he could see if a touch would kill someone or not. It wasn't the first time that Crona had proven her selflessness. She had access to an immense power but would be satisfied with only a small fraction of it. She was a marvel.

"So what now?" he asked.

His sister limped toward the backroom, and he followed. Crona picked up a Star of Saskia from the table and held it to her nose. "One inhaled flower equaled nothing," she said.

He frowned and rubbed his jaw. He was ready to end the experiment after Crona's first attempt, but he knew his sister well enough. She wasn't going to stop until she figured out how to make the flower work to her benefit. The best he could do was stay by her side, but he didn't like the idea of literally drugging his sister. "Maybe the scent isn't powerful enough?" Bronx walked to a cabinet behind his desk.

"Where are you going?" she called.

"Gimme a sec," he responded without glancing back. He shuffled through it until he found some smoking papers. There were some local herbs that, when smoked, helped with chronic pain, so there was always plenty of paper about. This was something he was more familiar and comfortable with.

He laid a sheet on the table beside where his sister lay, placed a few petals along the side, and rolled it into a long roll. He also produced a lighter and lit one edge, then handed it to his sister.

"You want me to smoke it?"

"Smell it, smoke it, both?"

Once a thin line of smoked wisped from the roll, she used her free hand to waft the smoke toward her nose. "The smell is stronger." She closed her eyes and waited for the visions to come.

After a few moments, she sighed. "They came, but the

visions were too faint. I can see actions but not people. The scent needs to be stronger."

Crona lay back in the chair. She studied at the unlit end of the roll, still between her forefinger and thumb. She then brought the end to her lips and inhaled. Bronx watched as she closed her eyes and slowly opened them again. He stood over her and watched her pupils dilate once again. She appeared as though she were looking through him, even though her eyes rested on his face. Eventually she lazily reached out and took the notebook from Bronx's hands and wrote. When she finished, her eyes refocused and she read the page.

*"To the people who loved the warrior slain*

*I promise you all, he will rise again . . ."*

The air rushed from Bronx's lungs as his sister crumpled up the piece of paper and ripped it from the book. "Hm, prophecy . . . still useless," she said, throwing it on the floor.

He closed his eyes and took deep controlled breaths before picking up the paper and straightening it out in his quivering hands. "What did you see?"

Crona ran a hand through her golden hair. "The visions were a little clearer, but not by much. Only this time, there were feelings that came along with what little I saw. I saw a figure split in two. I recognized him, but I couldn't tell his identity. I felt a sense of elation toward one half and serious dread toward the other. And then there was this prophecy. Does it mean that there's a warrior who is dead but will come back to life? What in the gods' name does that mean? Is there another Volocio we don't know about?" Crona glanced back at the dried plant and sighed. "Ugh. I really don't want to eat the damn thing again."

But Bronx no longer listened. His heart hammered in

his chest. He knew to whom the prophecy referred. A secret he carried for years. He tightened his hands into fists and then loosened them. They had already become sweaty.

He knew eventually he would have to admit the truth, especially to Rei and Arram, but he had hoped that day was a long way away. They thought that he was dead, but Bronx knew the truth. Niklaryn Ettowa was alive.

# CHAPTER 17

"WE HAVE GOT TO STOP MEETING LIKE THIS," SAID REI, watching Bronx shift through paperwork on his desk. It was late, the UV lamps were dimmed, and everyone was asleep. She leaned against the doorway to the medical bay and stood for several minutes enjoying the view. His jacket hung from his chair and the long sleeves of his dark blue shirt were rolled to reveal the chords of muscle that flexed as he moved.

Bronx smiled when he saw who spoke to him. "What would people say if they knew about our late-night meetings?"

"I'm sure it would be something scandalous!" She dramatically flung her hands in the air.

They both chuckled.

He gestured to the chair next to the desk. "Still can't sleep?"

"No." She sank into the seat. "Too busy digesting everything I saw today."

"Too much?" He found the light green box of mint tea in the drawer and showed it to her with shrug.

Rei nodded, then said, "Just a lot of info. I met Urius, I saw your sister's powers at work . . . the vision she had."

"Ah." He turned on the kettle, then leaned against the table. "My sister is under the impression our paths are intertwined with Infiernen's. What do you think it means?"

She shrugged. "I don't know. But I don't like that idea that I just watch him shoot you."

"No, I think if you wanted my demise, you'd do it your-self." He smirked.

She flushed. "Besides that. I want to prevent him from hurting anyone ever again."

"You mean to kill him."

She nodded.

His face fell as he sat down at the desk and scanned a few papers from a file before signing. Rei didn't understand his expression. She assumed he would want Infiernen's death as much as she.

"What did Urius tell you?" Bronx didn't look up from his paperwork.

"What's expected of me."

"Ah, the general that will lead our army to the battle to end all battles, right?"

Rei watched her hands and nodded. "With costumes and everything."

He winced. "I'm so glad I'm not you."

Rei furrowed her eyebrows. "Gee, thanks."

Bronx sighed and met her eyes, his shoulders hunched. "I'm sorry. I didn't mean it like that. I think it's too much responsibility to put on any one person." The kettle beeped and he stood to prepare the tea. "Even for the sake of a prophecy, it's simply unrealistic."

She watched his precise and fluid movements. She watched his hands—no gloves this time—and wondered if he put them away when he was alone. They had cuts and scars all over, which suggested that he didn't always cover them. They appeared strong—she imagined they were rough and calloused. She wanted to touch them to be sure, but she had to be satisfied with watching as he placed her mug on the desk in front of her.

She wanted to ask him about being Niklaryn's apprentice. He must have a reason for not mentioning it, but she wanted to know if he was there when her brother died—and why he didn't tell her. She gazed into his dark eyes and found herself wanting to trust him, but something about him not being up front gave her pause.

"What's wrong?" he asked.

She bit her lip before answering. "When you mentioned your apprenticeship, you forgot to tell me that it was my brother who mentored you."

Bronx studied her for a moment, as if surprised she had brought up the subject of Niklaryn. "Ah," he replied, and his beautiful smile disappeared. He moved the chair closer to Rei and sat down.

"That's a big detail to keep from your mentor's sister."

Bronx nodded. "I know." His voice was so quiet.

"Is that why Infiernen wants to hurt you?"

"Something like that." He ran a hand through his hair.

"Can you tell me about him? Niklaryn had never mentioned him before." No one had heard of Infiernen until Niklaryn was murdered. No matter how much she scoured the Nexus, there was little background information on the Negander.

"I only met Infiernen a few times before it happened. I don't know much, only that he was obsessed with your brother."

"Then why kill him?"

Bronx didn't respond.

Silence fell between them again. Rei's stomach turned in knots.

"When Infiernen took Nik from us," he continued, his voice low, "it was devastating. I mean, the way Niklaryn fought. He fought in a duel against Sagitan—"

"My grandfather?"

Bronx took another sip of his tea. "Yes, he fought him and won. We had never seen a fight like that. It was beautiful—they were both artists with swords. I remember wanting to be as quick as Nik."

"My Niko," she whispered, her eyes burning.

He tore his eyes away from her to stare at the vapor rising slowly from his tea. "He was really something. Stuff out of legends."

Rei held her own mug to her nose and watched the leaves float around. Niklaryn first introduced her to mint the last time he came home to visit. "The legendary Daer," she said to herself, but Bronx heard and gave her a smile.

"He was the best," he said proudly. "I trained on Kepler IV for a time before I was his apprentice. When we heard that Niklaryn Ettowa was being stationed there, they might as well have announced the coming of a god. Niklaryn was the man I wanted to be. The Daer we all wanted to be."

Rei's heart swelled with pride.

He scratched his chin, already coated with stubble. "He was a great teacher. I learned a lot from him, and we became close. Nik would often talk about you."

"He did?" she said quietly.

"Yeah. I was the only one who knew about you, the only person he could talk to. He really missed you. He had this photo of you with pigtails and you were missing your two front teeth."

Rei made a face. "Ugh. I hated that photo."

"I thought it was cute. But I must admit, when you first arrived, I half expected you to still have pigtails."

"I only wear pigtails on special occasions." She smirked.

"Like weddings?"

"And baptisms." She took a sip of her tea.

He raised an eyebrow. "Our second date?"

She choked as she laughed. She met his eyes and found them earnest. Her breath ceased completely for a moment, then she raised her mug. "By your logic, wouldn't this count as a second date?"

He laughed. She loved the sound of it. "You caught me, Miss Ettowa. Third, then?"

Her stomach fluttered as she caught the playfulness in his voice. "Just so you know, Mr. Manca, I will be expecting more than whispers and tea for our third."

"Then I vow to redouble my efforts." He winked.

Rei giggled once she caught her breath. She liked him. She really liked him. Every moment she spent with him left her only wanting more. "I can imagine how well you and Niko got along. You both like to pretend you're witty."

"Pretend? Ouch." He put a hand to his chest, a smile still on his face. "Right in the ego."

"I can tell Niko rubbed off on you. He said the same thing to me once." She threw her own hand to her chest. "Oh, betrayed by my sweet baby sister." She barely contained her laughter as she tried to imitate her brother's deep voice. "So dramatic."

It felt so good to talk about Niklaryn to someone who knew him like she did—not the legend, but the man. "Gods, I miss him."

"That was a great imitation." Bronx wiped his eyes as he chortled. "You sounded just like him." They stared at each other for a long time. Rei swore that he leaned closer to her. His gaze wandered down to her lips before he pulled away.

Bronx finished his tea and placed it on the desk. He stared at his empty hands for a long time and took a calming breath before continuing. "I remember being quite annoyed with him for a while, because he always found ways to talk about you. During staff fighting practice, he would go on about how far along you were with your own training. Or while we were in a bar, he would regale me with tales of how you drank him under the table, despite being seven years younger."

Rei laughed.

"Although," he continued, "I don't really know if that's something to be proud of?"

"In Ballarat, it was."

They both chuckled.

"I remember not being able to walk through the marketplace without him stopping and looking for something he'd thought you'd like."

Rei's eyes welled up. This sounded exactly like what her brother would have done. She never realized how proud Niklaryn was to be her brother. She didn't deserve it; she was more than proud to call him brother.

A tear dropped down her cheek. Bronx reached into his back pocket and produced a handkerchief. She took it gladly and wiped her eyes.

"You were always on his mind. I didn't really get it at the time. But I think I'm starting to understand."

"So you mean that you see me like a little sister, too?" Her heart sank, but she kept a grin on her face.

He held her gaze. "No. You're a wonder, and I'm very interested to see how far your star will rise." For a brief moment, everything around them fell away until her entire focus was on his dark eyes.

Rei snorted and wiped her eyes again. "You are such an awful flirt. I've heard my brother use that line on women before." She gave him a playful shove.

His breath caught. "Please don't touch me."

She pulled her hand away as though he had burned her. Dread pooled in her belly, and her face and neck grew warm as she cursed herself for being too familiar. He didn't like her, he was just entertaining his mentor's little sister. Nothing more. She placed the mug on the desk and stood. "I'm tired. I think I'll go to bed." She dared not look into those dark eyes.

"Rei." His voice echoed in the small room as she walked away from him.

"It's okay," she whispered, even though she felt anything but okay. She wanted to leave the room as soon as possible.

"I'm sorry." His footsteps grew louder as he approached her, but she couldn't bear to look at him.

"Good night, Bronx," she muttered before she left, the door hissing as it closed behind her.

# CHAPTER 18

REI PASSED BRONX STANDING OUTSIDE THE ARENA ON her way back to her room after breakfast. His tall frame leaned against the door as he watched whatever was going on inside the arena. His arms were crossed as if in defense, but she didn't know from what. His gaze turned to her as she drew closer. Her cheeks burned with the memory of the night before. She almost spun around to return to the mess hall, but she was never one to back down. She gave him a challenged stare, daring him to come up with a half-decent excuse.

"Please let me apologize for last night," he said. "I recognize you were trying to be a friend, and I mucked it up. I'm sorry."

She wrung her hands, not sure how to react. Whenever she fought with previous lovers, some managed to turn the situation around and blame her—or used the tried and true excuse: it's not you, it's me.

"It's not you, it's me."

And there it was.

"Do you pull away from all your friends?" she snapped. "Or just the women you flirt with?"

He looked down at his arms for a few moments before locking eyes with her. "My powers are unpredictable. I try to avoid contact wherever I can to keep my friends safe. So, yes, I do pull away from everyone who tries to get close."

Rei took a step toward him. He had yet to reveal what his powers were, and a part of her began to wonder if he would ever tell her. "It's hard to be your friend when you won't tell me what your gifts are."

"I know." He studied her. "I just can't bear to see the look on your face when you know what I am capable of."

"That bad, eh?"

He pursed his lips and nodded.

He was attracted to her—she knew that much. While she enjoyed their game, she hoped that he would make up his mind about what he wanted: keep her near or push her away.

She drew closer, wanting a glimpse of what had caught his attention before she arrived. The Daer Knights were performing their morning exercises. Ten of them stood in a diamond formation, moving in perfect harmony without weapons.

Rei had seen Niklaryn perform this routine every morning while he was with her in Ballarat, but she had never seen it performed with more than one Daer. It was beautiful.

"It's a drill on intuition." Bronx's voice brought her out of her reverie.

"Oh?"

"The Daer in the front corner of the diamond begins." He leaned in close and kept his voice down to avoid disrupting the knights. "The others have to predict the leader's movement. Eventually, all the Daer in the diamond turn, and the leader of that corner of the diamond is the new leader. Normally it's done with only four Daer, but ten certainly makes it interesting."

"Does it help you learn to dodge bullets?" she asked with a smirk.

"I can't give away all our secrets, Miss Ettowa." He gave

her wink. Rei felt the pressure in her chest lessen. She was glad they were back to their playful banter.

They continued to watch for several minutes. Rei found their movements more mesmerizing now that she understood the point of the exercise. She turned to Bronx and watched him as he leaned against the door frame, obviously preoccupied. She wondered what he would look like in the same robes the warriors wore. The black fabric with white trim was as recognizable on a Daer as their gladius and pistol. She imagined the cloth clinging on his frame quite nicely.

"Do you miss it?" she asked.

His dark eyes never left the fighters. "Sometimes."

She wanted to ask him more, but the Daer interrupted her thoughts as they finished their warm up and exited the arena, walking between Rei and Bronx and giving the Volocio a slight nod of acknowledgment as they passed. The very last one shoved past Bronx in a movement too exaggerated to be an accident.

"That wasn't graceful," Rei called.

The assailant turned, long black hair whirled around her like a fan, and she stared daggers at Rei before following the other Daer.

Bronx whistled. "If looks could kill."

"Who was that?"

"That is Kaz's loving sister and your darling cousin, Skylar. To say that she doesn't care for Volocio would be a gross understatement."

The woman continued to the mess hall. She had the same dark hair and light eyes as her younger brother. They certainly shared a familial resemblance with their sharp noses and prominent cheekbones, but Skylar seemed to have more creases in her eyebrows than her younger brother. Probably because Kaz didn't frown so much.

Suddenly, she and Bronx stood alone in the doorway. Now that the Daer had left, there was nothing to keep them standing there. Rei wracked her brain but couldn't come up with any idea to keep him from walking away.

"Come." He gestured her inside the arena.

"What?"

He entered and followed. "You were unknowingly raised by a Volocio. Surely you were taught weaponless combat. I want to see what you can do."

"Against you?"

"Yes."

They continued until they reached the center of the room.

She arched an eyebrow. "Didn't you just lecture me on how contact with you is unsafe?"

He held up gloved hands. "I'm covered. My powers need skin contact."

"Oh." She remembered his bare hands and forearms from last night.

They stood facing each other in the center of the arena. Even under her boots, Rei felt the rubbery mat give under her weight.

"Turn around." Bronx gestured to the wall behind her. She did so and found a large mirror. "Follow my lead. We're going to warm up." Bronx brought his legs shoulder-width apart and pushed both his hands forward.

Rei knew what he was doing: the same Daer drill they watched earlier. Niklaryn taught her the moves, but that was long ago. Hopefully her body would remember some of it.

Luckily, Bronx worked slowly, making sure that Rei

kept up. Each position represented a block or a blow. They didn't have clever names; they were simply first position, second position, and so on until they reached the tenth, only to return to one and start over again. They repeated the drill a few more times before Bronx turned to her.

"Very good. Now you will continue to carry out positions one through ten, and I will complement with positions ten back to one. Do you understand?"

Rei nodded but wasn't entirely sure what he meant. She started with the first position, which was a block, only to be met with Bronx's ten, which was a blow. Then Rei continued to second and Bronx to ninth. Now she understood.

They maintained the drill, each time forging ahead a little faster. By the time they were on the fifth repetition, they were moving at normal speed, and Bronx tried to surprise Rei with a new move here or there. By then she knew them and blocked each with ease.

She wasn't entirely sure how she knew them—whether it was from her years of training with Hotara, or what little Niko taught her, or perhaps even a memory from Micaela herself. Excitement bubbled inside her as she held her own against a Daer Knight. She tried her own punches and kicks, which Bronx also blocked. They were almost equally matched,

"Holy shit!" Rei heard someone cry.

She turned, only to have Bronx take advantage of her distraction, and with one sweep of his leg, knock her legs out from under her. Rei landed hard on the mat. Fortunately, the soft rubber broke her fall.

"You okay?" Bronx asked, his face beaming.

"Yeah, I'm fine. Just my pride."

"You were great."

"She was fantastic!" It was Bernie.

Rei lifted her head and saw Kaz walking toward the pair. The two must have been watching them skirmish.

"You are a force to be reckoned with. I didn't realize Hotara was so thorough with her training," Bernie said.

"I'm sure she's more impressive with lightning," said Kaz. "I would have loved to see her take down those Negander in Ballarat."

Rei stared at her hands. She wished she knew how to bring her powers back. It comforted her to know she held her own against Bronx, but the lightning was the extra kick she needed to ensure she defeated Infiernen.

"Too bad I can't call the lightning at will," she said.

"You'll get it," Bernie said. "You did it once, I'm sure you can do it again."

"Where does it come from?"

"Balance," Kaz said. "Something exchanged for another. Energy that is already available is constantly flowing. We Volocio are merely vessels, transferring energy from one object to another of equal value. Every Volocio's power works this equivalent exchange differently."

Kaz put a hand over his face, and when he uncovered it, Rei gave out a gasp. He had turned himself into Bronx. "I can take what's there and change it. Or I can change your perception." He tapped Rei's forehead. The scene around her changed and she was no longer in the arena but in the forest outside, surrounded by Negander in their scarlet cloaks.

Her heart hammered in her chest as she backed away. She expected the Negander to come for her, but they merely stared. Her eyes watered and she blinked furiously until the vision melted away and she was back in the arena.

"Wow," Rei whispered. She glanced briefly at her hands, now slightly red. "And the others?"

"They range," Bronx said. "My sister's powers are over time. Time is not something tangible, but it's always around us. Time is actually nonlinear. It's like a big ball of events jumbling together cohesively. It's happening all at once. Thus, Crona can see it. Manden manipulates plant growth, which you've already seen."

Yet he remained tight-lipped about his own abilities. Rei decided not to push it.

"Lightning, from my understanding"—continued Kaz—"comes from air. The bolts are charged particles. Manden told me that's why you fainted after the first time you used your powers; you took in more lightning than you can handle before discharging it. You'll need to learn to channel your energy so the next time you're in battle, you don't fry yourself after using your powers."

"And when will I learn how to do this?" asked Rei.

"I think you'll just have to sit down with Manden," Bernie said. "He helped the others when they learned. I am sure he'll know what to do."

Rei let out a loud breath. She didn't like this lack of structure in terms of training. Hotara would have had her learning to channel lightning the moment she awoke, but everyone in the Federation seemed unaware of the untapped potential of the Volocio. What Kaz was capable of was extraordinary, and she wondered how many people he could affect with his illusions. At least they utilized Crona's abilities, and then there was Bronx—someone deemed so dangerous that they would rather keep him as a medic than unleash him on the Dominion.

"So what am I expected to do until I learn?" Rei asked finally. "I am used to being busy."

"Let's spar," Bernie said. "I'd like to see if I can hold my own against the god queen."

Rei's jaw pained her from clenching too hard. She was not in the mood.

"Oh, come on, Rei." Bernie threw a punch at her and Rei leaned back out of the way and blinked. Bernie continued, and Rei blocked it again. "Take some aggression out on me."

Rei's annoyance simmered under the surface. Unfortunately, there wasn't anything better to do at the moment. Bernie was exact her in attacks, her style had less finesse than Bronx's, but Rei quickly discovered that Urius's niece was good. Bernie put her full weight into the punches and kicks. Rei felt the air of the ones she avoided, while the ones she blocked jarred her to her bones.

"I know you can do more than this," Bernie said. "You want to kill Infiernen? Show me what you're capable of."

Rei threw a must harder punch at Bernie; she almost didn't block it.

"Be careful, Bernie," said Bronx.

"She knows what she's doing," Kaz answered.

Rei barely heard either, all of her thoughts focused on her need to prove she was the right weapon against Infiernen.

"He killed Niklaryn," Bernie said quietly. The voice cut through Rei like a knife. Anger pulsed through her, hovering just under her skin.

"His dogs killed your grandparents."

Rei kicked harder and her punches were quicker, yet Bernie avoided Rei's attacks with frustrating ease. The cleansing white light appeared at the edge of Rei's vision.

"Imagine what Infiernen would do to Arram." Bernie's voice echoed in her mind.

They were the same thoughts that went through her head when she had seen Virga and Sagitan slumped on the ground as her town burned around her. They were the thoughts she tried to keep quiet, to keep her from going mad. Now they would not remain quiet. They were her enemy. They were everyone's enemy. She let out a ferocious yell and threw her hands forward toward the voice. Lightning danced across her hands and multiplied until there was only white light and a bolt burst forth.

# CHAPTER 19

For a horrifying moment, Rei watched Bernie fly through the air and land in a heap, her body twitching as little sparks danced across her back. Rei fell to her knees, breathing heavily, the faint scent of burned hair and rubber hovering in the air.

"Kaz, help me get Bernie to sickbay," Bronx said.

Rei stared dazed, lost in her thoughts, replaying what had just happened, remembering the way Bernie's body twitched. She felt sick.

She followed the men, holding onto the wall as she did. Her legs barely held her weight.

Bronx and Kaz carried Bernie and laid her on one of the beds in the medical wing. Rei made out a red burn mark down the side of Bernie's face, shaped like the lightning that had caused this mess.

Rei's heart thudded loudly in her chest. She knew it was her doing. After a few moments of Bronx checking Bernie's vitals, he confirmed that she had a pulse and was breathing, but they wouldn't know more until she woke up. If she did.

"I'm—I'm sorry," Rei stammered.

Bronx placed the heart monitor on Bernie's finger and listened for the beep. Her heart beat steadily.

"She baited me. I didn't mean to do it."

"Rei, shut up." Bronx whirled around, his face pale. "Can't you see I'm trying to help Bernie?"

She recognized that look and hated it. It was disgust—it had to be, and her heart broke in disappointment.

"I know," her voice was barely above a whisper.

Bronx returned to his patient. "Kaz, go to my desk and grab the burn cream."

Rei mentally kicked herself. She was so focused on using her powers to kill Infiernen, she didn't stop to think how much she needed to harness them first.

If she had, she could've stopped herself before she hurt Bernie. Now she'd created a rift between her and others. The look of disgust on Bronx's face was the last straw.

Just like that, what was between them disappeared as Bronx's dark eyes grew hard.

Rei took a step back. "I'm sorry," she said quietly to no one and fled to her room. She slammed the door with a resounding thud.

Rei sat on her bed, staring at the wall in front of her, still dazed. She couldn't believe what she had done to Bernie.

"Rei?" asked Arram from the other side of the door.

She didn't answer.

"Rei?" Arram asked again, softly knocking on the door. He must've already heard what happened. "Talk to me."

She lay down and shoved her face in her pillow. Arram sighed, followed by the soft click of his shoes on the marble floor as he walked away. A few tears streamed down her face, and she wiped them away with the cloth of her pillow and tried to sleep.

A few hours later, she awoke with a dried face, but she felt tear stains on her cheeks. She rose from her bed and gingerly opened the door. The hall was quiet, and the lights had dimmed to a soft glow. She walked down the hall, toward the bathrooms.

As Rei approached the door to the restroom, movement flickered to her right: Bronx approached from the medical wing, toward the stairs to the men's dormitory below. He seemed withdrawn, his eyes on the path in front of him. When he arrived at the top of the stairs, he noticed Rei.

She must have appeared a fright with her hair unbrushed, puffy eyes, and tear-streaked cheeks. They stared at each other for what seemed like an eternity. She wanted so much to know what he thought, but his dark eyes remained unreadable. He turned away, and her heart faltered.

"How's Bernie?" she asked.

He shook his head. No change.

"I'm sorry," she said quietly. "You know I didn't mean to hurt her. I'm still learning all of this. I'm doing the best that I can." Her voice shook as she spoke.

Bronx said nothing but continued to stare off into the distance.

"Please, talk to me." For a moment, Rei wasn't sure if he was even listening, then he met her gaze.

His lips trembled but only slightly. "You terrify me."

Rei closed her eyes and took a deep breath. The words were daggers to her chest. Her eyes burned again as the pain settled. She turned back to Bronx. "You were so worried about how I would react to your powers that you didn't stop to think about mine? I hate the way you're looking at me right now." She waited for him to say something—anything. She didn't understand him.

"Say something, please."

He didn't. His silence forced the air out of her lungs—just when she needed a friend the most. He of all people should understand what she felt. Why was he acting like this? And yet his face remained calm, his lips pressed into a line.

She rolled her eyes as another traitorous tear rolled down her cheek. "Well, fuck you."

Rei continued into the bathroom and stood in front of the sink. Bile rose in her throat, threatening to come out. She rushed to the toilet and threw up, praying her conscience would be as cleansed as her stomach. Her hands shook as she wiped her face. She sank to the floor and leaned against the wall, the cool marble permeated through her clothes, yet it didn't help the pain in her chest. Gods were supposed to be worshiped and feared, and it was only a matter of time before her friends realized the latter. Yet gods controlled their powers, only monsters hurt their friends. It was a title she more than deserved.

# CHAPTER 20

Bronx let go of the breath he held as Rei walked away. It took all his will power to let her, and he hated himself for it.

But it was for the best.

He squeezed his eyes shut, trying to forget the look in her eyes. The way they pleaded with him. *I'm doing the best that I can*, she had said. She was, and he didn't doubt that. Bernie shouldn't have bated her like that, but Urius's niece always loved to play with fire. Today was a wake-up call. Watching Rei's eyes glow white as she threw the massive bolt was a rude awakening about his own abilities. Both their abilities.

The Dominion had reason to fear them both.

"Nice work, asshole," came Crona's voice down the hall. She stood at her door, hand on her hip.

Bronx rolled his eyes and continued down the stairs to his room.

"I'm not finished with you!" Crona shouted from upstairs. "We need to talk." She followed him into his room, shut the door, and planted herself on his bed.

"Can't it wait until tomorrow?" he asked. He sat on the bed next to her and pulled off his boots.

"No." Crona rubbed her face. "I know that look on your face. You always make it before you shut down."

"I'm not shutting down."

"Really? The way you spoke to Rei sounded like you were pushing her away. You do it every time."

"Weren't you supposed to be sleeping?"

Crona stood and paced his room. "You know I'm a light sleeper. I was actually waiting for Rei to come out of her room. I wanted to talk to her about what happened, but you got to her first. You have such a delightful way with words." She shook her head. "How could you say that to her? Why would you tell her that she terrifies you? What the fuck?"

"I need her to hate me. I need her to not get close." He ran a hand through his hair. "You heard what she was capable of. I saw how Kaz looked at her, and her powers are deadly, but nowhere near as deadly as mine," he hissed. "Watching Bernie get hurt today reminded me how quickly things can go from wonderful to shit." He twisted the glove in his hands. "I say she terrifies me, and it's not entirely a lie. I can't stop thinking about her. The idea that she can electrocute me tomorrow, and I would endure it for her petrifies me. The idea of harming her—of killing her—scares me most of all. I can't bear the thought of using my powers on her." He sighed. "I used to hate the idea that we were reborn to find each other. To think that I had no say in my own destiny. But now . . ." He didn't want to say how he truly felt out loud. There was no point.

"So being an asshole is the logical course of action?"

Bronx sighed and took off a glove to rub his face. "No. No it isn't." The minute the words left his mouth, it dawned on him: if he could fear Rei, then what must other people think of him? He shuddered at the thought.

Crona pulled out the chair from his desk and placed it in front of him before sitting down. "I think it best you go and apologize to her. You of all people should understand what it's like to really hurt people."

Bronx didn't respond. He stared at the wall above his

bed, refusing to meet her eyes. Even if he ever finally gave into to those feelings, his powers prevented him from being normal. "I think it's best I keep my distance from her. She's proven herself to be as dangerous as I am. I think until we figure all of this out, I should just stay away."

Crona rolled her eyes. "Seriously? That's the excuse you're going to give?" She sighed. "Whatever." She stood and headed for the door. "I love you, but sometimes you can be so stupid."

"Stupid? For thinking it's better to have her hate me than to accidentally hurt her?"

"Stupid because you think those are your only options, idiot." Crona pinched the bridge of her nose with her thumb and forefinger. "The world is not so black and white. Intimacy is not just being physical with a person. Most of the time it's a connection of the mind. Of the soul." She sighed. "We're adults, Bronx. I've tried for the last few years to keep you from pulling away from people, but now I feel like I'm getting repetitive." She opened the door. "Do what you want. Obviously you won't listen to me." She walked out, and as she closed the door she muttered, "Dumbass."

Bronx sat on his bed for a few more moments, letting Crona's words sink in. Great, now Crona was angry with him. She had a point. All these years she tried to get him to stop distancing himself from people, tried to get him to stop being so hard on himself. He couldn't help it. His powers scared him.

Then he met Rei, and for a brief time, he almost convinced himself that he could have something normal again. He didn't think about his power; he was too entranced by her smile and her jokes. But the fantasy melted with Rei's attack on Bernie, reminding him that they weren't ordinary. The idea of her dying under his touch suddenly felt all too real.

He took off his other glove and threw both of them across the room, then lay down. He was still in his clothes but felt too shaken to take anything else off.

"I'm just going to have to take this one day at a time," he said quietly to himself before closing his eyes.

# CHAPTER 21



"Can't you get the door open yet?" Rei awoke to hear Manden's voice from outside her room. She barely remembered wandering back to her room that night.

"It's been a while since I've picked a lock, just wait."

Even though Rei couldn't see them, she swore Crona stared daggers at the redhead. She hadn't shown up for breakfast that morning, and a loud rumbling of her stomach reminded her of the decision. They must've been worried about her, and apparently even brought her breakfast. A medley of smells wafted under the door, making Rei's mouth water. She still wore the same clothes from yesterday, now wrinkled. Her stomach rumbled again, reminding her that her hunger currently outweighed her need for keeping up appearances. She rolled out of bed and opened the door.

Crona stumbled backward in shock; her tools jerked from her hands and hung uselessly on the knob.

"Yes?" Rei asked, her voice raspy.

"Are you okay? We were worried," Crona said.

"We brought you breakfast." Manden showed Rei the tray of hot sausage, scrambled eggs, buttered toast, and a mug of hot tea.

Rei wondered why they were so calm. After what happened yesterday, she didn't expect them to act so normal. "Come on in," she said as she walked back into her room.

Her room remained quite bare of decorations, except for the green scarf that Kaz had bought her, which she had draped over her chair. Manden placed the tray on the desk and pulled the chair out for Rei to sit. She plopped down on her unmade bed instead, where the tray remained still easily within reach. Manden joined her, and Crona took the seat.

Rei managed to eat a few bites of toast before she said, "The others?"

"We saw Kaz and Arram at breakfast, and Bronx is still with Bernie," Manden said.

"Any change?"

"Not yet. But I'm sure Bernadette will be fine. People have survived being struck by lightning before."

Rei winced. She had hoped to wake up to better news. "I'm sorry. I just feel terrible about what happened to Bernie." She continued to nibble on her toast.

Manden shook his head. "It was an accident, little lady. I mean, of course we are all worried about her, but we don't blame you."

Rei sipped her tea. She wanted to believe him, but she couldn't get the image of Bronx out of her head. The way he stared at her. *You terrify me.*

Crona reached out and touched Rei's hand, bringing her back to the present. "Hey, we're here for you. We don't want you to think that you have to go through this alone."

"Yet I feel like this is my burden to bear."

Manden inched closer and wrapped an arm around Rei's shoulder. "We all carry this burden. I should have done something sooner, even though my knowledge of lightning is also limited."

"I also have to pay a price when my powers don't work like they're supposed to," added Crona. "People have died when I'm wrong. My brother feels like he has to continuously pay penance for his abilities."

"You're not scared of me?"

Crona shrugged. "The truth? A little. But you are the god queen, destroyer of worlds or something like that. I would be worried if you weren't scary." She gave Rei a big toothy grin. "But if I had to choose a weapon to avenge my brother's death, I'd choose lightning."

But it was the same power that got her into this mess. Crona was right. She was a force to be reckoned with. She should stop feeling sorry for herself and learn her powers. She managed to call it twice now, a third time against Infiernen felt doable. She didn't need to be careful around him.

Rei offered her plate to the blonde. "Any luck with the flower?"

Crona took a piece of bacon and popped it into her mouth. "I see too much when I take the whole thing. I'm still trying to figure out the dosage, but I did see something."

Rei leaned in closer, though not as close as Manden. "Now I am curious. What did you see?"

Crona's eyes never left Rei's. "I saw you battle Infiernen. You were in a large crowded hall with cameras and light, but there were also trees and snow swirled around you both. I think you'll battle him at least twice."

"The two of you still want to continue this plan of stopping Infiernen before your other vision of Bronx's death is fulfilled?" Manden asked, nudging a piece of bacon in Rei's direction. "Eat."

Both women nodded as Rei took the bacon and chewed.

"What else did you see?" he asked. "Where will these battles take place?"

Crona leaned back into her chair and chewed on a fingernail. "The forest could be anywhere, but the hall was unique." She squeezed her eyes shut. "There were columns along the walls made of this deep-orange marble with veins of gold. I smelled earth, sweet with recent rain. I heard the murmur of people talking about a harvest, but of what, I didn't understand." Crona's hands relaxed at her sides, and she sunk deeper into her chair. "I saw a dragon watching two men fight at the steps of a temple. One succeeds and the other is left for dead. We should be happy for who won, but we're not. Something changed. The dead man was represented by four stars but replaced by an infinity." She opened her eyes and rubbed her face. "I don't know if that helped."

The mention of stars and temple steps tugged at her memory. Arram was very thorough in explaining all the recent events in the Federation to Rei, but she couldn't remember which planet he referred to. "Can one of you find Arram and have him meet me in the lounge? I want to change really quick. I think he may know which planet Infiernen will be heading to next." Rei tugged on her sleeve.

After Manden and Crona left, Rei put on a cleaner uniform, quickly brushed her hair, and pulled it back. She shoveled in the last of her eggs and tea and took the remaining sausage and toast with her, munching on them as she walked.

Arram waited with Manden and Crona in the lounge, his eyes full of concern. She had yet to spend time in this room. There were only a few faded gray sofas, chairs, and a low table between them. The wall boasted a few large touch screens, but they were off, reminding Rei of floating panes of glass. The smell of coffee hit her nose and brought her attention to a machine in the back corner with a blinking light, indicating something needed to be refilled or cleaned.

"Are you all right?" Arram asked when she sat next to him on one of the sofas.

"I am. I'll feel better once Bernie wakes up. But that's not what I wanted to talk to you about. You told me about a general who was killed on the steps of the Temple of Fiamatta."

"Of course," muttered Manden. "The dragon is the symbol of the goddess of fire."

"Yes," Arram said. "Representative Vaye of Trappist V was once a general, and he was recently killed on the steps of the Temple of Fiamatta."

Arram's mention of the planet recalled the list of information in Rei's mind—and the beginnings of a plan.

"Vaye was a representative for the Dominion," confirmed Crona, who sat on a chair next to them.

"Who's for the Federation?" asked Rei.

"Representative Canale," answered her brother. "She has no military background compared to Vaye's four-star status."

Manden stood and paced the room. "He was a rather violent type, if I recall."

"Right," Arram said. "He used to incite violence with his speeches, especially against Canale. Now that he's gone, it wouldn't surprise me if the Dominion replaced him with someone equally violent."

"Infiernen," said Rei. "There are elections coming up. The Dominion wouldn't dare try to have Infiernen elected as a representative."

"No, but he would try and keep Canale from being reelected." Crona's eyes grew wide as the final piece fell into place. "And if the planet becomes Dominion, they will set their embargo, and we lose our only source of Connocillin."

"I have a plan." Rei stood. "I need to get a message to

Urius first, but I think I know how we can keep the planet on our side."

"Urius is here," said Arram.

"He's in the Underground?" Crona sat up straighter. "He never comes here."

"He got wind of what happened to Bernie." Arram grimaced. "He took the risk. He should be in the medical wing."

Rei was not ready to see Bernie yet, but she had to talk to Urius. It was time to face the consequences of her actions.

# CHAPTER 22

"Brother, can you come with me to the lounge?" Crona asked. Rei had asked her to distract Bronx so she could get Urius alone. "There's something I need to discuss with you."

"Is everything all right?" he asked, his voice soft.

"Everything's fine." Crona approached Bronx and lightly touched his arm. "Let's just go, and we can also leave these two to talk." She gestured to Rei and Urius.

"Of course."

Rei snuck a glance in his direction and found him watching her, yet his dark eyes revealed nothing of what he thought. She pulled up a chair and placed it on the other side of Urius. He held his niece's hand, his hazel eyes remaining on her face, now half-covered with a red scar in the shape of a lightning bolt that reached down her neck and onto her collarbone. It was a punch in the gut to Rei.

"I'm so sorry, Urius," Rei whispered. Aside from the scar, Bernie appeared asleep. Rei prayed that no further damage was done; they couldn't afford to lose her.

"You should be." Urius finally looked at her. "Bronx told me it was an accident. But with you Volocio, accidents are always costly." He stroke his niece's cheek.

"Bronx told you?"

"Yes. He was very adamant that I not punish you. The young man takes protecting you very seriously."

But that didn't explain why he said those horrible things to her. Rei shook her head; she couldn't think about him right now. "Sir, I wanted to talk to you about Trappist V."

"What about it?"

"I think I know how we can help Representative Canale."

Urius studied Rei as though he already knew what she had planned. "I'm listening."

"I make my first appearance as the god queen. All of the Volocio, we go as a team. We show our support for Canale and announce to the star cluster that we are here."

"No." He returned to his vigil on his niece.

"No?"

"No!" he bellowed. "Trappist V is too volatile for a plan like that. There has been fighting between the Federation and Dominion for months. The council has already called the planet a loss. Even if that plan won us the planet, it's too dangerous for you; Infiernen could be there."

That was exactly her point.

"And if he is there, shouldn't I have a chance to avenge Niklaryn?"

Urius shook his head. "You will not fight Infiernen."

"He killed Niklaryn!" Rei stood, knocking her chair back. "Doesn't that mean anything to you? He was the hope of the Federation."

Urius's nostrils flared. "And his absence has left a gaping hole. But there is nothing we can do for Niklaryn right now. I know he would want you safe and in a position where you can be our hope. You have the potential to be so much more than him, but that means you need to be protected more. I thought you would be grateful for your role. No need to fight, just smile and look pretty."

Rei's heart stopped. She couldn't believe what she heard. "I have to do something," she said through gritted teeth. "Sitting pretty is not an option."

Urius loosened his hold on Bernie's hand and rose to

tower over Rei. "You want to be useful." His voice was dangerously low. "Find that final Volocio. Follow my orders and only then will I consider you well-behaved enough to be seen in public. My answer is no, Ettowa. That's final."

Rei scoffed and left the medical wing. She clenched her fists until her nails bit into her palms. This was unfair—how could he not think this was a good plan? She walked down the corridor toward the lounge. They couldn't afford to lose that planet, and Crona saw she would battle Infiernen there, which meant Rei needed to make it happen. She needed every opportunity to destroy him.

She arrived at the lounge to find the others waiting.

"What did he say?" asked Crona, wringing her hands as she paced.

Rei almost told them but held her tongue. Urius was an idiot if he thought they were just going to give up. Trappist V was vital, but killing Infiernen was more important.

"He thought it was a good plan. But we need to organize everything with Canale separately. We have to appear as though we have descended from Tas'und'eash to announce our arrival. It can't look like he planned it." Rei hated lying, but she needed to get on that planet.

"I'm impressed," said Bronx, yet his eyes lay on his sister's face as though he addressed her and not Rei. "I wondered when Urius was going to let this freak show commence. What do we do if we run into Infiernen? There's a big chance he might be there."

"We plan everything carefully," Manden said. "We only talk to Canale; we don't tell anyone else. Hopefully we can get on and off that planet without the Dominion figuring out and sending Infiernen."

"Even if he does show up," Rei said, "Urius thinks I should take the opportunity to avenge Niko." The lie slid too easily off her tongue. She probably shouldn't have said anything, but saying it out loud filled her with glee.

Bronx scoffed. Everyone turned to him.

"What was that about?" asked Crona.

"Nothing," he muttered before glancing in her direction. Rei narrowed her eyes; he didn't believe her. She watched her brother, Manden, and Kaz—they all had the same look of confusion on their faces.

"We should talk to the Daer Knights and organize an escort," Kaz said. "Our group should be small, but we should be ready just in case."

"Good idea," Manden said. "I will message Canale. She and I have worked together in the past, and she knows who I am. I say we get ready and meet at the *Luciernaga* as soon as possible. We should act now before the Dominion can suspect what we're planning." He glanced at Rei. "But I must admit, I don't like the idea of Urius allowing you to be paraded like some prized pig."

She nodded but ignored him. The group murmured their agreement, and all went their separate ways to prepare. Rei and Crona were the last ones out.

"Is there a way you can anonymously send messages to a few news stations on Trappist V?" Rei asked. "I would, but I don't have my own tablet. I think they would like to know there would be a huge announcement regarding the god queen coming up in the next day or so." Regardless of what they had planned, she needed Infiernen to come to her, and she didn't care how.

A knowing smile crept across Crona's face. "That'll certainly catch Infiernen's attention. I can find a way, leave it to me."

Rei returned to her room and grabbed her staff. She met

Manden at the entrance to the hangar tunnel. The redhead paced while tugging at the straps his bag.

"Hotara wouldn't like this plan," he muttered when he saw Rei approach. "The more I think about it, the more it makes me uneasy."

"Well, she's not here to contest."

He stopped and stared. "You seem rather relaxed for someone who is about to be led like a pig to the slaughter."

"Not if this pig is going to do the slaughtering." She smiled, thinking of how Infiernen would look before becoming a charred husk.

He shook his head. "The whole thing just feels wrong."

The other Volocio made their way to the hangar with Bronx being the last to arrive.

"The Daer who are escorting us are already at the hangar." Kaz gestured for the group to head toward their vehicle. "Sky has also volunteered to help us. She hand-picked her team of four."

Crona turned to Manden and Rei, rolling her eyes. "Oh great, my favorite Daer."

Kaz sighed. "I know you have problems with my sister. I will admit, she's not the easiest to get along with, but our parents pitted us against each other every time I came home growing up. Opportunities like these remind us that we are on the same team. She is one of the best, and we'll need her."

Rei had only had one brief encounter with her cousin, but it was enough to leave a sour taste in her mouth, regardless of what Kaz said.

Crona told the driver of the vehicle to move over and let her drive. The transport had an open top with seats in the back for at least seven people. When they were all situated, Crona punched down on the gas pedal and tore through the tunnel. The lights whizzing by made Rei dizzy.

Once at the hangar, everyone jumped out and headed toward Manden's ship. Only Rei stayed behind, still unsure if she wanted to enter such a hideous vessel. It didn't resemble a whole ship, but parts of several ships thrown together. Rei saw gears on the outside, along with sheets of metal in a plethora of colors: bronze, copper, and gold. She never thought that there were gold parts for ships. It was hideous. It reminded her of a face with its tongue sticking out.

"What do you think?" asked Manden to Rei as the others entered through the hull.

Rei grimaced, not knowing how to answer without being rude.

"Yeah, it's okay. I can tell by the look on your face that you don't trust it. I've had this baby for a couple of millennia now. She doesn't look the same as when I got her, since I've had to replace more parts than I'd like. But the soul of this old clunker is the same."

"What's her name?" Rei asked.

"*Luciernaga.*"

She recognized the word from the secret language she spoke with Hotara. "Lightning bug? Really?"

"Ah, so you speak Castelan?"

Rei shrugged. "Hotara taught me, but I always assumed it was something made up since no one else spoke it."

"Castelan is one of the official languages on Tas'und'eash. It evolved from Castellano, an old Earth language." Manden readjusted his pack over his shoulder and walked toward the ship.

Rei knew what *Luciernaga* meant, but she didn't know Hotara taught her a Volocio language.

"Luci is expeditionary and completely self-sufficient for long runs between planets, which is necessary for long trips between Tas'und'eash and here. I don't trust any other ship."

Rei followed, finally setting a foot on the ramp and expecting it to fall apart, but it didn't. She rested her whole weight on it to find it held. Inside, a large cargo hold spread out in front of her. A rusted staircase obstructed her path. There were several other people already inside. She didn't recognize their faces, but she did recognize the black and white robes: Daer.

She walked around the staircase to the cargo hold and expected it to be aptly named, but there was no cargo to be found aside from a few unmarked boxes. All around the outer walls were plants of every size, shape, and color.

"It's for protection," Manden said, still at her side. "If anyone tries to board my Luci, I have enough plants to protect myself and anyone on board." The UV lights that hung above the little space forest made Rei sweat.

She followed Manden up the set of stairs, maneuvering around the others also moving between levels, and found a dining area suspended above the hold. The sleeping quarters were located around the dining area with a small kitchen. The ship held a maximum of eighteen people, if they shared six to a room. There were more passageways with walls decorated in a collage of metal plates. Rei assumed they led either to the cockpit, the engine room, or the infirmary. She made a mental note to explore later. The inside looked better than the outside, which surprised her. It was still comprised of pieces from other ships thrown together, but the more she studied her surroundings, the more she got used to it.

She felt eyes on her everywhere she went. A few broke

eye contact when she caught them, while others simply stared or narrowed their eyes as though they wanted to dissect Rei with their gaze. She might as well get used to it once she announced her arrival.

For now, all that mattered was spending the next twenty-four hours getting herself ready to face Infiernen and to savor the sweet taste of revenge once she finally accomplished her mission.

# CHAPTER 23

Rei awoke, expecting to the sound of the ship's engine. The *Luciernaga's* hum was rather soothing and had easily lulled her to sleep earlier. But instead she heard something else—the murmur of voices punctuated with a roar of laughter.

She rose from her bunk, carefully avoiding hitting her head on the one that hung low above her. She'd already made that mistake.

The room boasted six bunks all along one wall, lockers just opposite, and a narrow passage in between. She'd claimed a compartment for her staff, only to find another set of Federation uniforms inside. It was good to have a spare. This was the unofficial "ladies bunk" since Rei, Crona, and the other Daer women slept there. No one was in the room. Perhaps the voices she heard were outside.

Rei pushed with all her weight to open the hatch. She stepped into what was the mess hall, where she found Bronx surrounded by the Daer, all laughing. But the sound died down as they saw Rei enter. They all, except for Bronx, bowed their heads slightly, and she swore that she heard more than one mutter the words "God Queen."

"Please, don't let me interrupt." Rei couldn't help but feel a little awkward. She watched Bronx, whose eyes were on the other Daer. Right as she entered, he was laughing, and her heart fluttered watching his eyes twinkle as he did. It was unfair—before it had been so easy for her to make him laugh. He used to find her funny and now she was terrifying.

"You weren't interrupting, my God Queen, we were just reminiscing with our old year mate here," said a young woman with long red-gold hair. Freckles dotted her milky-white skin, and her eyes were pale green like the grass on Gliese VI. The young woman very lightly touched Bronx's arm as she said "year mate." It wasn't enough that she actually touched him, but Rei noticed that he didn't pull away. Something told her that Bronx was more than just a classmate to her. Jealousy surged through her veins. She wanted to talk to him; she wanted to understand why he pushed her away. She needed to get him alone.

She opened her mouth to correct them on calling her god queen but caught herself. It made her feel superior to the Daer, even if she knew she was being petty. "I'm sorry," she said, "I didn't catch your name?"

"Sariah."

"Sariah, if your year mate isn't busy, I would very much like to continue what we started the other day. I wanted to learn some more Daer tricks to defend myself. Are you terribly busy, Bronx?"

Before he could answer, another voice did. "I have time."

Rei didn't see her right away as Skylar came into view. Now she saw her cousin's face more clearly. The Daer didn't have the same scowl from when they first saw each other, but her blue eyes were still hard.

Bronx's words flashed through her mind. Skylar didn't like Volocio, and her offer to help puzzled Rei. She glanced at Bronx and found him finally looking at her. He shook his head ever so slightly. Was that a warning?

Rei waited, perhaps too long, for Bronx to say or do more than just nod, but he did nothing.

"Sure," she finally said.

"Wonderful, let's work in the cargo hold. There's more room."

Just like Bronx before, Skylar had Rei begin with the Daer warm-up exercise. It didn't take long before they practiced with Rei starting at position ten and Sky at first. The Daer wasted no time with punches, jabs, and a leg swing here and there. Every time Rei blocked the hits—as if she could tell what her cousin's next attack was going to be. Rei had heard of the Daer intuition, but she was never able to predict Bronx's movements. Yet Skylar's were as obvious as if she had a large yellow sign over her head.

"You're quite good. How about we try with weapons?" Skylar reached for the gladius strapped to her back.

The onlookers roared in outrage. She could have sworn that she heard even Bronx bellow, "Bad form, Sky!"

"Don't worry, everyone," said Skylar. "She has proven to be a great student and could easily be one of us. I say we play a little game of First Blood."

"Oh, stop it, Sky," Sariah said. "There's no need for that."

"How does that work?" asked Rei.

"Whoever draws first blood wins." Sky flicked her wrist, and her sword slid across Rei's left forearm, leaving a crimson streak behind. "And it looks like I won!" The Daer laughed.

Rei didn't understand what in the gods' names just happened, but anger rippled through her core, followed by the rush of electricity. A bolt hovered around her fingertips waiting to be let loose. Her heart raced as she recalled the horrible scar covering half of Bernie's face. She couldn't let that happen again. She shook her hands, trying to free herself from the lightning's grip. She watched in amazement as the sparks listened and disappeared.

Rei took a few steps toward her cousin and punched Skylar in the face. She savored the rush of pain through her hand as her cousin's head jerked back, causing her to lose balance and land hard on her back while her gladius skidded away.

Sky stood and wiped the blood off her nose. Her blue eyes were wild, and she grinned like a predator eying her prey.

Rei looked up to her audience. "My staff?"

It was Bronx who complied, letting it drop from where he stood at the top of the stairs. The moment the staff touched her hand, she felt the call of lightning again, but she held back. She gave it a few experimental sweeps in the space around her before she took a swing at Skylar just in time for her cousin to block it. The Daer used her body to push Rei back and then attacked. Fighting against a sword was different than the staff training with Hotara that Rei was accustomed to, and yet the movements came naturally to her. It had to have come from Micaela—an echo of a surviving memory.

Skylar swung her gladius and Rei whirled away, slamming the butt of her staff into her cousin's spine. Skylar staggered but quickly swung again. Rei met the Daer's blade, pushing the staff into it and grimacing as the wood gave a splintered groan.

Skylar attacked with such ferocity that Rei began to think the other woman was actually trying to hurt her. Rei's heart pounded in her ears, and out of the corner of her eye, lightning faintly danced from her hands down to her elbows. The current murmured under her skin, whispering against her nerves like a lover's caress, begging to be released. She wanted to surrender, to feel the power flow through her, but she couldn't. She shouldn't. She would only use her powers to kill Infiernen. Yet her resolve waned.

Skylar evaded an attack and moved in too close, swinging her blade but missing Rei's face. She brought her staff up to block Skylar's weapon as the Daer swung again, and the staff shook in her hands as the sword nicked the hard wood. The air changed around her. Rei gained control and pushed the lightning down. Nausea riddled through her core. She shook as a small park remained. It was weak—exactly how she felt. It was now or never; her vision turned white around the edges.

Rei took her wounded arm and swept it out in front of Skylar, letting the bolt loose. It threw her cousin back, but she still managed to stand, singed clothes and all.

Rei let out a huge breath. She did it, she controlled her powers, even though it threatened to consume her from the inside.

Rei glared, daring the Daer to try again. But when her cousin's gaze turned to the other Daer watching them, she gave them a big smile.

"She is impressive, no?" Skylar turned back to Rei. "I wasn't sure you would actually use your powers. Glad to know you have the guts." Sky bowed. "It's been an honor, God Queen."

Rei knew the Daer didn't mean it. She would have said so, but she felt light headed, and the ship lurching beneath her feet didn't help. Little bolts lazily danced around the wood of her staff. A roar rang in her ears and her vision darkened. Luckily before her knees buckled and her eyes closed, she saw figures already at her side, catching her.

# CHAPTER 24

Rei awoke in her bunk. She assumed that she would have awakened in the medical bay below, but apparently it had been decided it was better for her to rest here.

The darkness in the room told her it was night, and her roommates were asleep. The only light came from a small red bulb near the door. She sat up and her head pulsed with a headache. Her left arm was wrapped in a bandage; a few dark drops of blood had seeped through, but they appeared long dried. She approached the door and carefully opened it with her shoulder. The door didn't creak, no danger of waking the other bunkmates.

She entered the kitchen and grabbed a small glass from one of the cabinets, filled it with water, and drank deeply. A noise from below startled her. She watched through the mesh floor at her feet to see Bronx, gladius in hand, doing drills. She refilled her glass and walked to the stairs to get a better view.

It never ceased to amaze her how anyone could move like that. A lunge, a swing, a flip and thrust—it was mesmerizing, like a dance. She had watched the other Daer train, but none of them moved like Bronx. A Daer performed feats through years of training, but Bronx was obviously born for this. His eyes were closed as he lost himself in muscle memory. His hands moved through the air with exact precision. He paused briefly to hold each position like a marble statue. The only other person who had such grace was Niklaryn, but Rei may have been biased.

Once Rei felt she had stared too long, she headed

toward the cockpit. Manden was there, working the controls. Rei gazed out the window in front of them. She had never seen the Alcubierre-Krasnikov warp bubbles before, the only way to travel faster than light. These bubbles spread out through the star cluster and allowed a ship to enter like a passenger entering a moving vehicle and hitch a ride at superluminal speed to a predetermined destination. While in the bubble, space is contracted in front of the ship as well as expanded behind it. It was how anyone in the star cluster reached any of the planets. The view outside could only be described as looking through a long tunnel of rolling clouds toward a white light at the end.

"We almost there?" she asked.

"Yup. We're just now entering the atmosphere. Cloudy day in the area it seems, so I'm taking Luci in slowly to avoid turbulence." He pulled a lever, and the tunnel melted away, but the clouds remained. He glanced in her direction. "You're looking better."

"Hm." Rei took a sip of her water and sat in the empty seat next to Manden, bending one of her knees against her body. The only lights shone from the keyboard under Manden's fingers. "I didn't realize controlling my powers can also cause me to faint."

"Damned if you do, damned if you don't. Unfortunately, you just have to learn to control your gifts. You have the capability of absorbing a lot of energy that you can then channel. It'll fry your circuits if you're not careful, and if you faint at the wrong time, they can capture you."

Rei didn't want to think about what would happen if she used her powers on Infiernen and they didn't work. If she fainted, she would be completely at his mercy. She had to hope they would work when she needed them. "Fry my circuits? Nice analogy. Did you stay up all night thinking about it?"

"Yup."

Rei chuckled. She watched him as he piloted his ship. It was the first time since she had left Earth that she was alone with Manden. So much had happened in the last few days, and yet in the silence of the cockpit, her head filled with questions—hundreds, thousands. But she had no idea where to begin.

"When we first met in Ballarat. You knew who I was. That I was Micaela, I mean."

Manden kept his eyes on the screen just above his keyboard as his hands flew a crossed the keys. "Yes. It was very unnerving how much you looked like her."

Rei stared at the glass she held in both hands. She took a sip of her water, feeling as if she needed to do something other than just sit and watch Manden fly the ship.

"And Hotara?" she continued. "She had to have known, right? She taught me to fight with a staff, she taught me your language, and she made sure I knew history, religion, and politics. She taught me everything Micaela would have already known. Like she had been grooming me my whole life for this." Rei said this more to herself than to her companion. It was as if her entire existence was one big plan: become Micaela.

"She knew," came the response. "She's a Volocio. She grew up with Mica; they were like sisters. She was the best person to prepare you for all of this."

Dread built in the pit of her stomach. All of this was a long time coming. Rei didn't want to think how far back her life was mapped out. Did Hotara plan this over the two-thousand years between Mica's death and Rei's birth? She wondered how much of her relationship with Hotara was built on her identity.

Glasses clinked together, the noise coming from the kitchen behind her. She leaned forward in her seat to have a better view down the hall.

There was Bronx, in a sweat-soaked gray shirt, drinking heavily from a full bottle of water. His back was to her, so he didn't see her as she watched. His muscles rippled through his shirt. Her mind dwelled on the thought of putting her hands on them. She could only imagine how taut he was. Bronx finished the entire bottle in seconds, then walked out of view. Maybe he was heading to the communal showers.

"You wanna talk about it?" Manden said suddenly, still clicking away at his keyboard.

Rei leaned back in her chair, her eyes never leaving the clouds. "I like him. A lot. I can't explain it. It's like I've spent my whole life being lost or having lost something important. But I didn't realize it until I met him. It was then that I felt I found it—him. I know it's crazy."

It was the first time she truly admitted her feelings about him, even to herself. Somehow, she felt lighter, freer. It felt right.

Manden smiled. "Sounds wonderful. So then, why are you confused?"

"Well... when we first met, there was a spark. We got along easily, and he knew how to make me laugh when I needed it." She smiled at the memory. "But ever since I struck Bernie, he's been cold and distant. He will either speak to me without looking at me, or he won't even utter a word to me." She shrugged. "Like I'm some weirdo. I terrify him. Yet he defended me against Urius." She growled in frustration.

"I'm sure you don't terrify him."

"He told me I do."

Manden sighed. "Jesus," he muttered. "Fucking moron."

"Jesus?"

"You don't know him," he said, typing away on the keypad in front of him. "If it's any consolation, I know he feels the same way about you, too, despite him being an asshole."

Rei scoffed. "Yeah right."

After a few more moments of typing, he stopped and turned to face her. "Rei, no offense, but you do understand that he may have more on his mind than just your pretty face?"

Rei's shoulders slumped. "Yes."

"You saw him out there doing drills in the middle of the night?" He gestured behind him.

She nodded.

"Nightmares. He has seen a lot of shit, including your brother dying, so just be patient with him. I'm sure it'll all work out."

Guilt weighed on her chest. It was vain of her to think that Bronx's actions had everything to do with her. She didn't know how she would react if she had seen her mentor die at the hands of Infiernen. She didn't even think about Bronx witnessing her brother's demise—but it was logical that they would have been at each other's side at the end. Remorse filled her thoughts. Niklaryn would have been more understanding of Bronx. He'd always had more empathy than she did. Perhaps she was being too harsh.

She gazed at the empty glass in her hands and thought back to the dream she had about Micaela and Atrius. Her gaze returned to the window where the clouds had disappeared to reveal the green earth quickly approaching them. "What can you tell me about Micaela and Atrius?"

Manden chuckled. "That's a long story."

She gestured at the slowly approaching ground below. "You said you wanted to avoid turbulence. We have time."

Manden sighed. He moved around in his seat, as if settling in for a long sit. "Well... they were in love with each other."

"I gathered this much."

"Yeah, well, I mean, they really loved each other. I wish I could've told them that it was a bad idea, but they would have never listened to me."

"Because she was married?"'

"Yes, Micaela was married to the last Emperor of Tyre."

"She was married to an ancestor of the Sovereign of the Dominion?"

Manden didn't respond right away. He pursed lips and narrowed his eyes. "Once he discovered their affair"—he eventually continued—"he declared war. Most of us stayed out of the fight. I didn't want to be involved in a marital dispute, even if she was my friend. Others did and they all died, including Mica."

As they continued their descent, Rei told Manden about the dreams she had long ago. She never got a chance to talk to Hotara about it, they had been attacked by Negander immediately after. She told him of the dream of Atrius and Micaela on the balcony and of Atrius's dying. Manden winced when he heard the latter.

"I'm sorry you had to relive that memory, sweetheart. It was so hard to see Micaela when it first happened. It broke my heart to see her after Atrius died. After everyone died. She was quite broken after that."

"How did she die?"

"I have my theories." Manden spent a few moments leveling his ship as he finally landed it on the ground. "But the official report says suicide."

Rei stared, stunned at this new revelation. "By the gods," she whispered. She would never have guessed. "Suicide?"

Manden nodded as he stood and rolled his shoulders. "As I said, I have my theories. She changed after that day, but suicide was unlike her. Unfortunately, I wasn't there. Hotara and I left her alone that night, and we have regretted it ever since. I'll tell you one thing: I will not repeat the same mistake. When I have a friend in need, I will do everything in my power to support them. I won't let them think they have to do this alone." He gave her a brotherly kiss on the forehead and smiled. "Please take comfort in that."

Manden stopped in the doorway of the cockpit and turned back. "Look. About earlier, I'm not trying to justify Bronx's shitty behavior. He has his own baggage to shift through without pushing you away like he does. But don't take it personally—he does it with everyone. I just don't want you to spend too much energy on him. When he's ready, he'll come to you. I'm saying this as a friend: focus on the mission at hand. We need you to be Micaela for the people of this planet. The rest will come."

"Are you sure?"

"The two of you are destined for each other." He turned and walked away. Rei heard his voice echo down the hall. "Wakey, wakey, children!"

Rei didn't stand for a few moments. Manden's last comment made her uncomfortable, and she didn't like the idea of being with Bronx simply because it was destined. Enough of her life had already been planned, and she didn't want it to extend to her love life. But she was here now, and her feelings for Bronx didn't appear to be changing anytime soon. She sighed. Manden was right, she should focus on this mission, and that's what she planned on doing. Everyone met in the center.

"Ready, Cousin?" asked Skylar, tying her black hair back, her blue eyes glowing against her porcelain skin. Rei would have found her cousin pretty if she wasn't such a bitch.

She turned to the Daer and gave her a sweet smile. "As ready as I'll ever be, Cousin." She gave that last word as much bite as she could muster.

She felt Bronx's eyes on her but refused to meet his gaze as she passed him, following the others out of the ship.

# CHAPTER 25

Two armored trucks waited for them at the port. An elderly man who appeared to be a butler or a high servant gestured for them to enter the vehicles. The six Volocio loaded into one truck, while the Daer piled into the second one.

The landscape in this part of Trappist V was quite similar to Gliese VI. There was green everywhere, but the hue seemed a little darker, perhaps because of the overcast clouds.

Upon further inspection, Rei noticed the trees were different. They didn't have the wide glossy leaves she had seen in her new home—here they looked more like needles. Even the air smelled different, crisper.

"I thought the forecast said it wasn't supposed to rain today," Crona said as rainwater streaked the sides of the windows, eventually obscuring Rei's view.

Canale's house was an older style made of stone with water staining the side walls. Iron in the shape of vines covered several windows; a high black wrought-iron fence around the perimeter made the building appear more imposing than necessary.

"Did you know that Canale was offered a position as a Daer Master before she went into politics?" Bronx asked as they piled out of the vehicles. "What do you think, Crona? Maybe you were right about me giving up the Daer life too soon. I could always go back, get a promotion, and buy a place like this."

Crona chuckled. "You've already lost a few years. What

if they make you start over? The Masters will think you're too old now." She leaned in closer. "I see those crow's feet becoming more prominent by the day."

"Ha. Ha. Everyone, my sister, the comedian," he said dryly.

"I can tell you from experience that Daer Masters don't normally live like this," Arram chimed in. "I don't think we ever had a house this nice before we had to go on the run."

The main entrance and staircase were made of a warm cherry wood with vases in reds and oranges. At the entrance was a small brass statue of the god queen with incense burning on either side. The scent of sandalwood hit Rei, flooding her mind with memories of her brother. He often lit sandalwood incense as an offering.

They entered a sitting room with various hues of deep blue curtains, cushions, and various adornments. There were several bookcases filled with books and a beautiful unlit fireplace. An imposing woman in a white pantsuit stood before the fireplace, her silver hair combed back into a severe bun.

"Hello. I'm Alma Canale," she said in a steady voice as her eyes took in the group in front of her. "This is my daughter, Camila." A younger woman with a plain face and watery green eyes sat next to her.

Canale appraised the Volocio as they filed into the room. Rei wondered what the woman thought. She assumed the group must have been an interesting sight, young and fresh-faced with hardly a scar among them.

"I wanted to be the first to welcome you to my home," said Canale calmly, her face showing no emotion. "I'm glad to have seen you in my lifetime. I wish to get to know each of you better, but we have much to plan and little time to do it. I would very much like a word with the god queen, the god king, and Kazimir. My daughter will show the rest of you to the kitchen. Please, help yourselves. I'm sure the cook can conjure something for you to eat."

Camila led the group out until only Manden, Rei, Kaz, and the politician were left.

Alma Canale indicated the sofa next to the stool where her daughter had sat earlier. "Please, sit."

The three took their seats while the representative remained standing. "It means a lot to have you here. I am glad to hear that Urius finally agreed that this election is too important to not announce your arrival to both the Federation and the Dominion. Tomorrow, our yearly fair will begin in the town square. It also marks harvest time for the nearby villages, and we normally pray to both the god queen and god king to give us another fruitful year of Connocillin. I think it would be the best time strategically to make your presence known and... well... bless the people."

Rei glanced at both Kaz and Manden, who simply nodded. Rei didn't have the slightest idea how she was supposed to bless people. She hoped it was figurative.

"So," Rei said, "we show up in costume and say a few words?"

"Basically," answered the woman, trying to give Rei a comforting smile, but by the look on her face, she was out of practice.

"And also show our powers," added Kaz. "How else will they believe who we are?"

Shit. He had a point.

She felt Manden's hand over her own. "We'll talk about what to do later," he muttered in Castelan.

She squeezed his hand and forced a smile. "Of course," she told Canale.

"Excellent," said the politician. "Tomorrow, my designers will come with the pieces they have already created for the three of you. I thought it wise that Kazimir also join you since he is already a recognized Volocio. We will get you fitted in time before you go on camera tomorrow."

Cameras. If Urius hadn't figured out that the Volocio had disappeared, he was going to find out soon enough. Both the Dominion and Federation would watch her destroy Infiernen. There was no doubt in her mind—he would be there. A twinge of guilt nagged Rei in the back of her mind, reminding her that she lied to everyone to get her to this point. But she was sure once Infiernen was no longer a problem, all would be forgiven.

"We have a procession every year, and the winners of the local dance competition usually get to dress as the god king and queen and ride in the parade. We thought about having you ride in the procession, but that would leave you too exposed. You will ride on ahead in one of our armored vehicles to the town hall. Filming will take place in the main hall with about a hundred locals, all winners of a recent lottery and a decent mix of classes. The camera will feed onto screens outside where the rest will be able to see. It's the best way to grant the most amount of exposure while still guaranteeing your safety.

"In the meantime, I ask you to join your comrades in getting something to eat. I hope you take advantage of my hospitality."

They stood together, and Manden reached out to shake hands with Canale, but the woman bowed to the three instead. Rei wasn't quite sure what to make of that, but she had a feeling that such gestures were only going to become more grandiose.

# CHAPTER 26

Rei tugged at the itchy costume as she gazed at herself in the mirror. The tunic cinched at the waist and flowed to her ankles, but the neck crept too high. Her hair was pulled back in a tight plait, already threatening to give her a headache.

The group was currently in Camila's room getting ready. On the far wall next to the door were three touch screens with downloaded paintings of the god queen, the god king, and the original Kazimir—all from the artist known as Benot.

Rei had seen a copy of the Mica's painting before through the Nexus. The billowing robe was breathtaking, hugging Mica's curves, yet giving her room to move. The dark green of the fabric brought out the color of her eyes, and the silver stitches around the wrists and the neck raced around like little bolts of lightning. It vaguely resembled the traditional Daer tunic, but somehow it appeared grander and more majestic—something a warrior goddess would wear. The costume allowed freedom of movement, perfect for taking down a Negander.

Unfortunately, the fabric necessary to create the look was also stiff and scratchy.

"You look uncomfortable." Crona helped Rei straighten the collar.

Rei only nodded. Dread filled her stomach at the thought of her powers not working when she needed it. She couldn't afford to fail.

"Well, my opinion was not asked for when they were

designed." Manden ran a hand over his own costume of copper fabric with gold leaves embroidered around the neck. "Or else I would have suggested that they use a more comfortable cloth." He chewed on his fingernails, worn well past the bed.

Kaz stood next to his painting, his deep blue and silver robe reaching onto the floor, covering his black boots. "It's uncanny, no? It's like they used my own photograph for the painting. It's hard to believe that it was painted almost two-hundred years before I was born."

Rei didn't dare draw closer to her painting. She saw her own likeness well enough in the artwork from where she stood, and it unsettled her.

Arram and Crona wore Daer uniforms, which consisted of a black wrap with white trim, gray trousers, and black boots. Apparently, Canale had decided that Kaz, Manden, and Rei announcing themselves was enough for now. The other three Volocio were expected to lie low in Daer uniforms and blend in.

Arram pulled her hand to him and inspected the embroidery.

"Is this real silver?" he asked.

"Yes," Manden said, coming in for a closer inspection.

"Well, no wonder she's uncomfortable. Silver doesn't make for forgiving thread."

"This was a recommendation I gave to Canale. It's not for show. The metal acts as a conduit. Silver helps the lightning Volocio increase the potency of their power."

"Really?" asked Rei. The tension in her shoulders loosened. She and Manden had spoken at lengths through the night about her powers and lack of control. She was grateful he thought ahead.

"Just like her staff?" Arram reached out next to the

mirror where her staff stood. "There's also metal infused into the wood, correct?" He held the staff in his hands, studying the intricate designs before handing it to Rei.

She took the staff. Manden had given it to her knowing it would increase her power. She remembered the immeasurable power that filled her before she killed the Negander. The doubt in her mind receded further. The tools she needed were there, but the last piece of the puzzle was Infiernen.

Manden's eyes wandered past Rei to someone behind her. "Where have you been?"

Rei turned to find Bronx leaning against the door frame, also in a Daer robes with the Daer sword at his back and a pistol at his hip. Her heart quickened—he resembled Atrius even more than before.

"Checking in with the others. Funny thing. I haven't even looked at this uniform in five years," he said, adjusting the strap holding his sword in place. "Never mind wearing it—and yet I'm torn. It feels so right to wear it again, but I'm still uneasy about the memories it represents."

"War has never been a pretty thing—despite what some may say," said Manden. "God knows you've seen your fair share of horrors. But Atrius was a Daer like you—you can't run away from your destiny."

"I don't know. I can run pretty fast." Bronx smirked.

His gaze fell on Rei, making her feel nervous. Goosebumps rose on her skin, causing the already itchy fabric to become even more unbearable. She wanted so much for him to talk to her again or at least to smile. She wanted to understand him. Yet all she heard in her head was his voice repeating the words *you terrify me.*

The Daer opened his mouth as if he wanted to say something to her, but his lips closed. The silence stretched on for what felt like eternity until he finally broke eye contact and walked out of the room.

Rei let go of the breath she held, then rolled her eyes. She didn't have time for his bullshit today. If only he didn't have this effect on her.

"Places, everyone!" Canale entered the room in a deep-blue pantsuit with gray panels and a pin of a twelve-pointed star over her heart—the colors of the Federation. She ushered them out of the room and into their positions downstairs. "Make sure you all have your headsets ready," she reminded everyone. Rei put a hand to her ear to make sure hers was still in place.

"Ready?" asked Manden, holding out a hand for her to take as they reached the bottom of the stairs.

Rei couldn't reply; her head felt weightless. She numbly took his hand and waited as the politician opened the door.

Her plan was set in motion, and she prayed it played out like she wanted. She squeezed her staff tighter.

They were fortunate. Only a few people, currently standing on the other side of the fence had figured out their escape plan. An audible gasp burst from the onlookers as both Manden and Rei became visible. A few of the onlookers whispered, "Goddess," "Mica," as well as a few saying, "Benot."

Through the crowd, a figure in a gray robe stood in the street, staring straight at Rei. He raised a gloved finger and pointed at her. She didn't see his face, but she knew. It was him, her brother's killer. If Infiernen was here, then so were his Infinity Dogs.

Her heart raced as her vision tunneled to the figure across the street. She clenched her teeth. Finally. She let the rush of anger flow through her until she felt lightning dance under her skin. Now she just needed that monster to sit still long enough for her to end him quickly.

"Infiernen is here," she said in a low voice into her headset, her heart pounding in her chest.

"Well, shit," came Crona's voice in her ear.

"We knew this was a possibility," Bronx said. "Just get them into the car."

Rei took Manden's hand and continued into the vehicle.

"Infiernen's tactic always required the element of surprise," Bronx continued. "Everyone be aware and focus."

Rei felt the tension in the air. Perhaps now was the time to tell them she planned for it, but she decided against it. Right now, they needed to focus on getting through this announcement, and Rei would take care of the rest.

THE TOWN HALL'S REDDISH-BROWN STONE STRUCTURE loomed ominously above them. Inside reminded Rei of Canale's house: warm polished wood and each room a vibrant color. The antechamber before the great hall was an orange so bright it hurt Rei's eyes. She silently cursed the color when she accidentally bumped into a large potted plant.

"You ready?" Crona said, coming to her side.

Rei looked at her shaking hands. "Honestly, I feel like I'm going to throw up. What do I even say?" She was so focused on destroying Infiernen, she didn't think about what she would say to the crowd.

"You have plenty to be angry about: What Infiernen has done to your family. What you saw when you were attacked in Ballarat. Use that anger and say what you feel. Chances are most, if not all, will have a similar story to tell."

The door to the hall was ajar, and Rei peeked through the opening. The room had the large orange columns just like in Crona's vision. Ahead of her stood a large wooden stage. On the platform, next to the microphone, stood Camila in a suit the same shade of blue as a Federation uniform. Just on either side of her stood life-size statues of the god king and god queen, complete with billowing clothes.

The Daer and guards lined the walls of the room while a hundred guests already hovered around the stage. The murmur buzzed all around Rei like a hive of bees. But she barely registered it. For now, her mind raced over the fact that she would have to speak, outweighing her nervousness concerning Infiernen's attack. There was no way he would enter into this room. He would probably wait for them to leave before making his move.

She took a deep breath. One thing at a time.

"Our long search is over!" began Camila, her voice carrying over the people. "Our god king and queen have returned together to help bring in a new age. The Age of the Federation!" An audible gasp met her cry, followed by the roar of applause. "Soon," she continued, "they will join the other Volocio and lead us to victory."

The crowd roared in response.

The door opened in front of Rei, leaving her exposed, and several voices in the crowd exclaimed once they saw her. Some surged forward, trying to get a closer look, but the guards kept the crowd back. Manden swooped in and took her hand to lead her to the stage with Kaz close behind. A large tree loomed above them as they approached.

Camila turned and bowed to Rei, Manden, and Kaz. Her cousin approached the microphone first. Rei hardly saw faces in the crowd as the lights from the cameras blinded her. The smell of perfume and sweat filled her nose; there were too many people in the room.

"My people," he began, "I am happy to show support to my god king and queen, as well as to the Federation. Together we will reunify the Tyre Star Cluster!" He raised his hands to the sky and used his power to create snow falling from the gold gilded ceilings.

Rei knew this was not normal snow—the snowflakes were so big she saw the actual crystal formation of each flake. The illusion only lasted for a moment until Kaz brought his hands down and the snow faded away to nothing. His actions were met with a round of applause.

Manden stepped forward. "It is good to come back from Tas'und'eash, and it pleases me greatly to see my god queen returned to us to finish what she started in ridding our world of evil." He, too, raised his hands to the tree behind them. It grew bigger and the leaves became a more vivid green. Rei wondered from where he retrieved the energy, but then remembered the large plant in the back. The crowd gasped, then gave him an ovation.

And now it was Rei's turn.

Manden took Rei's hand and led her to the microphone.

Rei stood before the crowd and drew a deep breath. Her mind froze. What could she say? Her gaze swept across the faces in front of her. People of all walks of life—some in their fancy garments, others in dust-covered clothes from the fields—all staring at her with wide eyes. She started breathing hard, as though the air had been somehow swept from the room. Cameras pointed at her from the back. Their lights were still too bright, blinding her—though it was better than trying to look the people in the eyes.

"Um. Hello," she breathed.

The rumble of thunder rolled above them. The hair on her arms rose as static built in the air. She continued to scan the crowd and found a familiar face. Her heart stuttered. She must've been seeing things. There was no way he was there. Yet seeing Niklaryn's smiling face as he beheld her made her eyes burn. He met her gaze with love and pride, and she knew she saw what her heart desired.

"I must apologize." She stumbled over her words with a smile. "I am not very good a public speaking, but—"

"No!" she heard Crona cry before the blonde knocked

her off her feet. The crack of a gunshot rang through the air, and Crona grunted as it tore through her. Rei's heart roared in her ears as she reached for her friend. The others surrounded them, weapons drawn. Screams tore through the crowd, followed by more gunshots. Rei clenched her jaw and looked up. It was Bronx who put his body between her and the crowd.

"You okay?" he asked his sister.

"My shoulder hurts like a bitch, but otherwise, yeah," she responded, hand over the wound.

The large back doors opened, and figures dressed in all red poured in, slashing at any who drew near. Screams echoed in the hall. The Negander were here, but Rei didn't see Infiernen. Rei's panic rose, along with the pandemonium. The crowd ran frantically and at random, as there was nowhere to go. It was a stampede.

Two more shots cracked, but Bronx blocked them with the flick of his wrist, his sword spinning in the air like magic. Rei flinched at the sound of the bullets hitting metal.

Rei helped Crona stand and scanned the crowd. Infiernen was close, she felt it. Anger rose inside her, and she thought about how she wanted to finish him.

She pulled the seer back to the tree just as a Negander woman climbed onstage. Rei shook as the memory came to the forefront of her mind. The Negander marched toward them, sword raised high. Rei moved to put herself between the fighter and Crona. Where were the others? They were busy with the figures in red. The Negander came faster now and brought down the weapon with a heavy swing. Rei raised her staff to block it, but Bronx was there first.

Bronx and Rei together attacked the Negander. The medic and the Negander were locked close in a heated battle while Rei's staff kept her at a safer distance. She circled and knifed at the Negander, but she easily swatted away her attacks. Rei gritted her teeth and tried to be faster. Bronx countered with his own attacks.

Another Negander tried to surprise Bronx from behind, but he blocked it. He continued battling the other Negander, leaving Rei alone with the woman. The Negander brought her sword down on Rei with alarming speed. She caught the sword on the broad side of her staff, avoiding the blade. Her heart pounded, and she wanted as much space between her the Negander as possible. The trunk of the tree stood steadfast as her back touched it. Nowhere to go now.

Rei roared as she continued to block, still not enough space to use her blade. Her arms grew tired. Each time the blade met her staff with jarring precision.

Crona came to her side, scimitar slicing at the Negander's leg. The woman screamed, but the sound stopped as Crona's blade plunged deep in the Negander's side. Bronx was back just as quickly, his hand around the woman's neck.

Rei gasped when she noticed that he wore no gloves. A plume of black smoke appeared, and the woman collapsed in a heap. Rei backed further into the tree, hoping the branches would envelop her.

"What the fuck was that?" she barked.

The Daer watched her, breathing hard, his dark eyes wide.

Laughter interrupted her thoughts. Rei turned to see a tall man with dark hair and light eyes standing at the edge of the stage. His gray cloak moved, making him appear like a specter.

"Rei Ettowa. This was far too easy." Her heart jumped against her chest. What Bronx had done was brushed aside. She recognized that face, that nose, the scar on his left brow, those eyes. Then she blinked and realized she didn't recognize him at all. But she knew who he was. She clutched at her staff and held it before her.

"Infiernen," Bronx growled.

"Hello, Bronx," he purred. "It's been a long time."

# CHAPTER 28

Rei stared at Niklaryn's killer. Finally. Her anger built, and the air crackled around her. She pointed her staff at Infiernen as a bolt of lightning flew toward him, but the Negander dodged it easily. She tried again, and a bolt grazed Infiernen's cloak, causing it to sizzle. He growled.

She swung her staff at his head, stepping too close to him. He immediately caught it, pulled Rei close, and head butted her. She fell to the ground, stunned. Her weapon skidded out of reach.

As Rei rose to her feet, Bronx barreled into Infiernen, both of them tumbling from the stage. Rei grabbed her staff and followed. She was ready to use more lightning, but Bronx stood in the way as he wrestled the Negander. Panic rose in her throat; this was her kill. Then she saw her opening. Infiernen kicked Bronx away from him as more Negander poured in and surrounded the medic.

Blood rushed from Rei's arm. She glanced at her crimson-soaked sleeve—she'd been cut, but it didn't matter. Lightning crackled in her veins, and she intended on using it.

She jumped from the stage and landed between Bronx and Infiernen. As Bronx took care of the other Negander, Rei whipped the staff through the air, hoping to catch Infiernen with the blade at the tip, but he parried her attack with a brush of his own. This only enraged her more.

"Get out of the way, Rei." Infiernen's attacks pushed her to the side, leaving Bronx open.

Rei surged forward, but he stepped aside with maddening ease. He retreated and removed his pistol, pointing it at Bronx's back. Her insides turned to ice.

Rei roared as she threw more lightning at Infiernen, and the force slammed him against the edge of the stage.

She took her stance between the Negander and Bronx. Infiernen should attack her, not Bronx. Blood pounded in her ears.

"I said get out of the way," Infiernen yelled.

"No." She swung at him, but the Negander blocked it and grabbed her staff, jerking it from her. She threw herself at him, but her small frame was no match for his larger size. She grabbed his hand holding his pistol and pointed away from Bronx.

"You killed my brother, you will not take him from me as well."

Infiernen stared as though his own heart stopped, but the moment was fleeting. He scowled as he used his weight to throw Rei off of him. A discarded knife lay near her line of sight on the stage, conveniently left where she needed it. She grabbed it and lunged at him, stabbing him in the leg. He roared and backhanded her across the face, knocking her to the ground.

Infiernen pulled the knife out of his leg and threw it aside. Rei screamed, reached over, and grabbed his other leg, lightning flew from her fingertips and shocked him, but it wasn't enough. He yanked her by her hair and kicked her in the stomach, knocking the wind out of her. Tears streamed down her face as the weight of the truth wrapped around her. She failed.

"Niklaryn is not dead. I am not your enemy, Rei!" he roared. "Back. Off."

Her mind raced trying to grasp what Infiernen said, but

Rei's lungs gasped for breath. She wanted it to be true, but there was no proof. It had to be a trick, yet she saw Niklaryn before. She expected another blow from Infiernen, but none came. Instead, he merely observed her until a bolt of lightning blew the Negander away.

"Don't you ever touch my sister again!" bellowed Arram.

*Wait. Arram?* she thought as her vision grew dark. She shook her head and breathed. A few moments passed before she tried to call her brother's name.

"Brother?" she croaked.

"I'm here," Arram said, wrapping an arm around her and helping her stand. She didn't mean Arram, but her mind was too fuzzy to think through everything she saw.

"Where's Infiernen?" she asked.

"He fled. They took Camila." Her head swam. She couldn't fully comprehend what he said. "We should go."

Rei looked to the crowd in front of her. The Negander were gone, which meant the chaos had quieted down, and the survivors were left having seen of the full extent of Rei's powers. She had done it. She had managed to show them her lightning, but the entire situation was a mess.

She had to salvage this. Infiernen yet again struck fear into their hearts, but she didn't want the Dominion to think they'd won.

She turned to find Bronx behind her, surrounded by the bodies of several Negander. He panted as he beheld them. Her eyes went to his ungloved hands, and the memory of the black smoke rose unbidden in her mind's eye. She finally realized why they wanted to keep a lid on what Bronx was capable of.

Yet she terrified him?

"Help me up on stage," she said to Arram.

"You're sure?"

"Yes. I have to address the crowd."

Her brother did so. Rei continued to take deep breaths until the dizziness finally abated. Once she reached the microphone, she pulled away from him, determined to address the people on her own two feet. Her legs shook but she willed them to keep her standing. She stared at the faces. Blood spattered the rugs, and a few people cried over fallen victims of the Negander. One of the cameras had been knocked off the stand, but the other pointed directly at her. The rest watched. She had their full attention.

She took a final deep breath before she began. "This war needs to end." She focused on the people, on their tired and worn faces. A few of them nodded in agreement. "The Sovereign, Anekris Praymer, has overreached his power and is trying to rule by fear. He let his Dogs loose to attack us because he thinks we are so easily controlled. But we are not. This must stop. He must be stopped. The Infinity Dogs must be stopped. Infiernen. Must. Be. Stopped."

Yet the Negander's words echoed in her mind. *I'm not your enemy, Rei.* He claimed he didn't kill Niklaryn. She shook the thoughts free.

A soft murmur of agreement rumbled from the crowd. "Even after today, we can't let the Dominion think they won. We cannot let their attempts for control be what defines us. We want unity, where the Dominion wants us divided. We just want to exist in peace, and yet the Dominion feels the need to slaughter us. They try to control us through fear because they know they are nothing without us." The murmuring grew louder. "I, too, am nothing without you. I may be the god queen, but I can't heal the rift between these factions alone. I need you. Alma Canale needs you. The Federation needs you. Tyre needs you." She reached her left hand out to the people. Blood flowed freely from her wound and covered her hand. "Will you help me?"

At first, there was nothing. Then a hand reached out her, then another and another until everyone in the room reached for her. She walked to the end of the stage and jumped off. As she landed, she felt the adrenaline flee from her body, and her legs turn to jelly, but she remained standing. She didn't care—her people needed her. She walked through the crowd, taking a hand, touching a shoulder, just as they reached back to her. As she did, she heard them murmur, "God Queen" or "Micaela" or "Long live the Federation."

Rei finally understood what Urius wanted, her role in this war. They needed her to be a symbol of hope, a conduit for their frustration. She managed to take down Infiernen, and she would do it again and win. Even if he hadn't killed her brother, he kept Niko from her and made her believe he was dead. She would make him pay for the pain he caused her, but she couldn't do it alone. She would need help, help from the Federation, as well as the Volocio.

After Infiernen, she would go after Praymer himself, and she would need an army. Suddenly her path was clear as day, and a weight lifted off her shoulders. She would put herself into a position where she could govern the change she wanted to see, and she had that position now.

"Oh, Rei," said a voice that chilled her to her core. Infiernen stood behind her with a knowing smile. He pulled out his pistol and pointed it above her head. She whirled around and saw Bronx onstage. Her heart leaped to her throat. Crona's vision had come true.

"Bronx, watch out!" she cried, diving back into the crowd toward Infiernen. Rei reached for her lightning again, but she was trapped. She couldn't use her powers without hurting everyone between her and the Negander. Infiernen winked, then shifted where he aimed his pistol. He pulled the trigger, and the gun cracked like one of her lightning bolts. Rei spun around and watched as Arram fell to the ground, hands clutching his stomach.

PART TWO
THE GODDESS

# CHAPTER 29

Bronx watched in horror as Arram fell. He didn't think about the fact that he didn't have any gloves on as he caught the young man. The thought only occurred to him long afterward. Kaz came to his side to take Arram's legs, followed by Manden, who took the young Ettowa's shoulders. Bronx was now free to use his sword to guard the Volocio as they made their way backstage.

But Rei was still in the crowd.

He scanned the faces for hers. His heart rate rose the longer he searched, but he breathed a sigh of relief when he saw Sariah with one arm around Rei as she led the god queen to meet the others. Infiernen had already made his escape.

Bronx was the last one in the backroom. They had already loaded Arram in one of the vehicles. They all climbed in and made their way to the *Luciernaga*. Luckily for them, the ship was only a few minutes away. Bronx helped Kaz and Manden load Arram into the infirmary and together they laid Arram carefully on one of the beds. Rei clutched her brother's hand as Manden put an arm around her, trying to hold her together.

"Arram, stay with us, okay?" she said with a ragged breath.

"Why is everyone upset?" Arram's eyes rolled into the back of his head. "Did the raiders come back?"

"Manden, can you assist?" Bronx asked, grabbing the tools he needed and laying them on the tray near Arram's bed.

"I can't, I have to fly us out of here. Infiernen can easily keep us grounded." Manden's voice echoed from the cargo hold as he headed to the cockpit.

"Of course. Kaz?" Blood leaked from the illusion Volocio's nose. Something else for Bronx to fix. But first Arram.

"Here, friend." Kazimir sniffed.

"What can I do?" Rei asked, her eyes red.

Bronx pointed behind her. "Breathing mask. We have to put him under."

She left to find it.

"Arram, you still with us, buddy?" Bronx opened Arram's eyelids and shined a light. Pupils constricted, normal.

"Just five more minutes, Grandma," he murmured as Rei put the mask over his face.

Bronx punched the gas setting at low. He only needed Arram slightly under. Kaz cut away the fabric from Arram's torso, and Bronx grabbed the extractor. He inserted the tool carefully into the wound, not wanting to cause more damage. His heart raced. If he nicked a major vessel, Arram was a goner. He found the bullet and carefully removed it, then watched the wound, hoping no more blood would seep out. It didn't. He breathed a sigh of relief. Nothing major was damaged.

"Heart rate?" he asked, looking at Rei.

"Uh—80 over 60?"

"Crap. That's low."

"It is?" Rei's voice was high.

"Kaz?" Bronx pointed to the cauterizer.

Kaz handed it to the medic, and Bronx inserted the tool back into the wound. There may be internal bleeding, but he had no way of knowing; he didn't have the equipment on the ship. He cauterized what he could. The rest was up to Arram. When he finished, he stapled the wound shut and covered it with gauze.

"It's up to him now," he said to Rei as he took off his gloves.

"Is there anything I can do?" she whispered. She appeared so small and frail. He hated seeing her like this.

"Pray."

Her gaze turned to her brother, and a tear rolled down her cheek. She quickly wiped it away. "Okay." She passed Bronx to leave and he touched her arm.

"Can you pray here? I still need to look at your wound."

They both glanced at his hand on her arm, and the memory of seeing her face when he used his gifts in front of her came crashing back. He pulled away quickly, yet her eyes remained where he had touched her. He wanted so desperately to know what she thought. But she only nodded and sat on the cushioned seat that ran against the wall. Crona also entered the room, hand covering her bloodied arm, and settled down next to Rei.

Bronx inspected Kaz's nose. "Nothing's broken." He placed a finger on either side and quickly snapped it back into place.

"Gods bless!" Kazimir gasped.

"Just kidding. It's really not broken now."

"You are so lucky we're friends," Kaz groaned as he stood and left the infirmary. "Fuck!" The illusion god's voice echoed in the cargo hold.

Bronx turned to his sister, who had already managed to pull the bullet out of her shoulder, her black uniform shone with blood. He cleaned the wound and stitched it closed.

"You alright?" she whispered.

He nodded.

"You did well, Brother. If he lives, it'll be because of you."

And if Arram died—he would still be at fault.

Bronx finally tended to Rei. He waited for her to pull away from him, but she didn't. Instead she offered her arm. He cut her bloodied sleeve and carefully removed it. He cleaned the wound and pulled her arm closer for inspection, all the while feeling those green eyes watching him and causing his pulse to quicken.

*Good, only three stitches needed.*

He finally dared to look at her to tell her, but those eyes of hers caused all the words to fly from his mind.

"It was very dangerous for you to go into the crowd like that after your speech," Crona said from where she sat, leaning against the wall.

Rei closed her eyes and breathed. "The stage wasn't safer."

"I know."

Bronx cleared his throat. "You'll need three stitches, okay?"

She nodded.

Bronx felt Rei's eyes watching him work when she spoke again. "It felt right to go out there. I finally get what Urius wants from us. I hope the elections swing our way. What happened today was surely broadcasted all over the Nexus."

"It was very inspiring."

"But we do need to work on our teamwork skills and definitely learn better combat, despite what Urius thinks," Rei muttered. "We could have better protected... Camila." Her eyes turned to her unconscious brother. "I could have done better."

Bronx felt bad for Canale's daughter. He knew why she

was taken. There were rumors the Sovereign collected women for his games. Although Bronx never knew to what end.

Crona sighed. "You're telling me. But Urius agreed that we should take this mission, and we all knew the risks."

Rei closed her eyes as more tears fell. He knew she lied about Urius. The Leader of the Federation would never have given Rei permission to avenge her brother's murder, especially when there was no murder to avenge. He was just as much to blame. He could have told Rei the truth and it may have been enough to prevent her from pushing this mission. But it was too late now. He wished he knew what to say to make her feel better; he wanted to see her smile.

Bronx dressed Rei's wound. "You should get something to eat," he said quietly.

Rei stared at him, and her lips parted.

"He's right. Let's go upstairs." Crona gently pulled Rei's arm.

"I can't leave Arram," she said, refusing to tear her gaze away from Bronx.

"I'll stay here with him," he offered. "I think you should rest and get food. Then you can come back and sit with him. Doctor's orders." He tried to smile, but she didn't return it. She followed his sister out.

The pain in his chest grew with every step she took away from him. He pulled his stool over to Arram's bed and sat down. He took off his gloves and threw them into the bin, already full from the several pairs he had already used for each patient. He rubbed his eyes, wishing the action rubbed away everything that happened over the last few days. He stared at the younger Ettowa.

"Come on, Arram. We need you to pull through." He took Arram's hand and squeezed it. He closed his eyes, imagining the thread he felt from his other victims. He imagined if given the choice, he wouldn't tug. He prayed and imagined tucking it back into place, weaving it several times before tying it off tightly in a knot.

He felt his legs go weak as adrenaline rushed from his body. It had been a long day. Maybe he should also get something to eat. He stood, but a wave of dizziness caused him to stumble. The day must've taken more out of him than he thought. He tried to reach the door, but his legs gave out from under him, and he suddenly got the notion that the floor would be much more comfortable.

# CHAPTER 30

Rei struggled to chew on the protein bar Crona handed to her. Every mouthful stuck to the roof of her mouth. She knew she had to eat, but her stomach turned in knots. Arram could die at any moment and she was not at his side.

"How is Arram?" Skylar asked as she passed their table in the kitchen. The Daer's eyebrows were drawn together and her lips pressed into a thin line.

"We don't know," Kaz replied. "We can only pray."

Skylar leaned against the sink, arms crossed. "Then I will pray for him."

"Why do you care, Sky?" Crona growled.

"I've always cared."

The scratch on Rei's arm from First Blood suggested otherwise.

Skylar stared at Rei's arm as though she knew what the other was thinking. "I'm sorry about our duel earlier, Cousin. Truly. When Nik and I used to train as kids, we were just as aggressive. We knew that our enemies wouldn't make a fight easy so why should we in practice? I was worried you couldn't take care of yourself against Infiernen, but you were ready."

"That wasn't your decision to make," Rei snapped. "I always knew I was ready."

Skylar held up her hands in defeat. "You're right. I just want to start over with you."

Rei didn't care what Skylar wanted. Her thoughts remained on Arram dying in a bed downstairs. It was all her fault. Her determination to avenge one brother almost cost her the other. She threw the rest of the protein bar on the table and wiped her mouth.

"I've lost my appetite. I'm going to sit with Arram."

Silence followed her as she walked down the stairs. She didn't want to admit it earlier, but a small part of her was grateful for Skylar's attempt. With Niklaryn still missing and Arram at death's door, she couldn't afford to lose more family.

"Bronx?" she called as she drew closer to the infirmary. It was too quiet. That was when she saw a figure crumpled on the floor.

She rushed through the door to find Bronx unconscious. Her heart leaped to her throat. She didn't want to lose him, too.

"Crona!" she yelled as she knelt at the medic's side. "Help!"

The sound of footsteps echoed through the cargo hold as Rei drew close to Bronx to hear his breathing. "Bronx?" His face remained relaxed, his eyes closed.

She knew she shouldn't touch him and that it likely had to do with that mysterious black smoke, but she didn't care. She grabbed his shoulders and pulled him to his side. "Bronx. Come on, wake up!"

"What happened?" Crona asked with a gasp. Kaz followed close behind, his mouth hanging open.

"I found him like this," Rei cried, her eyes burning. "Help me get him on the bed."

It took all three to lift him onto the bed. A lock of hair fell over Bronx's face and she tucked it away. She didn't care if his powers worked on her at that moment. The universe was already punishing her. She would have welcomed more. She had brought this upon herself.

Crona shuffled through a few drawers until she found a scanner. "Bronx showed me how to use this once," she muttered as she scanned her brother, lightly feeling around the man's head. "No blood and brain activity seems normal, but I don't know what else to look for."

Rei paced the tiny room. "Maybe one of us should let Manden know," she said. "What if he needs special medical attention?"

"Rei, calm down," Kaz said, leaning against a wall.

She felt anything but calm. Her hands shook and her heart thrashed in her ears. She was moments away from breaking and didn't know how to stop it.

"Where am I?" Arram murmured.

Relief washed over her and turned her legs to jelly. Tears welled up in Rei's eyes and fell freely as she stumbled over to him, threw her arms around him, and held him tight. "I thought I'd lost you."

"I'm all right," he whispered, hugging her back. "I have to stay alive if I'm to remain a pain in your ass." They both chuckled until he groaned, and his hand flew to his stomach.

"Take it easy," she said, cupping his cheek.

"We were worried for you, Arram," Kaz said, his eyes also shining.

Crona smirked. "If you had woken a minute later, you sister probably would have worn a hole in the floor with her pacing."

Rei flushed but her eyes never left Arram's face. He took her hand from his cheek and held it to his chest, giving it a gentle squeeze.

"Everything's all right now," he said. "No need to be upset."

Rei wiped her eyes as more tears fell. "I know. But it's my fault you're here, and I couldn't bear it if I lost you."

"But you didn't." He gave her a weak smile. "By the way, I had the strangest dream. Max came to me."

"Max?" Rei asked, pulling up a stool and sitting down. "As in previous life, Max? Micaela's brother, Max?"

He nodded. "It was a memory of Micaela explaining our gifts to him when they were children. It all makes sense now. I don't know how I didn't figure it out before."

"So you can help me with my powers?"

"We can help each other. Something clicked when I watched Infiernen hurt you. I had to act, and the lightning worked. I realized I didn't want to lose you. Being your brother turned out not to be so bad." He gave her a toothy grin and she laughed.

"I love you, too," she whispered and his violet eyes shined. Rei meant it, but she couldn't ignore the voice in her head, reminding her she still lied to her brother. She lied to them all. She would have to come clean soon. She just hoped they would forgive her.

# CHAPTER 31

Bronx jerked awake to find himself in one of the infirmary beds. Crona hovered over him, sighing with relief.

"What happened?" came Arram's voice, dry as sandpaper.

"He's fine," Crona said. "Not dead yet." She gave her brother a wink.

Arram still lay in the bed next to him, Kaz stood near the door, and Rei sat on a stool next to her brother. She sat up straight when their eyes met. His heart skipped a beat when he saw that her light was still there.

"You're alive," he whispered. He had dreamed. It was the same nightmare that had played over and over since the day he first laid eyes on Rei.

Her eyebrows furrowed as she glanced at Crona and back to him. "Are you sure the fall didn't damage his brain?"

Crona narrowed her eyes at her brother. "I don't think so."

Bronx couldn't stop staring at Rei. His heart hammered so hard that he feared it would burst. His hands trembled violently, and he rubbed his face, thinking how this last dream seemed more real than the others. Bronx wasn't sure what scared him more: Rei dying in his arms or the fact that when her lips touched his, he no longer cared that her life was in danger. He just wanted her.

He felt the eyes of everyone in the room watching him. He couldn't afford to let them see through his mask. He cleared his throat. "How are you feeling, Arram?"

The young man nodded. "Better, thanks to you."

"Thank you," Rei said, her voice drawing him to her.

Bronx muttered a "you're welcome" and stood. "Where did you find me?" He felt his head to see if there was blood. There wasn't.

"On the floor near the door," Crona said.

"Rei, Crona, and I had to lift you onto the bed," Kaz added.

"Eh?" He shot a warning look at his sister. After that dream, he needed more than ever to keep a distance. She waved her hand dismissively in his direction.

"You're heavier than you look," Rei said with a smirk. "You might want to lay off the sweets."

Bronx stifled a laugh. She still had some bit of humor after everything. He missed their banter. He missed their late-night talks.

But he had to stay away, even if she made it so easy to fall in love.

"I think I had low blood sugar." He moved to the door. "I'm sure I'll find something for my sugar fix upstairs." He glanced in Rei's direction. "Unless you need me for anything?"

"We're fine," she replied, her back to him. He watched her, hoping she would meet his eyes, but she didn't. "Wait."

He waited at the door, hoping she truly had more to say to him.

She rose from her stool and faced everyone. "I have to tell you all something." Her eyes remained on her hands as she wrung them. He had a feeling he knew she was about to say.

"I lied when I said Urius approved of the plan. He didn't. In fact, he made it very clear that I was supposed to remain hiding." Her eyes flicked to Arram. "I am so sorry. I was so determined to take on Infiernen, I didn't think about if anyone got hurt." She reached out and took his hand. "Or if I lost you."

Arram yanked his hand away from her. His mouth turned down in a sneer. "I can't believe you lied to me."

"Or to me," Kaz muttered. "I thought you had more integrity than this, Rei." He stormed out of the room and disappeared up the steps.

"I think we should leave these two alone." Crona stepped through the door and gestured for Bronx to follow. "Besides, I think I know where Manden hides his sugary drinks."

"Oh, goodie." Then he paused to give Rei one last glance. She met his gaze with desperation. She needed an ally.

"I don't blame you, Rei," he told her. "If I were in your position, I would have done the same thing." He gave her a small smile, which she returned. He followed his sister into the cargo hold.

She waited for him at the stairs and watched as Arram yelled at Rei. Neither heard what was being said, but they understood the voice of the betrayed.

"They certainly have a lot of baggage to work through," she muttered before she continued her ascent. "But I agree with you. Technically, I was in her position. While we waited for her to return with Urius's approval, I thought about what we would do if he said no. I can't let that vision come to fruition. I am not afraid to lie to keep you safe."

He smiled. "And I would do the same for you, Crona."

She gave him a toothy grin and didn't wait long before changing the subject. She whirled around and stopped him for proceeding further. "By the way, 'you're alive'? What did that mean?"

He sighed and met her gaze. "I thought I killed Rei."

"Ah. A dream. What were you doing?" She turned back and continued upwards.

He followed. "Well, er—we were..."

"You were?"

"Gods," he whispered. "Intimate."

Crona made a face. "Gotcha, say no more." She went into the kitchen and rummaged through the cool box. With an "ah ha" she found a couple of bottles of a brown fizzy drink hidden behind a few bottles of beer. She opened them and handed one to Bronx.

"I wish there was some way to help you with your power." She took a large gulp of her drink. "Arram seems to have an idea of how to help Rei. Did you see him throw Infiernen across the room?" She giggled. "Anyway, that's what they were talking about when you woke up."

He sighed, biting back the jealousy that budded underneath the surface. "There is no one who can help me. I'm the only Volocio with this type of power."

"What about Cesar?"

Bronx froze. Years ago, Bronx had asked Manden if there were other Volocio like him. "Reapers have kept their identity a secret for generations," was the redhead's reply. "There's only one I know. His name was Cesar, but I wouldn't know where to begin to find him." Cesar. The god of death.

"Well, unless I can get a hold of him, I have to stumble my way through this on my own. So until I know what I am doing, I need to keep my distance from Rei. It's for her protection."

"I don't keep my distance from you. You're obviously not doing that for *my* protection."

"You know the risks."

Crona let out an exasperated sigh. "Think about that for a moment. Because you told me what could happen."

Bronx rolled his eyes. "Lot of good that did me. You still keep trying to hug me."

"One day I will succeed." She wiggled her eyebrows.

He let out a soft chuckle and sipped his drink.

"You should tell her the truth," Crona said. "She needs to know."

He placed the bottle on the table with a satisfying thunk and turned it in circles with his index finger and thumb. The condensation dripped on and cooled his skin. "But what if she…"

Crona dug through one of the cabinets. She pulled out a can and started eating what appeared to be smoked jerky. "If she what?"

"Tries to… kiss… me?"

Crona chuckled. "Well, someone's thinking highly of himself."

He rolled his eyes. "What if she's like you? You know the risks but still treat me like some pet project, like I'm someone to be fixed. If you try hard enough, I'll finally let my guard down." He thought back to the dream. He told Rei the truth and she accepted it freely. Yet she was still willing to risk her life for a kiss. He knew he would never be able to deny her.

"I don't think you need to be fixed, Bronx." She tossed the can in his direction. He caught it with ease and dug in.

"You are smart to be wary of your powers, Brother. Of course they're dangerous. But we figured out that you're only dangerous with skin contact. You wear gloves, you wear layers—you're doing enough. You can still be normal… in a way. I just think you're taking this too far."

He avoided her gaze. He knew he was being extreme,

but all it would take was one moment of carelessness. It was exhausting to be aware of his body at all times. It was one thing to be a medic where death was just as much the job as saving lives. But he couldn't afford that luxury with his family, with those he cared about, with Rei.

He watched Crona down the rest of her drink and grab his. It was one of the few times she was faster than him.

She took another sip. "Let's just look at this practically," she began. "The five of us—well, six with Manden—have to do our thing as 'gods' for the Federation, right?"

"Right."

"That means we have to work together. We have to trust each other."

"Of course."

She shrugged. "Kaz, Manden, and I know the truth. Rei and Arram both deserve to know as well. We have to be a team."

He rubbed his face. He hadn't thought about that. He was so focused on avoiding Rei that he missed the most obvious. "Ugh. You're right."

"I'm always right," she muttered with a toothy grin.

"Fine. I'll talk to her. But after today, I'm not sure she'll want to talk to me." He gestured for his drink and Crona handed it to him. He stared at the bottle before he spoke again. "You should have seen the look on her face when I used my powers."

"I was right next to her. I saw it."

Bronx closed his eyes and remembered the fear he saw. *What the fuck was that?* she yelled. He hated himself, but if her fearing him kept her away, it would be worth it. Even after she would learn the truth.

"Hey," said Crona, "don't get lost in that head of yours."

Skylar walked into the kitchen and dug through the cool

box, pulling out a beer. She opened it and was about to take a sip when she noticed that she wasn't alone.

"No wounds for me to look at, Sky?" he asked.

She took a big gulp of her beer before walking away. "Fuck off, Manca."

Bronx watched the Daer leave. "Love you, too."

"That's one weird woman," Crona muttered with a snort.

The odd thing was that Bronx didn't remember seeing Skylar after they entered the town hall. He didn't remember seeing the woman at all during the presentation. Everyone else walked away with some kind of injury, yet she didn't. Bronx wanted to know why.

# CHAPTER 32



"Why did you lie to me?" Arram demanded. "Why?" He gritted his teeth as his hands clutched his stomach.

Rei took his hands. "Please. Don't hurt yourself, we can't let you open up that bullet hole." She wasn't sure if he was out of danger yet, and she would never forgive herself if he hurt himself further because of her. She had done enough damage.

Arram breathed hard and clenched his jaw. "Well?"

"I didn't think you guys would've followed me otherwise," she responded, her voice barely above a whisper. She felt ridiculous saying it out loud. She knew they all had the same goal; she should have told them the truth and let them decide for themselves if they wanted to take the risk.

Arram gave her hand a squeeze. "I get it. With our upbringing, it's hard to trust other people. But we have to trust each other. You and I need to be a team. One thing I cannot stand is being lied to by family—our grandparents did that enough. I also want revenge, not just for Nik, but for our parents and grandparents. You could have told me the truth, and I still would have gone with you."

Rei's cheeks burned as she cringed. "I'm sorry. Hotara always said I lose my head where Niko's concerned. Once I heard he might be alive, I lost sight of what I was even fighting for. I just jumped without thinking how my actions could have hurt someone else. If I had lost you—"

Arram leaned forward, still clutching Rei's hands. "Wait. Wait. Nik's alive?"

"I don't know. Infiernen told me. He says he's not my enemy," she said with a grimace.

"But he shot me."

"I know." Rei took one of the bloodied tools Bronx used to save Arram's life, then put it back. It clunked as it touched the metal tray.

"What the fuck?" Arram gasped, leaning back into his pillows.

"My thoughts, exactly."

"Do you think Bronx knows?"

Rei stared out the doorway where he'd left earlier with Crona. "If he ever talks to me again, I'll ask him." She hadn't thought of it, but he did say he couldn't talk about the day Infiernen "took" Niklaryn. He never said killed, but he never expanded on the topic further.

"Why do people who claim to care also lie to us?" Arram's voice brought her out of her thoughts.

That was the question. It wasn't just Bronx or their grandparents. Hotara had raised Rei knowing she was the god queen and seemed perfectly happy to let someone else reveal the truth to her.

"Hotara told me once she wanted me to have a normal childhood," she said. "I think she meant for me to be a kid, unburdened by what the universe had planned for me, for as long as possible. Maybe our grandparents wanted the same for you. Perhaps that was why they were hesitant to tell you your identity. It was their way of showing their love."

"Maybe," he said. "But it still doesn't explain why I didn't know about you or Niklaryn. We lived in Ballarat for two months and not once did they mention that the woman they wanted me to be friends with was my own sister. They could have led with that, you know."

"I know."

Arram scrubbed a hand over his face, his shoulders hunched. "It would have been nice to know when they were alive. The four of us could have enjoyed being a family before shit hit the fan."

Rei would have loved nothing more than to reminisce how life would have played out if she had known, but it was now an unreachable fantasy. "There's no point questioning it anymore, Arram. They're dead. Niko's not. We can have that with him maybe. If we find him."

"As long as we find out that truth."

Rei nodded, her jaw set.

"And we don't keep the truth from each other." Arram gave her a knowing smile.

"No more lies," she confirmed. A great weight lifted from her chest knowing she didn't lose Arram. Perhaps there was hope that Kaz wouldn't stay angry forever either. Not everything seemed bleak, at least not for now. All that was left was to survive Urius's reaction when she returned to the Underground.

# CHAPTER 33

When they returned to Gliese VI, Rei followed Bronx and another Daer as they carried Arram off the *Luciernaga*. Urius was already there, his face red with anger.

"What part of 'no' did you not understand, Rei?" he bellowed as he approached. "You were told to stay here where it's safe."

"We were going to lose the planet!" she snapped back.

"Trappist V may still be lost, the elections haven't taken place yet." Urius's nostrils flared.

"And when they do and we win, you'll realize I was right all along."

"Both of you should calm down." Manden stepped between the two, hands held up as though to stop either from coming to blows. "We can discuss this situation like adults."

"This is none of your fucking business, Walt," snarled Urius.

Manden neared Urius and spoke in a voice so low, only Rei heard. "You would be wise to remember that I am your ally, Urius, not one of your grunts. You are still addressing a king. Show some fucking respect."

Urius blinked. "An ally who has yet to deliver his army to us."

"An army that is waiting for her"—Manden pointed at Rei—"to be ready. She can't grow into her role if you keep her locked up here."

"Nor can she grow if she's captured and used by the other side." Urius's voice grew louder again.

"I'm still here!" Rei called, waving her hand at both of them. "Stop talking about my future as though I don't get a choice. Neither of you control me so you might as well accept that fact now. So shut up."

Everyone in the hangar stared, her words echoing in the silent building.

Rei breathed hard. "I am the god queen. I'm not the god pawn. I understand what you want from me Urius, and I agree that I can use my influence to help the Federation. But there was a choice that needed to be made and I did it. I almost paid the price with the life of my own brother, but I believe it was the right direction for us. We can't wait for all six Volocio to unite with the god king before we act, the war has gone on long enough."

Manden smiled proudly and slapped Urius hard on the shoulder. "You heard the little lady. Don't forget that when we win Trappist V."

"If we win," muttered Urius.

"We will," Kaz said, coming to Rei's side.

"Excuse me?"

Kaz put an arm around Rei. "She came up with the plan, but we all agreed to it. It's time to come back into the spotlight." He gave Urius a big toothy grin. "You know you can't keep us hidden forever."

Rei held her breath, watching the leader for his reaction.

Urius gave her a smile that didn't reach his eyes. "You're right, Kazimir. In the end, it worked out in our favor. I will make sure to consult the Volocio on such plans in the future." Urius pivoted on his heel and marched away.

Rei knew Urius didn't plan on working with the Volocio.

She let out a long breath. "Thanks, Kaz," she said.

He gave her a squeeze before letting go. "We're on the same team, Rei. I hope you realize that now. I want revenge for my cousin's death as well."

Rei's heart sank. How could she tell him that there was perhaps nothing to avenge? She needed to figure out if Infiernen lied or not.

Kaz's gaze turned to Arram, who waited in a nearby truck. "That was a close call with your brother." His voice was low.

"Too close," said Rei.

"It's a good thing Bronx is as skilled as he is." Kaz gestured to Bronx, who looked up at the mention of his last name.

The medic locked eyes with Rei and beamed. It felt like an eternity since he last smiled at her. There was no way for things to go back to before, but she needed everything to be okay between them.

"We're very lucky to have him," Rei said, more to herself, as she watched her cousin head for the car.

Bronx jumped out of the truck and approached her. As exhausted as she was, she hoped that maybe he would finally talk to her—she would put off rest a little longer if it came to that.

A roar shook Rei to her core. A group of shuttles floated into the hangar. The transporters had once been white, but the burn marks and dents indicated that it was a long time ago. The engines groaned as they wound down and a few sparks shot out from one of the hulls. Wherever the shuttles came from—it was not peaceful.

"I didn't get to message you before, Manca," Urius

bellowed over the roar. "There were several Daer wounded in a firefight with the Infinity Dogs on Kapteyn II. That's them now. There are too many and their medics are overwhelmed. Another medic is on his way."

Bronx's face fell and he gave Rei a fleeting glance before he raced back to the medical facility.

Urius greeted the newcomers, leaving Rei and the others behind. The Daer from the *Luciernaga* hurried to help transport the wounded from the shuttles. Skylar stood at the forefront, barking orders before joining Bronx in the facility.

Rei felt at a loss with what to do next. There were plenty of Daer to take care of their fallen comrades, while the Volocio slowly made their way to the truck where Arram and Manden were already waiting.

She wasn't ready to go back to the Underground. What she really wanted was to go back out there—to show her face. She wanted to work with her powers more, she wanted to question Infiernen more. She wanted a chance to talk to the people like she used to talk to the patrons at the bar. She was good at that. Now that she had a purpose, she wanted to keep the momentum going.

Rei growled in frustration, knowing she was trapped again. But she would bide her time until she found her next opportunity. The god queen would make an appearance again and she would be ready. She jogged to the other Volocio and jumped in the car next to Arram. As much as she wanted to accomplish everything on her list, she knew controlling her lightning should be the first priority until she found a way to get herself in a room with Infiernen and demand to know the truth.

# CHAPTER 34



"I'T's only been a few days, Rei. Be patient," Arram said. "Okay, watch me this time." He closed his eyes and slowed his breathing. Rei watched as his hands raised, palms facing up, then he dragged them lightly through the air. His skin glowed as little sparks danced all around his hands, flickering faintly but steadily.

Rei sensed the air crackling around them, making the hair on her arms rise. Unlike the crashing waterfall of electricity that came unabashed when she called lightning, this was soft like rain.

Arram reached out to the nearby circuit board and touched it. A soft flicker jumped from his fingertips to the circuit board, and the light bulb filled the room with a soft glow. He only performed this feat for a moment before pulling away from the bulb, and then it went dark.

When he opened his eyes, it was Rei who bit her lip and blinked several times.

"You make it look so easy."

"You just have to relax. I may understand the logistics, but I can barely get this amount to work. But you, you can command so much more. You're the inverse. You need to learn to control in smaller doses."

Rei studied the circuit board in front of her. Over the last few days since Trappist V, Arram had scavenged the hangar for parts. He made the little circuit board as an exercise for both him and his sister. Unfortunately, they quickly learned that her powers were exponentially stronger than his as each bulb they tested burst.

She gave an exasperated sigh. "Just go through it with me again."

"Of course. Remember the source of our power." He put a hand to his core. "It's here. It's what centers us. It holds us together when the lightning wants to tear us apart."

Rei nodded, putting a hand to her stomach.

"Once you've found your source, close your eyes and think of the air around you as alive. Every wisp, every breeze—feel the particles individually. They will feel like beads on your skin."

Rei did as Arram instructed, impressed by how much he had already gleaned, as well as disappointed in herself for not getting a handle on it as quickly.

She concentrated on her hands. A soft wind found its way into Arram's room and flowed over her. She tried to think of the breeze as individual pieces until the air grew heavy like glass marbles rolling across her skin.

"When you have it"—Arram's voice came softly into her consciousness—"drag those beads through the air. Imagine each bead causing a spark as they bounce off each other."

Rei continued, slowly opening her eyes to see small sparks flicker in and out around her hands. They weren't as vibrant and bright as before, but she did it.

He led her to the circuit board. The bolts jumped happily from her hands to the board and the bulb roared to life.

"I did it!" she whispered. The lightning reacted to her excitement and built up until, suddenly, the bulb shattered, plunging that corner of the room into darkness.

"Gods bless it," she said. "Sorry." She rubbed her face and groaned.

Arram chuckled. "Don't worry. I'm sure there's another

bulb around here somewhere. Glass bulbs clinked, hitting each other as he searched through a box.

"I'm sorry I keep breaking the bulbs."

"You don't need to apologize. I know you're distracted. Bernie still won't wake up and your handsome medic is busy so you can't stare googly eyes at him. Have you found any more news on Niko?" She heard him still rummaging for a bulb.

Rei shook her head. "I've scoured all of Nexus, and not once has Niko been seen since his 'murder.'"

"And we are sure he's alive?"

"There were plenty of people who were on the battle-field that day and I find it odd no one has come forward. I just wish someone would admit they know something. I'm getting sick of this vague crap."

"You and me both."

Rei helped shuffle through the bulbs, holding one to her ear and shaking it gently. The delicate filaments rattled against the glass—another broken one. She tossed it back into the box.

She had hoped to find an opportunity to ask Bronx about Infiernen, but there were still a few wounded Daer from the fire fight on Kapteyn II. Bronx had personally taken care of all of them without a single loss of life. She heard that was why his services were requested—he was the best corpsman they had. However, it meant he spent all his time at the hangar and not in the Underground.

"Googly eyes?" she asked with a raised an eyebrow.

"Crona's words, not mine," he responded with a chuckle.

"You talk about us?"

In the half-light of her brother's room, he watched her. "Nothing else is really happening. Watching the two of you dance around each other is all the entertainment we can get at the moment."

"Just the two of you?" Her heart raced at the thought of everyone watching her and the medic together. She didn't realize they were that obvious.

"Kaz and Manden are also in on it."

Rei's face grew red. "Oh gods," she gasped before they both dissolved into laughter.

"Success!" Arram cried holding up a bulb. "Found one."

Footsteps echoed in the hallway outside, growing louder as they neared. Kaz flung the door open as he entered, his eyes wide. "Bernie's awake."

# CHAPTER 35

REI RACED TO BERNIE'S SIDE IN THE MEDICAL WING. She took the woman's hand and squeezed it tightly.

"Bernie?" she asked.

Very slowly but surely, Bernadette's eyes opened. She smiled when she saw Rei looking down at her. The knot in her stomach slowly loosened.

"Hey there, beautiful."

Rei giggled and tears of relief streamed down her face. "How are you feeling?"

"I feel like I got kicked in the ribs by a horse." She groaned. "Shit the bed. How long have I been out?"

"Almost a week."

Bernie sighed. "That means my muscles have atrophied. Damn."

Rei laughed and kissed the scars on Bernie's hand. "I almost killed you, and your only concern is your muscle tone?"

Bernie didn't say anything for a moment, as if contemplating how to answer Rei's question. Then she replied, "Yes."

Rei laughed. "Well, then you won't be pleased to see the scar I gave you." She handed Bernie a mirror.

Bernadette only glanced at her reflection briefly before handing it back. "At least I can tell people that I've been touched by a god."

"You had us scared for a while there, Bernie," said a voice Rei had wanted to hear since they'd returned from Trappist V. Bronx approached to check on Bernie's vitals.

Dark circles shadowed the skin under his eyes, but he faintly smiled when he glanced in her direction.

Her heart fluttered. She didn't understand it. She had seen his powers at work and knew that she should be afraid of him. But her dangerous powers evened the game between them.

Rei watched him as he worked. Arram's googly eyes comment came to mind, and her cheeks reddened.

"I've called your uncle, he should be here shortly," Bronx said before returning to his work at his desk while Rei turned her attention to her friend.

Bernie's gaze darted from the medic to Rei. "What did I miss?"

"A lot," said Rei. "I made my first appearance as the god queen. I think it made a difference on Trappist V. The election is in a few days."

Bernie sighed with relief. "My uncle finally made the right decision."

"He didn't. I did. I had to do something." Rei shrugged.

"Don't tell him I said this, but I'm glad you did."

"He was already pissed off because of what I did to you. I think he wanted to punish me." Rei pressed her lips together. Relief continued to flow through her, releasing the tension she'd held over the last week.

"Well, I couldn't go to the Underworld just yet knowing I needed to save you from my uncle." Bernie winked at Rei, who blushed and rolled her eyes. "I'll always have your back, angel."

"I think I did more harm than I thought. I'm no angel." Rei squeezed the soldier's hand.

Bernie held her gaze. "No, you are. You may have been the last person I saw when you fried me, but you were the first when I woke up. After all that time, you're still by my side. I really appreciate it, my friend." Bernie gave Rei a mischievous smile. "Plus, it does wonders for my ego."

Rei barked a laugh. At least Bernie hadn't lost her sense of humor.

"Think what you like, but I only stayed by your side because I felt bad."

"Whatever. I'll take what I can get from you, Rei. But you gotta admit it, you did miss me."

Rei raised an eyebrow. "Of course. I missed your sass."

"Bernadette!" Urius cried, entering the medical wing and rushing to her side. His eyes were red with tears.

"I'll come by sometime later to talk to you more, okay?" Rei backed away to let Urius take her place at his niece's side.

"I'm not going anywhere." Bernie winked again. "And Rei? Thank you for being here with me. I'm grateful to know I wasn't alone."

"What are friends for?" A lump formed in her throat as she walked away from the bed.

Bronx leaned against his desk, arms crossed. She still found it shocking how dark his eyes were, like pools of ink. His lips parted as she drew closer.

"We need to talk," he said.

"I agree," she said.

"I have so many things to tell you, and I don't know where to begin."

She drew close, hoping no one else would head what she was about to say. "How about telling me if Niklaryn is still alive?" Blood pounded in her ears as Bronx's jaw dropped.

# CHAPTER 36

Rei held her breath, waiting for Bronx to respond. His eyes scanned the medical wing. They were alone save for Bernie and Urius. When he was satisfied no one overheard, he lightly tugged Rei and pulled her out into the hall, but there were still plenty of soldiers milling about. Her breath caught at his brief contact.

"Let's go for a walk," she said, leading him to the door to Urius's home and the forest outside. The sun set in the west, giving the forest a golden glow. Summer had reached its end, and a few of the leaves had changed from a lush green to the warm hues of red, brown, and gold.

"How did you find out?" he asked.

"Infiernen told me before beating the crap out of me."

He pinched the bridge of his nose with his fingers. "Urius made me promise I wouldn't tell a soul." His dark eyes returned to hers. "Not even you."

"He knows? What happened that day? What did you see?"

He shook his head. "I'm not sure what I saw. It happened so fast, and it was so horrendous that the details are hazy."

"Why didn't you tell me?"

Bronx winced and looked down at his hands, his shoulders hunched. "I didn't know what to tell you." His voice was low.

"You couldn't just say it? You couldn't just tell me that my brother didn't die that day on the battlefield?" she hissed.

He shook his head.

A few leaves fell around them as they stared at each other in silence.

She scoffed. "What could be so terrible that you can't tell me?"

Bronx stayed silent.

"Well?" Rei asked.

He bit his lip. He refused to meet her eyes.

"Bronx?" her heart broke with every second that he remained silent.

He held her gaze. "They left the battlefield together."

The ground beneath her lurched, and Rei's head flinched back. "Wait. What?"

"Infiernen came and overtook your brother. But they walked off that battlefield together."

"Are you insinuating Niklaryn was recruited for the Dominion?" she asked.

"That is what I don't know."

The air rushed out of Rei's lungs. She pulled at the collar of her shirt as she took deep breaths. Her mind raced, trying to grasp at all the information colliding together at once. "Maybe he was captured," she said with a shaky voice. "Is there a way we can find out? To be sure?"

Bronx bit his lip, his brows pulled in together in concentration. "Aside from going to Infiernen himself and asking him the details? No."

None of it made sense. Niklaryn fought the Dominion to avenge their parents, there was nothing in Rei's imagination that would have been enough justification to join the enemy. She had to be missing another piece of the puzzle. "Maybe I should ask him. Infiernen says he's not my enemy."

He narrowed his eyes. "He... he said that?"

Rei nodded.

Bronx shook his head. "I don't trust him. He wants me out of the picture and almost succeeded in killing Arram."

She would never get the image out of her mind of Arram falling, blood spilling from his stomach. He was right.

"But . . ." he began. "I think he and your brother share a common goal: protecting you. Maybe he doesn't believe he's your enemy."

"Yet Infiernen wants you and Arram dead." Her thoughts dwelled on the image of Infiernen pointing his pistol at Bronx's back. "I told him he couldn't take you away from me." The words passed through her lips before she realized it. Her heart raced, knowing she had revealed too much. But that door was open now and could not be closed.

Bronx froze, and a small gasp escaped his lips. "Rei," he whispered. "We can't—we shouldn't."

Rei growled in frustration. "We shouldn't what, Bronx? Tell me. Be honest with me."

He wrung his hands. "You're right. I'm sorry. Let me start from the beginning: I reacted badly after Bernie was injured. I shouldn't have said those things to you."

He said nothing for a long time, as if he were at a loss for words. "You see"— he rubbed his jaw—"what happened with Bernie didn't make me realize how dangerous you were. I already knew that. It reminded me of how dangerous I am." He paused. "I didn't know I was a Volocio until after I had graduated from the Daer Academy. I returned home to my father, who was very sick. He had a really bad coughing fit, and as I reached out to help him, this black smoke appeared." Bronx's voice hitched. "He died in my arms," he finished, his voice barely above a whisper. "Can you imagine that, Rei? The first time your powers come out is when you kill your own father?"

She thought back to when her powers first appeared. She killed the Negander who had destroyed her home. All the people she grew up with, everyone she knew. She may not have been close to them, but they didn't deserve that fate.

"Were you close with your father?"

Bronx nodded. "I didn't really know my mother until I was older. She was off raising Crona. He was the only parent I had, the only one I needed."

A dull ache grew in Rei's chest. She couldn't imagine how she would have felt if she caused her mother's demise. She looked up at Bronx, who stared out into the forest, lost in the thought.

"That's why you wear gloves," she said softly.

Bronx blinked, then met her gaze. "Yes. I'm scared what my touch will bring."

The sun continued to set. Its dying rays caught in Bronx's eyes. It was the first time she noticed that they weren't really black, but dark hues of chocolate and caramel that shone warmly as the sunlight hit them. She couldn't stop staring.

"I'm sorry," she said suddenly. "Manden told me to be more forgiving toward your behavior and give you space. He said that you had a lot of your own baggage to sift through."

"He's right about the baggage, but forgiveness is something I may not deserve. I had no right to take my anger out on you or anyone else." He turned and walked away from the sun, retreating into the cool shade of the forest.

"That's why you pushed me away?" Rei stepped in front of him to meet his gaze, but Bronx's eyes were cast down. "Because you're afraid you'll touch me? But you're a medic—you have to touch people to heal them."

"It's my way to repay the debt. Save a life to cancel out the ones I reap."

She tried to wrap her head around his logic, but something didn't add up. "What about your sister? You're close to her."

"My sister?" He sighed. "No matter how hard I push her away, she pushes back." He stopped and turned to stare further into the forest, refusing to meet Rei's eyes. "Crona's loyal to a fault. She loves me so much she can't stand the thought of me being alone. And as for me being afraid to touch you"—it was then that he locked eyes with her—"I am terrified of touching you, Rei, and yet it's all I want to do," he rasped. "Gods, it's all I think about." He reached out and gingerly took her hands.

The warmth from his touch radiated down between her legs. She thought back to when they first met, and she suffered a panic attack. He held her hands then and was equally gentle. The way his thumb brushed her knuckles stirred something inside her, tugging like a thread in her chest, drawing her towards him. It had been so long since she had been with a man that such a soft touch had that effect on her. But maybe it was all because of him. Everything in her life had pointed to him.

"I have dreams where you touch my face. Then I see that black smoke again and you die in my arms, just like my father. I want to be with you so much, but I can't even harbor such a thought in my mind because I can't have you the way I want."

"But we're holding hands now," she said. She drew closer to him, wanting more of his warmth.

"I know, but it can't be more than this. There always has

to be some barrier between us." He gently squeezed her hands, his eyes dropped to her mouth. "It killed me to see you holding hands with Bernie today. I was so jealous." He pulled away, letting go. The cold air kissed her skin where his touch was only moments before. "Here I am, running off at the mouth about my feelings and dreams, and yet I have no idea how deep your feelings run." He let go and turned to leave.

"No," Rei said, taking his hand again. She reached up to touch his face, but he flinched. She instead laid her hand on his chest, over his heart. "You know I feel the same way." His heart beat fast under her palm. "I'm sorry, I feel like such an ass. I got angry instead of trying to learn the whole story—"

"I should have told you everything instead of pulling away. That was never my intention. I do that with everyone, and I need to be better."

A calm, full silence fell between them. They stared at each other as the sun finally set. The air grew cold, and Rei moved closer to him until they stood inches apart. She shivered but not from the cold. Bronx took off his jacket and wrapped it around her shoulders. He pulled the button of the jacket, using it to bring her closer. His scent of rosemary, sage, and a hint of lavender enveloped her, consumed her. All of her thoughts narrowed in to the points of contact between them.

He let out a ragged breath. "I've tried to fight it. My attraction to you."

"Oh?" she whispered. Her heart lifted.

"A long time ago I had this dream. I know now it was a memory of Atrius, but it was something I could never shake. A balcony, a beautiful woman—"

"A kiss?"

His pupils flared. "Yes."

"Me, too," she purred.

Rei studied his face, wanting to commit to memory every angle and curve, how the light hit his eyes. His lips parted, and she felt the urge to touch them. She had to know if they were as soft as in her dreams.

"You are Niko's kid sister. I thought it was all a joke. But then we talked that night over tea, and I learned you were funny. I enjoyed being around you. I watched you beat Sky, and I knew I could count on you to have my back in a fight —you did when we fought those Negander. You were brave to take on Infiernen without hesitation."

"Some may call that stupidity," Rei said with a smirk.

He chuckled. "Some. Not me." He reached out and touched her face, his thumb gently caressing her cheek.

She closed her eyes, basking in his touch.

"You are so much more than a beautiful face," he whispered. "I didn't understand why reincarnation was possible or even necessary. But I can see how a bond between two souls can be so strong that they strive to find each other again in another life. The universe meant for us to find each other. My heart was already yours before we met. And even if I had a choice, I would still choose you."

She opened her eyes and gazed at his full mouth. She was so close to him, her lips moments from touching his. She ran a hand up his arm, feeling the thick chords of muscles under the cloth. The same arm snaked around her waist and pulled her close. They fit together so well, like pieces of a puzzle only made for each other. It was so unfair. The heat between her legs became a pounding need. She wanted Bronx, even if it consumed her.

"I want you to touch me."

His lips hovered just above hers. "I want more than a touch."

Rei couldn't think. Hunger ravaged her like a storm, leaving nothing but desire in its wake. She couldn't feel her arms or her legs—only his hand on her cheek and his fingers at her back, stroking lazy circles through the fabric of her shirt like he was casting a spell.

Bronx closed his eyes and smiled. "What are you doing to me, Rei? You're a temptation I can't resist." He bit his lip. "I'm afraid that if you get any closer—"

"You might lose control?" she asked in a husky voice. She wanted him to lose it. She wanted him to hold her, to caress her.

"Yes," he whispered, almost leaning in.

He drew closer to Rei and she felt the heat of his lips just a hair's breadth away. She wanted this. She needed this.

Bronx pulled away. Her body ached where he touched her, wanting to be touched again. A rush of cold replaced his fingers, leaving her shivering.

"We can't," he growled. He put a hand to his mouth, breathing hard. His dark eyes remained on hers, desire still visible. "I'm sorry, but I don't want you to die." He turned and walked back toward the Underground, leaving Rei alone in the cold.

# CHAPTER 37

It was quite late in the evening when Rei finally returned, still dazed, to the Underground. She shivered but was grateful that the cool air quenched the burning ardor in her core. Bronx was nowhere to be found, but she had a feeling he was in the medical wing. She veered toward the lounge to find Crona, Arram, and Kaz already there, sitting in chairs around a small table.

"You okay?" her brother asked, approaching her. "I saw Bronx come back alone."

"Yeah, we talked." Her cheeks burned at the memory. "I needed some time to digest it all."

"Talked, eh?" Crona asked from her seat, eying Bronx's coat around Rei's shoulders. "Did it by any chance have anything to do with his behavior?"

"Yes."

Crona's smile dripped with self-righteousness. "Good."

Rei took a seat between Kaz and Arram. "So what are you all up to?"

"We were trying to help Crona with her Star of Saskia project," her cousin said, at Crona's side.

"What's the problem?"

"It's a useless, stupid flower of . . . uselessness." Crona rolled her eyes. "Gah!" she yelled into the pile in front of her. "I'm trying to determine where Infiernen will be next."

"You said a forest before." Rei peered down at the small table. A crumpled up piece of paper lay next to several discarded pieces of the flower. In what she assumed was Crona's scrawled handwriting, she read aloud, "To those who loved the warrior slain/I promise you all, he will rise again."

"But now it's changed. Now it's some room with bright lights, shining weapons, and ribbon. Nothing gives me a clear vision except the whole flower." Crona held one of the stars between her thumb and forefinger. "I have tried each individual piece: the root, the stamen, the leaves, and now the petals. Every component only gives me a glimpse of a vision. Or a prophecy like the one you're holding."

Crona pointed at the paper in Rei's hand. "The only time I acquired the details I wanted was by ingesting the entire piece of shit." She tossed the star back onto the table, and it bounced several times, losing bits of pollen here and there until it stopped at the far corner.

"We know there are more options," Kaz said. "How else do the other seers do it?"

"Maybe I should grind it up into a powder and just snort it," Crona muttered to herself half-jokingly.

"Don't do that," a voice said from outside of the lounge. "I snorted something once, and it felt like my brain was melting." Bernie entered the room. "I don't recommend doing that as an extracurricular activity."

"You shouldn't be up. You're still hurt," Kaz said as he and Arram ran to Bernie's side. They led her to a nearby sofa.

"I'm fine, just restless."

Rei wasn't convinced, but she knew not to argue with stubborn people.

"What did you want to grind?" Bernie asked.

Crona sighed. "There's a flower that may help me use my powers. But there are no instructions on how much to take."

"Can I see it?"

Crona nodded and handed over the deep-red bud. The older soldier held it close.

"It's lovely. I've never seen anything like this."

"It's from the Volocio home world."

"I think it would make a very pretty tea if you had a glass teapot." Bernie lifted the flower to her nose and breathed in the scent. "Smells lovely. Reminds me of jasmine."

"What did you say?" asked Crona.

"Smells lovely?"

"No, before that."

Bernie furrowed her eyebrows. "Tea?"

"Yes!"

The group looked at each other in surprise.

"It's worth a shot," said Kaz. "I have certainly had to drink my fair share of teas while living among monks. Grab a pot!"

The small bar in the lounge had an empty tea set and kettle. Once the water boiled, Crona plopped the star into the pot, and the five watched and waited, watching the color of the water turn from clear to a deep blood red. All eyes turned to Crona.

"You sure you want to drink it?" Rei asked. If it were her, she wasn't sure she could do it. But then again, Rei remembered her desperation in learning how to control her powers—she couldn't really blame Crona.

"Yes." The seer poured herself a cup, downing it. She gasped.

Rei's pulse rose in panic.

"It's hot," rasped Crona. "It's just hot."

Everyone watched her for several agonizing minutes until the blonde's aquamarine eyes glazed over with a vision. Within moments, Crona's gaze cleared and she met Rei's gaze. Her eyes glistened and she smiled.

"What?" asked Rei.

"He can't hurt you as long as you're together."

"Say what now?" Rei's heart thundered loudly in her chest. With all the people hunting her, there was no telling what that vague statement meant. Her thoughts first turned to Infiernen. Had she been more forthright with her information and worked together with the other Volocio as a team, maybe she wouldn't have gotten hurt. Maybe Arram could have avoided the bullet.

A small voice whispered Bronx's name in her mind, and she wished it was true, but the wording didn't quite work. He could potentially kill her, not hurt her. Still she had to know. "Who's he?"

Crona gave her a wink. "*He* has many faces. There are some events that will happen soon, and your instincts will reveal his face when the situation is right."

# CHAPTER 38

When everyone slept, Rei crept through the halls to the medical wing. The adrenaline rushing through her veins made it impossible for her to sleep. Too many thoughts ran through her head, and if she didn't talk to someone, she worried she would go mad.

Sure enough, Bronx was still awake, sitting at his desk with a stack of papers. No patients remained in the wing, and the other medics were nowhere to be found. It was just the two of them. Alone. A smile crept across his beautiful lips when she entered.

"Shouldn't you be sleeping?" he asked.

"And miss our regular late-night meetings? Never." She smirked. Her heart drummed in her ears as she drew closer to him. "What about you?"

"My work is never done."

"Is that your way of saying 'nightmare?'"

"Possibly." His dark eyes were unreadable.

"Do you want to talk about it?"

"No."

Rei winced. She had hoped she could be someone he confided in. "Never mind. I'm sorry to have bothered you." She turned to leave.

"Please stay."

Her heart fluttered. She felt the pull in his voice and knew she couldn't say no. "I will."

"Good." His face lit up when he smiled. Bronx stood and walked closer to Rei, leaning against the desk.

"What I meant to say was that I'm not ready to talk

about my nightmares yet. But do you want to talk about why you couldn't sleep?" he asked.

She wasn't sure if she should tell the truth. Despite everything she learned today, her thoughts kept returning to the dream about Micaela and Atrius in a passionate embrace on the balcony of the palace. Yet this time the colors were brighter, the smells stronger, his lips felt softer, and his voice was less an echo of a memory and more reality. Because it was Bronx whom she was kissing.

"Dreams." Her eyes fell to his lips.

"Oh." His eyes were soft.

Rei took one of his gloved hands. "So can I still hold your hand?"

"Yes. In a way."

"But no kissing." She thought how close they were before.

"No."

"No sex?"

He sighed. "Tragically, no."

"Tragic indeed. Because you're 'dangerous?'" She inched closer. "So am I."

"My power is death, Rei. There's no gray area. There is dead and not dead. In your case, there is the possibility of death or being shocked." He sighed. "I just don't see how we can work this out."

"Why? Because we can't touch?" She shrugged. "Big deal. We work around it. It's not like we're short on time, being Volocio and all. We'll work with what we have. I can wait for the rest." She smiled.

He squeezed her hand. "Gods, I love you and I don't deserve you."

They both froze.

"What did you say?" she asked.

"Nothing."

"Say it again."

He shook his head, but his face broke into a beautiful smile.

"Please." Rei took both his hands, moving closer to him. She knew what he'd said. She was simply desperate to hear it again.

He looked at her, and she lost herself in those dark eyes. Those dreams were only a shadow compared to the reality.

Bronx smiled and said, "I love you."

Her pulse quickened. She returned the gesture, her smile broad and without restraint. "I love you too."

Bronx chuckled. "Very romantic setting, isn't it? Proclaiming our love for each other among bedpans, dressings, and scalpels."

"As long as I get to hear it."

The two stood in silence, eyes locked. Rei recognized the look in Bronx's eyes. The same yearning Atrius had in her dream, and she felt it, too. The tension between the two of them grew thick; the air was too tight, and a shiver rode down her spine. She wanted to feel his lips on her skin, to run her hands over his body, to taste him. Her mind overflowed with ideas of how and where she wanted him.

Bronx laughed uncomfortably.

"What?" she asked.

He smiled and pulled at the high neck of his tunic. "It's suddenly feeling really hot in here." He pulled off his gloves and began to unbutton the top of his shirt. His eyes never left hers. Her cheeks grew warm as heat flooded her, pooling into her stomach, then trickling between her legs.

She wanted to eat him alive.

She winked. "Yeah."

"Oh geez, get a room, you two." Ayres leaned against the door way. "The rest of us have work to do."

Bronx glanced at Rei, his expression tense, but he said nothing. He put his gloves back on and led Rei from the room. Her heart sank as he covered his hands, a reminder of what must always come between them. "Have a good shift, Ayres."

"Have a good night, love birds."

They walked in silence to the stairs. He stood so close his scent washed over her. Her time with him was always too short, and she scrambled for a way to keep things from ending.

Bronx took the first step down before he stopped. He was the same height as Rei now, and she held his intense gaze. His hand fell onto the railing between them. There always had to be a barrier.

"I think it's best if you go to bed." He let out a ragged breath. "If you keep looking at me like that, I may start begging to do things to you that I shouldn't."

Rei stopped breathing. What did he have in mind? Her imagination ran wild.

"And if I give you my consent? Now that I know the risks?"

"Gods," he whispered as he reached out and touched her face, tucking her hair behind her ear. "I love you." The warmth from the gloves threatened to consume her. "Even when we are together, I can't let anything happen to you. I would never forgive myself if I hurt you." He stopped for a moment, then rolled his eyes. "That sounded so much better in my head."

He smiled but she couldn't return it. She wanted him, and the ache grew with every second that he stared at her and did nothing.

"Good night," he whispered. He let her go, tearing his eyes from her as though it was the most difficult thing for him to do, and continued down the stairs.

She watched him walk away. She hated the barriers, hated being kept apart. And it was all because he was afraid of what could happen. But she couldn't blame him for his fear. If she were in his position, she would also do whatever it took to protect him, to keep anything from happening to him. She wanted as much time with him as possible, to be together in any capacity.

*He can't hurt you as long as you're together.*

Rei halted as Crona's words played in a loop in her mind. *He can't hurt you as long as you're together.* What the seer said made sense. It was so obvious. She focused too much on the literal meaning of the prophecy. She giggled as the weight of the realization hit her. That meant they could . . .

She ran down the stairs to find him at the door of his room. She strode to him, each step giving her confidence for the next one. She trembled with the need to touch him everywhere at once.

He saw her approach. "Rei?"

She reached out and touched Bronx's face. She expected him to jerk away, but he didn't. She stood on her toes, pulled him close, and kissed him before he could protest.

His lips were just as soft as she imagined, and her nerves were set ablaze as the kiss grew deeper. She had wandered a lonely wood for so many years, only to finally find her way back home again. She ran her fingers through his hair, and he moaned against her. His arms wrapped around her, crushing her against his strong body. His gloved hand pulled at her shirt, raking at the skin underneath, and her legs grew weak, no longer capable of keeping her standing.

Bronx hesitated before he pulled away, but he didn't pull away far enough. "We shouldn't have done that." His voice shook. "It's too dangerous for you." He leaned toward her, touching her forehead with his. She saw the fear in his eyes. "If something happens—"

She smiled. " Your powers won't work on me. Your sister saw it."

He let out a soft gasp. "Gods, I hope it's true." He leaned into her touch, causing her heart to break as she thought about how starved for human contact he must've been. "I can't bear it if it isn't. You know I can't fight you. I need you." His voice gave out as he whispered the word "need".

She thumbed his cheek, basking in the warmth of his skin. Her breath was shallow as she realized that they were standing at the precipice that destiny had been pushing them towards since they were born. They were meant to be together, she had never been so sure of anything in her life. "Then don't fight it. Just make love to me."

His dark eyes settled softly on hers. Then he gave a slight nod which quickly grew more vigorous as he appeared to reach the same conclusion as her. "As you wish."

He crushed his lips against hers, kissing her desperately, furiously, holding her tightly against him as he pulled her into his room and shut the door behind them. Her whole body felt as though it were made of live wire, becoming more electric at each point of contact between his body and hers. Her heart raced as liquid warmth ran down to her core. He pressed her against the door, his hard body connected with the soft curves of hers. He pulled away just enough to tug his gloves off, tossing them aside as if they were chains. His lips found hers again, his naked hands stole into her shirt to find more of her.

"You are so soft," he growled into her mouth and she moaned in response.

They moved together in a wordless dance as they helped each other remove their clothes. She couldn't kiss him fast enough or hard enough to soothe the need that grew inside her. The warms of his skin threatened to consume her.

He lowered her onto the bed, his hips heavy against hers. His lips moved away from hers to her neck, where he whispered her name into her skin, leaving her trembling. Her fingers raked along his back, digging into the muscles that lay beneath. Bronx groaned under her touch, the heat from his breath warming her neck before he returned to her lips. His hands roamed across her body, touching her in places that made her lose sense of time. Yet a small part of her wanted to slow down, to make this last, but the battle was already lost. His hand was well nestled between her thighs, his fingertips curling up and inward. She let out a gasp and rocked into his motion.

"Gods, the sounds you make," he rasped. "I want to hear you cry my name." His hand moved, edging her closer until she almost lost herself before he pulled back. "But not yet."

She let out a strangled laugh, still dizzy with desire. She shifted her leg, moving it up his hips, causing him to let out his own gasp. "You're going to cry my name first."

He let out a low chuckle before claiming her mouth again. "Rei," he whispered leaving a soft kiss on her neck. "Rei." He left another and another before their rhythm sped up again. Everything kiss, lick, gasp left her wanting more. She wanted everything. She wanted them to be one.

They were a tangle of limbs when they finally joined. Everything disappeared in a haze as he called her name. The world could have fallen down around them, and they wouldn't have noticed. Rei lost all sense outside the feel of Bronx, the smell of him, the taste of him. She let out a deep moan, then gasped his name as they both dove over the edge.

# CHAPTER 39

THE ONLY LIGHT IN THE AUDITORIUM WAS THE projected video covering election day on Trappist V.

Rei, from her seat in the far back, focused on the tense silhouettes wandering about in front of her. Crona and Urius spoke together in hushed voices while Kaz paced along the far-right wall. Arram rubbed his face and occasionally ran a hand through his disheveled hair. The other Daers in the room were in various stages of unease and restlessness. Manden appeared calm, but Rei believed he simply refused to show when he was stressed. Bronx remained a quiet rock at her side and gave her hand a gentle squeeze. He had taken off one of his gloves, and his calloused thumb gently stroked her knuckles.

While they waited for the final results, the channel continued to show looped footage of Rei diverting Infiernen's attack on Bronx. Large bolts of lightning flew from Rei's fingers and threw Infiernen to the side like a rag doll. Bronx had already taken care of three of the four Negander, and his eyes lingered on Rei for a heartbeat before he continued his attack on the last Negander. He ended the fight with the plume of black smoke before the warrior fell in a heap at Bronx's feet. Rei didn't notice before how he stared at her. She could've sworn his eyes were bright with pride.

That was when Infiernen told her Niklaryn lived, and he wasn't her enemy. She couldn't wrap her head around how he thought shooting her other brother would prove his loyalty.

The video continued, and Infiernen knocked the wind out of her. She lay on the ground, unaware as Infiernen lifted his pistol and fired two shots at his own Negander as they fought Bronx. The Daer used his black smoke to finish them. Infiernen's movements were so fast, she almost didn't catch them. Rei scanned the room, only to find several still pacing and others with heads bowed in conversation. Only Bronx saw it, his mouth hung open.

"He saved you," she whispered.

"I thought I killed them," Bronx replied, his gloved hand to his mouth.

Rei told the Negander to not take Bronx away from her and he listened. She squeezed Bronx's hand. Perhaps Infiernen meant what he said.

"I never thought I would see the Second Coming in my lifetime," said a young man on the screen being interviewed.

"Watching Mica stand up to Infiernen to save one of her own was an inspiration," said a woman.

"I agree," said the woman's companion. "Infiernen bleeds like the rest of us. Sovereign Praymer probably does as well. Fear shouldn't prevent us from striving for something better. Perhaps the Dominion isn't the right answer."

Rei smiled. She still couldn't believe she inspired people with a short speech. She imagined what more she could accomplish if she had more time with them. She always had a good rapport with the customers at Coronta Bar. She was probably more effective with one-on-one conversations with people.

Ideas swirled in Rei's head—the Federation needed more people, and she knew how to appeal to them.

Rei sensed movement next to her as Skylar joined them, her blue eyes sparkling with excitement. "Have they announced the results?" her cousin asked, unfolding a creaky chair before sitting down.

"Not yet."

Skylar put her palms together, with her fingers at her lips as though in prayer, reminding Rei of what she often did when she still believed in the gods. She missed the feeling of believing her prayers were heard. But she didn't think anyone would listen now.

"The voting is over, and the final tallies are coming in." The news reporter's voice dipped into Rei's thoughts, bringing her back into the present.

Everyone held their collective breath as they sat on the edge of their seats.

"Ladies and Gentlemen of Trappist V, I am pleased to inform you that Alma Canale has been reelected." The journalist beamed into the camera.

The room shook from the roar of the crowd. Everyone hugged and cheered again. Bronx drew Rei into a kiss, his strong arms held her against him as she ran her hands through his soft hair. Her heart brimmed with pride. Her path in the Federation had been cemented.

"I'm proud of you," he whispered when he broke the kiss.

"I'm proud of me too," she responded. "But we still have work to do."

She let him go to approach Urius and Manden, both enthusiastically patting each other on the back, but Skylar tugged on her arm.

"Now's not a good idea, Cousin."

"I need to do more of what I did for Trappist V," Rei announced. "I need to talk to Urius."

The Daer shook her head. "You made that already clear to him before. He's prideful and the last thing you should do is rub this in his face. He will say no just to spite you."

"But look at the videos and conversations on the Nexus!" Rei hissed, gesturing to the projector behind her just as it showed Canale at a podium. The cheers in the room grew louder as the representative approached the microphone.

"People of Trappist V," the woman bellowed. "You honor me with your votes. The god queen honors me with her faith. I promise I will do everything in my power to not let you down!"

The roar of the crowd drowned out anything else Canale would have said.

Rei gestured to the screen again. "See?"

"I agree with Sky," Bronx said. "Hard to believe, I know. But I'm concerned about Infiernen. He found you too easily. Someone betrayed us that day. Until we figured out who leaked your location, we can't afford another surprise. Perhaps it's best we stay hidden."

"That's ridiculous." Rei's face grew hot. She knew she was the one who betrayed their location by tipping off the media.

"Anyone could have told the media our location on Trappist V," he said as though he read her thoughts. "I'm more concerned with whoever let Infiernen and his Dogs in the building in the first place. Canale was thorough with her security detail. I think it's the same person who betrayed you in Ballarat."

Rei furrowed her eyebrows. "Ballarat?"

"Someone told the Dominion about Bernie and Manden's trip." Bronx slid his hands back into his gloves. "My guess is someone is working with Infiernen, and this mystery traitor told them where to find you. I'm afraid they may have leaked other valuable Federation information as well."

Someone was working with Infiernen to make sure he met Rei, to convince her they were on the same side. He saved Bronx, yet she would never forget what he did to Arram.

Everyone slowly trickled out of the auditorium to further celebrate, leaving Bronx, Skylar, and Rei alone as the projector continued to loop different videos from that day. One of them was Rei's first attempt at speaking before the attack. Her face grew red as she remembered how hard it was to find the words. She watched as her features went slack, then a small smile crept across her lips. That was when she thought she saw Niklaryn in the crowd. The video zoomed out to include more of the audience. Rei scanned the faces, heart pounding in chest, and let out a small gasp.

"Niko?" she whispered as she saw her brother's face. He was there, smiling at her. He was alive. Infiernen didn't lie about that either. Warmth radiated through her body as she laughed.

"Where?" asked Bronx, eyes darting across the video.

She pointed at the screen. In that brief moment, she forgot Skylar was also in the room.

"So it's true?" her cousin murmured.

Rei turned to Skylar. "You knew?"

"Of course, I was on that battlefield, Rei." Skylar's blue eyes darted in Bronx's direction. "I knew Nik didn't die. I just wasn't sure if he was still alive. How did you find out?"

Rei didn't want to tell her cousin what Infiernen told her. She didn't want anyone to think she was working with the Negander, not until she was sure about which side he truly leaned.

"Doesn't matter." Skylar waved her hand dismissively. "This changes things. I have to tell Urius."

"Should I come with you?" Rei asked, drawing closer to her cousin.

Skylar shook her head. "No. Keep that information close to your chest. Urius doesn't need to know that you do, and you may be able to use his ignorance to your advantage. I'll get in touch with you and together we'll figure out a plan to find Nik." She shuffled in between the chairs and out of the room.

Rei's attention returned to the news, where the same video looped again. Her brother was there and with a blink of an eye, he disappeared into the crowd. After all these years, he was still alive. Something in the universe had answered her prayers and hope bloomed in her chest. Yet doubt whispered in the back of her mind. Not once in the last decade did he try to contact her, to tell her he had survived and was in hiding. She had to know why it was important that everyone assume he was dead.

# CHAPTER 40

Rei landed hard on Bronx's bed after a long day of working with Arram. It had been two weeks since the election results on Trappist V, but in that time, Rei had made little progress. Even when she followed Arram's explicit instructions, she brought up tiny worthless sparks, barely enough to light the bulb. The frustration created a sudden surge that caused the bulb to explode, sending shards in multiple directions.

There was no balance.

Bronx was still on shift in the medical bay, so she waited alone in his room. They had spent every night together since their first time, and every moment with him left her hungry for more. They were careful—the last thing they needed was a child. The first time was reckless, but a quick trip to the apothecary took care of any accidents.

She spent more time in his room than he in hers. It was homey with his photographs of the Volocio, Rei, and his Daer year mates on the walls, plus random mementos scattered on his desk and nightstand. For a knight, he was quite messy. Niko was always organized.

As she waited, Rei lifted her hand and tried the exercise Arram taught her. She imagined the air like beads and moved her fingers through them in hopes that they would charge.

They didn't.

Only a faint blue spark appeared between her middle and fourth finger. She tried harder, but only the faint light remained. Her anger boiled again, and her hand became a blinding ball of light. She clutched her hand to her chest and tried to slow her breathing, praying that the lightning didn't cause some damage to Bronx's room.

"Damnit," she muttered.

When the light disappeared, she glanced around the room and found nothing charred or smoking. She continued to lay and stare at the ceiling. Bronx should be back soon. Rei reached over to his nightstand and grabbed her touchscreen to look at the time. It was already rather late; he should have been back already. Probably an emergency. She decided to skim through the newsfeeds.

The most recent news was of a woman claiming to be Tasya, the goddess of wind, and the last missing Volocio. Urius still pressed Rei to help him find her, but Rei didn't care about another Volocio. She dismissed the news notification. With the technology today, pretending to be the goddess of wind was easy. All anyone needed was a good fan. She had seen too many of these pretenders on the Nexus recently.

In all that time since Trappist V, the video footage of Rei fighting against Infiernen looped on the Nexus. There was also the footage of Rei walking through the crowd, but apparently the fight was the more popular. Her exposure had been a boon for the Federation and since then, the planet Tau Ceti II also voted to join the Federation. Yet Urius forced the Volocio to stay hidden in the Underground. Their only reprieve was the occasional visit to Yticol.

Rei growled. It had been weeks since Skylar first talked to Urius about Niklaryn being alive, and yet nothing moved forward. She didn't know what everyone was waiting for. Time ticked by, and she wanted to find her brother.

As if by magic, a notification from Crona popped up on the top right-hand corner of the screen.

*Just returned from a meeting and this was one of the topics we discussed. I wasn't sure if you were aware—here's a list of the leaked information.*

*Cheers,*

*Crona*

It wasn't much, just a list of her and Arram's previous addresses. That information was useless now, so why leak it? There were other names of family members, but no one of interest as they were already public figures. Her eyes stopped on a name she didn't recognize.

*Artema Ettowa—Fabrecido, Kepler IV*

Niklaryn's last known whereabouts were on Kepler IV. Perhaps there was a connection. She decided to ask Bronx. She found him and Bernie together in the medical wing. The medic leaned against his desk, while the blonde sat in a chair with her head in her hands.

"Who's Artema Ettowa?" she asked, showing him the list.

He reviewed the list then met Rei's eyes. "Nik's wife."

"Excuse me?" she asked. The floor lurched under her feet. Her brother was married and he never told her. She struggled to stay calm but felt lightheaded as her heart thrashed.

"You didn't know?" Bernie asked.

Bronx's eyes grew wide with worry. "I thought Nik told you."

Rei couldn't feel her face.

"I'm sorry, darling," Bronx said. "I thought you knew. Believe me, I would have told you if I'd known that was the case."

She sighed. "It's just so frustrating that I knew so little about my brother before he died."

"Not many people know."

"Who then?"

"Me, my uncle, and Bronx," said Bernie.

"Niklaryn and Sky were close, and Sariah was her apprentice," Bronx added. "We were all at the wedding."

*Sariah was more than that*, Rei remembered Bronx telling her about his past, but she bit her tongue. "But why the secrecy? I thought Daer can marry."

"That's true. At first, we didn't know either. But we think he wanted to protect her from Infiernen." Bronx inspected Rei's dead tablet before putting it on the table behind him.

"Not that it did her any good," muttered Bernie.

"How so?" Rei asked.

"Because when he captured your brother, Infiernen went to the apartment Nik and Artema shared and tried to kill her."

Rei's anger deflated, but her pulse refused to slow down. As if she needed more of a reason to hate this monster. How could he possibly not be her enemy when all he did was try to kill her family?

"So then what happened?" she asked.

"Well, she survived, and since then we've kept her in the Temple of Tasya for her safety," Bernie said. "The last thing we wanted was for Infiernen to realize that she was still alive and come back to finish his work. I traveled to Kepler IV every once in a while to keep an eye on her. I used to visit every year, but I haven't the last few because I became more involved in the war."

"Urius told Bernie about the leaked information before

you arrived," Bronx said. "They worried Infiernen might discover that Artema is still alive."

"I grew concerned and returned to Kepler IV after we found you on Earth," continued Bernie. "But she's no longer at the temple in Fabrecido. I tried not to panic, so I got into contact with friends to keep me up to date on a search for her while I returned to Gliese VI. Then of course, I was consciously out of commission." Bernie shrugged. "I finally got a message from one of my contacts today saying she left the temple four years ago, and no one knows where she went." Bernie sighed heavily. "So I came to Bronx for help because he was the only other person who knew her personally."

Bronx's brows furrowed. "We have to try and find her," he said. "Infiernen is bound to have seen the list and realize that she didn't die after all. He'll want to finish what he started."

All this time, Rei had a sister and she didn't know it. Artema. A connection to Niklaryn. A connection like this was precious; maybe she knew what happened to him. "I agree. But now the question is how do we get permission from Urius to go on this little field trip?"

"What field trip?" Urius asked, entering the medical area.

"Don't worry, Uncle," Bernie said, giving him her sweetest smile, "we're only discussing a day trip into Yticol tomorrow. Forecast predicts cloudy skies."

Urius pressed his lips together until nothing but a line a crossed his face. "Make sure it's only to Yticol. We can't afford to have you Volocio being seen."

Rei suppressed an eye roll.

"But what if we wanted to show ourselves, sir?" asked Bronx. "Despite the risks?"

"I can't allow that."

"Can't or won't?" Rei asked.

The leader whirled and met her gaze with simmering anger, a vein in his temple throbbed as his face grew beet red. Rei had a feeling that even his niece seldom stood up to him.

"Does it matter? You swore an oath to obey me when you joined."

Rei raised an eyebrow. "I don't recall swearing anything. I just woke up and here I was."

Urius gave her a smile that didn't reach his eyes, and Rei's insides turned to ice. She was on dangerous grounds and she knew it. "That is true. That does sort of make you an ally like Manden, yes? One who enjoys the safety of my army. Just don't forget our understanding, Ettowa. You need our protection from Infiernen and Sovereign Praymer until I deem you ready for the final battle. You may not have sworn an oath to the Federation, but these two"—he pointed to Bronx and Bernie—"they are sworn to obey me."

"My brother and I may need you," Rei said through gritted teeth, "but you need me more. Trappist V and Tau Ceti II are proof of that. Don't forget how I won you two planets."

Urius stared daggers at Rei. She had him. The hardness in his eyes told her that she would probably regret it, but she couldn't stand being a puppet, even if she had the same goal as her puppet master.

He opened his mouth as if to retort but instead turned to Bronx. "I expect you and the other Volocio to obey my command when I say that you are to stay on Gliese VI until I or one of my superior officers command otherwise. Understood?"

"Yes, sir," Bronx said, almost inaudibly.

Urius turned back to Rei. "If you decide to pull a stunt like on Trappist V, you're on your own. The Federation will not back you unless I decide it's to our tactical advantage."

"Duly noted," Rei sneered.

Urius turned to his niece. "Bernadette, I need you to report to my office at 0700 tomorrow. We have a video conference with the council on Proxima Centauri II."

"Of course, Uncle."

Urius nodded and left the medical wing with his chest puffed out and back straight. Bernie grabbed her cane and limped to the entrance, apparently waiting for her uncle to be long gone. "Shit the bed, that was awkward," she muttered before turning to Rei and Bronx. "What's going on in that pretty head of yours, Rei?"

Rei clenched her teeth. "I'm going to Kepler IV to find Artema. Even if I have to do it alone."

"You won't." Bronx took her hand. "I'll help you."

Rei smiled. She knew she could count on him. She also knew searching for Artema may bring her face to face with Infiernen. Perhaps she may finally discover the truth about Niklaryn. "What about Urius's command?"

"I'll deal with him. I'm another superior officer," Bernie said with a low chuckle. "Get the other Volocio. I'm sure the others will also want to join. When the jig is up, I'll tell him it was my idea. It's important we find Artema. It's easier to ask for forgiveness than permission."

# CHAPTER 41

The rest of the Underground slept soundly, so they had to be quiet when waking the others. It didn't take long for them to rouse themselves and sneak to the hangar without anyone noticing. Manden was already there working late to make minor repairs to the *Luciernaga*. When Rei told him they were leaving, he didn't ask right away—not until they were off Gliese VI.

"Niklaryn's alive," Rei told the others as they gathered in the cockpit.

Crona's mouth hung open, and she leaned back in her chair. "How do you know?"

"I saw them walk off the battlefield together," Bronx said, his jaw set.

"And there's video confirmation that he was in the hall with us on Trappist V," Rei continued. "He's still alive. Infiernen told me this information first and he claims he's not my enemy."

"That's a load of shit," Crona muttered.

"So where is your brother, then?" Manden asked, clicking away at the keyboard as he piloted.

"That's the question. I've scoured the Nexus for an inkling of his whereabouts but found nothing," Rei answered.

"Does that mean Niklaryn is working for the Dominion?" Kaz asked.

"No," Bronx said. "We don't know for sure. But we keep that information between us. Urius, Skylar, and Bernie are the only ones who know—we can't afford the Federation knowing until we have enough information."

"So we're heading to Kepler IV to find Nik, then?" Rei's cousin rubbed his chin.

Rei shook her head. "There's more to this tangled web. Niko was married." She sat next to the redhead in the cockpit.

"Really?" Arram asked, violet eyes wide.

She nodded.

"Did not see that coming," Crona said.

"She was Infiernen's second victim after Niko. She survived. Bronx and Bernie hid her in the Temple of Tasya on Kepler IV for protection, but she disappeared."

Rei looked at Kaz, who simply nodded as he digested this information. "Your brother certainly had secrets," he said. "He must've known Infiernen was dangerous. Too bad it didn't help in the end."

"It's very important that we find her," Rei said to Manden as she glanced out the window. An inky black with blurred stars passed them as the ship sailed through the sky. "She's our connection to Niko. She may be able to tell us where he is."

"I understand, little lady. We'll find her. But what did Urius think?"

Rei felt the lie on the tip of her tongue. No, this time she had to be honest. "He doesn't know."

Manden's green eyes grew wide. "Say what now?"

The other Volocio slowly trickled out of the cockpit, leaving Rei alone to tell Manden about the conversation with Urius, followed by her determination to go.

"And Bernie said she would claim it was her idea? He did say to only follow directions from him or another superior officer." Manden laughed. "Oh, serves him right. I told him promoting Bernie was going to come back and bite him in the ass. She finds a way around everything." His laughter turned into a chuckle. "He's going to be so pissed."

"Well, at least you find it amusing," she muttered.

"Oh I do, darlin'."

"How long before we arrive on Kepler IV?" she asked.

"Eh, six hours?" he said, scratching his head.

"Okay," Rei said as she left and headed straight for the ladies bunk. She passed Crona and Bronx in deep conversation.

She heard him laugh as she walked into the room and dumped her bag on her bed. She loved that sound.

Rei unpacked her things, humming as she did. She managed to accumulate more civilian clothes after a few trips to Yticol with Crona. In a hurry, she had stuffed her new clothes into her bag and now tried to fold them properly. When she turned, she yelped in surprise. Bronx leaned against the door frame.

"Yes?" she asked.

He crossed his arms and put a finger to his lips

A small smile formed. "I'm impressed with how well you've taken this news. I'd be pissed if I were you."

Rei shook her head. "I was, briefly. But in truth, I shouldn't be surprised at how much Niko kept from me. He was determined to keep me safe because of who I am, and that meant cutting me off from everyone. He had the luxury of leaving Earth and making a life for himself. I just wish he told me. Unfortunately, while he was on Kepler IV, I only received one letter from him. I guess he was too busy to tell me everything."

"But still—" Bronx began.

"It is what it is. The important thing is that Artema is

family, and we have to find her and protect her from Infiernen. She could possibly lead us to Niko."

Her eyes never left Bronx as he watched her, and he took her aback with his spell-casting gaze. Heat flooded her, pooling in her stomach as she let his spell take over.

What's more: they had six hours between here and Kepler IV and were alone in a room that locked from the inside. He bit his lip as he entered the room and leaned against the door. It shut with a resounding thud.

Rei raised an eyebrow. "What?"

"Nothing," he murmured, softly brushing his lips against hers. She closed her eyes as the room started spinning. She reached up to grab him, but he pulled away. Rei opened her eyes to find a satisfied smile on his lips.

She reached around him and locked the door behind them, breathing hard as she waited for his reaction.

Bronx's hand still lightly touched her face, and his thumb brushed over her lips. She closed her eyes and prayed for more. His caress made her body grow taut as heat pounded between her legs.

Then his mouth was on hers. She pushed him against the closed door, her hands went to his chest where his heart beat under her fingers, but he wore too many clothes. She moved her fingers to his jacket and began to unbutton it. She waited for him to stop her, but his hands moved to her own clothes.

The first layers fell in a heap around them, and Bronx crushed Rei against him. She loved the way her body fit against his. His kiss moved from her lips to her neck, his teeth lazily scraped her skin and a moan escaped her lips. He growled as he lifted her, moving her to one of the nearby bunks and lowering her onto the mattress with heartbreaking gentleness.

Bronx pulled his shirt over his head and revealed his beautiful body, his powerful muscles, and his battle scars. Rei held him close and kissed the one over his heart.

The heart that was hers.

She worked her way up until she kissed his neck and nipped at his ear. He shuddered under her touch.

"Now I'm wearing too many clothes," she whispered.

"Oh no." His lips moved against hers, and he gave her bottom one a bite, setting her nerves ablaze. "We'll need to do something about that." His hands slid under her shirt, and he peeled it away in one easy motion. He lowered her back onto the bed. His bare skin was so warm against hers—like she'd been out in a cold winter, and he was the sun on the first day of spring. She wrapped her legs around his back, hooking him closer.

Like cold water being splashed on them, Crona's scream pierced the air. The two rushed from the bed and threw on their shirts, leaving their jackets still discarded on the floor. Bronx pulled gloves from the floor and put them on. Adrenaline shot through Rei's legs as she followed.

Her thoughts moved to the last time Crona screamed, when she saw Infiernen shoot her brother. Rei's heart pounded in her ears as she feared what the seer saw this time.

# CHAPTER 42

Rei and others found Crona lying on the floor in the kitchen, staring at the ceiling, her eyes wide and wet with tears. She convulsed violently. A shattered porcelain mug lay next to her, along with a pool of water and a red flower. Bronx approached his sister and put his hands on the side of her face, trying to direct her focus on him. Her eyes kept darting around, unable to focus on anything.

"What's happening," Rei asked from the doorway.

"She's having a vision," Bronx said. "Crona," he muttered quietly. "Look at me, Crona."

She finally stared at Bronx, her light eyes locked with his dark ones, and in a voice that was not her own, she gasped, "Death!" Crona's trembling grew more desperate.

"Help me!" cried Bronx. Manden and Arram ran into the room and lifted her up, setting her down in a nearby chair.

"Has it been this bad before?" Rei asked, not knowing what to do as Crona continued to convulse.

"It's never been this bad," Kaz said.

Manden and Arram held Crona down onto the chair.

"Normally she goes blank for a moment and then she's fine."

Crona's convulsing stopped. She closed her eyes for a moment and then opened them.

"Are you okay?" Bronx asked.

She nodded. "I am now. That was intense. There were so many emotions going through my head."

"What did you see?" asked Kaz.

Crona paused for a moment before answering. But her eyes were red and full to the brim with tears. "A battle. Negander against us. There were so many of them. It was really chaotic, I can't see anything specific. Then I saw a forest, there were no leaves on the branches, but there was snow. In the center of a clearing, I saw Rei laying there, dead, and Bronx holding her." Crona glanced at Rei, tears flowing freely. "His gloves were off."

Bronx's eyes went wide and turned to Rei as her heart leaped into her throat.

"Anything else?" Kaz asked.

"There was more, involving other people, but I didn't recognize them."

Bronx nodded, then patted his sister on the shoulder. "All right. But you're feeling better?"

"Yes, thanks," Crona said.

No one else moved, shocked by the news. Bronx said nothing as he stalked away and took the stairs down to the cargo hold, heading toward the infirmary. Rei followed him. A tightness formed in her chest and she couldn't breath. She feared the thought that he may pull away again.

Bronx stood with his back to her, not uttering a word.

"Bronx," began Rei.

"Don't." He shook his head. "I can't believe this. She said it wasn't going to happen."

"You don't know what it meant," Rei said.

He turned to face her. "Something changed. You heard what she said. 'His gloves were off.' I'm going to kill you, Rei." A tear ran down his beautiful face.

They stared at each other. The silence became deafening as the meaning of the vision hung between them.

"So what do we do?" she asked.

"We? No, what am I going to do?" he whispered.

"It may not be set in stone. Crona told me her visions are sometimes like options. Maybe it's only a possibility if we're not careful."

"Exactly. We should be careful. I've had nightmares about it since the moment I met you. I've watched you die, but I've at least convinced myself they were the results of my fear. But the fact that I'm going to kill you means that at some point we are not careful." Bronx sighed. "I should never have said anything to you. We should never have kissed. We shouldn't have . . ." He put his hand to his lips, the hand that touched her. "I should have maintained my distance."

He refused to meet her gaze. His hollow dark eyes stared at the curtain of vines along the far wall.

"Don't, Bronx," she whispered. She knew that look. It was the same one he wore when he told her she terrified him. He was going to push her away. "Don't say it."

"I can't handle this. I think we should end it."

Pain pierced through her chest as her heart broke. Just like that, it was over. What hurt her most wasn't his fear of his power—it was that he didn't even want to try and make it work.

"No," she whispered.

"What?"

"I'm not leaving you."

His eyes were pained. "It's for the best."

"What is wrong with you?" she yelled. "You run away at the first sign of emotional discomfort. You fucking coward."

"And what is wrong with you, woman?" he called back. "Where in the gods' names is your sense of fucking self-preservation? Don't you get it? I'm going to kill you."

"Only when you touch me. Not when you speak to me,

not when you look at me." Her voice grew hoarse. "I don't understand you, Bronx. You're quick to help others when they start breaking down, but when you need help, you shove people away." She thought about how they first met, and the panic that struck when she saw all the blood on her. His touch was so calm and his eyes so comforting. His voice had helped her remember to breathe again. The light in her darkness. Why couldn't she be that for Bronx? "Being strong doesn't always mean saving others," she said. "Sometimes it means realizing when you need help, too." Tears fell down her cheeks. "Don't push me away."

He closed his eyes. "But I can't let you die. It would destroy me." He walked away from her.

With her last shred of dignity, Rei sighed. "Well, I don't know what to tell you, then." She turned and walked back up the stairs.

Hundreds of thoughts ran through her head, but Bronx's voice broke through, repeating, "I should have maintained my distance."

The agony that left a hole in her chest was worse than anything she had felt. She stopped and turned on Bronx. "You know what? I'm not finished."

He stopped but refused to face her. "What?" he whispered.

"First: Fuck you. Fuck you for thinking that you have to go through this alone."

"But my—"

"No." She breathed hard as she waited for him to turn to her, but he didn't. "You know I dreamed of Micaela and Atrius before we met. Just like you did. But what I didn't tell you was that I had to witness Micaela losing Atrius. I watched you die. I watched the poison take you in a slow death." Her voice broke. "That was the worst pain I felt in my entire life, and it was just an echo of someone else's. A memory. At least I thought it was the worst, until now. What hurts more is the idea that you walk this plane of existence—you are real—and I know you love me and yet . . . you won't even look at me right now." The last she whispered. The pain came in waves, and a new one crashed into her as tears streamed down her face.

Bronx finally faced her, his jaws clenched, his dark eyes pained.

"I'm going to die someday, Bronx." She took several calming breaths. Any minute now she would lose her resolve. "And if it's my time to go, I would rather it be in your arms and not at the hands of someone like Infiernen or the Sovereign. I don't want to end up like Micaela." She turned, unable to bear looking at him anymore. "I already told you that I am willing to wait. I have made my decision about us. So make up your fucking mind," she spat before she stomped upstairs.

Crona met her on the stairs. The two women stared at each other for what felt like an eternity before Crona reached and grabbed Rei, giving her a tight hug. Rei felt the dam break, and a shudder ravaged through her. She didn't want to cry here. Not now. But it felt good to be held, to have someone to comfort her. Luckily, the hug was brief. Crona kissed Rei clumsily on the cheek and continued downstairs to her brother.

Rei reached the top of the stairs and saw Arram, Kaz, and Manden near the kitchen. They must've heard everything but said nothing and allowed Rei to walk silently to the ladies bunk. She sat down on the bed, her back against the wall. Her chest hurt. Her eyes fell on the discarded jackets on the floor, and the memory of their short time together returned. Ecstasy to heartbreak all in a manner of minutes. It was a cruel joke. Rei choked on her own sobs.

Manden came by and leaned against the door frame. "You okay?" he asked.

Rei shook her head, and tears continued to fall.

Manden entered the room, shut the door, and sat down next to her. The two said nothing for a while.

"I'm sorry," said Manden quietly.

"For what?"

"For everything you and Bronx have to go through. It must be rough."

"That's a word for it. Rough." Rei's voice shook. "You're certainly a master word smith. Such words of kindness."

Manden winced. "Tara's better at these things. I wish she was here."

"I wish she was too."

"If it's any consolation, it can't get worse. In fact, I think it'll get better. Bronx will figure out how to use his powers, and the two of you can be together."

Rei said nothing. Manden was terrible at this. She rubbed her nose and sniffed. The weight in her chest made it difficult to breathe, but she kept taking deep breaths. Her body wouldn't allow for anything else.

Manden reached out and took her hand, squeezing it gently. "Just take it one day at a time."

Rei nodded but her eyes burned as they welled with tears. She sighed again and wiped her face. "I just wish the pain would end," she whispered. "I really don't need this shit right now."

Manden squeezed her hand tighter. "I know, kid. I know."

# CHAPTER 43



"Leave me alone, Crona," Bronx said to his sister, who stood in the doorway.

"No." She entered the infirmary and sat on the bed opposite him. She watched him as he pulled off his gloves and rubbed his eyes. "You two make quite the pair. You really know how to hurt each other."

"I fucked up," he breathed. "I panicked." He raked his hands through his hair. "I just can't control myself around her. I never realized how much I craved contact until she . . . until we . . ." He sighed. "I can't go on like this. I have to do something about these stupid powers. But to make her wait is unfair."

"Says you or her? Really think about what you're insinuating. Do you really want her to move on and be with someone else?"

"Yes? No? I don't know."

Crona scoffed. "Liar. You know exactly what you want. You just think you're being selfless."

"And is that a bad thing?"

"In this instance, yes. Be selfish, Bronx. What do you want?"

He said nothing as he studied his hands. He remembered how her skin felt under his fingers, how she moved against his touch. He knew what he wanted but couldn't muster the strength to utter the words.

"What do you want, Bronx? Say it."

He shook his head. It was better this way. Rei needed to be with someone who could give her the things he couldn't. No one should have to deny themselves like he did.

"Bronx?" Crona hissed.

"Her. I want her," he yelled. "I want her to be mine just like I will always be hers." A surprise rush of relief surged through him. The clouds in his mind cleared, and everything around him brightened. For the first time, he felt the smallest glimmer of hope. "I will always be hers," he repeated, almost inaudibly.

"You wanna hug it out?" His sister's self-righteousness knew no bounds.

He snorted. "Still determined for that hug, aren't you?"

"I told you, one day I will succeed." She smirked. "Good. Now that that's settled, I'm going to get to work." She hopped off the bed and headed toward the door.

"Where are you going?"

She turned around and leaned on the door frame. "Well, I told you that I saw a future where you learned your powers and didn't kill her. Now that I have this other vision —it means something's changed. I need to pinpoint that moment so we know how to keep Rei alive. I have some more flowers in my locker."

"Crona. You shouldn't take that drug anymore. We already know what changed."

"Oh?"

He hated to admit it. But not much time had passed between the two visions and only one thing had happened in between.

"We—she and I . . ." They should have taken it slowly, but he was too eager and he could never deny her.

"Bah." She waved her hand dismissively. "You're just grasping at straws. I've had plenty of visions since the two of you became an item. It's not that. I got it under control."

He and Crona shared the same stubbornness, so trying to convince her not to do something would only make her do the opposite. Still, he refused to give his blessing.

Rei's words rushed to the forefront of his mind. Don't push her away. She had told him that she could wait for the rest while he sorted things out. He knew she'd meant what she said. He had to have faith in her.

"I should go talk to Rei." He joined Crona at the door, but she stepped in his path.

His sister made a face. "You might want to wait. Emotions ran high just now, and I think for your safety, you should let her cool down first."

Bronx furrowed his eyebrows. "Okay," he said, feeling lost. Crona left him alone with his thoughts as he ran through hundreds of scenarios in his head. He didn't resurface until they reached Kepler IV.

Bronx stepped off the ship first, just as a blustery cold wind blew through his clothes, chilling him to the bone. Oh, how he hated winter here, especially because the people of Kepler IV were dependent on wood stoves and not a solar heating system like normal people. The tree huggers on the planet saw to that—they wanted to minimize the carbon footprint of Kepler IV so most modern technology was forbidden.

The port sat on the outskirts of the city of Fabrecido. People shuffled briskly, bundled up as white flakes showered them.

His heart beat fast. Snow. Just like in Crona's vision.

To his left, Rei stepped out of the *Luciernaga*; the powdery snow landed softly on her face and peppered her hair like a crystal veil.

"Cold," said Rei as if surprised.

Manden stuck out his hand out. "Ugh, snow. That's going to make nights outside unbearable."

"Agreed," Arram said as the others joined. "I can tell you from experience, it is as horrible as you can imagine. Living here was the coldest six months of my life."

Crona handed Rei and her brother heavy coats. "Thank you," Rei said as she put it on. The russet-colored leather had a thick fur lining.

"Where did these coats come from?" Arram asked.

"Manden's always prepared. In the cargo hold are trunks full of supplies for any weather on almost any planet."

Bronx felt those green eyes on him as he readjusted the straps to his pack. He met her gaze, trying to read her face—hoping that any damage he'd caused could be undone. The snow floated around them as though time itself slowed. They were Volocio. Time was on their side. She told him she could wait for the rest.

He reached out and took her hand. Even through the leather, he felt her warmth. When this was all over, he would hold onto her and never let her go. Detachment was no longer an option.

"I'm sorry," he said. "You're right. I want to make this work. I do think it's best that we hold off on physical contact for a while."

"I know," she whispered.

"But I'm still yours." His cupped her cheek. "Always. I hope you know that."

"You won't run away?"

He shook his head. "Never. If I run, it'll be to you, not away."

Rei smiled and his knees grew weak. "I'm going to hold you to that promise, Bronx Manca." She squeezed his hand.

"So where to next?" Crona asked, watching her brother and interrupting his thoughts.

"The nearest bar," Manden said.

"Shouldn't we start at the Temple of Tasya?" Kaz asked.

"After the nearest bar," said Manden. "I'm going to need a drink before I'm expected to deal with this cold."

"You're saying we shouldn't expect you to deal with this weather sober?" asked Crona.

"Exactly." Manden winked.

"Well, let's find you a bar and get this mission going," Rei's cousin said with a smirk. "Any suggestions? Bronx? Arram? You were the ones who were here before."

"There's the Crazy Horse," Arram said. "That has a good reputation."

Bronx remembered the bar but had no desire to return to it. His memories of his time here as a student swirled around him, tainted by the truth he wasn't ready to confront. He hadn't visited this planet since the Battle of the Fortress—the battle where he met Infiernen.

A little voice reminded him that he still needed to come clean about one more detail surrounding his mentor. He never told a soul about Niklaryn's connection with Infiernen, why he assumed Rei's brother walked away with the Negander that day. But he swore an oath to Urius that he wouldn't breathe a word to anyone. Niklaryn's image of the perfect Federation soldier was still important to the cause and the truth could devastate morale. Bronx agreed with Urius but for his own reasons. He didn't want to see the look on Rei's face if she ever learned the truth.

"I remember," Bronx said. "It's a bit of a walk. Are you sure you wouldn't rather visit another closer one? Jay's Tavern or the Bluebird?"

"Yeah, there are closer ones," said Rei's brother. "But

from what I heard, I think this occasion warrants a trip to the Horse."

"Why?" Rei asked.

Bronx turned to her and smiled. "That's where Niklaryn loved to go. It's where he met Artema."

The group weaved through a crowd until they reached the market square. Bronx led them from there to a small side street just as the snow began to fall heavier, and a thin layer of white crunched under his boots. Even though Bronx was no stranger to winter, he still felt it was unnaturally cold on Kepler IV. He wrapped his arms around his chest, trying to maintain some of his body heat.

Their current path brought them to another small plaza, and on the other side stood a small two-story tavern with a wooden outline of a rearing horse hanging outside. The lights on the second floor drew Bronx's attention. The windows were open, and the sound of boisterous laughter rang out into the cold air. He remembered celebrating quite often in those rooms.

Bronx opened the door, and a gust of warm air engulfed him. He brushed the quickly melting snow from his face and hair as he entered.

The bar stood off to one side with bottles of different liquors in a pyramid behind the bartender, while the other half of the bar was filled with tables, benches, and chairs.

"This reminds me of Coronta Bar," said Rei, appearing at his side.

"Where?" asked Bronx.

"The bar where Rei grew up," offered Manden.

They found a table large enough to fit all of them near the back and sat down. Within moments, a server came to take their orders.

"I want the strongest liquor you have—on the rocks," Manden said.

"Same," Rei said, rubbing her hands together, while Bronx and his sister ordered ales. Arram and Kaz ordered water.

"So, we've gotten you your drink," Kaz said. "When we're done, then can we go to the temple?"

Manden nodded.

Bronx took in the sight of the bar—it hadn't changed in the decade since he had last visited. He remembered coming all the time with his mentor. It wouldn't have surprised him to learn Niko liked coming here because it had also reminded him of this Coronta Bar. Or maybe it was because it was where Nik had met Artema.

In his mind's eye, he still saw his mentor standing at the bar, ordering a drink, his tall frame leaning against the counter, chatting with the bartender. Bronx saw him laughing at some joke, his bright blue eyes shining. Niklaryn always had a good sense of humor.

His breathing slowed as he lost himself in the memory. Those were good times. Back when everything was simpler: before Infiernen, before his powers. But it was also before Rei.

As the server returned with their orders, Crona pointed behind them. "Well, look at that."

The group followed Crona's gaze to a shelf with several lit candles, some random objects, a few small statues of Mica and Kazimir, along with a couple of small pictures. Above was a sign that read: *To those of the Federation who have fallen to free Kepler IV.*

"Is that what Niklaryn looked like?" asked Crona, pointing to a picture on the far left. Rei stood and walked over to the shelf to get a closer glimpse and Bronx followed suit. Sure enough, it was a picture of his mentor smiling. "This sure looks like an altar, worshiping these fallen heroes," Crona said. "As opposed to some kind of homage." Crona turned to Kaz. "Isn't that considered a kind of blasphemy?"

Kaz merely shrugged. "Well, the Prophet Jans once said that the gods were the 'The Lords, our Gods, that we shall not have any other gods besides them.' I'm sure that a fanatic would agree with you. But in this case, I think it's simply a way of paying respects to people who gave their lives for this fight. The god statues are there to ask that their souls are protected on their way to paradise."

"On that note," added Manden, "I knew Jans personally. I'll tell you what: the man was a drunk who stole that line from our own religion. I honestly wouldn't heed everything that man said."

"What? More of a drunk than you?" teased Crona.

Manden narrowed his eyes. "Ha. Ha."

"Did the one true god come from Tas'und'eash?" asked Kaz.

"No. It originated from Earth, but the Volocio still believe in the old religions, while those here in Tyre eventually worshiped us." Manden chuckled. "Oh, how the human mind works."

Bronx watched Rei. Her eyes never left the picture of her brother.

"Are you alright?" Bronx asked. She blinked before giving him a half-hearted smile.

"I'm fine."

"You miss him, don't you?"

She nodded. "Yes, very much."

He turned to the bar, half expecting to find Niklaryn there as he had always been. "I miss him too."

"He certainly was a handsome guy," Crona said, taking a sip from her ale when her eyes glazed over.

Everyone turned and watched her.

Crona blinked several times, her aquamarine eyes growing wide. "Oh shit," she whispered.

"What? What was the vision?" asked Manden.

She looked at Bronx with a question in her eyes. His heart raced. Had she found the moment they'd spoken of? A way to save Rei. She didn't even need to drink from the flower this time. "I think I have been drinking too much of that tea. I was probably hallucinating," was all she said.

"Oh yeah?" asked Bronx with a frown. "What makes you say that?"

Crona's eyes darted from the picture of the Daer on the shelf, back to her brother, her eyes unreadable. "Nothing."

Bronx's heart pounded in his chest. He had to know what she saw.

In fact, no one said anything. They sat quietly for a few moments more, sipping their drinks until they finished. They grabbed their things to leave, and each left a few coins.

As they left, Bronx pulled his sister aside. "What was in that vision?"

"Why do you ask?" she asked, trying to avoid his gaze.

"Because I have to know what you saw."

"All I remember was Niklaryn with a weird collar around his neck." She stared at her brother. "And you sat on top of him, punching him. Why did you do that?"

Bronx stumbled back. A collar? It was an odd detail to note. As for the rest, he could imagine a reason why he would punch Niklaryn. "We'll probably find him and join forces with him. Me punching him was probably us training together."

"The look on your face suggested it wasn't training. You were angry. And that collar . . ." She bit her lip. "That collar is important."

Bronx shrugged. "He always had a weird thing for jewelry. Maybe I'm angry because he has shitty taste."

Crona rolled her eyes. "You're such a terrible liar."

"What are you talking about?"

"That comment makes no sense. I think you know why you would want to punch your mentor."

His heart stopped. This was not the conversation he wanted to have with anyone. Ever. He turned and followed the others out of the tavern. The powder had turned to slush, and Bronx felt its cold bite through his boots, but he ignored it.

"Does Rei know?" Crona's voice pierced into his thoughts as she followed him.

The rest of the Volocio trudged quite a few steps ahead and well out of earshot. He turned to his sister, still in the doorway.

"What did you see?" he demanded. "What all did you see?"

"Enough to know we can't trust Niklaryn."

He said nothing, but a voice in his head screamed, *fuck, fuck, fuck, fuck.*

"Everything alright?" Rei asked, watching them.

Bronx tried to smile. "Yeah, we're fine. Just Crona telling me I'm an idiot. Nothing new."

Crona laughed, but it was forced. "Yeah, my brother's a moron!"

Rei furrowed her eyebrows, confused. "Uh . . . okay." She turned and continued along with the group.

Crona shook her head. "I need time to process all of

this." She picked up her pace and brushed past him to join the others.

"Please, don't say anything to anyone," Bronx said.

Crona turned and stared daggers at her brother. "How dare you ask that of me! We are here to find Niklaryn, to find where he's been hiding all these years, yet the answer was staring us right in the face." She walked away. "The others have to know."

Bronx reached out, grabbed her, and pulled her into a hug. Crona froze. "Please. Have I ever steered you wrong?" he whispered. "Please, trust me now. Promise me. Don't say anything. They can't know. Not yet." He slowly let his sister go. She looked up at him.

"You better not make me regret this," she snarled.

# CHAPTER 44

Bronx trailed behind, not paying attention to where they walked. Memories flooded him everywhere he turned.

As they entered the temple, Bronx remembered the Negander attack. He remembered how he and Niklaryn took down a big group of them. Negander threatened Artema on these very steps and Niklaryn had saved her. Everything reminded him of his former mentor, as well as the secret he had been keeping for the last several years. The guilt of such a secret weighed heavily on him with every step he took.

He believed Niklaryn betrayed them and joined Infiernen in the Dominion.

Now Crona knew. He didn't know if he felt relief or dread. A part of him hoped he was wrong. The idea of his mentor fighting for the other side hurt. Despite what his sister thought, now was not the right time to tell the others. Their goal was to find Artema, and they should focus on it. Maybe Artema could shed better light on her husband; she would've known him best. Until they found Artema, there was no point in shattering Rei's hopes, especially if there was a sliver of a chance he was wrong about Niklaryn.

There was more to the story of what happened to Niklaryn, but trauma tore holes in Bronx's memory of that day and the details remained hazy. Whatever happened, Bronx had done nothing to stop Niklaryn. He couldn't. At least that's what he told himself. That's what Urius said in a vain attempt to reassure Bronx when he told the Federation leader what transpired. The loud bang of a heavy knock snapped Bronx back to reality.

He stood on the all-too-familiar steps of the Temple of Tasya. The days following Niklaryn's disappearance were mainly a blur, but he remembered very clearly bringing Artema here after he had found her in the apartment, after what Infiernen had tried to do to her. She barely held on as Bronx carried her through the threshold to the other priestesses. He only stayed long enough to see if she survived, then he left and never came back. He didn't want anything to remind him of what he had seen that day.

He recalled the day being dark, the colors muted; however, today the sun shone and the falling snow brightened the room.

Head Priestess Mara greeted them when they entered the temple. Bronx remembered her, but the passing years were visible in the few strands of gray streaking her auburn hair. The laugh lines around her eyes ran a little deeper, but her smile never changed.

"Bronx! How wonderful to see you again after so many years."

"It's good to see you again, High Priestess."

"How many times do I have to remind you to call me Mara? We have been through too much together, helping Kepler IV gain its independence, to continue with such formality." The woman noticed Bronx's other companions, her eyes growing wide as she recognized them.

"The god queen and god king," she whispered as she bent to her knees in front of Rei and Manden, head down.

"Oh please, no." Rei tried to pull Mara onto her feet. "It's really not necessary."

Mara wouldn't look at Rei, but tears welled in her eyes.

"You will have to forgive me. I never thought I would see the Second Coming in my lifetime."

Rei moved more directly into Mara's line of sight, her hands still on the priestess's shoulders, and smiled. "Trust me. It's not all pomp and circumstance. We need your help."

Mara stared at Rei for several seconds before coming out of her reverie. "Of course. I was about to make coffee. Come with me. There's enough for all."

The group followed Mara out of the back of the temple to a small building in the back. Bronx remembered only having been let into the front room near the kitchen. Men were not allowed in the upper levels where the priestesses slept. The mostly bare stone-gray walls boasted a few paintings, the majority of the goddess Tasya with her midnight skin. A vibrant golden scarf, embroidered with green, yellow, and blue flowers, hid her dark hair. A Benot painting of Mica hung next to Tasya's painting.

The group sat along a large wooden table as Mara asked one of the other priestesses to make coffee for everyone. Bronx took the chair between Kaz and Arram. He wanted to sit next to Rei, but she had already taken a place between Manden and Crona.

Once everyone settled in, Mara began. "First, I am grateful that the Volocio have graced us with their presence. Ever since I saw the footage of your battle on Trappist V, I had hoped to be able to see you with my own eyes before I met the god of death. But I have to ask something." She gazed directly at Bronx. "Does your being here have something to do with Artema's disappearance?"

Bronx nodded but did it so minutely he wasn't sure that anyone else noticed.

"She's been gone for over four years. You're a little late."

The blood drained from Bronx's face. "Bernie and I," he stumbled, "we take blame for neglecting Artema."

"You more than Bernadette, I suppose? Since she at least came as often as she could, while you haven't visited since you brought her here to be healed."

Bronx's ears burned. Mara was always quick to point out the truth, even if he didn't want to hear it.

"I couldn't come back here. Not after everything that happened with Niklaryn. Not even for Artema."

"And yet here you are. Why?"

"We're worried about Infiernen finding her. We only discovered her disappearance recently, and we are here to help her and protect her."

By then, the lower priestess had returned with a tray of mugs filled with coffee. Mara pursed her lips and didn't respond as she placed a filled mug before each of the group members, leaving Bronx for last. He had received an "I ♥ the God King" mug. Life certainly had a sense of humor, he thought, as a vivid memory came to him of Artema drinking from that very same cup. It was right after Artema and Niko got married, and they had come to the apartment to celebrate, before Infiernen destroyed everything. The color had faded and the rim was chipped, but it definitely belonged to Artema.

"You will have to excuse me if I don't seem entirely convinced. You knew Infiernen could come back for her, and you did nothing. I am the one that kept her hidden and safe."

"Please," Arram said. All eyes turned to him. "We just recently found out that she is my"—he paused and looked at Rei—"I mean *our* sister-in-law. She's the only link Rei and I have to Niklaryn, and we want her safe just as much as Bernie and Bronx."

Mara looked over at Rei with mild surprise, but then narrowed her eyes as her gaze returned to Arram. "I recognize you. You were the young man branded outside the temple."

Arram's violet eyes grew wide. "You remember that?"

Bronx remembered Arram telling him the story of how his powers first manifested at the hands of Infiernen.

"Artema came to me that day, afraid Infiernen had found her. She must've thought he was hunting her. But she didn't disappear; she went into hiding," Mara finally said.

"Where?" asked Bronx.

"I don't know, exactly. She wouldn't tell me. But she went west, toward the Fortress of Riodan. She would have definitely made it to Ixchel, but that's the extent of what I know. She may have gone back to performing. She always did have a beautiful voice."

Rei scanned the rest of the group. "I guess we are heading to Ixchel. So? Shall we go?"

There was no point in wasting any more time. Bronx was the first to stand but the last to leave.

"Mara," he said, once everyone else was out of earshot. "I'm sorry that I didn't do more for Artema. But I intend to set things right, and I won't fail her again."

The high priestess nodded. "I know. I can see in your eyes that you have had your own burdens since that day. You are not the same young man who brought Artema to us all those years ago. I know you still care for her. When you do find her, please tell her that she is in our thoughts and prayers."

"I will. Thank you." He followed his friends. The midday sun hung high in the sky and, unlike earlier, the streets teemed with crowds of people.

The temple sat just off of another courtyard. There

were restaurants and cafes along the perimeter, all bursting with patrons. People filled the courtyard, despite the cold winter, and the smell of delicious food, the voices of the people, and the clang of utensils wafted out from the open doors.

"So what all do we need so that we can begin for Ixchel?" Rei asked, turning to Arram.

"We'll need horses," Bronx said. "And possibly a guide or even a caravan to ride with."

"Horses?"

"Yeah. Kepler IV has always been environmentally conscious in trying to protect the forests that make up most the planet," Manden said. "You may have noticed that there are no vehicles here. They don't allow many because it would ruin the landscape and their very fragile ecosystem. As a result, Kepler IV is a tiny planet that is the most under-developed in terms of technology, so we will ride while we're here."

Crona whipped out her touchscreen and began swiping. "To get to Ixchel, we'll have to go west, through the May Forest. If we keep up a good pace, we can make it there by tomorrow night."

"So why don't we split up? Rei, Manden, and I can procure rides," Kaz suggested. "The rest of you, why don't you replenish our supplies? We'll meet back here in . . . say . . . about an hour?" They agreed and went their separate ways.

# CHAPTER 45

Rei followed Kaz and Manden through the streets to a long line of stables, each owned by different families, each offering their horses for travel or as pack animals.

She raised her hood around her face. Attracting a crowd would not help their cause at the moment. She was glad she left her staff on the *Luciernaga,* in case it made her more recognizable, but she made a mental note to pick it up before they left town. The other two did the same thing—Kaz had experience living life in the shadows from his years of travel.

Someone grabbed Rei's shoulder and pulled her into an alleyway. Before Rei could yelp, a hand pressed against her lips. She recognized to whom it belonged.

"Sky?" she whispered as her cousin lifted her palm.

"What are you doing, Rei? What if someone saw you? You know there is a traitor in the Federation that would love to sell your location to the Dominion."

"I'm trying to be careful." Rei pulled her hood across her face, hoping to retreat further into its shadow. "How did you find me?"

"I followed you with my shuttle. You weren't very good at sneaking out of the Underground and Manden's ship is hard to miss."

Rei's pulse raised. "Does Urius know?"

Skylar shook her head. "No. I thought I would come here first and defuse the situation before he found out. This better be important. You don't want Urius as an enemy."

"We're on a mission. Please say you didn't see me." Rei narrowed her eyes.

"Sister?" Kaz asked, placing a hand on Sky's arm, which she shrugged off. Manden stood a few steps from them.

"Kaz," sneered Skylar before facing her younger brother. "Why are you guys being so reckless? You know Rei's being hunted."

"It was my idea," said Rei, her voice low. "They're just following me."

"You are indeed Nik's sister. Idiots with your recklessness." The Daer shook her head, a small knowing smile on her lips. "What's the mission?"

"We're looking for Artema," Kaz responded before Manden or Rei could stop him.

"Kaz!" Rei exclaimed.

"It's fine, Rei. We can trust my sister."

Sky's blue eyes stared into Rei's green ones. "Artema?" Skylar's eyebrows furrowed, and Rei could have sworn that her cousin's lips twisted as though saying the name of Niklaryn's wife left a nasty taste in her mouth.

"She is in danger of Infiernen finding her. That's why we're here," Kaz continued.

Rei desperately wanted to know what Skylar thought, but the woman's pale eyes remained unreadable.

Manden approached and laid a protective hand on Rei's shoulder. "What are you thinking, Skylar?" the redhead asked.

"Do you need help?" she said finally.

The three Volocio blinked in surprise. Rei didn't expect Sky to want to help them. While she and Sky got along well enough, she couldn't shake the feeling that there was history between Artema and her cousin.

"No, thank you," said Rei. "We should get going." She then stared pointedly at Kaz.

He nodded and approached a nearby stall with the name "Paraise" at the top. One of the stable hands stared, mouth open, as Kaz, Manden, and Rei all entered. Kaz spoke with the young woman, leaving Manden and Rei with Skylar, who didn't appear to want to leave Rei's side.

"Why offer to help us, Sky?" Rei asked. "I know you don't like the Volocio."

The Daer winced. "I like you, Rei." Her eyes flicked in Manden's direction. "To be honest, I was jealous. I've worked my whole life to be a Daer, and yet we are no longer Urius's favorites. You are. The Volocio."

Rei scoffed. "That's it? Excuse me, but I have to call bullshit. I don't believe your coldness toward someone like your brother is a product of jealousy."

"Why not?" Sky shrugged. "He's our parents' favorite—ever since he was recognized as a Volocio. He brought fame to the family whereas my hard work didn't."

"Being Urius's pet has been anything but beneficial to me." Rei clenched her fists until her nails bit into the palms of her hands. "I'm treated like some fragile doll to be hidden away and then paraded when it's convenient for him. I have spent my whole life learning to fight—to protect myself—only to be locked up. The others don't like it either. Trust me when I say the Volocio want to fight alongside you. We should be a team."

Skylar pursed her lips. "It means a lot to hear you say that. Perhaps I have let my jealousy blind me."

Relief flooded Rei. "We really need you as our ally, Sky."

"Trust me, Rei. I'm not your enemy."

Rei grew cold again as Infiernen's voice echoed the same words in her head.

"Great news, our cousin has enough horses for us." Kaz returned, beaming.

"Another cousin?" Rei asked Manden with a raised eyebrow.

Kaz pointed to the sign. "One of our aunts, she married a Paraise. They aren't here, but the stable hands were more than happy to give us a family discount."

Rei scoffed. Arram was right—there were Ettowas everywhere.

"You're heading to Ixchel, then?" asked Skylar.

Kaz nodded.

"Let me come with you. I want to help, and it'll be better than sitting here waiting for my informants to respond."

Rei turned to Manden and noticed he was still uncertain as he tapped his food and bit his lip, but he answered Sky. "We're happy to have you." The snow began to fall in bigger flakes. "Let's meet up with the others and get going. It's getting colder by the second."

# CHAPTER 46

The snow finally stopped long after they rode out of the town of Fabrecido. The cold still permeated into every possible opening in Rei's clothing, and she couldn't think of what else to do to make it better.

"Now you see why I hate snow," Manden said with a smirk as he rode next to her. "It rarely snows in Munda. It's my paradise."

It didn't snow in Ballarat either, Rei wanted to say. She pulled her coat tighter around her as she grumbled.

"I told you." Arram straightened on his horse, which meandered beside hers. "The cold is as terrible as you can imagine."

He rubbed his hands together vigorously. She remembered from their talks that he had lived in places colder than this. She didn't know how anyone could ever get used to this level of freezing.

"Winter here is the worst," muttered Bronx.

"Oh yes, having to wake up in the middle of the night to put more wood into the stove was one of my favorite pastimes," her brother commented dryly.

"Your powers first manifested when you lived here, right, Arram?" asked Crona from where she rode in front of Rei.

He nodded. "My grandparents and I had been living in Fabrecido for about six months. I was rarely allowed outside and only with an escort. I never understood why until Infiernen found me—when he branded me."

"At the Temple of Tasya?"

"Correct. Now that I think about it, I remember meeting a woman named Artema when I was there. She was very kind. Sharp tongue. She healed my brand."

"That information would've been helpful before, Arram," Crona grumbled.

"How? We left Kepler IV almost immediately afterward, and apparently she ran off around the same time. The last time I saw her was at the temple."

"What did she look like?" asked Rei, her breath coming out in puffs. She was desperate for any conversation to draw her focus away from her chattering teeth.

"Statuesque with dark skin. Her hair was up in a thousand tiny braids." Arram scratched his chin.

"She also had a mean left hook," Bronx said with a chuckle. "She was very sweet, but she was not someone you wanted as an enemy."

Rei twisted in her saddle to Skylar behind her. "You knew Artema, too, right? What did you think of her?"

Sky shrugged. "She always seemed to think she was better than everyone else. I didn't care for her."

Rei's eyes flicked in Bronx's direction. His eyebrows drew together, indicating that he also puzzled over Sky's comment, but he said nothing.

They rode silently through the trees. In the dead of winter, no other sound carried through the forest, as though the snow absorbed it all. Rei only experienced this all-consuming silence one other time: when she ventured into the Badlands outside of Ballarat.

She caught Bronx watching her more than once. He always smiled when their eyes met. She still wanted nothing more than to lean in and feel his lips on hers, but with Crona's vision looming over them, she knew to keep her distance.

At one point, they rested under a large tree, its branches spreading wide, keeping the snow from reaching the ground. There they found enough dry twigs to build a small fire. Bronx used the opportunity to show Rei a photograph of the wedding on his touchscreen.

Niklaryn beamed with his arms wrapped around a beautiful woman with dark skin, black hair, and a white flowing dress. Rei couldn't take her eyes off of him. Her mouth dropped open when she saw who the other guests were: Skylar, Urius, a young eighteen-year-old Bernie, and a sixteen-year-old Bronx with a baby-faced Sariah hanging on his arm.

"I didn't realize that you and Niko were so close, Sky," Kaz said, studying the photograph over Rei's shoulder.

"We were year mates. We were quite close growing up, and Nik always came to stay with our parents when our classes weren't in session. You were still living at the Temple of Aladonis at the time."

Rei remembered Niklaryn telling her stories of his holidays with family. She never told him how jealous she was of the opportunity.

"She was with us on Trappist, right?" Arram pointed to Sariah. "She's looking rather cozy with you, Bronx."

Bronx shrugged. "Sariah and I have a history. We've known each other since we were children. She's from this planet, actually. She was glad when we were stationed here. She loved the idea of coming home."

"Nik and I thought Bronx and Sariah made a beautiful pair," Sky said. "We even joked about what their children would look like with Riah's blonde hair and Bronx's dark eyes."

Rei's cheeks burned at the comment. She knew it was more than jealousy that burned like fire through her veins.

"I feel like there's some unwritten misogynistic law that binds me to ask you if that history would affect my sister," Arram said to Bronx. "You know, in case I'm supposed to fulfill from brotherly duty to defend her virtue or something."

Arram winked at Rei, trying to hold in a laugh. She was grateful for the joke.

"You and I both know your sister needs no one to defend her honor," said the medic. "But no, there's no threat. Sariah and I were young, children almost. Things are different—I am different. The universe had already decided my path long before I was born, and it led me to Rei."

Everyone groaned, making both Rei and Bronx laugh. Rei couldn't have loved him more than in that moment.

"Gods, Bronx," Manden said. "If you were any more saccharine, I'm sure you would've given me a cavity." He stuck his finger in his mouth and jumped. "Ach! You did!"

"You okay, Crona?" Kaz asked, sitting next to her on the other side of the fire. She had been mostly quiet since they had left town. Rei assumed she was just as cold as Rei, but now, by the warm fire, she wondered if it was something else.

"Fine," Crona growled, staring daggers at her brother.

Rei watched as Bronx's face fell. She recalled them arguing outside of the Crazy Horse earlier. Crona had always been very open about her feelings but had yet to utter a word about what transpired between them. It must've been something big. Rei had hoped Bronx would talk to her about it, but then assumed—like all things with him—one must wait. Eventually their break ended, and they decided to cover more ground before nightfall.

# CHAPTER 47

That evening, they found a cave just off their path, big enough for the whole group. It was carved into a lone mountain, one that wouldn't have taken more than a day to walk its circumference. To everyone's relief, Manden announced they would make camp here for the night. As the sun continued to set, the temperature dropped by the second and they were desperate for a reprieve.

Rei's teeth chattered violently as she attempted to untie the straps to her horse's saddle. She didn't understand it. She told her fingers to move, but they refused to listen. They were so stiff.

"I got it," Bronx said, coming to her side. He put his coat over her shoulders. It was deliciously warm and laced with his scent. She had to admit that sage had quickly become her favorite fragrance. He pulled her staff from its straps on her saddle and handed it to her. She watched him untie the saddle with ease.

"I thought you didn't like the cold," she remarked.

"I don't." He pulled the saddle from the horse. "But your lips are turning blue, and I like that less. Go into the cave. I'll build a fire."

Some of their group had already gathered some wood; others were out hunting. The rest set up their belongings well into the back of the cave.

It didn't take Bronx long to get the fire going, and soon Rei basked in its heavenly warmth.

Crona had captured a few rabbits and, between her and Arram, had them skinned and roasted over the fire in minutes. Rei found that the little horrid beasts no longer frightened her, and she smiled at the thought.

The group ate in silence, still too tired to start talking right away. Manden eventually broke the ice as he lightly hummed, then sang ballads from Tas'und'eash. Most were in Castelan but all were beautiful.

"How did you and Micaela meet?" Crona asked as Manden finished.

"On the battlefield. But we technically met before that time as children. We didn't remember much of each other at that point. Her father and my mother had fallen in love and run off together, causing a rift between our countries, so there weren't many diplomatic trips between Munda and Dinay.

"Before they left, my mother bestowed upon me the secret of the possible location of origin of all Volocio: Earth. Micaela's father told her the same, and she acted on the information first. I found it shortly afterward, and what resulted was the Battle of the Badlands.

"What we didn't know was that Earth was not only still inhabited but also part of the Tyre Empire—before there was a Dominion or a Federation. We found out the hard way when we were both captured by Emperor Tynan Praymer, an ancestor of Sovereign Praymer."

Skylar pulled out a wineskin. "So what made you become friends?" She took a sip and passed it to Arram.

"Well, we definitely weren't friends at first," he contin-ued. "But we quickly became allies to survive our capture and escape. Fortunately for us, they came to see us as gods, and out of fear for our wrath, they let us go."

So that was it. That was how the religion started—because of a misunderstanding between two differently evolved groups of humans.

"So you mean to tell us that the whole reason we believed in the gods was because it allowed you to escape imprisonment?" Rei asked.

Manden shrugged. "It was a small price to pay to get out of there alive. We may wield great power, but we are grossly outnumbered. We never abused that information to take advantage of the people, except to maintain a certain distance. Micaela was the only one to cross that line and marry a non-Volocio. But she had her reasons."

They sat in silence, passing the wineskin around, listening to the crackling wood as it burned in the fire. As always, Manden left a lot to think about when he dumped a world of information on them concerning their previous incarnations' histories.

When it was time to turn in for the night, Rei made sure to lay her bedroll next to Bronx's. She kept enough of a distance so that they couldn't accidentally touch while they slept. Though the idea pained her—she missed sleeping in his strong arms.

"I hope the conversation about Sariah didn't upset you," he whispered when the cave grew quiet, aside from a few snores. Manden stood at the mouth of the cave, taking first watch.

"How so?"

"Because I didn't wait for you. You weren't my first love."

"I didn't wait for you either." She scoffed. "I know we're supposed to be a part of this epic love story, but we are both still human. We are allowed to have other relationships before meeting the one."

"But Hotara must've known."

Rei thought back to all the late nights she stayed up with her mother. She told Hotara everything: the good, the bad, and the mediocre. "She believed in experience. If she ever had a problem with my relationships, she never told me. But after every heartbreak—the ones I received or inflicted—she would always remind me these experiences would prepare me for something greater in the future."

Bronx rubbed the bridge of his nose with his thumb and forefinger. "If she could see me now, I would probably be a major disappointment." He looked at her. "I'm sorry for all the pain I've caused you."

"I think she expected Atrius. She didn't know what would happen. You and I both know we are not carbon copies of our previous selves."

"And what did you expect?"

The firelight caught in his eyes, reflecting the brown in them. "I don't know." She wondered how Micaela and Atrius met. "But I wouldn't change a thing."

They were so close now. She wanted so desperately to reach out and touch him. To kiss him. If she were fast enough, she could probably steal one. But Crona's vision hung like a veil between them, keeping them apart. There always had to be a barrier, and the reminder weighed heavily on her chest.

"Goodnight, sweetheart," he said, his gaze full of the love he couldn't show by touch.

"Goodnight, my love," she responded, before laying her head on her pillow. She watched him close his eyes with a smile on his lips.

The next day proved warmer. The light reached their side of the mountain. The sun felt delicious on Rei's face. She decided to saddle hers and Bronx's horses, not wanting him to feel like he had to do all the work.

The sun had risen well above the trees when they were

finally packed and saddled up. The light hit the top of the mountain, and only then did Rei notice the ruins.

"What's up there?" she asked, pointing upwards.

"Just old ruins," Bronx said, already ushering his horse forward.

The group glanced up, all except Bronx who fidgeted with his reins. It was as though he wanted to look anywhere but up.

"What is it called?"

"The original name is long forgotten, but now it's known as the Fortress of Riodan," Skylar said.

"The Fortress of . . .?" Rei's voice failed her. She turned to Skylar to find a pained look in her eyes—she knew this place.

Rei clicked her tongue to drive her horse and rode around the side of the mountain. She found a break in the trees that appeared somewhat like a path. She heard the others call her name, but she ignored them. She needed to see this place for herself.

Rei jumped off her horse, tied the creature to a nearby tree, and began her hike. Snow made the steep path slippery. She continued on, using tree branches to hoist herself further up when necessary. Each step caused more dread to fill her belly, and her heart raced faster and faster.

Eventually the path opened to a road, mainly cobblestone and fallen into disarray. Rei assumed no one had wanted to come back after the battle all those years before. She never stopped moving. The slope of the road evened out, but her breath still labored.

The road came around a bend and she saw it: a large stone edifice that towered above her. It was a miracle the behemoth had been overtaken. She knew the Daer and Federation stormed the citadel, but it was obvious the

Dominion and their Negander easily protected themselves and used whatever weaponry they had to take care of their "problem." And yet, the Federation had won, and the planet eventually voted to join their side.

The road continued on through a tunnel that ran under the belly of the beast—the only entrance. She heard one of her companions catching up to her, but she didn't wait to see who. The tunnel wasn't long and opened on the other side to a large courtyard. To her right was a breathtaking view of the valley before her. To her left, the fortress sprawled along a higher peak like a sleeping giant. Most of the stones had crumbled away, while others had been weathered by rain, covered in moss. The courtyard held nothing but open space with a layer of snow. Off in the distance a mound stood tall and Rei approached it as her companion entered the courtyard.

"Rei?" asked Skylar, but Rei didn't acknowledge her. This place was not what she had expected. In her mind, she had always pictured this fortress to be dark and gloomy, filled with so much negative energy that it would strangle her with grief. And yet, despite the light snow that fell, it was peaceful. It was quiet. It held such a violent history and led to the bloody end of too many people, but the energy around her was tranquil.

"We can't be too long. We still have a ways to go if we want to arrive before the sun sets," she heard Sky say. Snow crunched until the Daer stopped at her side. "It's a mass grave," she said, gesturing to the mound before them.

Rei's eyes grew wide. "Of both Dominion and Federation soldiers?"

Sky shook her head. "No, just Dominion. The Federation identified theirs, and the bodies were sent back to their families. Well, the ones they found, anyway."

Rei knew what she meant—they had never found Niklaryn's body, since there was no body to find. Her hand lightly touched her collar where Niklaryn's ring still hung around her neck. She knew they couldn't stay much longer, but she wasn't ready to leave. This place was the last place her brother had seen. Before he disappeared.

She studied her footprints in the snow. Is this the very spot where Infiernen struck him down and captured him? She wanted to know more but felt her time running out.

"What are you hoping to find, Rei?" Skylar asked.

"Something that could tell me more about what happened between my brother and Infiernen. What did you see that day?"

Skylar reached down and picked up a clump of snow, rolling it into a ball in her hands. "Nothing I would want to burden you with."

"Learning what happened to my brother is not a burden."

The Daer fumbled with the ball, tossing it aside. "Infiernen didn't hurt Nik, as far I know. They left the battlefield and I haven't heard from Nik since. I assumed he perished until you pointed him out on the video. How did you know to search for him? Who told you he was alive?"

Rei breathed hard as she debated how to answer. She still wasn't sure she wanted to trust her cousin, but she was desperate. "Infiernen told me," she answered barely above a whisper.

Skylar's head flinched back. "He did? What else did he say?"

"We didn't have an opportunity to sit down over tea. We were in the middle of battle, and he only told me because he wanted me to stop attacking him." Rei fidgeted with the buttons on her coat. "I don't understand what

Infiernen wants. He saved Bronx from his own Negander, shot Arram, and still claims to not be my enemy." The last part slipped out. She didn't mean to reveal that to her cousin. Sweat pooled around her neck and under her arms, despite the chill in the air.

Skylar's mouth hung open. "You seem determined not to believe him, and given his actions, I wouldn't believe him either. Yet you appear unsure."

Rei flung her hands in the air. "I don't know. Maybe because he never killed Niklaryn. They were best friends, so it had to account for something. I fear Infiernen is more important to Niko than I am because he stayed with this monster all these years and never once tried to come back for me." Rei's lips trembled and her eyes burned. She had never uttered that dark thought, not even to Bronx, and she never wanted to believe that Niklaryn willingly abandoned her.

Skylar wrapped an arm around Rei's shoulders and gave her a gentle squeeze. "I don't think Nik would have ever left you behind without a good reason. Nik loves too strongly to do something like that."

"But there's no way to ask. That's why I have to find Artema. Who would know better than his wife?"

"Who indeed." Her blue eyes remained on Rei as she bit her lip. "We should get going. The sooner we get to Ixchel, the sooner you can ask her."

Skylar passed Rei only to be stopped. "What is your problem with Artema?" Rei asked. "I know you don't like her."

Skylar met her gaze and gave a smile that didn't reach her eyes. "Call me protective, but I always thought Nik could do better than Artema. We should leave. We still have a long way to travel."

# CHAPTER 48

The party arrived at the sleepy town of Ixchel well into the evening and after the sun's last rays disappeared over the horizon. They found a hotel just on the outskirts with a few rooms still available. The pale blue half-timbered facade was still visible in the failing light. Rei had never seen a building that color before.

Crona and Bronx entered first to organize lodging. They worried about drawing too much attention from other guests if Rei, Manden, or Kaz showed their faces. Much to Rei's relief, there weren't many guests. A few were scattered among the large benches in the restaurant while another small group settled around a huge circular hearth with a roaring fire.

The owner, a portly young man with thinning hair, led them down the hallway and away from the restaurant. Velvet tapestries covered the hotel's stone walls—most depicting little cherubs frolicking in a meadow, but one tapestry depicted a shining knight with dark hair. He kneeled before a woman in green robes that suspiciously resembled the costume Rei had to wear on Trappist V.

They continued up to the second floor to their rooms, one for the women while the other, down the hall, was for the men. The women's room was a wash of vibrant blues, greens, and purples, or as Crona later described, where peacocks came to die.

"I don't know if I have signal here," Skylar said, lifting her touchscreen toward the ceiling. "I'm going to head downstairs and see if it's better. Hopefully my informants will have more news for me."

Crona waited until Sky closed the door behind her before she spoke. "I don't like Skylar being here," she muttered as they unpacked. "I don't trust her."

"Bad feeling as in vision or instinct?" Rei asked.

"It doesn't matter, something's not right."

Rei understood Crona's concern, but after their moment on the mountain, she saw her cousin differently. Maybe her friend and cousin should sit down and talk. They were on the same side of the war, so surely they could find more common ground.

When they finished unpacking, the group met downstairs at a large bench in the dining hall for dinner.

Rei wanted to ask the hotel owner a few questions. Bronx joined her, and together, they found him at the front desk. The young man's eyes grew wide when he recognized her.

"Hi." She gave him her biggest smile. "I was wondering if you could help us find someone?" She gestured to Bronx. "Can you show the photograph?"

"You are looking for another Volocio, aren't you?" the owner asked. Both Rei and Bronx shook their heads.

"No." Bronx placed his tablet on the desk. "We're looking for this woman." He showed the gentleman the wedding photo and pointed at Artema, his finger conveniently over Nikalryn's face. "She may be a singer or a performer."

The man squinted for a moment before reaching behind the desk for his large glasses. He placed them on his small nose and studied the photograph again. "I know her. She's a singer. Her name is Willow, and she works at the Feather of the Peacock, best club in town. I can get you tickets for tomorrow if you'd like. Tonight is already sold out."

"That would be lovely," Rei said. "Thank you."

Bronx pulled his hand away from the photograph. "We'll need enough for seven."

"Oh, he looks familiar," said the man as he noticed Niklaryn's face.

Bronx quickly yanked the touchscreen away. "He probably just looks like one of your regulars."

The man nodded absentmindedly. "Yeah, a regular."

The pair returned to the others, weaving through half empty benches until they reached the group already seated with pitchers of beer and large chunks of crusty bread between them.

"Apparently, she works at a club." Rei sat next to Arram, who handed her a piece of bread. "We have tickets for tomorrow night." She reached for the glasses of beer Crona had filled for both her and Bronx.

"For all of us?" Crona's eyes darted in Skylar's direction.

"Yes," Bronx replied.

"Is that wise?"

Rei shifted in her seat. Crona had her reservations and had no qualms letting tension between her and Skylar escalate. But Rei couldn't allow that to happen; too much depended on them working as a team.

"I trust Sky," Rei said. "She's aware of the situation surrounding Niko's survival and our fear that he may now be a member of the Dominion. I confided in her about Infiernen and his claiming to not be my enemy."

"I know we've had our disagreements," Skylar said, "but I hope we can put aside our differences for the sake of Nik. I think we should find out the truth about him as well as if Infiernen meant what he said. Perhaps Artema will be helpful. If not, we find a way to contact Infiernen. If he is truly for our side—or at least Rei's side—he can be a powerful ally against the Dominion."

"That's a big 'if', Sky," Kaz said. "Infiernen hasn't done anything to earn our trust over the years. I still don't understand why we are even considering trusting him?"

"He saved Bronx from his own Negander when Rei made it clear he was not to be harmed. I have a feeling Infiernen and Niklaryn had a common goal to make sure Rei was safe. She is the key. Perhaps she can influence him." Sky placed the beer on the table with a satisfying clunk. "We should find a way to get her alone with him."

Rei's face tingled. It never occurred to her that she had leverage with Infiernen. Bronx had said the same thing about Infiernen's and Niklaryn's mutual feelings for Rei. Perhaps there was some truth to it.

"Not alone, but maybe Rei should talk to him," Manden said. "If only we can get him alone without his Dogs."

"If we can discover Infiernen's true motives," Arram added, "maybe we'll understand Niko a little more. I want to know what made our brother follow him."

Rei wiped off some of the condensation from her glass as it dripped onto the table. Her thoughts kept coming back to why Infiernen made enemies of Bronx, Arram, and Artema in the first place. They were a threat, yet Rei was to be protected at all costs. Maybe threatening their lives was what kept Niklaryn bound to Infiernen as a guarantee her brother did whatever the Negander asked. Whatever their bond was, she believed her brother was not a willing participant. If that was so, maybe her influence over Infiernen could free him.

# CHAPTER 49

Bronx dreamed again about the golden forest. The black trunks reached high into the heavens before branching out into thousands of golden leaves. A few fell lazily in front of him, landing on the path before him. Where it led, he didn't know.

The scent of lavender tickled his nose, and the ground absorbed his footsteps as he walked. Something told him that if he continued on this path, he would find others. Others like him.

"Atrius?" the echoing voice called him. He turned to see where the voice came from, but he was alone. He was always alone.

But something changed.

To his left stood a gate. He had seen it before in his dreams but was never close enough to inspect it. As he drew closer, he saw that each rail shimmered like a white pearl fresh from the sea. He reached out and touched it. It was smooth and cool under his fingers. He tried to be gentle—the pearls appeared fragile. Gods knew what would happen if he broke one.

"Atrius," the voice called again. He spun around to find that scene had changed, and he stood on a battlefield.

He knew this place: The Fortress of Riodan, where he'd first met Infiernen. He remembered it vividly. The smell of blood that ran from fallen friends and enemies was still fresh in his memory. His arms tingled as everything around him played out as it had every night since that day. He grew dizzy, knowing he would be unable to stop it.

His body jumped back in the courtyard, and the rest of the fortress loomed to his right. Blood covered him, most of it not his own. Off in the distance, the leader of the Negander, Riodan, struck Niklaryn down. Bronx's heart leaped into his throat. Not again. He couldn't lose Nik again.

"No!" Bronx yelled, running to his mentor's aid. Nik suffered a blow to the head, his temple red from fresh blood. Bronx lifted his pistol to fire, but Riodan knocked it out of his hands. He swung his sword, grunting as Riodan easily deflected the blow and parried. Bronx gritted his teeth. He had to be faster this time.

He made a wide sweep of his sword, and Riodan took up the defensive. He deflected, feigned, then thrusted so hard that he pushed Bronx back. Sweat beaded on his brow and stung his eyes. He couldn't stop—Niklaryn depended on him.

The Negander, with his bright red hair and purple sash, towered over Bronx. He roared like a great beast that shook Bronx to his bones. The Daer apprentice attacked, but the Negander whirled away, taking his dagger and slicing at Bronx's thigh. Bronx clenched his teeth as the blade cut through flesh, the pain causing him to stumble to the ground, into the mud. Riodan stood over Bronx, his sword held high, ready to give Bronx that fatal blow. Bronx closed his eyes—as he did every time.

He failed again.

Somewhere, Bronx heard Niklaryn bellow from behind Riodan, ready to strike. Bronx opened his eyes and saw that it wasn't his mentor who saved him.

Another man had appeared.

Bronx remembered how he had never seen this man before: tall with curly hair, bright eyes, and a Daer uniform. The man struck down Riodan with a crushing blow. The stranger took his sword and hacked at the man's face until Riodan was no longer recognizable, save for the sash. Hot blood sprayed onto Bronx's face. He wanted to wipe it away, but shock froze him to his place on the ground.

When he finished, the newcomer locked eyes with Bronx, his face crimson from his victim, causing Bronx's stomach to churn. The man gave Bronx a maniacal smile as he jumped over Riodan's carcass and landed next to Bronx. The man's face was inches from his.

"Who . . . w-who are you?" stammered Bronx. He now knew who it was, but the dream always played out as he remembered it.

The man's blue eyes glowed. "I'm Infiernen. And you're Bronx."

Bronx's heart hammered in his chest. His vision centered on the killer in front of him. The rest of the battle raging around him felt muted. "Where's Niklaryn?"

Infiernen tilted his head to the side as if he did not understand the question. Then he raised an eyebrow and gave Bronx a toothy grin. Bronx had to fight back a wave of nausea as he saw that Infiernen had blood between his teeth.

"Niklaryn is gone."

Bronx's eyes snapped open, and he sat upright, covered in sweat. That dream still haunted him after all those years.

He rose from his bed and shivered, frisking his bare arms. He pulled on a short-sleeved shirt and headed for the door. Kaz, Arram, and Manden still slept in their cots, and Bronx didn't want to wake them. He gingerly opened the door and tiptoed out.

He continued down the hall, wary of creaky floorboards as he passed the women's dark and silent room. When Bronx went to sleep earlier that evening, he heard Rei talking and laughing with his sister and Skylar. It was already late, but apparently there was much to discuss. He smiled at the thought that Rei was able to surround herself with such loving people. Yet he still felt uneasy about Sky. He had only met a handful of Ettowas in the years he'd known Kaz, and despite their notoriety on the Nexus, the majority had only shown him kindness and generosity.

It made Sky's behavior more enigmatic.

He walked to the staircase and descended. He didn't wear any gloves, so he took advantage of letting his hand run down the soft, varnished wooden handrail.

As he headed toward the dining hall, he saw a faint glow from the hearth. Someone else was awake.

He entered and stopped in his tracks as he saw Rei sitting on a stool next to the fire, reading. Her back was to him, her hair loose and un-brushed. He wanted so much to run his fingers through it. He remembered how soft it was. He took a step forward and the floor creaked. Rei saw him and gave him a big smile, which he returned.

"We have a weird habit of finding each other when everyone else is asleep," he said.

"I like our moments." Rei put the bookmark in her book and closed it.

"Why are you up?" he asked, standing on the other side of the hearth. With not only his hands uncovered, but his arms as well, he was an even greater threat to Rei. He didn't want to run the risk of brushing up against her, despite wanting desperately to do so.

"I couldn't sleep. You? Nightmare?"

"You know it. You want to talk about it?"

She shook her head. "What about you?"

Bronx dropped his hand to his side. He wanted to tell her about his dreams. His heart beat rapidly in his chest. He hated himself because he knew he wasn't going to tell her, not yet. She didn't need to know what kept him awake most nights.

He forced a smile. "The usual, getting chased by a lobster with loafers."

Rei chuckled, then stood. "I was about to make some tea. Would you like some?"

"Yes." Bronx gave her a genuine smile, glad to change the subject. "I would love some."

A small shelf sat next to the hearth with a pitcher of water, a cast iron kettle, and a few boxes of tea. Bronx assumed they weren't the only guests to want tea in the middle of the night. Rei put a kettle of water on the rack next to the fire, while Bronx pushed open the door leading to the kitchens.

"What are you doing?" she asked.

"To find us a snack."

"Are we sure that's allowed?" she asked.

He shrugged. "I don't think the owner would deny his god queen sustenance."

He found a block of cheese and a heel of bread, which he quickly sliced into smaller pieces. He returned and placed them on the small table next to the hearth.

"What a feast," Rei said, taking a slice of cheese and placing it on the bread to nibble. "Can you cook?"

He shrugged. "Sort of. Not very well."

"After suffering through Niko's attempts, I'm pretty sure that they don't teach cooking at the Daer Academy."

He chuckled. "He was awful." He watched Rei. "The only other thing I know how to do is order at restaurants."

Rei giggled. "I am quite good at that as well."

"And can you cook?"

"Yeah. We served food at the bar sometimes, mainly two

or three stews made in bulk for the day—nothing too fancy. Hotara was the real brains behind the kitchen, but she taught me what she could."

"You're a real wonder."

Rei blushed. "Cooking a meal is not magic. Anyone can do it."

"True. But cooking brings sustenance. As a Daer I was taught to take care of my body. One would think that would include knowing how to cook a proper meal."

They sat quietly for a few moments—the only sound between them was the soft crackling of the fire. Then Rei asked, "So what's Artema like?"

Bronx picked at the crust of his bread. "She's very sweet, incredibly intelligent, and loyal almost to a fault."

The kettle whistled. Rei took the kettle from the fire, careful not to get too close to Bronx, and poured the water into two mugs as he continued. "She grew up in the town of Fabrecido, near the Temple of Tasya. Her mother had disappeared, and her father grew sick and died. I met him briefly. He was in the final stages of dementia. It drove her to the temple because of their mental health healing arts. She had given up a life of performing in order to take care of him full-time. She had hoped to learn something to help him, if only to help ease his pain. She was very devout and was about to take her vows when she met your brother." He smiled at the memory.

"Where did they meet?"

"In a bar of all places. The Crazy Horse." He chuckled.

"I remember you mentioned that. A would-be priestess in a bar?"

"I'm sure there's a joke in there somewhere." He smiled. "But no, she didn't believe in denying herself the little pleasures in life. She enjoyed a good hard drink from time to time."

"I hope it is her at this club. I would very much like to meet her."

They ate in silence, enjoying each other's company.

"I'm sorry I couldn't make something more." He gestured to the bread and cheese.

"It's fine, but I'm sure we'll have the chance later." Rei looked at Bronx and he smiled. Gods, he loved her optimism. This could work, they could work.

His eyes roamed over her face, trying to commit every angle and curve to memory. Those green eyes penetrated into his soul as if she knew what secrets he held there.

Then the smile disappeared from her lovely face. "Bronx," she whispered. "There's something I need to ask you."

His heart raced—she figured it out. "What?"

She bit her lip as though contemplating how to say it. "Why do you think Infiernen wanted to kill you? I'm trying to understand where Infiernen draws the line between friend and enemy."

He wrung his hands as he thought of an answer. He knew he couldn't tell her the complete truth. But he told her what he could. "I am a threat. I witnessed what happened that day and lived to tell about it. I also confronted him after he almost killed Artema and I vowed to destroy him. I don't think he took kindly to my threat."

Those green eyes continued to study him. He swore she knew he omitted. "What did you see?"

"That's the problem. Trauma does weird things to the mind. I have a memory of what happened, but I don't know if what I saw was real or not. The rest is a blur."

Rei put her plate down on the edge of the hearth.

"You're not sure if the memory is real or something your mind created to protect you from the truth?"

He nodded.

She took another piece of cheese and nibbled on it thoughtfully for a few moments. "I hope you can tell me about that day when you're ready." She gave him a small smile. "His animosity toward you makes sense. I have a feeling it's the same with Artema. But I still don't understand Arram. The sister is to be protected, but the brother must die? Neither of us met Infiernen, so I'm at a loss for a motive."

"Your guess is as good as mine."

They watched the fire as it slowly died, bringing with it a chill. Bronx found more wood and threw it into the hearth.

"What do you think of Skylar?" she asked. "She seemed to like the idea of having Infiernen on our side."

"I don't trust her."

Rei smirked. "Neither does your sister."

"And do you? Trust her?" His cheeks warmed as he waited for her answer.

"I want to."

"How can you even think of trusting her? Or did you forget your little skirmish on the *Luciernaga*?" He stood but kept his distance. Despite his question, his voice was soft.

"Her actions have left me confused. Her reasons for being a bitch were petty. But I don't think they were petty enough to betray us or the Federation. I think she still believes in the cause. She believes in it enough to want to protect it." She remained in her chair.

A small smile escaped his lips. "You are just as much an optimist as Kaz." He ran a hand through his hair. "But Sky's animosity toward me came long before she discovered what

I was." He sighed. "To be honest, I also believe Sky is a true believer of the Federation. I hate to admit your brother being right, but she's an Ettowa and most usually have an ulterior motive. She wanted to hurt you and now wants to be your friend. Why? I can't shake the feeling that she's up to something. It drives me nuts I can't put my finger on what it is."

Rei touched his knee and gave it a squeeze. "Maybe we should get some sleep," she said. "We can think about it better when we sleep."

Bronx shook his head. "I won't get any sleep now."

She gave him a beautiful smile. "Then I'll stay up with you. You look like you could use a distraction."

He returned the gesture. "What sort of distraction did you have in mind?"

She shrugged. "I don't know. Our usual means of distraction is not the best idea at the moment." She gave him a wink.

Bronx bit his lip. "You and that mouth." He took a few steps away from her. "You really know how to tempt a man."

"And I look forward to the day we can resume our dance. But for tonight . . . what do you normally do when you can't sleep?"

"I do exercises."

"Can you teach me then? At least the basics? I have to admit, I have seen you do them some nights when I couldn't sleep. You make it look like a work of art."

Color rose in his cheeks as he blushed. "You've been watching me?"

"I haven't been able to take my eyes off you since the day we met."

His broke into a grin. He loved her so much. "Let's get started."

# CHAPTER 50

Rei was so nervous about running late she was already dressed and waiting in the lobby well before anyone else. Apparently, the club had a strict dress code, and she and Crona had spent most of the day shopping. They returned with just enough time to get ready. She wore a green dress from one of the shops they visited, as well as a pair of satin slippers she bought elsewhere, which would do nothing to keep her feet warm from the snow falling outside.

Luckily, she had purchased a cloak and wore it with the green scarf Kaz gifted her what felt like ages ago, which complimented the dress perfectly. Rei reminded herself she had only been with the Federation for a month. As she waited, she fidgeted with Niklaryn's Daer ring that she still wore around her neck. Her other hand held her staff against her body, and her thumb ran over the carvings.

In that time, Skylar walked passed Rei on the way out the door, toting a full rucksack.

"Where are you going?" Rei asked. "We still need to talk."

"Sorry, Cousin," said the Daer. "I have to get back. There's been reports of Dominion soldiers lurking about in Fabrecido. They know they shouldn't be here. I should head over there and check it out."

"Is Infiernen among them?"

Skylar shook her head. "He hasn't been seen since Trappist V."

Rei furrowed her eyebrows. "Where could he be?"

"I don't know, but don't worry about him. I need to go and make sure none of those soldiers come this way."

"Then stay with us. Order others to come and take care of the problem."

Sky let out a low growl. "But what if they come this way?" She met Rei's eyes. "I can't let anything happen to you."

"But if they're in Fabrecido, they won't make it here tonight," said Rei with a shrug.

Sky readjusted the straps of her rucksack. "You don't understand. The report is already twenty-four hours old. They could be on their way as we speak."

Rei's body tingled at the idea of having Dominion soldiers descend on them here tonight. She felt exposed in her fancy gown and wrapped her cloak tighter around her body like a shield.

"You're staying," Rei said finally. "If they come, they come. We'll need your protection."

Skylar sighed and rubbed her face. "Fine. I'll meet you at the club. I'm sure no one has thought to scout it beforehand."

Rei nodded and then Skylar was gone, leaving a cold draft from outside to bluster past Rei. She let loose the breath she was holding once the door shut behind her cousin.

Rei saw movement out of the corner of her eye. It was Bronx and Crona coming down the stairs. The latter wore a fiery-orange dress she found from one of the shops. Crona had convinced the shop owner to tailor the dress to fit her small frame, and she currently showed the fabric to her brother. The blonde literally danced in place, grinning uncontrollably over her purchase.

Bronx wore a light gray tunic over a pale blue shirt with

a v-neck. He had even managed to find gloves to match the ensemble. It was one of the few times Rei had seen him wear anything other than the Federation uniform, and the lighter colors suited him. She approached him as he put on his long coat.

She felt a pang in her chest as she thought about Sky's news. She hoped her cousin was being paranoid. They didn't want another onslaught like Trappist V.

"What's wrong?" Bronx asked.

"Skylar just told me there's a possibility of Dominion soldiers headed this way."

Bronx pinched his nose with his fingers. "Who could've known we were here?"

"It could be a coincidence. Dominion soldiers skulk about on Federation planets all the time."

He sighed. "I don't believe in coincidences. If they do come here, it's because someone has been giving the Dominion your position. How old was the report?"

"Sky said twenty-four hours."

Bronx chewed on his lip. "That means they couldn't be on the road longer than that. We have another day if they are headed this way."

The two stared at each other. The dress she wore was too tight to hide a knife if something happened. She quickly glanced over to Bronx again, hoping he was armed in case of trouble. Fortunately, he did have a pistol on his hip and a gladius at his back.

Voices echoed throughout the hotel as the rest of the group made their way to the front door where Rei and Bronx currently waited.

"What do we tell the others?" she asked.

Bronx shook his head. "I don't know. We may be panicking over nothing. I say we keep it between us for now, okay? But I think it best we get through tonight, then we pack up and keep moving."

Rei nodded. Get through tonight.

She felt his hand take hers and squeeze. She looked at him and he grinned. Clearly, he didn't seem worried about tonight. Perhaps she was just being paranoid. Ixchel was not easily accessible. Even if Infiernen knew where they were, he would still have to arrive on the planet and make the trek here to catch them. Rei was quite sure they had a great head start, and they could handle anything else that came. The goal was to reach Artema first.

"You look very handsome," Rei said, drinking in the sight.

His eyes shone with desire. "And you look stunning."

Her face grew hot, and she reached up to tug on one of her crystal earrings. "I've never worn anything so pretty in my life."

Bronx grinned. "It suits you."

Manden entered, also wearing green, making the red in his hair more intense. He, too, wore two blades at his back. Arram and Kaz were the last to arrive, each wearing black with their own guns on holsters at their hips.

"That's a lot of metal for a club," said Crona. "Do you think we will be let inside?"

Bronx nodded. "It's legal to carry. I checked."

When the carriages finally arrived, the group left the building, only to be immediately bombarded with the bright flashes of cameras. Several voices yelled questions in quick succession:

"What brings you to Kepler IV?"

"What are you wearing, Rei?"

"Why are you dressed for a night out instead of getting ready for the final battle?"

They hurried inside and shut the door. All eyes turned to the hotel owner who sheepishly gave them a grin. "I'm sorry. I couldn't help myself," he said with hands raised. "I never thought I would have the real Volocio stay in my hotel."

Crona shook her head. "If Urius didn't know our whereabouts before, he certainly does now."

"We'll worry about him later. Bernie already said she would help us, and we knew this was a possibility," Rei said with a shrug. "But if they know we're here, the Dominion won't be far behind." She met Bronx's gaze and knew he thought the same thing.

"Skylar heard a report that Dominion soldiers were already spotted on the planet. We need to be on our toes tonight."

"Gods bless it," muttered Crona.

"I'll see if I can get the photographers to go away." Kaz opened the door and approached the photographers with his hands raised. "Please, we ask that you give us privacy. We are on a diplomatic mission of utmost importance and would appreciate if you let us be tonight."

But the flashes continued, and Kaz turned to the group and shrugged. "Usually that works, but this was a risk when we decided to be out in public."

"I have an idea." Rei made her way to the edge of the porch and gave them the same smile she had given the patrons back at Coronta Bar, a toothy grin and stern eyes that said, "I can be nice, but don't cross me."

"Ladies and Gentlemen," she began. The camera flashes came quicker, almost blinding her. "As my cousin said, we have important work to do tonight, and it would be really helpful if you didn't follow us. So I propose this: if you allow us some privacy this evening, we will agree to a group photo."

"And what if we don't agree?" asked a voice from behind the lights.

Rei raised a hand, praying that maybe her powers would work now. A few sparks danced between her fingers, not enough to be useful, but it was somewhat threatening. "Then I fry your equipment, and you walk away with nothing."

She approached one of the photographers with a particularly small camera and snatched it. "I'll be taking this," she said with her biggest smile. She put it in the small purse she had wrapped around her wrist. If Infiernen did come for her tonight, she was going to get him to admit what happened to Niklaryn, and she was going to get proof.

The flashes stopped, and it didn't take long for the reporters to agree. After several minutes of the group standing together and smiling long enough to make their cheeks hurt, they finally piled into the carriage and were whisked away toward the center of town to the club.

# CHAPTER 51

The snow fell heavily, and Rei was grateful to share such a small carriage with Manden, Crona, and Arram. Bronx and Kaz chose to sit outside with the driver.

"So much for secrecy," Crona said.

"Well, we didn't try very hard to hide Kaz, Rei, or myself." Manden shrugged. "Secrecy was not going to be a long-term option for us."

"Then let's hope our sister-in-law is the singer." Arram watched the snowfall outside their carriage window. "If not, we move on—and quickly."

When they arrived at the main street, Manden held a hand out to Rei and helped her step out of the carriage. The snow covered the road in white, and it already seeped into her thin slippers. She turned and watched as Bronx leaped down gracefully from the carriage and dusted the quickly melting snow from the hood of his cloak.

A few photographers waited for them outside, but the group simply ignored them. It was too late to try to hide at this point. There was no need to keep it from hindering their mission.

They followed the signs around a few corners until they stood at the entrance of The Feather of the Peacock. It was in a dark narrow alley, and the door barely hung by its hinges. The outside of the building was unimpressive; in fact, it appeared quite shabby. The only sign it had was a faded outline of a red peacock.

"This is it?" asked Bronx.

"Apparently," Kaz said, giving a soft rap on the door.

They waited a few moments as the snow fell in larger clumps around them. Kaz knocked again and the door opened, revealing a dwarf in scarlet robes. He studied each person in the group as if sizing up what they wore. Then he saw Rei and Manden and smiled broadly.

"Welcome God King and Queen!" He opened the door wider. "It is an honor to have you with us tonight." He invited them in and bowed. "And I see that you've brought friends."

Cherry-wood benches with carved vines sat against the wall. Hanging lanterns flowed faintly against the deep maroon walls.

"Please, let us take your cloaks," said a man at the coat check with an extended hand.

They handed him their outer garments and followed the dwarf down the hall to a russet curtain. Their host pulled it back, revealing a large open room with garnet and black tapestries on the walls, short tables with pillows scattered about the floor, and a grand stage that jutted out among the tables.

Rei spotted Skylar against the back wall. She nodded at Rei when they locked eyes. A wave of relief washed over Rei. They were as prepared as possible. If the Dominion soldiers were indeed spotted in Fabrecido twenty-four hours before, then they needed another to reach Ixchel—they still had time.

A shapely brunette strutted up to them and led the group to a table on the far right of the stage, near the back. Rei placed her staff against the wall behind her before taking a seat. The table was large enough to seat the Volocio comfortably, and a contraption sat in the center with a red and gold glass base, a metal rod protruding from the top and hoses coming out of several sides.

"A water pipe!" exclaimed Manden. "I didn't know they were brought to Tyre." He picked up a card the brunette had left with them. "I wonder what flavors they have."

Everybody read through their menus. According to the owner of their hotel, this place served a light dinner and drinks before the show commenced.

Their server returned within a few moments to take their orders. They ordered several appetizers to split among themselves as well as a pitcher of the local ale.

"Can you please bring some mint tobacco and a coal!" Manden called as the server left.

While they waited, crowd around them murmured with the occasional pointed finger in their direction. She remembered long ago when the people of Ballarat would also talk about her. It bothered her then, when it mattered what they thought about her. But that was before she realized there were more important things in life than the opinion of people who have no impact on her or those she cared about. She had a place where she belonged with people like her, who accepted her. She smiled, her heart full.

The server returned with their food and drinks, as well as the mint tobacco and hot coal for the water pipe. A short melody of bells sounded, announcing the commencement of the show. The lights dimmed, and the faint outline of dancers became visible as they made their way onto the stage. The lights brightened, revealing a group of women in crimson robes, each holding a pair of thick swords. A small band of women in orange silk fluttered about further upstage.

They played their string instruments, plucking rising and falling arpeggios. The dancers posed in their first formation and began their dance. Their movements were precise and fluid, reminding Rei of the Daer routine. Some flipped and twirled with a sword in one hand, while others had a pole with long colorful ribbons in the other hand. Then the women paired off and half began to juggle the swords, while the other half danced with the ribbons, creating a kaleidoscope of color. The swords shone in the light and flickered while being tossed and twirled. The audience clapped in amazement.

The swordswomen pranced offstage, replaced with a singer in a golden gown that shone against her dark skin. Her long black hair twisted in a million little braids that fell halfway down her warrior body.

The audience quieted, waiting for her to begin. When she did, it was in a deep, rich voice that reached into Rei's soul as if to awaken something within. Every note of her ethereal voice hung in the air in perfect harmony, complementing the next one that floated to join it.

No one understood the lyrics to the ancient language. According to the program, the song was about a maid who found the love of her life, only to watch him die in her arms. Rei glanced around the room and found many patrons holding handkerchiefs to their eyes. Even Rei's eyes burned as she remembered her dream of Atrius dying in her arms. The waves of heartbreak came crashing back into her consciousness.

She looked over at Bronx to find his eyes on the stage. Then, as if he felt her watching him, he turned to her. It took everything she had to not lean in and kiss him. She loved him so much, and the thought of losing him was unbearable. The audience broke into applause, interrupting her thoughts. The singer finished and left the stage.

Bronx leaned in, and she felt his heat as he spoke into her ear. "That's her. That's Artema."

Rei turned and met his gaze. So it was her. She glanced

back at the stage and tried to remember what Artema looked like. But all she thought about was the woman's voice.

"Are you sure?" she whispered.

"Your brother fell in love with that voice. You don't forget that kind of music."

She had to go to her. She wanted to meet her sister. She began to rise, but Bronx touched her arm. "Wait. We'll go during the intermission."

Rei didn't want to wait. She wanted to go now. She worried that if she didn't, then Artema would disappear again. She let Bronx take her hand and keep her grounded, even if she no longer focused on the following acts.

There were more dancers and singers on stage—their performances bleeding into each other as the band continued playing until eventually it was the wind dancer's turn.

The woman stepped on stage as it rained pink petals. They fell onto her long black hair and dotted it like silk stars. The flowers kissed the pale skin of her outstretched hand. She raised her arms to the heavens, and a couple of petals rose and floated in the air. Soon all the petals moved individually around her. She raised a leg in the air and began her dance, and the petals followed.

Rei watched the show in awe, amazed at how the petals moved of their own accord. She sensed something in the air. The air moved about her with an ebb and flow, making the hair on her arms stand on end. This woman was a wind Volocio. Of course. Lightning sparked the air, and that's why she sensed the energy. Rei glanced over at Arram; she could tell by the look in his eyes that he sensed it too. Her gaze then turned to Bronx. His eyes were transfixed, his mouth opened in amazement.

The clap of the audience brought Rei back to the present. The dancer had already gone backstage, and the house lights brightened. Another band had taken the place of the previous and began to play during the intermission. They allowed the patrons to step on stage and dance.

Crona twisted in her seat and faced the group. "That wind dancer was amazing. It was like she was really the goddess of wind."

"Except that Tasya was a woman of color." Manden shook his head. "She looked more like that singer than the wind dancer. In fact . . . that singer looks exactly like Tasya."

"No. She can't possibly be that last missing Volocio," Kaz said.

"The singer is Artema," Bronx added. "It can't be that easy."

But the look on Manden's face made Rei think otherwise. He was the one who knew their previous counterparts. He knew Rei immediately when they met. The prophecy stated the six reincarnated Volocio would find each other and work with the god king, but the prophecy didn't say it couldn't be convenient.

"You're sure?" asked Arram.

"I think we should ask her," said the redhead.

# CHAPTER 52

Bronx stood. "I'm going back there to talk to her."

"Why you?" Crona asked.

"Because I need to make it right between us." Bronx made his way toward a curtain next to the stage.

"I'm coming with you," Rei said, restless at the thought of meeting this long-lost sister-in-law.

Rei grabbed her staff and followed Bronx through the tables, a wave of whispers trailing them as they made their way to the stage entrance on the other side. A few flashes from cameras also blinked in her direction, only making her stand straighter.

Out of the corner of her eye, she felt the tug of something familiar. She saw his smiling face again. There was no way Niko was here, yet there he was. His blue eyes twinkled, and he had a beard now, but he was still the same handsome man she loved. Her eyes burned with tears of joy and she smiled.

"Rei?" Bronx's voice pulled her back to the present.

She turned to point out her brother, but Niklaryn had disappeared. Or maybe he wasn't there to begin with. Her heart sank.

"I'm coming," she whispered and they continued to the curtain where they were met by a heavyset, balding man who sat in a chair much too small for him.

As Rei and Bronx tried to pass, the man stood to block their path. "You can't enter this way."

"Please, sir," said Rei. "We're old friends of Artema."

The man narrowed his eyes. Then after a moment, he said, "Let me go and ask her. What are your names?"

"Just mention the names Ettowa and Manca," Bronx said. "She'll know."

The man left, quickly replaced by an even larger man.

"For a dance hall that doesn't allow men backstage, there sure are a lot of them here," Rei muttered to Bronx.

"We're eunuchs," growled the new guard.

Bronx nodded. "Ah, that makes sense."

Rei looked over at him and raised an eyebrow. "What?" she mouthed. She didn't understand what eunuchs had to do with dancers.

Bronx leaned in. "The women here are sworn to celibacy so that they can concentrate on their art. I think the eunuchs protect their virtue."

Now that made sense.

The first man returned and gestured to the pair to come toward him. The second man put a hand to block Bronx's path.

"Sorry," the first man said. "Just the lady."

Rei turned to Bronx. "It's all right. I'll be back." She gave him a big smile before following the eunuch to the back room lined with mirrors and girls running back and forth, changing garments, putting on makeup, or fixing hair. The eunuch led Rei to a woman in the far back right, perched in front of her own mirror. He pulled a chair out for Rei and placed it next to Artema.

Artema Ettowa sat quietly for a moment, removing her makeup. She didn't notice her guest right away. But when she did, she jumped in her seat.

"Mica?" she breathed.

Rei shook her head, watching the woman's dark eyes in the mirror. "No. I'm Rei. Your sister-in-law."

Artema smiled. "Of course. I know who you are." Her eyes continued to watch Rei through the reflection, eventually flicking to Rei's staff.

The singer picked up a small bottle of sandalwood oil and dabbed the contents on her wrists. "I had always wondered if Niko had told you about us."

Rei shook her head. "He didn't. I guess there wasn't a chance to tell me before . . ." Rei didn't know where to start. She had so many questions, but she decided to stick to her goal. It didn't matter if Artema was a Volocio or not, she came here to ask about Niklaryn. Those answers were more important. "Before he left with Infiernen."

Artema winced. "So you know." She turned to face Rei. She was so close, Rei saw the remnants of gold powder on her midnight cheeks and lips.

"That's actually why we're here," Rei said. "You're the person who knew my brother best. I have so many questions, but we don't have a lot of time. We want to take you to the Federation with us."

Artema shook her head and returned to removing her makeup. "I'm not ready to join the battle yet."

Rei furrowed her eyebrows. "We're not asking you to join the battle." She noticed Artema's choice in words. Maybe she knew more than she was letting on. "Tasya?"

The singer's jaw dropped. "How did you know?"

It was true. "The god king recognized you." Rei tightened her grip on her staff.

"Manden's here?"

Rei leaned back in her chair, her turn to be surprised. "You know him?" Artema knew her history, while Rei grew up as a Volocio in total ignorance. "You know what? That doesn't matter right now. We just need your help in finding Niko."

"Nik isn't ready for my help, and I prefer my life here."

Rei didn't understand what that meant. "I'm afraid you won't have much of a choice. I fear Infiernen knows you're alive, and he will most likely come for you."

Artema studied Rei's face as though searching for an answer to a question she hadn't asked yet. "Infiernen's coming here?"

The wind dancer walked by, and Artema briefly glanced in the woman's direction before turning back to Rei. A few of the pink petals landed near Rei's feet.

"I think so," she said with a nod.

Artema reached for one of her many braids and fidgeted with the end. The gesture reminded Rei of Hotara and how she performed the same gesture when she was thinking.

"You said 'we.' I also heard Manca mentioned along with your name."

"Yes," Rei said. "Bronx is here, too."

Artema's face lit up. "I always remembered his laugh. How is he?"

Rei tried to come up with a reasonable answer. "He's well," she responded with a forced smile. She didn't understand what Artema was trying to accomplish. "I don't mean to sound rude, but we don't have much time. Do you think you can you help us?"

A blood-curdling scream rang from the main hall.

Rei recognized Crona's voice yelling, "Rei, run!"

She jumped to her feet. Soon more screams joined.

"What's going on?" Artema asked, standing.

Rei narrowed her eyes and blood rushed in her ears. "I think I know." The soldiers were closer than they thought. "We have to get out of here. Can you use one of those swords from the first act?" Rei held her staff and reached for the call of lightning, feeling it simmer under the surface.

"This way." Artema led Rei farther back to where the props lay.

Her hands shook as chaos erupted around her, undercut with flashes of metal and ribbon. Performers ran with no direction, and a few grabbed weapons. Boots thudded heavily to her right. Rei turned and came face to face with Infiernen.

"You!" screamed Artema.

"Well, I didn't expect to see both Rei and Artema in one place." Infiernen stared at Artema. "And I'm very disappointed you're still alive, whore."

Infiernen swung his gladius at Artema, but Rei jumped in and knocked the woman to the side. The metal stung as it nicked her neck. Rei touched the wound, and her hand came with away with a little blood, but the cut wasn't deep.

"It was not for you!" cried Infiernen.

Rei's fighting instincts kicked in—she couldn't allow herself to panic. She brought up her hand and waved it in front of her face, charging the air around her. But before she could attack, Artema threw her hands forward. The wind picked up around Rei and flung Infiernen back into the wall.

Artema took her sword and pointed at Rei's dress. "Cut."

Rei cut the fabric of her dress from ankle to thigh, giving her more freedom of movement.

Artema grabbed Rei's hand. "We go now," she said, leading Rei out the back door.

They ran through the nearest door and out into another alleyway. The snow fell in larger clumps, and within moments, soaked Rei's thin slippers. She mentally kicked herself for not having dressed for the weather, but now was not the time for such thoughts.

They ran out onto the street, along with others who ran, screaming, in all directions. Photographers stood on the sidelines, their cameras flashing like little bolts of lightning.

The lights stopped as the Negander cut them down. There were at least four, but Rei knew she could take them on. She flicked her wrist and called a bolt, throwing it at two of the Negander. Their clothes smoked in the cold snow as their charred corpses hit the ground.

Artema never let go of Rei's hand, pulling her away from the crowd before she handled the other two. "This way."

"Why? I have this under control."

"We have to get away from Infiernen. I know where we can hide. Come on."

"But I was supposed to save you." This was not at all how Rei had planned this night to go.

They ran across a large street into an arboretum and continued through the trees, taking care to not trip over the signs. Artema gestured for Rei to follow before running off the path to an area with bigger trees and larger overhanging branches.

"What was that?" breathed Artema

"Negander," gasped Rei. "They must've followed us."

"Not that. I meant the lightning. You already have your powers?"

"So you know who I am?"

"Of course. You see, I'm really Tasya. Not a reincarnate. I never died."

"Wait, what?"

Before Artema could respond, screams filled the air.

"No time," Rei said, taking the singer's hand. "Let's go."

They ran until they came to an area with a beautiful willow tree, heavy with snow, and in front of a small frozen pond. Rei tripped on a root and fell, hitting her knee on a stone. "Damn," she cried.

"Are you okay?" asked Artema.

Rei gritted her teeth and stood, balancing her weight on her good leg. "I'll be all right."

"Rei!" Infiernen's voice rang out in the distance.

"Shit," muttered Rei. She raised her staff and readied her stance. "Artema, go back and get help."

"But I can help."

"No. I came here to find you. To protect you from him. He's mine. We shouldn't have run from the others, but it's too late now. Find Bronx or Manden."

Rei watched as Artema hesitated.

"Go!" Rei yelled and the woman disappeared into the woods.

The snow fell harder as she waited, and her heart jumped to her throat. This was it—she would take on this monster, and this time, she would win. She thought she would be more merciful if she came face-to-face with him again. But watching those innocent people being killed by his Dogs reminded her of Arram clutching his stomach as his lifeblood spilled out. She didn't care what he had to say, he was her enemy. She took the camera from her purse and hobbled to a tree with low branches, placing it where it could film everything.

She prayed it worked. She just had to get Infiernen to talk before she killed him. She wanted to prove to the star cluster that Infiernen didn't kill her brother through a confession. Niklaryn was alive and everyone should know. The Negander came into her line of sight, his light eyes wide and chest heaving as though he fought for his very breath.

"Rei," he gasped.

Rei didn't respond.

"Where's Artema?"

"You'll have to get through me if you want Artema."

Infiernen scoffed. "What makes you think I came for her? I'm here for you, but we don't have much time."

"Much time?" Rei raised an eyebrow. "Are we in such a rush for whatever it is you're planning? Do you plan on throwing me in the same dungeon as Niklaryn?" Her heart pounded her ears.

"I told you, Rei. I'm not your enemy."

"I don't believe you." Rei lunged at him, swinging her staff.

Infiernen brought his gladius up and blocked it, pushing the blade into the wood as it groaned. Rei roared as she pushed him back.

She released and limped away from him, never taking her eyes off her brother's captor. Anger surged through her veins and kept her standing.

She swung her staff and Infiernen dodged it, whirling around to Rei's side—quicker than she could blink—and punching her bad knee. Rei yelled as pain racked her body. This was harder than she imagined it would be.

She swung her hand around in a circle, and the air crackled as she put her hand on Infiernen's face, but no sparks came—the pain in her knee caused her to lose focus, replaced by panic. She punched him and he fell.

"Stop fighting me!" he cried, jabbing at her bad knee again. "Stay down and let me explain!"

Rei gasped in pain as she fell to the ground. Her heart raced as fear began to take over.

With her other hand she tried to charge the air again, but Infiernen stomped on her arm. He grabbed her by the shoulders and threw her against a tree, knocking the air from her lungs. She wouldn't give up. Not now. Not ever.

She winced and stood, clapping her hands and throwing them forward. Lightning shot from her fingertips toward Infiernen and threw him to the small pond. The ice broke under his weight, and within seconds, the water soaked through his clothes. She almost cried from relief for the reprieve.

"Rei, please," he said through chattering teeth.

"Fight me!" she screamed. Her knee still throbbed, but she held her ground as she brought her staff up. "Your Dogs killed my grandparents, you tried to kill Arram while keeping Niklaryn away from me. I owe them vengeance."

Infiernen raised an eyebrow. "It was all for you, Rei. Everything I did was to keep you safe long enough to fulfill your destiny. I never meant to keep Nik from you, but I had to stow him away for safekeeping. I can't afford to let him loose."

Rei's heart flew up to her throat. "What? Where is he?"

"You don't know? How delicious." He limped toward her, shivering. "Well, I won't spoil the punch line, Rei, but he's a lot closer than you think."

Rei wanted to respond, but her tongue grew heavy and thick. Warm copper dripped from her nose, its metallic taste filling her mouth. She touched the cut on her neck and whimpered—the blood had turned black. Drops of Jupiter. His blade was poisoned.

"Rei!" a familiar voice cried just as white blinding pain ripped through her, and her legs gave out from under her.

Yet it wasn't the Negander who caught her as another wave of agony pierced her consciousness. It was Niklaryn. The familiar scent of sandalwood washed over her as he held her. She barely felt his ice-cold body. "Fucking Infiernen," he cried. "Rei, I'm so sorry. He meant the poison for someone else."

Rei screamed as electricity coursed through her body. Each crest worse than the last, leaving her an empty trough.

She trembled as she waited for another wave of pain. The veil lifted just enough for her to see her brother's face, his blue eyes red with tears.

"Infiernen?" she asked, her voice hoarse.

"I fought him off for now."

"Why?" she whispered. "Why try to kill them? Arram? Bronx? Artema?" She arched her back as her nerves blazed again with fire.

Niklaryn held her tighter. "They are all threats to my agreement with Infiernen. But not you, my darling. You are special. Infiernen and I vowed to keep you safe. We had to protect you from the one hunting you, the one who was always hunting you. Even if I had to sell my soul to Sovereign Praymer to do it." A sob wracked through him. "But I failed. I'm so sorry."

Rei barely heard him as her vision blurred. Her body grew colder as the snow continued to fall, in her hair, her eyes, and her face. Her nerves were dead, and she couldn't feel anything. *Niko?* she thought, wanting the word to pass through her lips, but it was too late. Rei was gone.

# CHAPTER 53



"Rei, run!" Crona yelled, her otherworldly voice returning.

Bronx whirled around and found six Negander standing in a row, faces covered and swords drawn.

People backed toward the stage, and Bronx fought his way through the crowd, wanting to put himself between the Negander and the audience. He reached for his gladius and readied his stance. Skylar appeared at his side, her own gladius in hand.

Bronx saw Manden and the rest of the group out of the corner of his eye. He could take on the five by himself, but he was sure there were more waiting. Infiernen and his Dogs never left anything to chance.

"Manden, make sure everyone stays back. Be ready." Bronx turned his head slightly to ensure Manden heard him, but his eyes remained on the Negander.

"Everybody, please stay calm and stand back. We'll take care of them," said Manden. Yells and whimpers from the crowd drowned out his voice.

Bronx took a step forward. He almost told the Negander to leave, to give them a chance to escape. But, of course, they weren't going to listen. He took off his gloves, keeping his expression calm, but his heart pounded in his ears. If there was any time for his powers to work, now would be it. Once his gloves were off, he let them fall to the floor. He readied a fighting stance as the first Negander attacked, sword raised high.

Bronx let his body take control of his actions. He

ducked at the first swing of the sword and punched the Negander in the stomach. With another flick, he took down the first Negander by slicing him in the throat. Bronx grabbed the wounded Negander's wrist as the ever-recognizable black smoke appeared, and the Negander slumped over. It was the first time Bronx didn't feel dread at the energy surging through him—the first time his powers felt like a gift. He was powerful. He was death incarnate, and he would make the Negander regret dancing with him.

Another Negander attacked Bronx from behind, but Skylar was there first and slit the Negander's throat. A different warrior connected her temple with the hilt of his sword, knocking her down. Anger coursed through Bronx's veins. He made a wide sweep of his gladius, and the Negander took up the defensive. Bronx whirled around and stabbed the Negander with his blade. He raised a naked hand against the Negander's face; the black smoke returned, and the Negander collapsed. Bronx grabbed Skylar's arm to help her stand. It felt good to fight alongside another Daer again.

"You all right?" he asked and she responded with a nod.

Out of the corner of his eye, Bronx saw more people enter the club—Dominion soldiers. He didn't bother to count how many and kept his mind blank as he lost himself in the act of killing.

"Bronx, are you alright?" Crona asked.

Bronx closed his eyes. The battle was over, and in the end, he took many lives with his powers, but that was not all. He was still a conduit like the other Volocio, but instead of transferring the energy, he absorbed it as the person died. With nowhere to go, the vitality of those victims now coursed through his body, giving him the strength of thirteen men—one for each life he had taken by touch. He tried to steady his breathing, but his veins were on fire.

In answer to Crona's question, he did not feel all right.

"Yes," he lied, not opening his eyes.

Shortly after the Negander fled, the reporters poured in. Kaz spoke with them now, his silhouette surrounded by thousands of blinking lights.

Arram sat on the edge of the stage. "Has anyone seen Rei?"

"She's not backstage?" asked Skylar. She stepped over the ruins of their table on her way to joining the others at the stage.

"No, I asked a dancer. She said that one of the Negander came, and Rei fled with Artema."

Bronx's sister winced. "I hope they're safe."

"I'm sure they are," Manden said. "Rei's much more confident with her fighting powers than the last time she confronted a Negander. She can take care of herself."

"But what if that Negander was Infiernen?" asked Crona.

No one had an answer to that.

A door creaked open and slammed shut, and someone panted heavily as they stumbled toward the group of Volocio. Artema appeared on stage, her clothes wet from the snow, still melting, and her eyes red and filled with tears. She saw Manden and ran to him, stumbling as she fell at the edge of the stage. Bronx joined her with the rest of the group.

"Manden, you have to come quick!" she cried.

"Tasya," the redhead said with a gasp. "W-what happened?"

"Infiernen came and . . ." Artema's chest rose and fell

with heavy breaths. "And Rei fought him and . . ." Tears streaked her cheeks.

"And Rei? Where's Rei?"

"She's . . . she's—I'm sorry. I couldn't do anything to save her."

"Where is she?"

"The arboretum. She needs help. I may already be too late. Drops of Jupiter."

Bronx's world spun. He felt numb, and his heart pounded. The energy in his body surged through him. He would kill Infiernen for this.

"Where?" he asked.

"Under the willow tree, next to a pond."

Bronx was out of the room and the building faster than anyone else could react. He raced down the alleyway onto the street.

People from the audience, the ones that the Volocio helped escape, huddled in the snow outside. He ran past them and quickly spotted the sign that read "Arboretum of Ixchel" across the street. The Volocio called to him, asking him to wait, but he didn't listen. The energy of those thirteen men gave him the strength to run faster than he had ever thought possible. He could probably run forever, but he didn't want forever—he just wanted to get to Rei.

He crossed through the trees, off the path until he found the willow tree next to the pond Artema had spoken of. At the foot of the tree, partially covered in snow, lay Rei.

He reached her, fell to his knees, and scooped her into his arms. Her eyes were closed as if asleep, but the crimson lifeblood streaming from her nose and ears suggested otherwise.

"No," he whispered. "No, no, no, no, no." He touched

her face, stroking her cheek. "Rei?" he called. "Darling, wake up. Please, wake up."

His vision blurred with tears. He sat there, not knowing how to react. He felt numb. The pain that wracked through him left him blind to everything else. He touched her face, her skin soft but ice cold. He wiped the blood from her chin, still a little warm. She had only died moments before.

"Bring her back."

Bronx's head snapped up and his heart stopped. Niklaryn crouched on the other side of the lake, his face wet with tears.

"Nik?" Bronx whispered. "How? But how?"

"I don't have much time. Bring her back."

"My powers don't work like that."

Niklaryn crossed his arms. Bronx noticed his old mentor's wet clothes and the little crystals that formed on his uniform.

He pursed his blue lips. "I call bullshit, Bronx," he growled as his teeth chattered. "I don't believe the universe is so cruel to gift us someone like you—one who can take life and yet cannot give back? Where the fuck is the balance in that?"

A little voice questioned if Niklaryn was right. But he didn't know where to begin with no one to help him.

"I don't know how," Bronx whispered, his heart breaking at the thought that maybe, just maybe he could do it, but he hadn't tried hard enough to learn how.

"So you're going to give up? I taught you better than that."

The medic's eyes met those of his mentor. "What if I can't?" Grief strangled him, and his voice broke.

"You can. I know you can." Niklaryn threw a camera at Bronx's side. It was the camera Rei took from the reporters earlier that evening. "No one can know the truth about Infiernen and I. Not yet. But I promise you he won't threaten your life again. I won't allow it. I still fight for the Federation."

Crona called Bronx's name, her voice echoing in the woods.

"I have to go," said Niklaryn. "I can only keep Infiernen away for so long."

Hot tears streamed down Bronx's face. He didn't want Nik to leave.

"You better be right about Infiernen." Bronx's voice was hoarse.

"You'll have to trust me." Niklaryn shared a pained look with his former apprentice before disappearing into the trees.

Bronx wept as he held Rei close. This was so unfair. Here he had the lives of those Negander, and he couldn't use them to bring back the one he loved. He put his forehead against hers.

"Rei?" he asked, knowing the act would be useless. Her eyes remained closed. Her lips never moved, and she didn't reach out to touch his face like he prayed she would.

"Please, gods," he whispered. "Let me go instead. All I bring is death. I've lied to those I care about. Rei is so good and kind, and she deserves so much more and so much better than me. Please." He squeezed his eyes shut and willed himself to death.

"Bronx!" Crona called from behind him. The group had finally caught up, but he didn't listen.

He felt Rei's body drift away from him. Panic gripped him as he held her tighter, not wanting to let her go. But she faded into mist, leaving him alone and with pain ripping through his heart.

# CHAPTER 54

Bronx's heart hammered in his chest as he opened his eyes. Rei was gone. His panic quickly turned to confusion when he realized where he stood. He rubbed his eyes, unable to believe the scene before him. He was no longer in the arboretum, but he was still among trees. Ahead of him lay a long winding path and a gate.

The Daer walked up to the gate to get a closer look. Each gate column was made up of a single pearl. He reached out and touched its smooth surface. Then his gaze turned to the forest in front of him, past the gate.

The trees had long trunks that didn't start branching out until several feet up. Everything around him had a golden hue, which unnerved him since the dirt beneath him and the tree trunks around him were black as night. It was the forest of his dreams. But what was he doing here now?

"Can we help you?" said several voices in unison behind him.

Bronx whirled around and came face to face with a group of five soldiers, one woman, and four men wearing long black robes with the hoods pulled back. They had similar features: a thin face, high cheekbones, fair skin with contrasting dark hair, and even darker eyes.

"Who are you?" they asked in unison.

Bronx almost took a step back. "Bronx Manca. Who, er . . . what are you?"

"We are Reapers," said the woman. Suddenly, the five cocked their heads to the side as if they heard something, yet Bronx heard nothing. Watching them move as one disturbed him immensely.

"Reapers," Bronx breathed. Manden had told him about this group before.

The five returned their attention to him. "Like you, Atrius," they responded together.

"We have many names: Death, Psychopomps, and Daemons," said one of the men, "but we are Reapers. We transfer energies from the dying to the living. We take life and give life. And those whose souls arrive here must follow us to the ship on the river—to Annan."

"And where is here?" Bronx asked.

"Hamastagan," the woman said.

"The Land of the Dead," said the man in the middle.

"How did I get here?"

"A Reaper can see through the veil. We have sensed you peeking through for a long time, but today you wanted it enough."

Bronx pondered the Reapers' words. "We can give life, yes? Say . . . I can bring someone back to life?"

"Technically, but few have succeeded. A life for a life."

Relief flooded Bronx. "I can do this. I've taken several. I need to find Rei Ettowa." He wouldn't allow himself to dwell anymore.

"Rei?" asked the woman.

"Micaela Roya?"

The group parted to either side of the path. The woman pointed down the path.

"Pray that she has not already arrived at the boat."

Bronx ran harder than he ever had in his life, weaving in and out of trees, up and down hills, his legs moving for what felt like forever. Off in the distance, a pale figure walked with another dark-robed fellow.

"Rei!" he called.

The figure wore sheer white flowing robes that shimmered as they moved.

"Rei!" he cried again. He ran to the pale figure and pulled back the hood only to find an old obese man. Bronx recognized him. He must have died during all the chaos at the club.

No time to wait. Rei was still out there.

He continued down the path. The farther he ran, the more pale-robed figures he saw. At first, they each had a dark-robed Reaper leading them. But then he noticed fences on either side of the path, and the population of Reapers decreased as the souls increased. More and more figures in white cloaks gathered around him. He breathed hard as panic rose in his throat. He worried he wouldn't find her in time.

He pulled the hood off of those within his reach and none of them were Rei. He wanted to scream. This was taking too long. He let out an exasperated sigh. There were too many souls around him.

Bronx peered between the white figures toward the other side of the fences where Reapers just stood, watching the souls move like cattle within the fences.

"A little help?" Bronx asked to no one in particular.

"What do you need?" asked a voice to his right.

Bronx turned and found an older man on the other side of the fence. He couldn't see him very well through all the dead souls, but he saw that the man waved to him to come closer. Bronx pushed through souls until he reached the man, who extended a hand.

"I'm so happy that you've returned, Atrius, or, is it Bronx?" The gentleman scratched his gray hair, combed to the side in a neat part.

Bronx looked into the older gentleman's light brown eyes and he knew this man was far older than any Volocio he would ever encounter. "Sir, I don't have much time. I need to find a young woman."

"Rei?"

"Yes!"

"This way." He waited for Bronx to hop over the fence, and the two ran along the trail of souls until they reached a large clearing. Off in the distance and down a small hill, the path of herded souls arched away from Bronx and his companion, then came back to a dock that stretched out before them. The ship was at the end. It was a large, rickety wooden ship with a huge rudder in the back. Water stained the peeling dark panels.

Bronx scanned the crowd quickly, but the souls were so crowded together that he barely saw where one ended and another began.

"How are we ever going to find her in time?" he asked in a panic.

Bronx's companion said nothing as he scanned the crowd quietly, then he reached up and scratched his stubbled chin. "Patience, child. We'll find her."

"But how do you know?"

"I just know."

"Oh." Bronx waited but inside he was ready to scream at his companion, to tell him to hurry. The man led Bronx down the hill where a larger crowd white-robed spirits congregated. "How did you know my name?"

"You look just like Atrius," said the man, his dark eyes never leaving the crowd before them. "He was my son."

Bronx stared at his companion. "That would make you?"

"My name is Cesar Duque."

Bronx's heart stopped in his chest. The same Cesar who knew Manden.

"You give life and take life?"

"Yes, just like you." Cesar's eyes continued to scan the crowd, eventually moving closer to the fence.

"But we don't get to choose, right?" While Bronx was desperate to find Rei, he wanted answers to his questions. He didn't know how much time he had in this place and he needed to take in as much as he could. He needed to know if it was possible to bring Rei back.

"The decision is made by a higher being, but we can sense death coming. When it's their time, we feel their freedom and take their energy.

"Once our numbers were many—enough to help everyone to a peaceful passing. Now our numbers have dwindled, and receiving a peaceful death from us is now merely a blessing. Most die without a final rite." Cesar watched Bronx, who twisted his fingers together so tight it hurt. "It's a very lonely death."

Bronx thought back to his fight with Rei. She told him she would rather die in his arms than at the hands of someone like Infiernen. His eyes burned at the memory of how he had failed her. He let her die alone in a forest. Alone with Infiernen.

"How do I bring her back?"

"She's dead and here now. You can only give life to those at the edge."

"There's a way. I know it—that's why I'm here." Bronx found it difficult to breath. It wasn't the end for Rei, he wouldn't let it happen.

Cesar shook his head, his dark eyes pained. "It may be possible. But it comes with a price."

"I will pay it."

"It will cause you great pain."

"There's no greater pain than the one I feel right now," Bronx whispered. "To walk this life without her."

Cesar sighed and patted Bronx on the shoulder. "Very well," said the older gentleman, grabbing Bronx by the arm and leading further him down the hill. "Listen, my son, our job is not an easy one, but it has to be done. When we release a soul, it's a release for them. Believe it or not, it makes their death easier, less painful. Don't fear for your loved ones. Just live your life. Take comfort in that."

They arrived at an overly crowded area of the fence.

"She's there."

Bronx couldn't imagine how Cesar pinpointed Rei out of all these souls.

"You sure?" asked Bronx.

"Yes. When you return, I can teach you more."

"Return? But how?"

"You have now seen beyond the veil, you can do it again. Now go."

"But what do I do?"

"What do you see right before you touch someone? Before the black smoke appears."

"I see a patchwork with a loose thread. I either tug it, or I put it back in its place."

"That's good. This may work." Cesar studied the trees above them. Several golden leaves fell around them, glittering in unseen sunlight. "You will have to rebuild such a cloth for Rei. The price for such energy will come from you. How much, I don't know. It could kill you."

Bronx smiled as relief rushed over him. "Thank you for helping me."

He didn't care about the price. He would pay it long before he knew what it was.

Cesar pursed his lips. "Don't get too excited. What you're about to do has rarely been done. You're risking your very soul for her. But I can see by your expression you are determined to go through with it, anyway. Find her and you'll know what to do."

Bronx climbed over the fence and pushed his way into the crowd. Souls pressed against him, almost suffocating him. He felt guilty as he shoved his way through but quickly remembered they were dead, and therefore, impervious to pain.

The number of souls in his direct vicinity seemed endless. They felt solid but more were crowded in this small space than humanly possible. He found it difficult to breath as the bodies pressed around him. He clenched his jaw and dug his heels in as he pushed through the souls with all his weight. The souls together moved like a current, and if he was not careful, he would be swept away, but he pushed on further and further into the crowd until he was in the thick of it.

Cesar said to let his instincts guide him.

Bronx closed his eyes and thought about Rei, the way her hair shone in the sunlight, her eyes when she watched him, the feel of her skin, and the memory of the kisses they'd shared. He thought about how much she meant to him. What he would give up to bring her back.

His pulse spiked. Even though closed eyes, Rei's soul was like a bright light in a sea of darkness. He opened his eyes, and her soul shone. Bronx moved toward her. He shoved past more souls—he was so close. A surge moved through the crowd, almost pulling Bronx away.

"Rei!" he called, using one more push to grab her hand and pull her toward him.

She resisted. Maybe the dead were drawn to the ship. He pulled a little harder. She still resisted.

"Rei, look at me." He put his will behind the words.

She must come back. She turned, hood still covering her face. Bronx drew it back. Her green eyes sparkled as they met with his. Her gaze remained on his face as Bronx pulled her through the crowd toward him. As she inched closer, he put his other arm around her waist, pressing her against him. Their noses softly touched. Bronx let his lips gently brush against hers. Her arms reached up around his neck and she laid her head on his chest.

He held her close and kissed the top of her head. "Live," he whispered, concentrating on using what energy he had to transfer to Rei.

He closed his eyes, letting his body and instinct take control. He was still unsure about what he was doing, but somehow it was working.

The pain started like a knife carving his heart from his chest. He clenched his jaw as he advanced. He would carve himself to pieces if that's what it took to bring her back. The cost was a piece of his soul, yet he didn't know how much. He didn't know and didn't care.

A gasp escaped his lips as the pain in his chest continued to build. He would give her his entire soul, if necessary. Her grip on his arm tightened. Her head rested in the crook of his neck, as they fit together like two puzzle pieces. After this, they would be one, not only in body, but in spirit.

"Come back to me," he whispered.

As if on cue, he felt his energy being drawn from him. In his mind's eye, he saw a golden thread between them, knitting itself back together into a beautiful tapestry of Rei's life. The agony in his chest grew as the tapestry stitched every minute of her history up until Infiernen's blade struck her neck, and the unraveling began. Bronx tied a secured knot—the poison would not take her again.

His knees buckled, and he fell to the ground without letting go of the woman now in possession of a piece of his soul. He felt the cold bite of snow as his knees hit the ground.

Rei took a large gasp of air and coughed. Bronx opened his eyes and drew her close to him. His vision cleared and the golden leaves and blacked trees were gone, replaced by the pure white snow that fell in large tuffs around them. They were back in the arboretum where the rest of the Volocio stood watching.

"I brought you back," he whispered, cupping her cheek.

"She's alive!" Arram gasped.

Rei groaned. "I feel like I've been kicked in the ribs."

"It's all right," Bronx said.

He laughed and kissed her. When he pulled away, he noticed something different. Niklaryn's ring was gone, replaced by a necklace with a brass infinity symbol.

His blood ran cold at the sight of his old mentor's mark.

Rei shivered against him, her dress soaked from the snow. All of his thoughts centered around getting her somewhere warm.

The photographer's flashing lights surrounded them. They must have followed the group here. They had watched him bring Rei back to life.

Bronx tried to lift her, but his knees were weak and he fell back down, still holding Rei tight in his arms.

"Little help?" he asked.

Manden stepped forward and took Rei.

"We should find a doctor," Arram said.

"I'll go on ahead to try and find a carriage," said Artema, running ahead of the group.

The reporters followed, asking questions, but he couldn't hear them. Kaz and Skylar drew attention away from the pair by answering as many as they could.

Crona eyed him suspiciously. "What in the gods' names happened just now?"

"It's a long story." He smiled broadly. "And I promise that I will tell you everything. But right now, I just want to warm myself and get Rei to a doctor." He reached out a hand. "Can you help me stand? My knees still feel a little shaky."

Crona didn't move from where she stood. "But you're not wearing gloves."

Bronx glanced at his extended hand, then back at his sister. "Yes. Yes, you are right."

# CHAPTER 55

Rei opened her eyes and found herself on a familiar ledge—the mouth of Finner's Cave, just a few kilometers outside of Ballarat.

The sun set, the eternal expanse of the badlands stretching out before her in a golden glow. She sensed movement to her left and turned to find Niklaryn sitting next to her, munching on the last of the sunflower seeds he brought from Wolf X.

This was exactly what she and Niklaryn had done the night before he left.

"This has to be a dream," Rei said.

"You are right, little sister," Niklaryn said.

He took an empty shell from his mouth and threw it over the ledge, then handed her the bag. She took a seed and opened the shell with her front teeth. As she munched on the salty seed inside, her eyes never left her brother. He looked just the way she remembered him, hood up, covering his hair. He smiled at her, his blue eyes squinting as he did. This was the last time she had seen him before he left for Kepler IV and disappeared with Infiernen.

She remembered Infiernen had said something before she died. Died. She was dead. Rei shook her head. One thing at a time.

She thought back to her last memory.

Infiernen's blade was laced with Drops of Jupiter, and she had fallen to the ground, blinded by pain. The last thing she remembered was the smell of sandalwood and juniper. Niklaryn was there. Then she was in a place of fog and spirits. There had been a forest and a path, then mist. She heard Bronx's voice. She wanted to ignore it, but something stronger forced her to listen.

Bronx said *look at me*.

Rei listened, and when she locked eyes with him, all her mind focused on was of returning to him.

*Come back to me*, he said.

Niklaryn's loud munching at her side brought her out of her head.

"I'm not dead?" Rei asked.

Her brother shook his head as he popped more seeds into his mouth. "Nope."

"Where are you?"

Niko tilted his head to the side as though he didn't understand the question. "Right in front of you."

Rei thought about what Infiernen had said to her before she died: *It was all for you, Rei. Everything I did was to keep you safe long enough to fulfill your destiny. I never meant to keep Nik from you, but I had to stow him away for safe-keeping.*

"Can't afford to let me loose," Niklaryn said out loud.

"What?" Rei asked.

"You don't know? How delicious." Her brother raised an eyebrow. Rei felt a cold chill. For a moment, her brother looked exactly like Infiernen.

"Well, I won't spoil the punch line," said Niklaryn. "But I'm a lot closer than you think."

Rei snapped awake to discover she was lying in a bed in the hotel. Moonlight shone through the curtains. Its light guided her gaze to the soft glow of a table lamp to her right. Bronx sat in a chair, reading from his touchscreen.

He glanced at Rei and smiled, his dark eyes filled with relief. He put the tablet down, leaned in, and kissed her.

"Well, hello to you too," she said.

Bronx said nothing, but his eyes expressed the same desire that had drawn her from the fog while in Death. There was also hunger in those dark eyes—one she was more than willing to help satiate.

"You brought me back, didn't you?" she asked.

"I did."

Rei tried to sit up, but her body was too weak. Bronx was at her side, an arm around her, helping her up—with gloveless hands.

Once settled, she gingerly touched Bronx's hand, expecting him to pull away, but he didn't and instead, interlaced his calloused fingers with hers. Her heart drummed at his caress.

"I love you, Rei Ettowa," he whispered.

"I love you, too, Bronx Manca," she returned, her heart bursting with emotion.

Bronx sat down on the bed next to her, and Rei leaned in to press her lips against his. She missed this, she missed him. She raked her hand through his hair while he wrapped an arm around her, drawing her close. Rei couldn't concentrate on anything except for the feel of his hands on her body—she felt each graze of his fingers like a jolt of energy, warming her to the core.

"Ahem," said a voice to Rei's left. Bronx broke the kiss and turned toward the owner of the voice. "I would have appreciated if you'd waited until I left the room before you two decided to physically express yourselves." The faint glow of the table lamp shone on Arram's face as he laid in a cot, tightly wrapped in a quilt.

"Sorry, Arram," Bronx said with a smile before getting off the bed and sitting in the chair. "I thought you were still sound asleep. We just got carried away."

Arram stood. "Obviously." He gave Rei a kiss on the cheek and threw his arms around her.

"I'm so glad I didn't lose you," he whispered.

"And we have Bronx to thank for that," said Rei, returning the hug. They pulled away, and Arram settled on the bed next to his sister.

"What happened, Bronx?" she asked.

"I found the Land of the Dead, Cesar, and other Reapers like me. I discovered the truth about my abilities: I wasn't the cause of any deaths. They happened naturally, and I just helped them die peacefully. The Negander I killed had already suffered a killing blow at my hand, and my gift made it final." He took a deep breath. "Also, I can bring people away from the edge of death."

"Like me?" Rei asked.

"Like Arram. Others."

Rei knew what he meant. She was dead, not at the edge. She shivered as she wondered what he had to do to bring her back.

Bronx reached out and cupped her cheek. "I paid a price for you. One that I would gladly pay again."

"What price?" Arram asked.

"No offense, Arram, but it's something I would rather keep between your sister and me." He met Rei's gaze. "I'll tell you everything later."

She touched his hand on her face. "So you're no longer afraid?"

Bronx smiled. "I did a lot of thinking while you slept. I remember the names of each life I took, except the Negander from this evening. They were at the brink of death and were suffering horribly: my father, Prue, others . . . My touch allowed them to die in peace and be released from their misery. It's comforting to know there's a sense of balance in my power. I didn't cause anyone's death, and I also enabled others to live."

Rei sunk into her pillow, digesting this new information. A great weight lifted from her chest knowing Bronx embraced his powers and no longer feared them.

"So Crona's vision was right all along?" she asked. "You were never going to hurt me."

"She also said, 'he had many faces.' Her vision also applied to what happened tonight. Infiernen was able to hurt you because you split off from the rest of the team. I shouldn't have let you go." His eyes were bright.

*He can't hurt you as long as you're together.* "Prophecies are only useful after the fact."

"Infiernen won't be pleased when he finds out you're still alive," Arram said. "I want to end that man's life for what he did to you. To us."

Rei met Bronx's intense gaze. After talking to Niklaryn in those moments before her death, she understood her older brother a little better. It was no wonder Bronx thought his mentor betrayed them. Her brother sold his soul for her protection, and Infiernen was also bound to follow suit.

"I don't know how I feel about Infiernen," she said with a sigh. "He didn't want me to die. Infiernen isn't our enemy. At least that's what Niko said, or maybe he was a hallucination from the pain. My dying mind merely trying to give me some sense of peace."

Arram's mouth hung open in shock while Bronx wore a pained expression.

"Niklaryn was there," Bronx said.

He reached out and touched the object that hung around her neck.

Rei touched it as well. Niklaryn's ring was gone. She unclasped the necklace and brought the charm to the lamp where she could better see the infinity-shaped brass piece. It was the symbol of Infiernen.

"I saw Nik as well," Bronx said. "He promised me Infiernen wouldn't be a threat to us anymore."

Rei's eyes burned as the truth hit her. Her brother was there; he was there at her side at the end. She found him, and she could find him again.

"He held me," she whispered. "He told me Infiernen only attacked you, Arram, and Artema because you are a threat to his deal with my brother."

"What deal?" Arram asked.

Rei shook her head. "I don't know. Do you, Bronx?"

"I don't know about a deal. But threat, I believe," he said.

"Is our brother working for the Dominion?" Arram asked.

"Not of his own free will," Rei said. "He and Infiernen are bound in some way, and our brother sold his soul to protect me."

"To protect you from whom?" Bronx asked.

"This is a conversation that should involve the others." She didn't care that it was the middle of the night. Her purpose was still clear, and she was just beginning. This war went beyond her and Infiernen now.

Bronx carried her downstairs to the dining hall while Arram woke the others. They gathered together in a circle around the empty hearth.

Rei stood. What she wanted to say was important to her, and the message would be more powerful if she were on her feet. It was hard—the muscles in her stomach were sore, but she held herself up. Her eyes wandered to each of her comrades. Some smiled, while others were still caught in the remnants of sleep, but she had everyone's attention.

She met Artema's gaze. "First, I want to welcome Artema to our ragtag crew. We came here to find a sister-in-law but walked away with Tasya. The real Tasya." Rei chuckled. "The fates certainly wanted us to find each other."

"The fates indeed," Manden said. "I would love to know the story as to why you now go by Artema and no longer Tasya."

Artema winked. "Another story for another day."

"Regardless," Rei began, "all six of us are united, and that means we can prepare for the final battle that was prophesied."

"A battle that's likely purely symbolic," Kaz said.

Rei shook her head. "It's not. I understand why I have to lead against Sovereign Praymer." She pressed both palms onto the cold stone surrounding the hearth. "I'm sure Bronx told you he saw Niko when he found my body."

The others nodded. Bronx's pained expression reminded her that seeing her dead was not something he wanted to remember.

"I saw him, too, and he said something interesting. All these years, I thought it was Infiernen hunting me. I thought he was the reason I had to stay hidden on Earth. I thought he murdered my parents. But I was wrong."

"Infiernen is your brother's age," Skylar said. "He would've been too young to murder your parents."

"Then who?" asked Arram.

"The Sovereign," Rei said. "Anekris Praymer." She turned to Bronx. "You told me when we first met that Praymer knew the prophecy of my coming meant his destruction. He's been hunting me since I was a child because I am a threat to him."

"It runs deeper than that," Manden said.

"You never told her?" asked Artema.

Manden shook his head. "Up until today, her only enemy was Infiernen. I couldn't get her to focus on anything else. You'll see, she's just like Micaela in her stubbornness." He met Rei's gaze. "But now you understand what Praymer did to you and your parents, and you should understand what Micaela did to him."

"Micaela?" Rei asked.

"He's Mica's husband."

Rei grasped a nearby chair and sat down before her legs gave out. "But that would mean he's also several thousand years old. Is he a Volocio, too?"

"No. I don't know what he is or how he managed to live this long," Manden said.

"He's an abomination." Artema's voice was dangerously low.

Rei's stomach churned and bile rose in her throat. She lived in fear her entire life, her family was destroyed, her brother became a slave to the Dominion, all because of a woman making a cuckold of her husband two thousand years before.

"What a petty bitch," she said finally. "All the more reason why I should take him down."

"Let's not forget about another issue," Crona said.

"What's that?" Rei asked.

"How Infiernen managed to find us tonight."

Kaz's blue eyes turned hard. "He came because the press found out about us."

"They arrived around the same time. Even if he had found out through the Nexus, he would already have to have been on the planet to begin with. Either way, it begs the question: why was he on this planet and how did he find out about us?"

Rei looked at her friend. Crona had a point. This was the third time the Dominion was told of her position. The third time she was betrayed—even though Infiernen was not the threat.

"I told Infiernen," Skylar whispered.

An audible gasp escaped from the group.

"What?" Kaz asked, hand to his mouth. "Why?"

"Infiernen and I have been working together for years. That Negander has been playing the long game. He and Niklaryn have been working for Sovereign Praymer in hopes of getting close enough to kill him. But to get close, they've had to play parts."

"Infiernen plays his part too well," muttered Crona.

"Why couldn't you tell us this before?" Bronx asked.

"Not even Urius knows Infiernen is my informant," said Skylar. "I can't let my part in all this be known. Infiernen was supposed to come alone and convince you that he's an ally and that's it. Sometimes he's able to travel alone, but he brings his Dogs with him when he tries to keep Sovereign Praymer from getting suspicious." Skylar let out a loud breath. "That's what happened tonight. Both Infiernen and Niklaryn are playing a dangerous game, but I trust them completely. But if Niklaryn says he is fighting for the Federation, I guarantee Infiernen is as well."

"So we have men on the inside," Manden said. "It's a start, but I don't understand why Urius doesn't know."

"The fewer who know, the better," Skylar responded. "I am trusting you to keep this information secret. Urius knows I have an informant who has proven very useful. That's all he needs to know for now."

"Okay," Rei said. "We will deal with everything as it comes, but the important thing is we will do it together."

Her gaze fell over each of her friends, her cousins, her brother, and finally, her lover.

Excitement coursed through her veins as her next plan formed in her mind. Having Infiernen as an ally instead of a target certainly changed things, but her path had never been clearer. "Let's just take tonight as a victory, and we will work to deal with everything. We'll strike against Praymer. Perhaps with Infiernen's help, we can find a way to break Niko free from his bondage. But until then, we get ready. Together we will lead the Federation in the final battle."

**Continue Rei and Bronx's story in *The Last Imperator***

HOW MUCH WILL SHE SACRIFICE FOR PEACE?

After six months of campaigning, Rei and the other Volocio have barely convinced half the star cluster to vote for the Federation.

Activist groups from all sides are calling for a war Rei is destined to declare, but she won't do it. While she wants to kill the Dominion Sovereign - Anekris Praymer - she wants to destroy him herself. She can channel lightning - she is the god queen - she doesn't need more than that and the whole star cluster doesn't need to go to war for it.

But tensions are rising beyond both their control and when both Rei and Anekris are trapped together after an attack - they strike up an uneasy alliance.

As time progresses, Rei finds herself wondering - will they remain enemies or will they join together and finally unite the Federation and Dominion?

# GLOSSARY

A

- **Alcubierrre-Krasnikov**—the drive used to allow ships to travel through premade tunnels in order to travel faster-than-light.
- **Alexia**—the goddess of time, prophesied to return in **The Second Coming**
- **Alma Canale**—representative for the **Federation** on the planet **Trappist V**.
- **Ama**—the goddess of ice
- **Anekris Praymer**—sovereign of the **Dominion**
- **Ara'nden**—planet capital of the **Dominion**, capital city: Corincancha
- **Arram Ettowa**—reincarnation of **Maximilian Roya**, a lightning **Volocio**
- **Artema Ettowa**—**Niklaryn Ettowa**'s wife, also known as **Tasya**
- **Atrius Duque**—a reaper, lover of **Micaela Roya**, prophesied to return in **The Second Coming**
- **Ayres**—a medic for the **Federation**

## B

- **Ballarat**—town in what was once California, USA. Resting spot enroute to holy city of **Escalante**
- **Benot**—painter, famous painting of the god queen
- **Bernadette "Bernie" Boyard**—soldier of **Federation**, niece to Federation leader, **Urius Boyard**
- **Bronx Manca**—reincarnation of **Atrius Duque**, a reaper

## C

- **Camila Canale**—daughter to representative **Alma Canale**
- **Castelan**—one of many official languages of **Tas'und'eash**
- **Cesar Duque**—reaper and father of **Atrius Duque**
- **Connocillin**—preferable antibiotic of both **Dominion** and **Federation**, only grown on planet **Trappist V**
- **Coronta**—purple liqueur produced by **Hotara** in **Ballarat**

- **Craegus**—god of animals
- **Crona Sandern**—reincarnation of **Alexia Vagner**, a time **Volocio/seer**

---

## D

- **Daer**—knight of the **Federation**
- **Dominion**—political party of the **Tyre Star Cluster**
- **Drops of Jupiter**—a poison

---

## E

- **Escalante**—holy city of the **Volocio** religion, located in the Death Valley of the former United States
- **Ettowa Starline**—biggest producer of the star ships for both **Dominion** and **Federation**

---

## F

- **Fabrecido**—capital and port city of planet **Kepler IV**
- **Federation**—political party of the **Tyre Star Cluster**
- **Felix Royalt**—famous author and historian
- **Fiamatta**—goddess of fire
- **Fortress of Riodan**—fortress where famous **Daer Niklaryn Ettowa** was murdered by **Negander Infiernen Jessar**

---

# G

---

- **Gliese VI**—planet in the **Tyre Star Cluster**, home of the **Underground**

---

# H

---

- **Hamastagan**—another name for the Underworld, the Land of the Dead
- **Hotara Quin**—bar owner and adopted mother of **Rei Ettowa**, also known as **Tara**

# I

- **Iarann**—goddess of metal
- **Infiernen Jessar**—**Negander** knight of the **Dominion**
- **Infinity Dogs**—**Negander** knights who follow **Infiernen Jessar**
- **Ixchel**—town on the planet **Kepler IV**

# K

- **Kapetyn II**—planet in the **Tyre Star Cluster**
- **Kazimir "Kaz" Ettowa**—reincarnation of **Kazimir Roya**, an illusion **Volocio**
- **Kazimir Roya**—god of illusion, prophesied to return in **The Second Coming**
- **Kepler IV**—planet in the **Tyre Star Cluster**, origin of antibiotic **Connocillin**

# L

- **Luciernaga—Manden**'s ship, over 2,000 years old.

---

# M

- **Manden Walt**—the god king, a plant **Volocio**
- **Mara**—priestess in the Temple of **Tasya** on planet **Kepler IV**
- **Maximilian Roya**—god of lightning, prophesied to return in **The Second Coming**
- **Micaela Roya**—the god queen, a lightning **Volocio**, prophesied to return in **The Second Coming**

---

# N

- **Negander**—knight of the Dominion
- **Nenen**—god of water
- **Nexus, the**—an intergalactic system of interconnected computer networks within the **Tyre Star Cluster** that communicates between networks and devices

- **Niklaryn Ettowa—Daer** knight for the **Federation**

## O

- **One True God**—main religion of the **Dominion**

## P

- **Proxima Centauri II**—capital planet of the **Federation**, capital city: Madu

## R

- **Reapers—Volocio** who can manipulate energy of living beings
- **Reina "Rei" Micaela Ettowa—** reincarnation of **Micaela Roya**, a lightning **Volocio** and the god queen

- **Rose House, The**—popular restaurant in town of **Yticol** on planet **Gliese VI**

---

## S

- **Sagitan Bronto**—**Daer** Master and maternal grandfather of **Arram**, **Rei**, and **Niklaryn**
- **Sariah Bray**—**Daer** knight, year mate of **Bronx Manca**
- **Second Coming, The**—a prophecy that states that six of the murdered **Volocio** will return to war against the **Dominion** sovereign
- **Seer**—a **Volocio** that can predict the future
- **Skylar Ettowa**—**Daer** knight, sister to **Kaz Ettowa**
- **Stars of Saskia**—flower native to **Tas'und'eash**. **Seers** use them to amplify their ability to see the future

---

## T

- **Tara**—goddess of the earth
- **Tas'und'eash**—the **Volocio** homeworld

- **Tasya**—goddess of wind, prophesied to return in **The Second Coming**
- **Tau Ceti II**—planet in the **Tyre Star Cluster**
- **Trappist V**—planet in the **Tyre Star Cluster**, home of the fungus **Connocillin**
- **Tyre Star Cluster**—a group of planets split between two political parties: **Dominion** and **Federation**

---

# U

---

- **Underground, The**—a secret **Federation** base
- **Urius Boyard**—**Federation** leader

---

# V

---

- **Vaye**—**Dominion** representative of planet **Trappist V**
- **Virga Bronto**—maternal grandmother of **Niklaryn**, **Rei**, and **Arram**
- **Volocio**—humans with a longer lifespan and the ability to control the elements, believed to be gods

# W

- **Wolf X**—planet in the **Tyre Star Cluster**, home planet of **Bronx**, **Crona**, and **Kaz**

# Y

- **Yticol**—tourist town on the planet **Gliese VI**

ACKNOWLEDGMENTS

It has taken me almost two decades to find the right way to tell my story about Rei and Bronx. There is not enough space to fit all the people I want to thank.

A million thanks to my editor Tiffany White at Writers Untapped - you helped me become a better writer and I can't wait to continue working with you.

To Kirsten Olson, April Smallwood, Anna-Sofia Le Noac'h, L. S. Matthews, Jon F. Chaddock, Hannah Jane - my awesome critique partner, Elizabeth Hejl, Luralee Kiesel, Kirk M, and Kristin Yodock. Thank you all for taking the time to read my book and having a hand in helping make *The God Queen* what it is! Your feedback and support gave me the courage to keep going.

To my sister, Samantha - thank you so much for the tools for my book cover. I would have not known where to start without you. Thank you for your honest feedback in my more o-target ideas. You helped set the foundation for what my cover looks like today.

Meg LaTorre - Thank you for dealing with every minute change I did with the final stages of my book cover! I'm so grateful for your patience and support.

To my parents, John and Maria - you guys have been my biggest cheerleaders since you first heard of my project when I was thirteen. Thank you for your love and support.

And lastly, to my husband, Thorsten - you are amazing

and I'm so grateful to have a partner to who supports my dreams of being a writer. *Ich liebe dich, Schatzi!*

Mari, a native Hoosier, currently lives in southern Germany where she entertains people with her adventures as an American expat in the Land of Beer and Pretzels on her blog and YouTube channel Adventures of La Mari.com as well as the adventures of her pugs, Abner and Roxy. When she's not writing, Mari cooks, snowboards, dances to the beat of her own drum, reads late into the

Author Photo © **Tobias Vogt**

night, and binge watches Netflix with her husband. *The God Queen* is her debut novel.

tiktok.com/@mltishner

instagram.com/mltishner

youtube.com/mltishner

bsky.app/profile/mltishner.bsky.social

facebook.com/mltishner

**The Rebirth Saga**

The Knight and the Goddess (Book 0.1)

The God Queen (Book 1)

The Last Imperator (Book 2)